The
Wretched
and
Undone

A Novel

J. E. Weiner

ISBNs: 978-1-963452-11-2 (pb);
978-1-963452-10-5 (hc);
978-1-963452-12-9 (eBook)

Book Cover Design: The Book Cover Whisperer, OpenBookDesign.biz
Interior Book Design: Inanna Arthen, inannaarthen.com
Peacock image designed by rawpixel.com / Freepik
Map Design: Annika Wooton, annikawooton.com
Library of Congress Control Number: 2024921548

First Printing: 2025
Printed in the United States of America

Publisher's Cataloging-in-Publication
(Provided by Cassidy Cataloguing Services, Inc.)

Names: Weiner, J. E., author.
Title: The wretched and undone : a novel / J. E. Weiner.
Description: [Minneapolis, Minnesota] : HTF Publishing, [2025] | Includes bibliographical references.
Identifiers: ISBN: 978-1-963452-10-5 (hardcover) | 978-1-963452-11-2 (paperback) | 978-1-963452-12-9 (ebook)
Subjects: LCSH: Polish Americans--Texas--History--Fiction. | Families--Texas--History--Fiction. | Ghost stories. | Good and evil--Fiction. | Blessing and cursing--Fiction. | Generational trauma-- Fiction. | Death--Fiction. | Texas--History--Fiction. | LCGFT: Historical fiction. | Gothic fiction. | BISAC: FICTION / Historical / General. | FICTION / Gothic. | FICTION / Literary.
Classification: LCC: PS3623.E432438 W74 2025 | DDC: 813/.6--dc23

For Eitan Michael. I miss you. Every day.

When we lay in sin polluted,
Wretched and undone we were:
All we saw and heard was suited
Only to produce despair.
Ours appeared a hopeless case:
Such it had been but for grace.

— 'When We Lay in Sin Polluted,'
Reverend Thomas Kelly, 1831

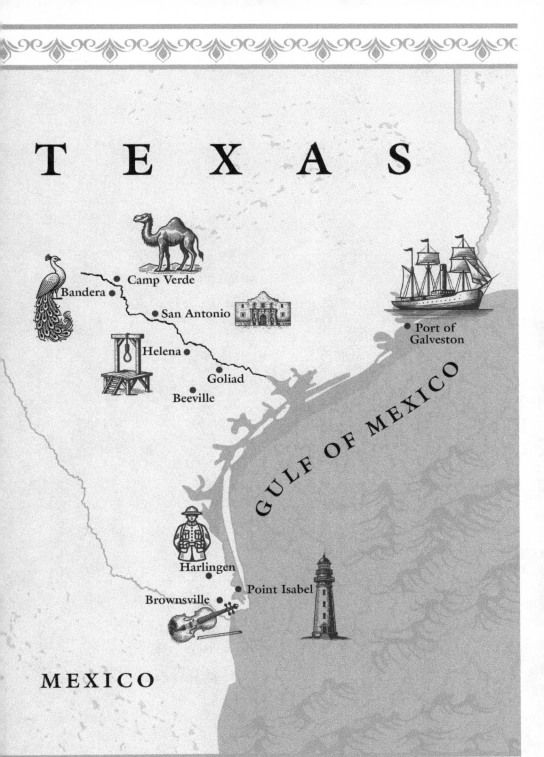

PROLOGUE

Bandera, Texas, 1987

The crunch of gravel and the thump of a car door alerted the proprietor of the Frontier Times Museum that he had company. He poked a gnarled index finger between the slats of the wood blinds he'd been dusting, widening the space between them, and peered outside. A rusted pickup slowed along Thirteenth Street, the driver's attention attracted, no doubt, by the shiny black Cadillac parked out front. The bells atop the entrance tinkled, and sunlight flooded into the museum's dim interior. An elegant woman slipped over the threshold, letting the heavy cedar door slam behind her. The star-shaped window carved into the door's center panel framed her face like a halo.

The visitor who had come to call was most unexpected. Truth be told, any visitors to the Frontier Times were a rarity of late. The proprietor, also the museum's self-appointed curator, did not know the woman, but she seemed familiar. He searched his brain, sorting the detritus of memories from a life lived well past the age of ninety.

"Hello?" she called out.

The curator continued to observe the stranger from behind a display cabinet containing a stuffed two-faced, four-eyed baby goat that had come to the museum's collection after a run at the county fair fifty years prior. He wanted another moment to recall where he had seen this woman before.

His visitor wound her way through the teetering and wobbling exhibits, which were equal parts tribute to Bandera's legacy as the Cowboy Capital of the World and the long-standing local obsession with taxidermy. She wore less makeup than was the fashion of the times, and soft freckles kissed the bridge of her aquiline nose.

The curator's breath began to fog the cabinet's glass, which caught the woman's attention. He shuffled behind the counter as if he'd popped in from the back room. "Can I help you?" he asked, stuffing his feather duster into a bucket on the floor.

The visitor stepped closer and bent over the glass countertop, surveying the artifacts on display beneath. Wisps of raven hair fell across her cheeks, and she instinctively tucked them behind her ears. She straightened and smiled. A spark of recognition bridged the man's shriveled synapses. He realized he'd seen that face splashed across the newspaper's front pages and flashed across his television screen over the years. There'd been a buzz across the county for weeks that some country music starlet had bought the old Ander-wald place, seeking refuge from the melee of infamy. But something else tugged at the curator's memory, a flutter beyond his cognitive grasp.

"Yes, I hope you can," the woman said. "I bought a ranch near here a few months ago. It's out on Highway 16."

"Mm, hmm," the man nodded.

"The thing is," the stranger hesitated. "Shoot, you're going to think I'm crazy," she laughed nervously.

"You'd be surprised, ma'am. My bar for crazy has always been pretty darned high." The curator grinned, hoping to put his visitor at ease.

"I think it might be haunted," she said, leaning in close like she feared being overheard.

"Ah, yes. Peacock Bend. Out on the Old Bandera Road. Yep, I know," the man said.

Suspicion sparked in the woman's eyes. "You know I bought it, or you know it's haunted?"

The man shrugged. "Bandera's a small place. You'll need to get used to a fair bit of gum flappin' around here." Or, he thought to himself, the petty impulses of those who relish any chance to sit in sanctimonious judgment of their fellow man.

"I see," she said, still wary. "Maybe you can tell me something about the family who used to own the place? All those graves on the hilltop?"

The curator pursed his lips. Where to begin, he wondered. "As a general matter, the intrepid pioneers who built this town didn't last long in those early days. But the poor souls of Peacock Bend had a disproportionate share of loss over the four generations that lived out there. That's for sure."

The visitor began to say something else but was distracted. Her gaze fell upon two ragged photographs hanging askew on the wall beside the counter. "May I?" she asked, pointing at the splintered frames, cobwebs draped at their corners.

"Be my guest," the curator said.

The woman lifted the first photo from its hook and brushed it off with the sleeve of her jacket. A pair of wild-eyed Arabian men and a grubby Confederate soldier were posed astride camels, grimacing into the lens. "Would you look at that," she muttered and replaced the frame on the wall.

The mysterious caller took the second photo from the wall and gently blew the dust from its surface. She began to cough and sputter. A stern young woman who appeared to be in her early twenties stood on a riverbank, staring out from many lifetimes ago. The image was degraded at the edges, leaving the impression that the subject was floating across the water. A name and date were etched on the bottom of the picture: Agnieszka Nowak Anderwald, 1861. The visitor gingerly ran her finger over the figure's light-colored hair and round face, the detail about the eyes beginning to dissolve. "I know you," she whispered.

The curator cupped a hand around his ear. "I'm sorry, I didn't hear what you said."

"I've seen her," the visitor spoke up, but her voice was thin, and her hands trembled. "At the ranch. And I've also seen that thing," she said, pointing at a dark shadow hovering in the photograph's background.

A chill raced along the curator's spine. "Now I see why you have come," he said. "We all figured the curse of the Anderwalds had lifted after the last of them died out, but maybe not."

"A curse? You're not serious," the woman scoffed.

"I may have spun a yarn or two in my day, but when it comes to the Anderwald family, I never waiver in my faithful commitment to the facts," the curator insisted.

"I'm sorry. I just...a curse?" The visitor raised an eyebrow.

"I will do my best to explain, ma'am, but as is true of all the best stories, folks don't always agree on the who, what, where, and when. That said, I am probably the only person left alive who can make any sense of it all for ya."

"Please tell me. Everything," the woman said with a note of urgency. "I need to know."

The curator pulled a stool from behind the counter and patted the seat. After all these years, he relished the chance to set the record straight and lift the burden from his heart. "Why don't you sit down," he said. "I'll get us some coffee."

PART ONE

The Lord is long-suffering and abundant in mercy, forgiving iniquity and transgression; but He by no means clears the guilty, visiting the iniquity of the fathers on the children to the third and fourth generation.

—Numbers 14:18

CHAPTER I

In the Beginning

The first whiff of trouble for the Anderwald family swirled on a sweltering Sunday in July 1860, when a rattlesnake dropped out of the rafters during Mass at St. Stanislaus Catholic Church. Father Piotr Mazurek was already sideways of his exhausted congregation that morning as he attempted to deliver his sermon. The priest's letters home to the villages of Upper Silesia had promised an exotic new world of faith, fertile soil, and freedom in this land called "Teksas," but it had been five long years of hardship and misery for one and all. Doubts had arisen, and more than a few parishioners blamed Father Mazurek for their trials and tribulations. Lately, there was talk he had mismanaged some of the church's funds. While the flock would never falter in its faith in the good Lord, their confidence in the good Father waned.

"Dear friends," the priest began, mopping his brow with the greasy hem of his vestment.

"Father sure has got his dander up," a boy tittered in the back.

"Yeah, and at full chisel. You'd think the Pope hisself was here," another replied.

Marcin Anderwald heard this exchange and half-hid a smile behind his hand. His wife Agnieszka reprimanded him with a sharp look and a sharper elbow, her patience nearly depleted in the last month of her fourth pregnancy in less than five years.

"Ow," Marcin mouthed with a scowl.

"I am reminded of John the Baptist's return from the wilderness," Father Mazurek forged on; his jowls dripping with sweat and his slight falsetto rising. "He preached that for those who make ready the way of the Lord, 'every valley shall be filled, and every mountain and hill shall be brought low.'"

The congregants stirred in their seats, and a quiet grumble began to build among the pews. "We need work, Father, not empty promises," one man said.

"I beseech you," the priest replied. "I know this past year has been difficult, but God will reward our efforts. Our hardships will soon be behind us."

"Or six feet above!" another woman cried.

Father Mazurek frantically looked around the room in search of the hecklers. The cleric frowned and opened his mouth but appeared to reconsider the rebuke he was poised to issue. He pressed a chubby fist against his lips and cleared his throat. "The Lord will show us—" he started again but was cut short by a loud swish exploding from above.

All eyes darted to the rafters above the priest's head. Sound muted, and time slowed as a giant diamondback tumbled through the air and landed smack dab in the middle of the altar. The church's prized silver chalice and candlesticks scattered across the floor. The snake was stunned for the briefest of moments before it curled into a warning posture, its rattle announcing an intent to strike. The ominous buzzing ricocheted off the bare log-framed walls of the makeshift sanctuary as if a legion of serpents had alighted upon the gathering.

"Boże mój!" Father Mazurek screamed and tumbled forward, landing on an elderly woman in the front row, his face smashed between her ample thighs.

"It's the Devil!" she wailed.

Parishioners recoiled in panic, some crawling on their hands and knees until they could reach their feet. Marcin pulled his three young children onto the bench and threw himself across Agnieszka's swollen belly.

"Tato, what's happening?" the eldest child Zacharias said, clutching his father's arm.

"Mamusiu!" his younger sisters Victoria and Beata bleated like startled lambs.

Marcin could feel Agnieszka's petite frame trembling beneath him.

"Stay calm, Aga," he said and leaned into the center aisle, blood pulsing behind his eardrums.

Marcin watched the serpent slide over the altar's edge onto the floor. The rattler gently lifted its head and advanced, its forked tongue navigating the distance between them. A burst of white light glanced off one of the candlesticks lodged under the opposite pew and distracted Marcin's attention. He lunged from his seat and, with one swift arc of his muscled arm, grabbed the altar ornament and brought its heavy base down with a thunderous crash, severing the snake's head with one blow. Complete silence fell over the church. Marcin remained perfectly still, watching the snake's blood ooze around the tips of his boots and between the cracks in the floorboards.

"It's a sign!" someone shrieked at the rear, and the congregation sprang back to life.

Agnieszka grabbed Marcin's wrist. Her ragged fingernails tore at his skin. "We must leave this place," she panted.

"Yes, we will go," Marcin replied, but his attention remained fixed on the dead reptile at his feet.

"Now," Agnieszka insisted. "The baby. It is coming."

CHAPTER 2

The Confederacy Comes Calling

M arcin jumped when he heard Zacharias shouting outside the barn. "Come, Tato!" the boy cried, fumbling desperately with the heavy iron bolt on the door.

Marcin rushed outside. It was unlike his son to be so excitable. "Zachek, what is it?" he asked, stroking Zacharias' dark curls and trying to calm him. When he saw the fear on the boy's face, he immediately understood something was very wrong. Marcin grabbed his shotgun. "Is it Mama? The girls? Tell me!" he insisted, loading two shells into the gun barrels.

"Żołnierze!" Zacharias exclaimed.

Marcin squinted across the pasture. Two men on horseback veered off the bridle path running along the bank of the Medina River and wound through a small herd of longhorn cattle grazing on tender shoots of spring sage grass. The brass buttons on their uniforms and the hilts of their swords gleamed in the sunlight as they headed up the hill toward the house. "God, help us," Marcin mumbled and crossed himself.

The continued squabbles at St. Stanislaus paled in comparison to the troubles brewing on the eve of a most uncivil war. The election of Abraham Lincoln in November of 1860 had set the wheels in motion for Texas' resounding secession the following February and the outbreak of hostilities two months later between the North and the South. Although Marcin and Agnieszka Anderwald did not understand the roots of the conflict, they understood it was best to keep quiet and keep their heads down. Life in Poland had taught them that there were no good choices in times of armed conflict, only degrees of acquiescence.

Rumors of forced conscription of fighting men to the Southern Army spread like wildfire after a boy from church named Anton Knappick was swept into a Confederate infantry regiment. He had been leading a new group of arrivals to Bandera from the Port of Galveston, and no one had heard from him since. Even more terrifying were the stories of brutal and indiscriminate retribution for any form of resistance to the Southern cause. So, when the Confederacy came calling that warm spring afternoon of 1861, Marcin feared the worst.

"Zachek, run as fast as you can and find Mama. Tell her soldiers come," Marcin ordered.

Zacharias sprinted toward the house with Marcin a few steps behind. Agnieszka was nursing their youngest, little Lena, on the front porch swing, rocking the bench back and forth with the tips of her bare toes. She was startled when she saw Marcin and Zacharias and pried the child from her breast, eliciting a sharp cry of protest.

"Mamusiu! Żołnierze!" Zacharias announced.

The soldiers were now only a few yards from the gate. Agnieszka scrambled to button her blouse and replace her feet into her boots. The baby was bawling.

"Where are the big girls, Zachek?" Marcin was doing his best to remain calm.

"Inside, Tato."

Marcin pushed the boy toward the front door. "Good. Go with Mama and stay in the house," he instructed and hurried to greet the uninvited guests.

"Afternoon," the older of the two men said.

"Dobr—," Marcin stumbled in his native tongue. "Who are you?" he managed, holding fast to the rifle at his side.

The younger soldier snorted and spat a large glob of sticky saliva onto the ground. "Sarge, what we got ourselves here, ya figure? German or Polish? Can never tell with them funny accents."

The older man, who appeared to be in charge, ignored the question. "Private Brewer, I'll do the talking, thank you," he snapped before turning back to Marcin. "Kirby's the name," the man said, tugging the brim of his cap. "Sergeant Curtis J. Kirby. And this here is Private Augustus Brewer. Who might we have the pleasure of speaking with?"

"Marcin Anderwald," Marcin replied, remaining suspicious.

"Mr. Anderwald, I'm glad to finally make your acquaintance. Your reputation as a master carpenter precedes you," Kirby explained. "A local man, a Mr. John Stanard, sings your praises."

Marcin furrowed his brow. John Stanard and his wife Eugenia were the closest thing to royalty in Bandera. Their families had come from old cotton money in Galveston, and they owned the largest cattle ranch in the county. The odd carpentry jobs Mr. Stanard had sent Marcin's way, and the sewing piecework Agnieszka did for Mrs. Stanard made it possible for the Anderwalds to buy their small homestead off a Mormon named Hawley a few years back. Marcin considered their dealings with the Stanards a fair trade of goods and services, and there were no debts to be settled. It was no secret that Stanard had political aspirations and was courting both sides, waiting to see where the winners and losers might land in this great conflagration, but to Marcin's mind, the man had no right dragging him into the mayhem.

"Might we sit a spell and talk?" Kirby continued. "We could sure use some refreshment. It's been a long ride."

Marcin held fast to the gate, eyeing the soldiers as they dismounted and tied their horses to a fence post. It was clear they were coming in regardless. Marcin reluctantly released the latch and followed the two men onto the front porch.

Sergeant Kirby had a few years on Marcin, who had celebrated his twenty-fifth birthday the month prior. The sergeant was clean-shaven, but that was the only thing clean about him. When Kirby removed his filthy army cap, Marcin was shocked to discover the enormity of the man's skull beneath his long, oily locks. His stained jacket and pants appeared to be from two different uniforms. Private Brewer looked to be just shy of eighteen years and was in an even worse state of presentation than his sergeant. The young soldier had scaly, sunburned skin slathered in some kind of ointment that glistened and wide-set eyes an eerie shade of bright green. His too-short pants revealed a pair of mismatched boots, one larger than the other, and each with different colored laces.

"Sit. I will bring you some food and drink," Marcin said. He retreated into the house and closed the door firmly behind him. He returned with a plate of biscuits and a pot of tea, slamming them on a small table when he discovered Private Brewer trying to peek through the window.

Brewer winked and limped toward the porch swing, favoring his left leg. "So," he grunted, settling into the seat, "where did that little blond filly get to?" The private didn't wait for an answer. He grabbed a biscuit and took a bite. "Mm, mmm, mmm, these sure are tasty," he said, pieces of food flying in all directions. "Anderwald, you are one lucky man to have such a beautiful wife who can also bake like this."

Marcin bristled, and the young soldier burst into a nasty, self-congratulating cackle.

"That's enough now, Augie," the sergeant intervened with a frosty glare in his companion's direction. "Mr. Anderwald, you'll have to excuse Private Brewer. These ruffians we've recruited into our ranks from various homes for wayward youth are in serious deficit when it comes to manners, let alone military discipline."

Private Brewer rolled his eyes and picked at his teeth with a grubby fingernail.

Sergeant Kirby returned to the subject at hand. "Mr. Anderwald, I trust you are aware that the Republic of Texas has pledged loyalty to the Southern cause," he said. "Your skills have come to the attention of my commanding officer at Camp Verde, Colonel Thomas Peters, and I am here on his behalf to enlist your services."

Marcin's breath caught in his chest when he heard the word *enlist*. "What is it you want?"

"We desperately need transport wagons to supply our troops further west. Seein' that we got ourselves a bunch a Union prisoners with idle hands up at the camp, Colonel Peters has decided to put those men to good use to build those wagons. We need someone to oversee the work." Sergeant Kirby paused, expecting a response, but proceeded when there was none. "It's an unusual kind of project, though."

Marcin cocked his head.

"The thing is, we also got some curious livestock underfoot. You know, the kind of beasts o' burden you probably read about in the Bible," Kirby continued. "Dromedaries, or is it dromedians? Aw, heck. Camels. That's what we got. Forty-five stinkin', gruntin', and spittin' camels. Oh, and a coupla Arab wranglers to keep 'em in line. Those animals can go for days without water over the toughest territory. Makes 'em perfect for hauling provisions."

"I am to build special wagon for them?" Marcin asked.

"Exactly. Plus, some regular ones for oxen to pull."

Marcin went quiet again.

Kirby scratched his head. "That about sums up what I come to ask ya, Mr. Anderwald."

"You pay me, or I am prisoner?" Marcin probed. He was unsure he'd understood the terms of this proposed arrangement.

The sergeant seemed taken aback by the question. "No, sir, you are not a prisoner," he said. "We are prepared to pay you five dollars a week. I expect you'll be with us for at least a coupla months, maybe more."

"Hey, Sarge, we almost done here?" Brewer interrupted. "You promised me a stop in town. I gots a card game and a bottle of whiskey waitin' on me, and I don't aim to pass those by," he said as he stuffed two more biscuits into his pocket.

"Hold on, Augie. We'll be on our way soon enough," Sergeant Kirby said, still watching Marcin closely. "Mr. Anderwald, we're at the Riverside Inn for another two days. We leave for Camp Verde at daybreak on Monday. Do we have a deal?" The sergeant extended his right hand.

Marcin did not immediately offer his. He considered the life he wanted to provide for his family but still could not. The extra money would change things, so this sergeant was making an offer that could not be refused in good conscience. Marcin also considered the possibility that refusal was not an option. He took a deep breath and shook Sergeant Kirby's hand.

* * *

Marcin tossed and turned in the bed. Agnieszka lay beside him, snoring. She had cried herself to sleep.

"What in God's name have you done?" Agnieszka's question replayed in his head.

Marcin had tried to reassure his young wife. "Don't worry, kochanie. I won't be away for long."

"How can you leave me alone like this?" she had pleaded.

Marcin leaned over Lena, who was sleeping between them. The baby was a whir of constant motion now that she could crawl. She'd soon be walking. Marcin always loved those first steps, and he would likely miss them. And then there was Agnieszka. Marcin watched his wife's chest rise and fall with each snuffled breath. Aga was right to worry about being alone, but Marcin felt he had no choice in the matter. He brushed back a lock of her wheat-colored hair and kissed her forehead, careful not to wake her. She tasted of tears, sour breast milk, and dust. The blanket fluttered at the end of the bed where the other three children were curled around his feet, and Marcin felt another pinch of guilt.

"Tato, do you have to go?" Zacharias had asked.

Marcin winced as he remembered the exchange. Zacharias stood in the doorway with his arms around Victoria and Beata, listening as Marcin and Agnieszka argued after supper. Marcin saw so much of himself in the boy, always protecting his mother and sisters, defiant and stubborn to a fault.

"Yes, Zachek. I must go. It is too much money. You will help Mama and the Hawleys will come."

Marcin smiled as he thought of Mormon Hawley and his wife. He had felt a close kinship with the family since purchasing their land a few weeks after the snake incident at St. Stanislaus. He recalled the day a fellow parishioner told him Hawley was looking to sell part of his farm.

"Them Mormons are in a bad way," the man had shared with a hint of glee. "Hawley might be of a mind to sell. But don't go yammerin' on about it," the man advised. "People are skittish about those folks from the Mormon Camp, but that's to be expected. Nobody wants to do business with heathens."

Heathens? Marcin thought. The same or worse had been said about his kind.

One of the girls murmured in the darkness. Beata was talking in her sleep. Marcin placed his foot gently against her back, and she quieted. He, too, finally nodded off with a yawn, but his mind remained restless, and he began to dream. He was standing on the riverbank with Zacharias. The Medina's blue-green waters sparkled like a blanket of gemstones in the sunlight, and endless rows of bald cypress lined each of its banks as far as the eye could see in either direction.

"And the river went out of Eden," Marcin said.

"Tato? Tato!" Zacharias was pulling on his father's sleeve. "Why is the stick moving like that?" The boy pointed at something in the middle of the river. A dark black cottonmouth was swimming toward them, its head drifting above the waterline.

"Zachek, this is not a stick," Marcin said, yanking the child away from the water's edge. "It is a dangerous snake. You must run away when you see one."

The serpent undulated back and forth across the surface. It appeared to consider Marcin before turning upstream and disappearing beneath the roots of a tree growing over the riverbank. Marcin looked at his feet. The tips of his boots dripped with blood.

Marcin gasped and bolted awake. The sheets tangled around his long limbs bound his body to the bed. He blinked in the pale morning light, seeking some kind of assurance it had only been a bad dream. But what did it mean? Was it another sign? He was not sure he wanted to know. He crossed himself and pressed his hands together with such force they shook. "I will fear no evil, for thou art with me," he prayed.

CHAPTER 3

Then Cometh the Devil

The three men set out for Camp Verde at dawn, heading due north through Bandera Pass in a single file, Sergeant Kirby in the lead, followed by Marcin and Private Brewer. The steady beat of hooves and the staccato of woodpeckers echoed through knotted branches of scrub oak, sending white-tailed deer scattering into the surrounding hills. The hoofbeats soon fell into a hypnotic rhythm, broken only by periodic explosions of profanity from Private Brewer.

"Goddamnit, Jackass, if ya don't git a move on, I's gonna kick the cussed piss outta ya," Brewer snarled at his stubborn pack mule. The animal had stopped to feed on a dandelion peeking out from a thin crack in the ground.

Marcin shook his head in disgust. He had already grown weary of the young soldier's childish tantrums.

"What's yer problem, Polack?"

"Nothing." Marcin wanted to avoid a pointless confrontation.

"Private Brewer," Sergeant Kirby called back over his shoulder, "it could be that your foul language is offending our guest, who, unlike yourself, is a respectable, God-fearin' man. Yet, for reasons I cannot fathom, you are hell-bent on taking the Lord's name in vain at each bend in this here road."

"Hold on now, Sarge. I have no intention of listnin' to anything this Bible thumper has to say. He don't have no 'thority over me."

"You're right, Private," the sergeant replied, "but as we've discussed time and again, I do. I'm only gonna ask nicely once."

"I'm only gonna ask nicely once," Brewer mocked under his breath. "Who does he think he is? My pappy? Ha! That bastard's long gone."

"Private, you got somethin' on your mind?" Kirby was losing patience.

"No sir, Sergeant Kirby, sir!" Brewer chaffed with an exaggerated salute.

The men forged on in silence. Over a steep rise five miles further along the parched trail, they came upon thirty white wooden crosses aslant in a clearing. A light breeze rustled through the mott of ragged mesquite trees surrounding the graves like the whispers of the dead beneath the freshly turned soil.

"I guess them Comanche are good for sumpin', huh," Brewer said. "Took care of these Yankee vermin for us."

Neither Sergeant Kirby nor Marcin reacted.

"Oh, you see there, Jackass," Brewer turned to his mule, "you're the only one listnin' to anything I has to say."

Kirby raised a closed fist to signal stop, scanned the tangled scrub brush dotting the surrounding hills, and waved all clear. "Let's rest a bit, gentlemen," he ordered. "Not much shade after this."

The men dismounted and headed for the trees.

"I gotta take a crap," Private Brewer groaned, unbuttoning his pants as he jogged toward a fallen trunk a few yards off.

Sergeant Kirby took a swig of water from his canteen, or what Marcin assumed was water, and looked out over the improvised cemetery. "Damned barbarians," he said. "It was a slaughter, you know. Them Comanche snuck up on these Union soldiers and killed every last one of 'em. Some they did even worse."

Marcin reached out to touch one of the crosses. It bore no name. He jerked his hand back like he'd touched a hot poker and lowered his head.

"What's with the Holy Father, Sarge?" Private Brewer snickered, his mission beyond the tree trunk accomplished.

"Shut up, Augie," Sergeant Kirby sighed. "Have some respect for the dead."

"To hell with these blue coats. They had it comin'." Brewer turned back to Marcin. "Boy, oh, boy! Comanche git ya quick, Anderwald. Slice yer eyelids off and stake ya into the ground facing the sun afore yer even dead." The young soldier's narrow tongue flicked in and out of a toothless gap in his lower jaw.

Marcin had had enough. He wanted to get this trip over with as soon as possible. He headed back toward the horses, clipping Brewer's shoulder hard to make his point.

Brewer struggled to regain his balance, his left leg tender under his full weight. "Now, wait a goddamned minute," he protested. "Did you see what he done, Sarge?"

"Enough, Private Brewer," the sergeant cautioned. "We got a long ride left ahead, and I'm nearly sick to death of your nonsense."

"Seriously, Sarge," the young soldier protested. "Are you takin' that Polack's side over mine?"

"I said that's enough!" Kirby bellowed. A flock of sparrows burst out of the treetops. "Damn," the sergeant said, looking toward the horizon. "We better get moving."

* * *

Marcin and his escorts reached the remote Confederate outpost nestled on the northern bank of Verde Creek by late afternoon. The crossing was smooth, and even Brewer and Jackass arrived without further incident. Camp Verde lay before them, fortified around the perimeter with solid picket defenses. Men and horses crisscrossed a dusty parade ground surrounded by one-story limestone buildings. A guard who was no better outfitted than Kirby and Brewer relieved Marcin of his horse and showed him to a sparse room resembling a jail cell in the rear of the commissary. A rickety cot stood in the corner, and light trickled in from a narrow window, dust dancing along the rays of sunshine penetrating its thick glass panes.

"I'll be back in a half-hour to take you to Colonel Peters," the guard said. "That should give you time to get washed up. Water pump's right out back."

The door slammed shut, and Marcin peered through the window. In an adjacent pen, he caught his first sight of the creatures Sergeant Kirby had spoken of. They were a strange and bewildering breed. The largest of the herd, presumably the males, were at least twenty hands tall from the ground to the top of a massive hump along their spines, their grunts and snorts like an alternating mix of cow, donkey, and wild hog. Marcin wondered how he would be able to sleep with such a racket right outside of his window. He yawned and stretched out on the cot, intending only to rest for a moment, but loud and persistent pounding on the door dragged him from a sound, dreamless slumber sometime later. The intensity of the knocking evidenced the extreme irritation of the person on the other side.

"Mr. Anderwald!" the caller urged.

"Yes, coming," Marcin croaked, not yet fully awake.

"The colonel is waiting for you, sir," came an impatient reply followed by the thud of heavy boots and metal spurs retreating.

Marcin rushed to catch up to the soldier who escorted him to the camel pen to meet Peters.

"Mr. Anderwald, I trust you are settled," the colonel said, feeding a handful of hay to one of the animals.

"Tak, um, yes," Marcin replied, taking in the impressive man before him. The officer's boots were worn but spit-polished, his threadbare uniform was ironed, and his beard was trimmed close along his pronounced chin. As Peters spoke, Marcin saw the whitest and fullest complement of teeth he'd ever seen in a man of fifty or so years.

"I'd like you to start work straight away," Peters said, getting right to business. "We commandeered this camp four weeks ago and are expected to be fully operational before the end of the summer. Follow me."

The colonel and Marcin pushed through the gate into the corral, where the camels converged, expecting more food. One large bull greeted them with a blustery burp. The rancid smell of the fermented, half-digested hay was overwhelming.

"A word of advice I should have heeded myself," Peters said with a wry smile, "these beasts don't take no for an answer. Best not to start feeding them, or they'll never leave you be." The colonel slapped several dusty backsides, trying to scatter the animals. "Go on, get!"

A moment later, shrill whistles rang out from the far side of the enclosure. The herd backed away as two stable hands drove the animals to one of the corners. Marcin could not help but stare. The men wore flowing robes and open leather sandals, revealing toenails bruised and bloodied when not missing altogether, and gestured violently with their hands, speaking in a language he did not recognize.

Colonel Peters answered the question Marcin had not yet uttered. "Never mind those two. They're the camel hands we inherited from our captives. One's Khalil, and the other's Ahmad but damned if I know who's who. I don't much care so long as they tend to these brutes and keep the stables clean."

The colonel continued through the barn, past stalls filled with worn-down horses and piles of Union army gear, to the back pasture where several soldiers stood guard at the edge of a ravine. "This is where we keep the prisoners," Peters explained, pointing into a deep gash in the landscape.

About forty men were being held at the bottom. Some were smoking and chatting, and others were cooking something in a pot over a campfire. Several more were covered in bandages and lay on blankets under a shabby army-issue tent. Even from above, Marcin could see that all the men were covered in filth, and most looked emaciated.

"How can they work when they are so weak?" he asked.

The colonel started to respond when a gunshot rang out, the men below diving for whatever cover they could find. A soldier standing on the other side of the ravine was pointing his weapon at the prisoners. He was clearly drunk and could not steady himself or his sidearm. Marcin recognized the twisted form. It was Brewer.

The guards glanced over but did not move to intervene. Colonel Peters also hesitated before calling out, "Stand down, Private. That's an order."

Brewer complied and slithered back into the underbrush. The guards resumed their watch, and the prisoners returned to their activities. The drill was over.

*　*　*

Within a couple of weeks, Marcin had recruited and trained his crew and designed a prototype for a camel cart. The cart was inspired by an etching he had seen in an old newspaper of a Kiowa brave on horseback, pulling a sled-like contraption piled high with skins. Of course, field testing the design was a serious challenge. The men were subjected to fierce kicks by the bulls and repeated bites on the buttocks by the mares. One day, after several prisoners were injured, Khalil and Ahmad approached, cooing and clucking to calm the animals before buckling the sleds around their midsections. The two stable hands quickly proved beneficial additions to Marcin's detail, and both he and the prisoners were much obliged for a reprieve from the beasts' assaults.

"How a Polack, two Arabs, and a bunch a Yankee prisoners made such expert and efficient work of those wagons is a mystery, but I am impressed," Marcin overheard Colonel Peters remark to Sergeant Kirby after an inspection. Marcin seized the opportunity to request that some leftover bits of venison and bacon be added to the prisoners' rations, and to his surprise, Sergeant Kirby endorsed the idea, and the colonel agreed. The additional food was a godsend for the men.

Marcin and Kirby slowly circled one another at the worksite, and a quiet trust began to form between the two men. The sergeant was not like the other Southern soldiers at Camp Verde. Marcin could not say precisely why, but there was a flicker of humanity about the man despite the grim brutalities of the war. Marcin was less nervous when Kirby was around, both for himself and for his men. Late one evening, after the prisoners were secured for the night and Khalil and Ahmad had retired to their quarters, Marcin and Kirby sat together by a campfire near the barracks. The sweet smell of the smoke from the mesquite logs was intoxicating. Marcin tilted his head back and inhaled as the sergeant stoked the embers with a thick branch. The flames flared, and more smoke began to billow into the air.

Kirby also drew a deep breath. "The Apache think the smell of mesquite attracts good spirits. Sure hope they're right," he said with a yawn.

Marcin nodded.

Kirby tried again to break the silence. "Mr. Anderwald, you don't say much, do ya?"

Marcin shrugged. He had been thinking about Zacharias and the girls, their sweet laughter, their innocent faces. He also thought about Agnieszka and how difficult his absence must be for her.

"I've been meanin' to ask," Kirby said. "Why are you so concerned about them Union boys? They're our enemy."

Marcin opened and closed his mouth several times before speaking. "Sergeant Kirby, to be honest, I do not understand why you fight."

"I guess it comes down to the principle of things," Kirby replied.

"What are these principles, Sergeant? Starving prisoners and letting your soldiers attack defenseless men?"

Kirby grimaced. "Well, principles are complicated, Mr. Anderwald."

"I do not understand what 'complicated' means," Marcin challenged. "Maybe it is my English, but I know what the Bible says. You must not repay evil with evil. It is God's to avenge."

The sergeant hesitated. "Mr. Anderwald, I don't mean to offend, but I'm not so sure about all that love your enemy nonsense anymore, let alone what God does or doesn't want from me." Kirby took an ornate silver flask from his breast pocket, unscrewed the top, and took three swift gulps. Marcin eyed the flask. "It was a gift. From my late wife," Kirby explained. "Amelia was her name. She died of smallpox. Along with Katie."

"Katie?" Marcin asked.

"Our little one," Kirby choked.

"I am sorry to hear this," Marcin said, pulling his jacket tighter around his chest.

Kirby poked at the fire and watched the sparks float into the night. "As for what happened with Augie today, he is a menace, no doubt, but you gotta keep in mind where he's come from. His mother died when he was barely a boy and left him with a father who beat him senseless. Finally got sent off to the House of Refuge up in Louisville, which was anything but. Them delinquents set upon the poor kid straight away. Broke his ankle in a brawl, which left him lame. Didn't leave much room for good in that boy's spirit. He does try occasionally, though."

Marcin was not convinced Private Brewer was worth all the effort. His compassion was in short supply when it came to the vile young soldier. Marcin frowned as these thoughts crossed his mind. He'd never considered that his own principles might be complicated as well.

"Anyway," the sergeant continued. "Seein' as I ain't got a family no more, and I can't seem to make heads or tails of this damned war, I figure I can try and help by taking Brewer under my wing."

Kirby took another sip from his flask and offered Marcin a swig. Marcin did not usually imbibe, but it had been a long day. The cheap spirits burned the back of his throat. He returned the flask to the sergeant, who took another long drink before passing it back.

Marcin raised a hand. "No, thank you, Sergeant Kirby."

"Call me Curtis," the sergeant said with a sad smile.

Marcin blinked. "And you must call me Marcin."

✳ ✳ ✳

Sergeant Kirby was due to make his regular run to San Antonio to secure provisions for Camp Verde. Marcin was already preparing for the worst in the sergeant's absence. With few men to spare, Colonel Peters assigned Private Brewer to take Kirby's place guarding the Union prisoners on the work detail.

"I'll be gone for ten days at most, Marcin, but while I'm away, you gotta steer clear of Augie," Kirby urged. "And not to worry. I will stop through Bandera and check in on your family." The sergeant tucked the list of items Marcin asked him to buy for Agnieszka and the children into his saddlebag.

"Thank you, Curtis," Marcin said, handing over a small pouch of coins.

Kirby shook his finger in Marcin's face. "I'm serious. Do not give that boy any cause for violence. He won't be able to resist the temptation."

"I understand," Marcin muttered and headed to the worksite, steeling himself for the days ahead.

Private Brewer greeted Marcin outside the stables with a wicked grin. "Looks like you and me will be workin' together long as the Sarge is away," the young soldier said. "And don't think I won't frisk your men at the end of their shift. I've heard talk you been aidin' and abettin' the enemy prisoners with extra rations," he taunted.

Marcin ignored him and set to work with his men, while Brewer spent the entire morning sneaking sips of what the soldiers referred to as bark juice from a bottle. By noon, he was so drunk from the homebrew that he was laid back against a tree, sleeping. However, when the workers' lunch arrived, the private sprang to attention and jumped to the front of the line, grabbing most of the meat for himself.

"Private Brewer, what are you doing?" Marcin asked.

"We're all hungry here, Polack, and I'm not passing up the chance for some extra grub," Brewer said, stuffing his face in front of the hungrier men. When finished, he threw the remaining bread on the ground and forced the prisoners to crawl in the dirt to retrieve it. "Go on, you Yankee scum. That's it," Brewer smirked, kicking several men with vicious force in their ribs and backsides.

"Stop this now!" Marcin shouted.

Everyone, including Brewer, looked stunned by the outburst. The prisoners slowly moved between Private Brewer and Marcin in a line of defense and defiance.

Brewer dislodged his weapon from its holster. "Fuck you, Anderwald," he slurred. "And you sonofabitches," he said, pointing at the other men, "stand aside, or I'll shoot."

The private stepped forward but caught his foot on a tree root and fell, losing a grip on his pistol. As he tried to stand, Brewer's back suddenly arched, and he vomited with three mighty and uncontrolled heaves. After the last, he sat back on his heels and wiped his chin. The meat and booze he'd gorged on seeped into the dirt before him.

"Private Brewer, you must stop." Marcin now spoke calmly but forcefully, edging toward the gun. A puff of dust floated up beneath his boots and betrayed his intentions.

Brewer pounced and grabbed his pistol. "Anderwald, what in blazes d'you think yer doin'?" he seethed, aiming directly at Marcin. "And who are you to take that tone with me?"

"I don't understand. What have I ever done to you?" Marcin asked, hoping to reason with the soldier.

"There you go again, you sanctimonious lickfinger! Talkin' down to me. You think cause you got that beautiful wife, them kids, your precious Pope—hell, everything—that yer better than me, don't ya. Well, I ain't gonna stand for it, Anderwald. Where I come from, that calls for takin' a fella down a peg or two."

Brewer raised his weapon, his hand shaking. Without warning a shot exploded from the barrel, and a bullet whizzed past Marcin's ear so close its heat seared his skin. The young soldier froze, and Marcin and the prisoners backed away, their hands raised above their heads.

From somewhere in the rear, a thundering roar rang out as Colonel Peters charged toward the group, two guards at his side. "That is enough, Private!"

Brewer remained on his knees.

"Get up and hand over that weapon," the colonel demanded.

The guards grabbed the young soldier and forced him to his feet.

The private stood meekly between them. "Yes, Colonel," he said, proffering his gun to the commanding officer.

Colonel Peters tucked the weapon into his belt before launching into a severe and public rebuke. He stood before his charge, hands on his hips. "Private, I believe I was clear after the incident at the ravine the other day when you fired upon unarmed prisoners of war, was I not?"

"Yes, sir, you was," Brewer replied.

Peters turned to address Marcin. "Mr. Anderwald, did Private Brewer intentionally fire at you?"

Marcin looked hard at Brewer. He could not be sure whether what he felt was hatred, nor did he want to be. And though his faith taught him that he should turn the other cheek, he could not bring himself to do so. The bullet's graze began to throb.

"Yes, Colonel," Marcin replied. "And he threatened me and the prisoners many times before."

Private Brewer lifted his head and stared at Marcin, his gaze searing and desperate in equal measure.

The colonel turned back to the accused. "Private, you've crossed the line for the last time. Sergeant Kirby can no longer come to your pathetic defense. You will be held accountable for your flagrant insubordination and breach of protocol. Gentlemen, escort this sorry excuse for a soldier to the guardhouse."

The guards dragged Brewer away.

"Get back to work," Peters barked and headed to the barracks.

*　　*　　*

That night, Marcin tried desperately to settle his mind, but thoughts of the young soldier intruded, and he did not sleep a wink. The confrontation at the worksite left no doubt in his mind. He had tried to be reasonable, but if there was a bad seed, a sinner so foul they must suffer God's wrath, it was Private Augustus Brewer. Marcin prayed for vengeance for the first time in his life, and in reply, a faint murmur sounded in his head, "Cursed above all." He could only make out a few words, but he recognized the scripture. God's charge to the serpent in the Garden of Eden.

Ice pulsed through Marcin's veins. "What have I done?" he pleaded into the blackness. He knew that God had cursed not only the serpent but also Adam and Eve and their son Cain. "Zachek," he whispered. "Could such an imprecation be more than you can bear?"

"Yes," came a disembodied growl.

"Who is there?" Marcin called out, beginning to worry that exhaustion was giving way to delusion.

No one answered.

As daybreak approached, a great commotion erupted outside.

Marcin made his way out to the stables and joined a group of enlisted soldiers talking excitedly with an officer from another division.
The man was strange-looking—pale like a ghost with a thick mop
of red hair and copious eyebrows of the same hue. His deep voice,
laced with a curious sibilance, was also notable. "I'm tellin' you,
boys, it was a terrible scene. Our patrol came upon a family of home-
steaders butchered on their ranch along the Guadalupe River," the
man reported.

"Sonofabitches!" one soldier yelled.

"There's word them murderers are camped to the west on a
bluff above the river," the fire-haired man explained. "Those savages
must be hunted down and brought to justice."

"Count us in!" several more soldiers cried.

Colonel Peters approached, and silence fell over the crowd. A
guard was pulling Brewer along. The private looked like hell.

"Boys, if we're gonna catch these bastards, we must make haste
now that the sun is up. I'm gonna need some volunteers—" the
colonel paused and turned to the stranger. "What's the name again,
Sergeant?"

"Josiah T. Gaines, sir," the man replied with a whoosh at the
end like he'd said "Gainsh."

At least ten hands shot into the air.

"Sergeant Gaines, you'll be in command, and this man here
will be your scout," the colonel said, pointing at Brewer. "Private,
tie your boots and button your coat. You're going with Gaines and
these boys. You'll head out first."

"You can't send me out there! I's lame, Colonel. No way I can
ride fast enough, sir," the private protested, his look of impudent
incredulity quickly giving way to terror.

"That's an order, Private. You can get on your horse or join the
prisoners in the ditch. Your choice." Colonel Peters did not wait for
a reply. He pushed past, leaving Brewer sputtering.

Brewer bent to tie his ill-fitting boots, his hands shaking. He
stood up and checked his sidearm before limping to the stables. He
mounted his horse and started toward the camp's entrance. Marcin
followed to ensure the soldier did not try to escape.

At the main gate, Brewer pulled back on his horse's reins and turned to Marcin. "I see you there, Anderwald, you stinkin' turn-coat," he seethed. "You ratted me out to save your own hide, but you'll pay for it you hear? When I get back, yer mine!"

Brewer's threats rang hollow, for it was no longer hateful contempt he conveyed. It was fear. Marcin was unmoved. The Devil had surely cometh to Camp Verde and must be cast out. Of this, Marcin was certain. Marcin's response was drowned out by the whoops and whistles of the other riders who galloped up from behind. Private Brewer's horse startled and took flight across Verde Creek at full speed, the disgraced soldier holding on for dear life.

*   *   *

A weary and much-diminished detachment crossed back over the creek two days later. Of the sixteen men who set out together—fifteen of the Confederacy's best and one of its worst—only three returned, and Sergeant Gaines was missing in action. Those who'd fallen were piled into a wagon, their boots peeking out from under a tarp.

Colonel Peters and the other soldiers gathered on the parade ground. Marcin approached from the worksite, followed by Khalil and Ahmad. The colonel drew back the tarp to reveal faces already starting to bloat and distort from the summer heat. By the process of elimination among the living, Peters and his remaining men worked to determine who had perished, but Marcin was sure of one casualty. A pair of feet in two mismatched boots was at the bottom of the putrid jumble of bodies.

"Khalil and Ahmad, start digging some graves," the colonel ordered. "And the rest of you, help me lay out these poor boys."

Most of the dead had been killed in combat, with arrows entering their chests and abdomens from the front. Private Brewer, however, had been shot twice in the back, and his attackers had beaten him most fiercely, crushing his skull and exposing the gelatinous brain tissue beneath. But what disconcerted Marcin more than anything else was that Brewer had also suffered the gravest and most humiliating personal violation. His severed member protruded between his split and bloodied lips, having been forced down his gullet with extreme malice.

"What the hell happened out there?" the colonel interrogated one of the returning soldiers. He was pointing at Brewer's corpse.

All three survivors exchanged uncomfortable looks.

"Mm, hmm. I see," Peters said, his brow furled. "I guess we'll have to talk about that later, then. We have more urgent matters to tend to," he grunted, lifting another body beneath its arms. "Somebody grab his feet."

Again, distant murmuring rose up like it had the night before, "You will crawl on your belly and eat dust all the days of your life." Marcin began to tremble. Were his darkest prayers being answered, and if so, by whom or by what? Or was he simply losing his mind?

Marcin stood over Brewer, the private's dulled, unblinking eyes looking past him toward the sky. He knelt and reached out to lower the soldier's eyelids. Heat seared Marcin's fingertips the instant they brushed against the young man's lifeless skin. At the exact same moment, he heard a muffled howl rise from deep within the rotting body. He spun around, sure others had also heard, but there was no reaction among the men. Marcin looked down again to find Brewer's eyes reopened. Their pupils, restored to a vibrant green color and divided by the narrowest of vertical slits, were cast in his direction.

Marcin collapsed onto the ground. "Boże pomóż! God help me!" he begged.

CHAPTER 4

And So, Follows the Shadow

No one at Camp Verde spoke of the curious circumstances of Private Brewer's demise, and Colonel Peters never inquired again. Although the tell-tale brutalities Comanche were known to visit upon their enemies—soldiers, settlers, and fellow Native Americans alike—were evident on several of the bodies, it could not be denied that the injuries Brewer suffered appeared overly gratuitous, even for a Comanche warrior attack. Nevertheless, the fact that the young soldier had been shot twice in the back at close range and apparently in retreat didn't seem to cause too much consternation, and most of the men appeared content to let sleeping dogs lie.

It was not so easy for Marcin Anderwald. His was a crisis of conscience on a hair trigger. His testimony had been truthful, but Marcin's quiet intentions had been vengeful, and his prayers were offered with a heart filled with hate. Sleep remained elusive as he desperately sought to reconcile his role in the boy's grisly death. And then there was what he had seen and heard on the parade ground that now tormented him. Private Brewer had been dead and buried for nearly two weeks, but horrific visions of the young soldier appeared each night in varying degrees of decomposition, his countenance accusing, pleading. At first, Marcin refused to believe what manifested before him might be some kind of spirit, and dismissed the vision, its skull shattered, and bone fragments and blood smeared across its cheeks, as either a symptom of delirium or a nightmare. But when the figure began to speak to him, Marcin understood darker forces were at play.

"You best know, Anderwald," the apparition threatened, "I will call upon the Devil himself to hold you and your filthy kin to account both here on earth and in the hereafter."

In the hierarchy of curses, earthbound or otherworldly, this one was extraordinary in its scope. Marcin had never been so frightened in his entire life, and he was not sure prayers would help, but he prayed nevertheless. "Forgive me, Lord," he entreated as blood-curdling screams tore through the camp. He thought he was dreaming again, and the screams were his own, but he quickly realized they were coming from the stables.

"Shabah!" one of the Arab wranglers howled.

Marcin dressed quickly and rushed toward the noise. "Khalil! Ahmad!" he shouted to the men.

White with fear, the stable hands jumped the corral fence and grabbed at Marcin. They continued screaming, "Shabah! Shabah!"

Inside the barn, the terrified horses roared and kicked the sides of their stalls, and outside in their pen, the camels backed away from something unseen beyond the door, pawing frantically at the ground. Something caught Marcin's attention, a flutter in his peripheral vision, and then a long shadow glided across the opening. Nothing defined, only a denser patch of black within the blackness.

"I don't understand," Marcin said, trying to release himself from the men's grip.

"Brewer. Shabah," the wrangler Ahmad panted.

"Brewer?" Marcin asked in disbelief. "No. It cannot be."

The noise had woken Sergeant Kirby and two other soldiers who'd returned from their provisions run earlier that evening. The men approached from the barracks in haste.

"What the hell is all this racket?" Kirby grumbled. "I'm dog-tired from the road and don't appreciate bein' dragged from my bed in the middle of the night."

"These men saw something in the barn," Marcin reported. "They are terrified, and so are the livestock."

"Shabah," Khalil repeated, pointing toward the building.

"I think shabah might mean ghost, Curtis."

"They are certainly scared 'bout somethin'," Kirby said, waving his colleagues forward. "You two, go check it out but be careful. Might be thieves comin' for the horses."

The men crept inside, guns drawn, but returned a few minutes later, shaking their heads.

"Not sure what to say, Sarge. No thieves or boogeymen lurkin' in there, best we can tell," one said.

The other added, "I think all that yellin' was what set the horses off. Damn, Sarge, those boys scare me half to death when they get to yammerin' on."

"Yeah, yeah," Sergeant Kirby interrupted. "Marcin, I'm sorry these two disturbed you. Khalil and Ahmad, stop all this nonsense and get back to your bunks."

The stable hands retrieved their blanket rolls from the barn and retreated to a small grove of trees near the ravine.

"Suit yourselves, you crazy Arabs," the sergeant laughed. "If the ghost don't get ya, the 'skeetoes will!" Kirby smacked the back of his neck. "Marcin, I think we're done here for tonight. I'm off to bed and suggest you do the same."

Marcin stared at the entrance to the barn, crossing himself twice for good measure before returning to his lodgings. Unable to fall asleep, he stared at the ceiling. He could hear Khalil and Ahmad talking to each other, and after a short time, he realized they were praying. Marcin added his own appeals to the chorus floating into the heavens.

*　*　*

Three weeks after the incident at the stables, Marcin gathered his few belongings and prepared to head home. His job was completed, and he could not wait to escape Camp Verde. A cloud of intense disquiet had settled over the camp. It was clear to Marcin that he and his family were in terrible danger from forces beyond his control. As he prepared to head to the stables, there was a knock on the door.

"Anderwald, you still here? You best not have left without say-in' goodbye." It was Sergeant Kirby. "Open the damned door!"

Marcin found Kirby on the other side, a mug of coffee in each hand.

"Morning, Curtis."

"You look like shit. Here, drink this." Kirby handed one of the mugs to Marcin. "And sit. I gotta talk to you. Didn't wanna burden you after all that ruckus with Augie, but there's somethin' you need to know."

What now? Marcin frowned. He was not sure he could take much more.

"I done what you asked me and stopped through Bandera to check on Mrs. Anderwald and the children. By the by, that boy of yours is something to be proud of, Marcin. He sure is takin' good care of things. And them Mormons, they are doin' right by your family, too. Good people, the Hawleys. But your wife—" Kirby paused and took a sip from his mug. "Thing is, she's been missing you somethin' awful, and it's taken a toll. You will need to tend to her closely when you get home, you hear?"

"Is something wrong with Aga? Is she sick?" Marcin was not sure he fully understood the sergeant's concern.

"I can't explain it. It's just a feelin', and I needed to ruminate on it before sayin' anything."

"Tell me, Curtis."

Kirby cleared his throat. "I think your wife has had a tough time with you bein' away. Might be a bit broken, as they say. I'm sure everything will settle when you get home, but it didn't feel right not to warn ya."

Marcin stood up. "I must go."

*   *   *

At midday, Marcin reached the final stretch along Bandera Pass, and the clearing where the grave markers stood came into view. A sickly-sweet smell of decay hung in the air, and something moved in the tall grass along the roadside. A threatening growl rose from the same direction, spooking Marcin's horse.

"Easy, Miko," Marcin said, pulling back on the reins. He steadied his rifle across his lap, clicking the double barrels into place.

The stench intensified, and the growling grew louder. Marcin knew he was being stalked. When all fell unusually still and quiet, he panicked and kicked his horse with all his might. Upon reaching the next rise, Marcin looked back. His chest tightened as a dark shadow slid out of the tall grass and into the road a quarter of a mile behind. The figure floated atop a hillock, its body twisted, and its head concave where the top had been crushed. A soft breeze began to stir again, shepherding a raw and menacing wail through the air.

Marcin fumbled with his shotgun, raising the barrel and trying to level his sight, but sweat dripped from his brow and blurred his vision. "For God's sake, what do you want from me?" he pleaded, his cracked lips trembling.

The shadow cocked its mangled skull. "You are mine," it said.

"Please, no," Marcin begged, slowly backing his horse further down the road.

The figure began to laugh. "Mine," it repeated and started toward him, its laughter growing louder. "Forever, Anderwald. You and your children, and your children's children."

"Diabeł!" Marcin screamed and raced toward home. He did not slow again until he saw the rooftops of Bandera.

CHAPTER 5

The Home Front

Marcin edged off the road and onto a dirt track that ascended a familiar hilltop. Three ancient oak trees stood sentinel at its crest, their knotted and twisted boughs extending into the cloudless sky as if in supplication. Soon, the stunning bend in the Medina River would be revealed in the valley below. Marcin had been drawn to the river by a force he could not identify from the first moment he'd seen its waters cutting a majestic path across the rugged landscape. He longed to walk along its banks once again, to listen to its current gurgle around the jagged boulders anchored in the riverbed. Home at last.

The Hawleys' wagon was parked in front of the house, and the children scurried back and forth in the yard. Marcin stopped and watched from a distance. Zacharias, Victoria, and Beata were playing hide-and-seek with the Hawley brood, and the adults were seated in the shade of the front porch. A blond head popped up from the swing. It was Lena.

"Tatuś!" the little girl chirped.

"Yes, Lenka, Tatuś will be home soon," Zacharias assured his baby sister.

The toddler giggled and pointed, "Tatuś! Tatuś come!"

All heads turned in Marcin's direction, and he quickly dismounted and jogged toward the gate.

"Lookee there, Anderwalds," Mr. Hawley said. "The little one is right."

"Oh, Agnieszka," Mrs. Hawley exclaimed. "God has brought your Marcin home."

"Tato!" Victoria and Beata shouted as they pounced on their father.

"Who are these princesses?" Marcin said, hugging both girls at once.

Agnieszka was a half-step behind. She threw her arms around Marcin, clutching him tightly. He could feel how thin she was and see the purplish-blue circles of exhaustion under her dark brown eyes, damp with tears.

The Mormon and Mrs. Hawley followed Lena, who insisted on walking all by herself, her pudgy arms extended to each side to maintain her balance. "Tatuś!" she repeated.

"Who is this beautiful maiden walking and talking so nicely?" Marcin sniffed as he greeted his youngest daughter.

Zacharias remained a few paces back. The boy had grown taller in the nearly four months Marcin had been gone. Marcin stood and reached out to shake the boy's hand but immediately embraced him. "Zachek, my son. Tell me you are not too big to hug your father," he said.

Zacharias beamed and squeezed his father's waist.

"We'll be on our way," Mr. Hawley interrupted. "Let you all enjoy your reunion. Holler if you need anything."

"Charles, I cannot thank you enough," Marcin replied.

"Happy to help," Mr. Hawley said with a tip of his hat, his wife shooing their children into the back of the wagon.

The Anderwalds waved goodbye, and the Hawleys headed toward their homestead further along the river path.

After supper, when the children were in bed, Marcin watched Agnieszka tidy the kitchen from across the room. The two had exchanged no more than a few words the entire afternoon. "Kochanie, I have missed you," he said softly.

Agnieszka turned to face him, wringing a towel in her hands. The light from the two small candles on the tabletop flickered, illuminating her creamy white skin.

Marcin eased closer. "What's wrong, Aga?" he said. "You look so troubled."

"I am tired, Marcin. So tired. I cannot sleep."

Marcin wrapped his arms around Agnieszka. He could feel her breath catching as he extracted the pins from her long braids and combed through her tresses with his fingers. He began to sing their favorite song, the one about the young village girl dancing in the forest. "Będziemy, będziemy. Tu tańcować," the words skipped across his lips.

Agnieszka began to sob, mournfully humming along to the familiar tune.

"Aga, we will also dance again," Marcin said. They began to sway back and forth. He kissed Agnieszka's cheeks and chin before touching his lips to hers. At first, Marcin was tentative, but when Agnieszka reciprocated, her lips parting, he was overcome by longing. Marcin touched her breast through her shift.

"Moja, mine," he moaned.

"Twoja, yours," she replied.

*   *   *

The relief of homecoming was short-lived for Marcin and Agnieszka. In those first weeks back, Marcin felt a slow but steady distance growing between them. Some days, Agnieszka was combative; others, she was sullen. Marcin understood she was angry that he would not discuss his time at Camp Verde or the nightmares, but he had no intention of ever sharing what haunted his slumber.

"Tell me," Agnieszka insisted after a night of arguing that left Marcin silent and defeated.

"It's nothing," he insisted and turned away. It was hard to lie to Agnieszka's face, to see the helplessness that weighed upon her.

"You left me here to worry and wonder, and though you have returned, you are lost to me, Marcin," she spoke into the rift between them. "Something happened, and you have changed. Tell me, kochanie. Jestem tutaj," Agnieszka pleaded, wiping the sweat from Marcin's shoulders.

"I know you are here, Aga," was all Marcin could bring himself to say.

Agnieszka soon stopped asking. She withdrew from Marcin and the children, rarely speaking to them. "Mamusiu," little Lena would call out, wandering the house in desperate search of her mother. The older girls would ask questions and receive no response, retreating in frustration or seeking out Marcin for answers he did not have. Agnieszka acted as though she was deaf to her children's pleas.

Zacharias took matters into his own hands, stepping into the fray when his mother was at her worst. Marcin observed his son closely and remembered what Sergeant Kirby said about Zacharias caring for everyone. "Hold my hand near the water, Bea," he would insist as his sister skipped from rock to rock on the riverbank. "Vicky, be careful. Miko will kick you," he repeatedly cautioned when his other sister would approach their horse from behind. "Lenka, do not go under the porch. There are snakes," he would warn and pull the toddler away from danger.

Agnieszka's apathy was occasionally overtaken by an all-consuming mania, only to return with greater intensity and unpredictability. One hot September morning, Marcin watched her scurry around the house in preparation for a visit from John and Eugenia Stanard, who had become regular customers. Mrs. Stanard had sent word through one of her ranch hands that she and her family would be stopping by to retrieve a recent order Agnieszka had completed—a dress of magenta-colored silk trimmed in indigo lace. Even Marcin understood Agnieszka had created a work of art.

The Stanards arrived in a light two-horse carriage, the rear platform piled high with trunks and two tall birdcages covered with a blanket. Squawks like no bird Marcin had ever heard and the frantic rustling of feathers and rough scratching came from the cages. Mr. Stanard pulled the horses to a stop, and the children bounded from the back seat, squealing with excitement. The young Stanards were notable, indeed. Like her mother, Mary Rose was a stunning beauty, and Robert was his father's beguiling and jovial spitting image. Liza, the youngest Stanard, was the most remarkable, however, for she was as wide as she was tall. After formal welcomes, the Stanard children hesitated by the carriage, glancing at their father, who winked to signal they were free to proceed into the yard. They promptly ran off to play with Zacharias and his sisters.

"Please come in," Marcin said. He eyed John Stanard, still wary of the man who'd sent Kirby and Brewer his way.

Stanard's tall form dipped as he crossed the threshold, and his broad shoulders, draped in the finest haberdashery, brushed the door frame as he entered the house. The faint scent of cologne from freshly shaved cheeks and a professionally trimmed beard followed in his impressive wake.

"Much obliged," Stanard acknowledged Marcin with a nod before turning to Agnieszka with a bright smile. "And good morning, Mrs. Anderwald. It's lovely to see you again."

Marcin noticed the hint of a blush sweep across Agnieszka's cheeks.

"Hello, Agnieszka," Eugenia Stanard said, emphasizing Agnieszka's Christian name. "We shall not be here long."

"What a delicious smell!" John Stanard raved and seated himself at the kitchen table where a pastry steamed at its center.

"Um, yes. It is szarlotka, a family recipe from my homeland," Agnieszka replied with obvious pride.

"Might I trouble you for a piece?" Stanard asked with a longing glance.

"Mrs. Stanard?" Agnieszka gestured for Eugenia to take a seat as she sliced the pie.

"No, thank you. It looks lovely, but I am always watching my waistline, so I must decline," Eugenia replied, unabashedly surveying Agnieszka's form.

Marcin watched Agnieszka touch her stomach and brush the pleats in her dress. He stepped closer and gently squeezed her elbow in quiet support. He had never liked this Stanard woman.

Eugenia pursed her lips and inhaled through her nose. "We do not have much time, dear. I think Agnieszka and I should get to my fitting," she said, and the two women retreated into the bedroom.

John Stanard pinched off a piece of the pastry Agnieszka had served him and popped it into his mouth, eyeing Marcin as he licked the remaining sugar off each of his fingers. The birds on the wagon outside crowed, which was followed by the sound of the children's shrieks.

"We better get out there and make sure those kids don't let the birds loose," Stanard said, heading for the door.

Marcin followed. He, too, was curious.

"Hey, kiddos, how about we take a peek?" Stanard offered.

The children jumped to see into the cages. "Oh, yes!" they gushed.

John Stanard hurried toward the carriage. "Hang on. Let me get this blanket off."

What was revealed beneath took Marcin's breath away. He had never seen anything more beautiful in his life. Two dainty birds were pacing in their cages.

"Whoa, Tato, look!" Zacharias said, pressing his face against the metal bars.

"Yes, Zachek. They are something." Marcin also bent down to take a closer look.

"Daddy, tell 'em the story about these birds," Robert insisted.

"All right, then," Stanard said, glancing at his pocket watch. "I think we have some time before your mother is finished."

"The *whole* story, Daddy," Liza chimed in.

"Will do, Liza Lou," Stanard said with a playful squeeze of his daughter's plump cheek. "Here goes. These drab, ordinary birds were going about their business in a faraway land over the ocean called India. They were hunting for bugs, worms, baby snakes—"

"Snakes?" cried Victoria and Beata. "Ewwwww!"

Stanard smacked his lips. "But one day, those birds got more than they bargained for. They stumbled upon a big nest of serpents that were riled up and ready to strike."

"Daddy, is this a true story?" Mary Rose asked.

"'Course it is, Rosie," Stanard said dismissively, reengaging with the others. "Anyway, those birds were tough, indeed. When one of the snakes started at the papa bird, he got to pecking and chasing the darned thing. Before that reptile knew what was happening, the bird gobbled him down headfirst."

"Whoopee! Git 'im!" the boys cheered.

"Funny enough," Stanard grinned, "while the snake didn't get a chance to bite the papa bird, it was still filled with poison, which started seeping into the bird's belly. But guess what happened?"

"This is gonna be good!" Liza said, pulling at Zacharias' shirt-sleeve with excitement.

Stanard leaned forward, eyes wide, the children hanging on his every word. "All that poison worked its way out into the bird's skin and all the way out to the tips of its feathers, transforming them from the ugliest brown into the most beautiful combination of blues and greens you ever saw. Another bunch of feathers took on the shape of an eye—round, like the snake's eye. The females ate the babies, and since there wasn't much poison in them, the hens only got a bit of color on their breasts. So, that's how peacocks and peahens came to be."

"I had no idea," Marcin said, equally entranced. He could not stop looking at the birds.

"These peafowl were an unexpected gift from my mother-in-law," Stanard explained. "And though they are something to behold, they make an awful noise when startled. I understand they are superb snakers, though, and keep the bugs away. I figure they'll be of some use to us on the ranch."

"We have many snakes here," Zacharias piped up. "Under the house and in the barn. Tato, maybe we should get birds like this, too?"

Marcin shot Zacharias a stern look.

Stanard laughed and tousled the boy's hair. "Your son has given me an idea, Mr. Anderwald. Seems like you could use these creatures more than we can. Might you do me a favor and take them off my hands? If I'm honest, they make Mrs. Stanard a bit anxious."

The birds were in the yard before Marcin could utter a word of resistance.

"John, what in the Lord's name is going on out here?" Eugenia interjected testily, emerging from the house, Agnieszka in her wake.

Marcin hadn't noticed the women approaching over the birds' racket.

"Keeping the little ones occupied so you can try on your new outfits," Stanard replied. "How do they look?"

Marcin caught Agnieszka's eye. She could not hide her deep desire for affirmation from Eugenia Stanard, some recognition of her hard work, nor her utter disappointment when it was not forthcoming.

Eugenia did not answer and continued her directives as she walked toward the carriage. "It will be dark soon, so we best be getting home. Kindly give Agnieszka her wages. Oh, and next time, I will bring the children's drawers and socks for mending."

John Stanard withdrew a small pouch of coins from his jacket pocket and handed them to Agnieszka. "We're much obliged, Mrs. Anderwald," he said apologetically. "Here's four dollars per our agreement, plus a little extra, given I expect you spent more time and effort than you let on."

Agnieszka frowned.

Marcin stepped in and reached for the purse. "Mr. Stanard, it is not necessary to pay more than agreed."

Stanard firmly placed the coin pouch back in Agnieszka's palm, and folded her fingers closed. "Consider the extra my gratitude for taking those birds off my hands." Stanard pointed toward the cages as he helped his wife into her seat. "Let's go, chickabiddies," he beckoned to his own children. "Time to skedaddle!" As the carriage departed, Stanard tipped his hat. "Much obliged, Mrs. Anderwald. You take care, kids."

The Stanard children chattered in the back, promising they would return soon. Eugenia Stanard looked straight ahead without saying goodbye. Agnieszka remained still, her hands clasped in front of her, and her head bowed. Marcin knew well the look of burning humiliation on his wife's face.

"Aga, don't pay her any mind," he said.

Agnieszka tucked the coins into her apron and turned up the path. "It is time for me to go back to my place," she replied.

CHAPTER 6

The Picnic

Marcin decided the family needed a day of rest, complete with a picnic on the banks of his beloved Medina River. He invited the Hawleys to thank them for their assistance during his absence. It was a spectacular fall afternoon, still hot in the open but cooler under the trees. A light breeze rustled the delicate branches atop the towering bald cypresses, releasing the first of the season's slender bronze leaves into the cloudless sky.

With blankets spread and food assembled, Marcin, Agnieszka, and their guests relaxed for the first time in months. Zacharias and two of the Hawley boys were casting their lines off a large boulder on the opposite side of the river, and the older girls were playing dolls under a nearby cedar. Lena and the Hawleys' youngest, Tobias, played beside Agnieszka, who was napping in the sun. The toddlers studied a colony of black carpenter ants at work and tried to coax them over a bridge they had fashioned from a long, thin tree branch between two mounds of dirt. Marcin sat further up the hill with Mr. and Mrs. Hawley playing cards.

Something attracted the little ones' attention closer to the river. "Mamusiu, baby birds! Come see," Lena said, pulling Agnieszka's arm. This was the bevy's first venture beyond their nest near the farmhouse. "Mamusiu, come!" Lena begged but quickly lost patience. She and Tobias ran after a peahen and her five peachicks, waddling through the tall grass toward the riverbank. The peacock greeted his stalwart mate and their first progeny. "Eee-iu, eee-iu," the bird trumpeted through the trees.

"Wait for us," Beata said, and the big girls joined the viewing party. The older boys were also waving and shouting something from their perch.

A wisp of movement flickered among the trees on the opposite bank, catching Marcin's eye, and he noticed the little ones wandering closer to the water. "Aga, are you minding them?" he called.

Agnieszka offered a limp wave, and Marcin returned to his game. A moment later, something again darted in and out of the brush. When Marcin looked up, Lena and Tobias had already reached the river.

"Aga, they are too close to the water," Marcin warned, but Agnieszka made no move to get up from the blanket. "Fine," he grunted and stood up. "Children, be careful!" he shouted and set off down the hill.

Mr. and Mrs. Hawley rose to join him, but Agnieszka remained stretched out on the blanket, her feet bare and arm draped over her face. She did not stir when Marcin and the Hawleys passed. All at once, the children's laughter spiraled into panic.

"Lenka, stop!" Zacharias cried. He jumped into the water and frantically waded across the strong current. "Tato, help! Help her!"

The other girls were howling and running back toward Marcin and the Hawleys, who sprinted to the riverbank. They had all seen Lena run after the baby birds and tumble headfirst into a deep pool near a cluster of trees. Marcin arrived breathless at the water's edge and, to his horror, saw the child writhing beneath the surface. She looked to be trapped among the tree roots growing over the bank. There was little time, and, upon closer inspection, Marcin understood he might already be too late. It was not a tangle of roots but a nest of water moccasins into which Lena had fallen. The snakes flailed back and forth and raised their heads above the surface, bearing the cottony interiors of their massive jaws and exposing their long, sharp fangs with each strike. Even after the child stopped struggling, the snakes continued to attack.

"Zachek, stay away! Get out of the water!" Marcin ordered.

"Mrs. Hawley, do not let Aga come here. Keep her back."

Mr. Hawley grabbed a long tree branch, and the two men hooked it onto Lena's pinafore and dragged her from the river into the grass. Marcin began to strip off her clothes to search for the punctures. There were six pairs—two on her upper right arm, three on her torso, and one on her left calf.

Agnieszka tore barefoot down the dirt path, screaming, "Nie! Nie! Nie!"

Mrs. Hawley blocked her way. "Agnieszka, no. Marcin and Charles have the baby. They are trying to save her. You don't want to see."

Agnieszka twisted her way free. "Lenka!" she wailed and threw herself down beside the child, clawing at her, slapping her cheeks, and trying to shake her awake.

"Aga, nie! Stop!" Marcin snapped and shoved her back. "Mr. Hawley, get the doctor. Tell him to come now! Mrs. Hawley, take Aga!"

The Hawleys dragged Agnieszka back up the path, kicking and sobbing, "Marcin," she continued to scream, "he was holding me down! I couldn't move!"

Marcin drew a small knife from his boot and made an incision between the entry points for each pair of punctures. He secured his mouth over the cuts and began to suck with all his might to try and draw the poison out of the wounds. Footsteps approached from behind. It was Zacharias, who, seeing what his father was doing, knelt at Lena's side and began pressing his lips against his sister's flesh, frantically drawing and spitting her blood onto the ground. Marcin continued to check whether Lena was breathing. Her respiration was almost imperceptible, but she was still alive. Marcin lifted the girl into his arms, keeping her head and chest elevated. Zacharias ran along beside him, holding her limp hand.

Doc Adolph arrived soon after dark but could do little for the child. Her stomach, arm, and lower leg had swollen tight, and the area beneath each bite was nearly black from the hemorrhages expanding beneath the skin's surface. The little girl's pulse was also weak, and her breathing remained shallow. He told Marcin to prepare for the worst. "I am mighty sorry, Mr. Anderwald. I fear Lena will not make it through the night."

"Yes, I understand," was all Marcin could muster by way of a response.

The doctor signaled to Mr. Hawley, who took his cue to summon Father Anton Adamietz, the young priest assigned to St. Stanislaus after Father Mazurek was relieved of his duties. Doc Adolph turned back to Marcin. "I am also worried about your wife, sir. She is in terrible shock," he said.

Marcin peered through the bedroom door and into the kitchen, where Agnieszka remained crumpled on the floor, shaking and moaning. She had not spoken a word since the accident and, despite Mrs. Hawley's best efforts, refused anything to drink or eat.

The doctor also expressed concern for the other Anderwald children huddled together in the front room, Zacharias holding tight to his little sisters. "Mrs. Hawley, I think it might be best if the children got some rest, don't you?" he suggested.

"Yes, yes. I'll see to it," Mrs. Hawley replied, guiding Zacharias, Beata, and Victoria to their beds.

* * *

The peacock trumpeted from the yard. Marcin's head jerked up from the mattress, where he'd dozed off at the bedside. The nub of a candle and its dying flame quivered on the bureau. Angry shadows darted across the ceiling, and dark smoke billowed into the air. Marcin sensed a heaviness in the room, followed by the now familiar voice.

"It begins," it wheezed.

Something Agnieszka said at the river echoed in Marcin's head. "He was holding me down," she had wailed. Marcin gripped the blanket. "God, please, no," he whimpered.

Night fell like an ax, and stillness followed, only to be broken by one final rattle of air releasing from within the tiny body at the center of the bed like a gentle sigh.

* * *

"Here, Tato," Zacharias insisted, pointing at the ground. "That way, Lenka can see us and won't be scared."

"All right, Zachek," Marcin answered, pushing his spade into the earth.

Zacharias collected rocks to place on top while Marcin dug a small grave on the rise under the three oaks. The physical exertion brought distraction and release. Marcin could not bear to be in the house where Lena lay wrapped in a blanket on the table, a small package of all that was good and light in the world but no more. The weight of preparation for the funeral was also suffocating. Father Adamietz was trying his best to shake Agnieszka from her grief-induced stupor, quoting endless lines of random Bible verses. Mrs. Hawley was tending to the girls, and Mr. Hawley was busy building a small coffin and fashioning a simple cross to mark the grave.

With the last scoop of soil, Marcin felt his knees weaken. "Zachek, run and wash up," he instructed. "Help the girls put on their Sunday dresses so Mrs. Hawley can try and get Mama ready. And see that Father Adamietz has had something to eat."

Zacharias set off toward the house. As soon as the boy was out of sight, Marcin sat down at the grave's edge, staring into the emptiness. How could he possibly face what was to come? The Mormon and his wife would stay on for the burial that afternoon and take the remaining Anderwald children back to their farm for a few days, but what about Aga? Marcin did not have the strength to tend to her, nor to forgive her failure to protect their beloved child.

Marcin swallowed hard and wiped the tears from his cheeks. The question of forgiveness would have to wait. A more somber task was at hand. He stood up and stumbled after Zacharias.

* * *

The grim funeral procession assembled in silence on the hill-top. Father Adamietz began his remarks with obvious trepidation. He'd confessed to Marcin that it was his first funeral for a child, and it showed. "The Lord hath given. The Lord hath taken away. Blessed be the name of the Lord," he said tentatively.

No one among the small gathering reacted or looked away from the wooden casket. Zacharias stood closest as if to keep the coffin from tipping into the open grave. Mrs. Hawley held Beata and Victoria close, and Marcin and the Mormon Hawley struggled to keep a disheveled Agnieszka upright. They had carried her from the house, her feet dragging so heavily that one of her boots had torn through at the toe.

Father Adamietz continued, "Our Lord Jesus said to the Pharisees: 'Let the little children come to me and do not hinder them, for to such belongs the Kingdom of Heaven.' Dear God, lead us, who grieve at this untimely death, to a new and deeper faith—"

The moment the word "faith" crossed the priest's lips, Agnieszka collapsed, clawing at the collar of her dress, and released a cry of pure anguish. "I am to blame!"

Marcin tried desperately to pull Agnieszka to her feet. "Aga, please," he implored.

"Lenka, I failed you! Take me, God, take me!" she howled over and over again.

CHAPTER 7

Jestem Tutaj, I Am Here

Little Lena's grave was the first of two Marcin would dig in the Anderwald family plot that autumn of 1861. Twenty-eight days after laying his youngest child to rest, a broken and bereft Marcin buried Agnieszka.

The picnic by the river was the last time Agnieszka would drink or eat anything herself, and the bits of food and drips of water Marcin forced down her throat, not without tremendous effort and frustration, couldn't sustain her. That terrible afternoon along the Medina would also be the last time Agnieszka spoke to their children, and her final words to Marcin would be on her deathbed a few weeks later. Those words would follow him for the rest of his life.

"Kara," Agnieszka rasped as Marcin wiped her brow with a wet cloth to keep her skin moist and cool. Her withering body could no longer sweat even in the oppressive heat of the Texas summer's last gasp.

"Kochanie, what do you mean punishment? For what?" Marcin pleaded.

Agnieszka turned toward him. "Kara," she repeated.

"Aga, I beg of you. Don't do this," Marcin said, caressing her bony hand.

Agnieszka licked her cracked lips with great effort. She moved her desiccated tongue around in her mouth, desperately trying to communicate. Marcin put his ear above her mouth, so she didn't have to struggle. "I failed her. I am to blame," Agnieszka whimpered.

The following morning, Mrs. Hawley dressed Agnieszka in a white muslin dress and braided her hair, and Mr. Hawley and Marcin lifted her dead body into a wooden crate perched atop the kitchen table.

"We'll give you a few minutes," Mrs. Hawley said, and she and her husband retreated to the front porch where Zacharias and his sisters sat, numb and silent, awaiting the signal to come and say their goodbyes.

Marcin stroked Agnieszka's cheek and brushed back a lock of hair that had come loose from her braid. The pain that had twisted his wife's face at the end had finally released. Marcin was relieved. It would be easier for the children to see her now.

"Aga. Kochanie," he wept.

Agnieszka was not alone in blaming herself for Lena's death. Marcin, too, was certain that his own failings and transgressions had led to the loss of his child and his wife's terrible demise. He had prayed for vengeance and asked God to bring suffering to another man. And it had been so. Now, the taunting presence of the dark figure continued to intrude upon his waking thoughts and stalk his dreams. Marcin feared this was only the beginning.

"Tato?" Zacharias said. "May we come?"

Marcin nodded, and the children filed in quietly, Zacharias leading the way. Beata and Victoria had each picked a bouquet of wildflowers and bound them with bright yellow ribbons. Zacharias lifted Beata, who placed her bouquet in one of Agnieszka's hands, and Marcin helped Victoria put hers in the other.

"Is she sleeping, Tatuś?" Victoria asked, the child's soft brow knitted in confusion.

"Yes, Vicky, sleeping with angels," Marcin answered.

"Will she come back when she wakes up?"

"No, Mamusia is going to sleep forever," Marcin strained.

"Is she with Lenka?" Beata said, clutching Zacharias around the neck.

Marcin's heart sank. "Yes, Bea, they are in Heaven together. Forever."

"Good. Then Mama won't be lonely." Beata looked at her mother for the last time.

Victoria bent over the casket and brought her face close to Agnieszka's. "Mamusia looks so beautiful," she said.

"Yes, she is," Marcin mumbled, setting the child down.

Zacharias released Beata. The boy stared at Marcin, tears brimming in his azure eyes.

"Come, Zachek. Help me," he said, and together, they secured the flat wooden cover with several nails to the top of the coffin.

It was time to head up the hill.

* * *

That evening, Marcin lay alone on the porch swing. He could not face the bed he and Agnieszka had shared. Not tonight. The peacock's cry floated through the trees from the river. "Hee-yelp! Hee-yelp!" it cawed.

Marcin began to drift off. The next thing he knew, he was running through the black night toward a speck of light in the distance, tripping over sharp rocks in his bare feet. Thin branches covered in long thorns sliced his forearms and face. The faint sound of sobbing, disrupted by an occasional sharp cry of distress, surrounded him. He approached what looked to be a clearing and saw a small campfire at its center. Violent thrashing followed by a hostile rattle shook the surrounding brush. Marcin's instinct was to run away, but an unseen force drew him toward the red and orange glow of the fire's dying embers. A long, serpentine shadow slithered forward into the dim circle of light and slowly turned toward the river.

"Hee-yelp," someone yowled. "Help me!" The cry became more insistent.

Marcin was compelled to follow the shadow. When he reached the riverbank, the clouds parted, and a full moon illuminated a dark figure standing on the other side, watching him. Marcin sensed movement at his feet. What looked like blood seeped from the muddy bank between his toes, over the tops of his feet, and over his ankles. He fell to the ground and prayed. "Forgive me, Father," Marcin begged. "And forgive the boy. Please show him mercy and let him rest in peace."

The calls for help began to fade, and somewhere in the night, Marcin heard laughter. It was wicked, not joyful laughter. He was soon distracted by a slow ache beginning to work its way up his legs. Marcin started to shiver and realized he was now fully awake, kneeling waist-deep in the river. He had no memory of how he had gotten there from the house. He continued the prayers he'd begun in the fog of half-sleep. "Dear God, forgive me for my sins. Let me be cleansed," he chanted.

Marcin threw himself forward, surrendering to the Medina. Turning onto his back, he floated along, his face barely above the water's surface. Stars twinkled through the dense foliage of the tree branches above. When his arm caught on a large rock at the river's bend, Marcin grabbed hold and dragged himself onto its flattened top. Gazing into the clear night sky, he listened to the ripple of the current.

A light wind picked up, and Marcin felt a chill race through his body. As he turned onto his side and curled into a ball, trying to keep warm, he saw an ethereal specter in white, standing at the water's edge. It was a woman, her arms extended toward him. She was humming a familiar tune.

"Aga!" Marcin cried. "Don't leave me!"

"Jestem tutaj," the woman replied. "I am here, and I will protect you all."

A deep, rumbling growl sounded in reply. Marcin squinted into the darkness. The shadow paced feverishly back and forth among the trees.

The woman in white raised her fists in the air. "Leave him!" she howled.

Marcin watched the ghostly figure swirl into the air and float toward him across the water's surface.

"Aga," he croaked.

"I am here," she whispered, slowly dissolving into the night.

CHAPTER 8

The Castoffs

In the wake of Lena and Agnieszka's deaths, the Anderwalds sought refuge in isolation, but the centripetal force of their collective suffering was intense and steady. Before long, like the whirlpools at the edges of the Medina collected the flotsam and jetsam of the river, so, too, did the Anderwald ranch—now known as Peacock Bend in honor of the curious fowl parading its grounds—draw in the castoffs of Bandera County.

But it was not only the lost and hopeless among the living who found their way to Peacock Bend. The sinister shadow and the fiercely protective woman in white also saw fit to take up permanent residence along the riverbank and among the hills. Both spirits set about recruiting their earth-bound surrogates and were soon locked in a desperate struggle for the hearts, minds, and souls of Marcin Anderwald and his family.

The Hawleys were the first to wade into the vortex, helping Marcin and the children at every turn, but they had only been biding their time to see if peace would hold with the North and the Comanche before heading to the Utah Territory. Life in Bandera had never been easy for the Mormons, especially after their spiritual leader, Elder Lyman Wight, died suddenly after having a premonition of the looming hostilities on the eve of the war.

"It's been a rough patch, Marcin," Charles Hawley had

confided. "Most folks around here prefer to deal with their own, you know? I can't see how they'll ever change their minds."

"You cannot go alone, Charles," Marcin advised. "It is too dangerous."

"No, no, you're right. I won't risk harm to Rebecca or the children. We'll head north with one of the spring cattle drives and join a wagon train heading to Salt Lake along the railroad line. I think that's the only way," Hawley replied.

"But your farm?" Marcin asked.

"That's something I wanted to talk to you about. Might you be in a position to buy me out?" Hawley raised his hand to keep Marcin from replying straight away. "Now, I know it's a lot to ask, but I'll give you a good price, and I can think of no one else I'd rather have the place. You know it's a fine piece of land, and it's right alongside yours and the river."

Marcin scraped together every spare penny he could find to buy the Hawleys' homestead, but the acquisition was bittersweet. On the morning of the Mormon's departure for Utah, the depth of the gaping hole they would undoubtedly leave in the Anderwalds' daily lives was overwhelming. "Be safe, Charles, and thank you for everything," Marcin said.

The Mormon Hawley smiled and withdrew a large brown envelope tied with string from his coat pocket. He pointed at the word "deed" printed on the outside. "That right there is thanks enough, Marcin. I wish you better luck with that land and this town. Pray for us, will you?"

The first weeks after the Hawleys' departure were the most difficult. Marcin often retreated to the family graveyard to be alone. It was the one place where he could collect himself and navigate the complexities of grief and the harsh realities of raising three children alone. He could never have imagined how much more complicated his life was about to become.

One April afternoon, Marcin brushed the dirt and leaves from the weathered wooden crosses on the hilltop, his fingers tracing the letters he had carved into each: *Agnieszka Nowak Anderwald, 1836-1861*, and *Magdalena Maria Anderwald, 1860-61*. He gathered several stones that had tumbled into the sage grass growing nearby and placed them back on top of the graves. A flock of great-tailed grackles screeched as they foraged on the edge of the pasture below, their black and purple feathers iridescent in the afternoon sun. It had been six years since he dug those graves, but it felt like yesterday.

The peacock shrieked from the roof of the barn, "Eee-you, eee-you."

"What is it, damned bird," Marcin barked, irritated by the interruption.

"Oh, wow," the cock rejoined.

"Guess I should see what this is all about," Marcin said, scanning the parched horizon to see what might have triggered the alarm. He spotted Zacharias running up from the house.

"Men are coming," the boy announced.

"Do you know them?" Marcin asked.

"No, I don't think so."

A large cloud of dust rose along the road, and shouts and shrill whistles bounced back and forth across the hills. Three men on horseback came over the rise with a small herd of creatures. Two of the riders were circling back and around the beasts, whistling and poking them with long poles. The travelers were only twenty yards away when Marcin and the children reached the front gate.

"It's the soldier who took you away," Zacharias said. The boy was trembling.

There was no mistaking Curtis Kirby with his colossal forehead, reddish-purple with sunburn, or the two camel wranglers, dark as night and hairy as wild hogs pulling up the rear. "Not to worry, Zachek," Marcin said, smiling for the first time in a long while. He could feel the deep creases in his brow twitching and slowly releasing. "These are long-lost friends."

Zacharias squeezed his nostrils closed with a thumb and forefinger. "What's that awful smell!" he groaned.

Beata and Victoria sheltered behind Marcin, pointing. "Tato, are those monsters?" Victoria asked.

"No, not monsters, Vicky. Camels. Camels and friends." Marcin raised his arm in greeting.

"Marcin Anderwald, you are a sight for sore eyes," Kirby shouted.

"Sergeant Kirby, welcome," Marcin said, nodding to the other men. "Khalil, Ahmad, it is good to see you."

The brothers bowed in greeting from their saddles.

"I'm not officially a sergeant no more, Marcin. Didn't ya hear? We lost the war. I'm plain old Curtis Kirby from here on. Farmhand for hire. But I'll still answer to Sergeant if you like," Kirby saluted. His attention quickly turned to Zacharias. "Forgive my manners. Who might this young man be?"

Before Marcin could speak, Zacharias stepped forward. "I am Zacharias, sir. Don't you remember?"

"Zacharias, I remember a little boy running around this ranch, not the nearly grown man standing before me here," Kirby grinned. The sergeant noticed the girls eyeing the animals. "Them beasts are mean, so best keep your distance, little ones. They bite like the Devil and spit somethin' awful." Beata and Victoria backed away, mouths agape, clinging to each other. Kirby laughed. "You ever seen a camel before, ladies?"

The sisters shook their heads and said, "No, sir."

"They're like horses—sort of. They come from Egypt, and these here are my friends who care for 'em," Kirby explained. "Khalil is the tall, taciturn one on the right, and his brother Ahmad is on the left. They only speak a little English, but they're good men. Don't you be frightened."

"Are they Injuns or Negroes, Mr. Kirby?" Zacharias asked, inspecting the curious men closely.

"Neither son. Them boys come from Egypt, too. They're what you call *Ay-rabs*."

A loud thud followed by an angry bellow rang out from somewhere among the throng of foul-smelling beasts. The largest of the bulls had kicked a smaller one who had gotten too close. The girls shrieked, and Zacharias jumped behind his father. Ahmad said something under his breath and began to snicker.

"Leave it, ya akhi," Khalil replied.

"Hey, you two," the sergeant said. "Get them animals outta here. Marcin, could we use your cattle pen for a night or two?"

"Yes, of course."

"Khalil, Ahmad, get on up to the barn."

"Yes, sir!" Ahmad saluted exuberantly as his brother began prodding the restless herd.

"Tato, can we go watch?" Zacharias asked.

"Tak," Marcin said, and the children followed the wranglers and their charges.

Kirby waited for a beat before turning back to Marcin. "I was sorry to hear about Agnieszka and the baby. I guess I'm one man who can truly know your pain," Kirby said. "How you doin'?"

Marcin sighed but did not reply.

"Right, well, you got yourself a fine boy, Marcin," Kirby said. "And those two little beauties are precious, I must say. Even after all these years, I still think about my Katie..." The sergeant did not finish his sentence. He reached out and squeezed Marcin's shoulder.

"Thank you, Curtis," Marcin said, patting the sergeant's hand.

"And I'm here. If you need to talk. Understand?" Kirby smiled.

Marcin sensed a flutter of what felt like breath along the curve of his ear. "I am here," Aga sounded in his head.

*   *   *

After the girls' weekly bath and a bedtime story, Marcin and Zacharias joined their guests on the front porch. Zacharias had been asking to stay up with the men since supper, and Marcin finally agreed. A late evening breeze offered the first real relief from the searing heat of the day. Kirby tipped back his shiny silver flask, and Khalil and Ahmad passed a pipe filled with sweet tobacco back and forth. Zacharias took a seat, and Ahmad offered him the pipe.

The boy shook his head. "No, thank you," he said.

"Al-walad khayif!" Ahmad clicked his tongue and laughed.

"Uskut, ya akhi," Khalil scolded.

Zacharias turned to Sergeant Kirby. "What'd they say?"

Khalil himself replied, "My brother, ya akhi in our language, say 'you so scared, shit is running into your pants,' and I say to him 'shut up.'"

"Easy," Kirby said. "Ahmad, he's a little young for a smoke, don't ya think?"

Khalil grabbed the pipe from Ahmad with a stern look. "Ya ahmaq," he muttered.

"Hey, English when you're in company, you two," the sergeant admonished.

"I sorry, Sergeant. I say 'you are idiot' to my brother," Khalil translated with a hint of a smirk.

All but Ahmad began to laugh. After a few minutes the group settled again, and Marcin turned to Kirby. "Tell me, Curtis, why are you here?"

The sergeant took a sip from his flask before answering. "I need your help, or should I say, we need your help." Kirby paused, and the wranglers looked nervous.

"What can I do?" Marcin asked.

"Simply put, the three of us got nowhere to go. My family is gone, and these two ain't ever going back home. I'm not sure how long they'd last on their own in these parts in any case." Kirby scratched behind his ear. "Anyways, I was wonderin' if you might require some hands here on your ranch."

"I need help, but I cannot pay much," Marcin said.

"You needn't worry about that. We'll work for a roof over our heads and a meal here and there if that would be agreeable." The sergeant turned to Khalil and Ahmad, who both bobbed their heads.

"Yes, of course. There is a small house closer to the river where you can stay. It was my friend's, but he is gone to Utah. It is not as nice as Camp Verde, though," Marcin cracked a smile.

"Marcin Anderwald, did you just make a joke? Well, I never!" Sergeant Kirby cackled and turned to Zacharias, shaking his finger. "I mean that, Zacharias. I have never known your father to tell a joke. Always serious, that one."

"Tell me about Camp Verde, Sergeant Kirby. My father has never said much about the place or what happened there," Zacharias said. Marcin could see the boy was avoiding his glare but did not intervene.

The mood shifted. Kirby glanced sideways at Marcin. "Zacharias, war is no laughing matter. I can't say it was the nicest of places or the best of times. I also think this might be a subject best left to menfolk."

"Sergeant, I'm nearly thirteen," Zacharias protested.

Marcin stared at Zacharias long and hard before turning to Kirby. "Tell him, Curtis."

"You sure about this, Marcin?"

"Yes, I am sure." Marcin still regretted keeping his secrets from Agnieszka. He would not push Zacharias away, too.

Sergeant Kirby took a deep breath and sat forward in his chair. "My commanding officer, Colonel Peters, sent me to fetch your father to Camp Verde to help build wagons for them camels I brought with us today."

"Who was that other soldier who came with you?" Zacharias interrupted.

"Ah, yes," Kirby said, "that was Private Brewer, son."

"Where did he go after the war?"

Zacharias' question was met with uncomfortable silence. Kirby coughed, and Khalil puffed more vigorously on his pipe.

"He's dead, Zachek," Marcin snapped.

"Oh, I'm sorry," Zacharias replied.

"I am not." Marcin's clipped tone intended to make clear that he was not inclined to discuss the topic further.

Zacharias crossed his arms over his chest and looked at the sergeant expectantly.

Kirby appeared to be waiting to see if Marcin would say anything else. "Truth is, Zacharias," he finally continued, "Private Brewer never did like your father much." The sergeant again looked at Marcin, presumably to seek his permission to say more.

Marcin blinked but did not offer any objections.

Kirby pursed his lips. "One thing led to another, and bad went to worse when your father showed Private Brewer up in front of the colonel..." The sergeant's voice trailed off, and he fell silent.

"Sergeant Kirby?" Zacharias pressed.

"I think that's enough for tonight," Kirby said, taking another slug from his flask.

Zacharias frowned and fidgeted in his seat. He took a deep breath and tried again. "What do you mean by 'showed him up'?"

Kirby shot Marcin another look.

"Please, Sergeant," Zacharias slammed his fist on the arm of his chair. "You came here and took my father away. Something happened to him at that camp, and he was not the same with Mama or me and my sisters when he got back. I want to know—no, I need to know—what it was, sir."

"Zachek, calm down," Marcin spoke up at last.

"It's all right, Marcin. The boy's been through a lot. I understand," Kirby said.

Marcin ignored the sergeant. "Zachek, it is enough."

"No, Tato," Zacharias insisted. "You left us and didn't come back the same. Why?" Marcin could see his son was on the verge of tears.

"Zacharias," Sergeant Kirby quietly intervened. "Thing is, Private Brewer was tortured somethin' terrible, and we're not exactly sure by whom. But no matter, it was a gruesome death." The sergeant paused again and looked at Marcin. "And I believe your father may blame himself for young Brewer's demise."

"He was a boy," Marcin sputtered. "A stupid, stupid boy."

"Marcin, we all got our regrets. But you know that Augie surely would've done hisself in at some point anyway. You need to leave it be."

Kirby offered his flask to Marcin, who drank generously from its contents. Marcin could feel Zacharias staring at him as he gazed into the darkness and took another sip. "And you, Curtis? You have regrets?"

Sergeant Kirby pulled out his pipe and packed it full of tobacco. "More than a few," he began. "Things were calm for a bit after you left, but as the news from the east trickled in, it was clear that defeat and disaster would soon be upon us. About six months before the end, the army command in San Antone decided to rotate some of our regiment further west, including Colonel Peters. A new commanding officer arrived soon after. Someone you might remember."

Kirby struck a match against the porch post and took a long drag from his pipe. He held the smoke deep in his lungs for almost three counts before exhaling through his nostrils.

"Gaines was the name. Josiah Gaines. Got promoted from sergeant to major and returned outta nowhere with several lackeys. We'd assumed he was missin' in action after that Guadalupe River mission, but he'd given chase to them Injuns and ended up at a post near Galveston. Anyway, those new boys yessir'd whatever that man said, right or wrong. Sure enough, all hell broke loose, I tell ya."

The sergeant paused to pull a small leaf of tobacco off the tip of his tongue and rolled it between his thumb and forefinger before flicking it onto the ground.

"It started with gambling among the officers, and not too long after, we were gettin' complaints of speculation and outright looting from some of our patrols. None of Colonel Peters' men, mind you, but those who'd come with Gaines. There was always cause to suspect one person or another of conspiring with the North. And for the brave few who fought back, it was ugly."

Kirby took another puff of his pipe and blew white smoke rings into the darkness.

Marcin leaned in closer with each word. "Curtis, tell me what happened."

The sergeant raised his flask again. "There was a farmer named Johnson who was found hanging from a barn beam with his throat slit ear to ear and a sign pinned to his chest that read 'Yankee Traitor.' Now, anybody who knew anything about Elias Johnson knew for damned sure he would never conspire with the enemy in a million years. And things got worse toward the end of the war. Never mind what Major Gaines and his men did to them poor Comanche, and believe you me, I never expected to give a spit about any of them."

The sergeant finished the contents of his flask and wiped his mouth with the back of his hand, which had started to shake.

"One day," he continued, "a patrol brought back a couple of Mexican vaqueros suspected of horse thieving by one of the local ranchers, a gambling buddy of the major's. Gaines marched those wretched fellas through camp, tied the nooses hisself, and strung 'em up in the live oak off the parade ground."

Sergeant Kirby went quiet and remained so for some time. Khalil repacked his pipe and handed it to Ahmad, who lit the fresh tobacco, smoke twisting around his head.

"Didn't even try to break their necks with a fall," Kirby said. "Wanted 'em to suffer, I think. Forbid anybody to cut 'em down and left 'em to the buzzards. A good number of us suspected they weren't even guilty. Wrong place at the wrong time, I guess."

"What about the prisoners?" Marcin asked, fearing the worst.

Sergeant Kirby looked away, and Marcin noticed Khalil and Ahmad exchanging knowing glances. "A number of the men were paroled soon after you left, Marcin, but a dozen or so remained in the camp, mostly those too sick or lame to join Confederate regiments or travel home." The sergeant paused and took a deep breath. "It took almost four weeks for the news of General Lee's surrender to reach Camp Verde. When it did, Major Gaines and several of his men drank themselves into a rage and began to recruit troops to continue the fight. A right fearsome posse they were, and that sadistic bastard Gaines was the worst. He was possessed by the Devil himself. And that laugh." Kirby shuddered.

"And the Yankees who were left? What happened to them?" Zacharias prompted.

Kirby shook his empty flask. "Them vigilantes' first victims were those poor soldiers in the ravine. A group of ten or so men, with Gaines in the lead, set off with shotguns and sidearms at full tilt and shot every man. Thank goodness Khalil and Ahmad heard the ruckus and hid themselves across the river. I fear they may have been next."

Kirby looked at Khalil and Ahmad, who both shifted uncomfortably on their stools.

"The following morning," the sergeant continued, "we awoke to find the major had deserted his post with the men loyal to him. Some weeks later, we heard they met their match near Uvalde. Not clear if it was a tussle with Mexican smugglers or Comanche horse thieves, but rumor was that Gaines didn't make it. Never was no proof, but he didn't come back." Kirby rose and spat over the porch rail. "Good riddance."

"Curtis?" Marcin said.

Kirby turned back. "Here's the last thing I'll say on this matter, as it is right difficult for me to own the things I done and those I didn't. I am not proud of the fact that none of the rest of us stepped in to help them Mexicans or them Yankees, but we all would have ended up in that tree or face down in that ravine if we had. My punishment was to get the bodies and give 'em a proper Christian burial, but for the rest of my days, my penance will be seein' those men's faces every time I close my eyes."

Sergeant Kirby stiffened and abruptly headed to the barn. Khalil and Ahmad followed closely on his heels.

CHAPTER 9

Chief

A most unorthodox family unit was forged that spring evening of 1867, six years nearly to the day after the Anderwalds first spotted Sergeant Kirby and the loathsome Private Brewer on the river path. Curtis Kirby, Khalil, and Ahmad were soon permanent fixtures at Peacock Bend, and in their own way, this curious assemblage of aggrieved persons filled the void left in the wake of the tragedies that had befallen the Anderwalds. On those desperate nights when he was plagued by fits of sleeplessness, Marcin often spoke to Aga and wondered aloud whether she had sent Kirby and the camel wranglers to watch over the family. She never answered, but somehow, he suspected she had.

"Marcin? Zachek? You in there?" Kirby boomed from the yard.

Zacharias sprang from the table, nearly toppling the last of his breakfast to the floor. "Can we go, Tato? Sergeant Kirby said I could help you finish the fence."

"Yes, but grab the sandwiches the girls made for the men. They will be hungry."

Zacharias grabbed a straw basket from the counter and pushed Marcin out the door.

"Get a wiggle on, Anderwalds," Kirby urged. "We gotta finish that gate today before Stanard's boys bring yer new longhorns in from Fort Worth."

Much work had been done to clear the fields around the Hawleys' old homestead and build accommodations for the Anderwald
family's expanding livestock. Marcin and the men hurried to build
fences, and in the meantime, the peacocks and the camels proved
unexpected assets when it came to fending off cattle poachers and
coyotes. At the slightest rustle, the peacocks would raise an alarm
from above, and the camels would disperse themselves around the
perimeter of the pasture, facing out into the darkness, grunting, and
pawing forcefully at the ground, preparing to charge. Rumors had
spread among prospective rustlers that the Anderwald place was
possessed by demon beasts whose bites could tear a man limb from
limb, so they steered clear. The coyotes would circle wide, but they,
too, never dared approach.

The camel wranglers were waiting for Marcin and Zacharias
in the field. "Ya za'im! Chief!" Ahmad waved with a toothy grin.
"Come!"

Ahmad had taken to calling Zacharias by this name, and Khalil
quickly followed suit. At first, Marcin assumed it meant Zacharias in
their language, but one afternoon, Khalil translated. "No, ya akhi,
this means 'chief.' Ahmad say the boy is the chief." Marcin understood the brothers were having a bit of fun, but this was also their
way between each other. A nickname meant you were one of them,
and when he saw how his son beamed when the men addressed him
in this manner, he knew he could never stand in the way of such
happiness.

Ahmad relieved Zacharias of the basket of food and led him toward a shed, where Khalil stood next to a massive bull camel. A thick
woven blanket was fastened between the two large humps along the
camel's back, with a leather strap cinched by a heavy buckle beneath
its belly.

"Today, you ride camel," Khalil declared.

Zacharias whipped around in search of Marcin. "Tato!" he
cried.

"Go on," Marcin said, pointing at the camel as Ahmad grabbed
the boy under the arms and dragged him toward Khalil.

"No!" Zacharias pleaded. "I can't!"

"Chief, the boss always ride biggest camel, and Bakr is biggest,"

Khalil teased and helped Ahmad boost the boy onto the blanket. The older wrangler kept the beast still by jerking the reins back. "Waqaf ya, jamala. Whoa, Bakr," he ordered.

"But my father is the boss, not me. He should ride," Zacharias protested.

Khalil and Ahmad looked over at Marcin.

"No, no, Zachek. You are the boss today," Marcin said, trying to stifle a laugh.

Zacharias lurched forward and wrapped his arms around the hump in front. The camel began to buck and kick, rearing its head back and releasing a torrent of spit and snot over its head and straight into Zacharias' face.

"Whoa, Bakr!" Ahmad ordered.

"Chief, hold tight," Khalil instructed, yanking the camel's head toward the ground and beginning to pull it in a wide circle. When the animal's gait smoothed, he loosened his grip and handed the reins to Zacharias. "Pull tight to stop and kick to make go. Like a horse."

"Go, Chief!" Ahmad cheered and slapped the camel's hindquarters.

Bakr launched into a lumbering gallop, and Zacharias panicked, jerking back on the reins and yelling, "Whoa!" When Bakr did not respond, Zacharias spoke to the animal in the same way Ahmad and Khalil spoke to each other. "Stop, you idiot!"

Sure enough, Bakr halted, and Khalil and Ahmad burst into uncontrollable howls. Zacharias glared at both men.

"Do not be angry," Khalil said. "You became real chief today."

"Chief, Chief, Chief!" Ahmad chanted, pounding his fists against his chest.

"That's enough, you two," Marcin said, approaching from the shed. "Come down, Zachek."

"Did you see me, Tato? Did you?" Zacharias was out of breath.

"Yes. You were very brave. Let's get you cleaned up." Marcin led Zacharias toward the river.

"Fun's over, boys," Kirby announced. "Get back to work. We need to finish the fence before it gets dark."

"Yes, sir," Ahmad saluted.

*   *   *

"We go?" Ahmad held the reins, waiting dutifully for Marcin's orders.

"Yes, we can go," Marcin said, climbing onto the wagon.

Zacharias had been begging his father for months to sign him and his sisters up for school in town. "Tato, we need to learn our letters and numbers, like all the other children," he insisted one morning while working at the Stanards' ranch. "It's only two dollars a term."

Marcin frowned, irritated by his son's boldness. "And how do you know this?"

"Liza told me."

"Yes, yes, Liza. She says many things."

Liza Stanard had blossomed into a lovely teenager with more than a single helping of pluck. She was a constant presence and distraction whenever Zacharias joined Marcin for carpentry work at her father's ranch. Zacharias pretended the youngest Stanard confounded him, but Marcin suspected his son was more than a little bit sweet on the girl.

"How will you get to school?" Marcin pushed back.

"I'm old enough to hitch and drive the wagon. I'll take us."

"No, it is too dangerous."

"Then Sergeant Kirby, Khalil, or Ahmad can take us." Zacharias was clearly not going to take no for an answer.

"I will think about it, Zachek."

Marcin finally did agree to send the children to school on the condition that he and one of the men would accompany them. The Comanche were restless again along Bandera Pass, and vigilante groups continued to run roughshod and harass travelers along the Hill Country back roads. He was not going to take any chances with Zacharias and the girls. They were all he had left.

"Chief, come." Ahmad slammed his palm on the seat beside him. "We go."

Marcin and the wrangler started toward the Bandera Road, Zacharias between them and Beata and Victoria playing in the back of the wagon. Zacharias had taken it upon himself to help his friend with his English during their trips to and from school.

"Shu hadha?" Ahmad pointed.

"What's that? Um, an oak tree," Zacharias said.

Ahmad pointed again at the sky. "Wa shu hadha?"

"And that? Yeah, that's a cloud. You gotta say it out loud," Zacharias instructed.

"Kwah-ood," Ahmad repeated, and the girls started to giggle. "Please," Ahmad pleaded his case to Marcin.

"Girls," Marcin said gently, "be polite."

Zacharias burst out laughing.

"Chief, no you," Ahmad scolded, shaking a fist in Zacharias' face.

"Pull up, Ahmad," Marcin interrupted, reaching over Zacharias for the reins.

The wagon and its cargo jostled to a stop. Ahead on the road, five men came into view. Three were on horseback, and two drove a battered army ambulance wagon in the rear.

"Halt!" the man in the lead ordered, raising his hand. He wore an old gray wool uniform jacket, with the epaulets removed but most of its brass buttons still intact. The man's crew was similarly outfitted in ragtag pieces of old Confederate uniforms, giving the group an official air. All were armed to the teeth, carrying both side arms and long-barreled, formerly army-issue shotguns.

Ahmad maneuvered to the side of the road to let the men pass. Marcin felt for the shotgun under the seat, but it had slid too far under the bench to be retrieved without notice. Zacharias leaned forward to see if he could reach the weapon, but Ahmad extended an arm to stop him. "No, Chief. Bad man," he said under his breath, visibly nervous.

The girls popped up from behind to see what was going on.

"Bea, Vicky. Sit back and be quiet," Marcin said.

The man who issued the order to stop and another in his crew dismounted and approached on foot. The group's leader walked toward the front of the wagon, his gait purposeful and strong, and the other moved around to the rear. The leader tipped his hat in greeting and revealed a full head of bright red hair underneath.

"Good morning," he said. "I am Josiah T. Gaines of the Bandera County Vigilance Committee. Who might you be?"

Marcin recognized the name and the voice, its deep timbre vibrating inside his ears. The man also had a familiar manner of speech, with consonants cushioned by a swishing of tongue against teeth, Josiah T. Gaines sounding more like Choshiah Tchee Gainsh.

"I'm Marcin Anderwald, sir," he replied.

"Where are you headed, Anderwald?" Gaines inspected the back of the wagon.

"We're off to school, sir," Zacharias said.

"Son, I was not talking to you." The man turned back to Marcin, smiling with his mouth but not his eyes. "I was addressing your father."

"I am taking my children to school," Marcin replied.

"And who's your friend here?" Gaines tried to engage Ahmad, who continued to stare at the floorboards of the wagon.

"He's Ahmad, sir, my ranch hand."

Gaines paused, his lip curling. "Ahmad, eh," he huffed, staring intently at the wrangler. "I thought I knew that face. Ahmad, didn't realize you were still skulking about in these parts?"

Ahmad did not answer.

"Major Gaines, I think this one might not be showin' you the proper respect due a person of your position," the second man said as he approached from the rear, his hand hovering over his sidearm. "Where you from, boy?"

Ahmad remained silent, but Zacharias jumped in again. "He's from Egypt, sir."

"Don't this fella have a tongue in his own head?" The second man stared at Ahmad. "Ee-jipt, what in the hell kind of place is that?"

"Sir, we are from back down the road. Peacock Bend. This here is our hand," Marcin tried again to explain.

The second man ignored him. "Major Gaines, looks a bit curious him here with these nice white folks. Are we sure they ain't bein' kidnapped? Maybe this Ak-Mad or whatever he's called has a ransom in mind?"

Ahmad grabbed the reins from Marcin. "To school! To school! We go," he cried.

The third man on horseback dismounted and walked toward the group. The two others in the ambulance pulled forward and blocked the road.

"Get out of the wagon, boy," Gaines ordered.

When Ahmad did not respond, the second man drew his sidearm and aimed at the wrangler's chest. "You heard the major. Get out!"

Without a word, the third man grabbed Ahmad by his collar and threw him onto the ground. The wrangler began to fight back but was subdued with a swift kick to the gut. The girls huddled in the corner of the wagon bed and began to cry. Marcin stood up, prepared to intervene.

"Anderwald," Gaines snarled, "you stay put."

"But you have no right to do this," Marcin insisted.

The unnamed men tied Ahmad's wrists behind his back, dragged him to the back of the ambulance, and lifted him inside.

"You sonofawhore," Ahmad howled, fighting to break free. He was still kicking violently against the wagon panels when they slid the lock across the back gate. "Marcin, Chief, help! Get Khalil! Get Kirby!"

"Where are you taking him?" Marcin demanded.

"To the sheriff for questioning," Gaines said, adjusting his hat and pulling at his riding gloves.

"Why? He's done nothing!"

"Mr. Anderwald, that ruffian has assaulted an officer of the court who asked a simple question that only required a simple answer. We cannot let violent men like that threaten our fragile peace."

"Please, this man is innocent!" Marcin protested in vain.

"I'd stand down if I were you, Anderwald," Gaines warned and set off with his men in the direction of town.

Marcin turned back to Peacock Bend, whipping the horses with all his might. The short sprint home felt like an eternity. The wagon finally crested the hill and thundered toward the house at full speed. "Curtis! Khalil!" he shouted at the top of his lungs.

The men came running from the field. "What happened?" Khalil demanded.

"They took Ahmad!" Zacharias panted.

"Who? Who took him?" Kirby asked as Khalil scrambled to the barn to assemble the horses.

Marcin was breathless. "That man Gaines from Camp Verde."

With the mention of the name, Kirby grabbed his arm. "Marcin, how many men did this man Gaines have with him?"

"Four others. Two on horseback and two driving a cart."

"Where did he say they were gonna take Ahmad?"

"To the sheriff. For questioning," Marcin replied, jumping out of the wagon and lifting his hysterical daughters to the ground.

"Marcin, this is bad. It's those goddamned vigilance boys. You, Khalil, and me gotta catch those bastards. Zachek, get the girls into the house and then ride like the wind to fetch Mr. Stanard. Tell him to bring his foreman and as many of his men as possible. Tell 'im Gaines got Ahmad. You understand?"

"Yes, Sergeant," Zacharias replied.

Khalil returned with two more horses saddled for Kirby and Marcin and immediately headed toward the main road.

"We best go quick, Marcin. No tellin' whether he'll make it to the sheriff at all," Kirby said.

The men kicked their horses hard and followed Khalil.

✳   ✳   ✳

Gaines and his men were assembled in a grove of trees west of town. Marcin, Kirby, and Khalil were crouched behind a small hill fifty yards away, preparing a rescue plan.

"There's Stanard," Kirby said.

John Stanard turned off the road with four of his men, Zacharias bringing up the rear in the wagon. They all dismounted and crawled on their bellies to where the others were lying flat on the ground.

"What have we got, Sergeant?" Stanard prompted.

"Thanks for comin'. Until you got here, we were outmanned by two, and we may still be outgunned by who knows how much. Haven't seen Ahmad yet. Looks like them boys are talkin' somethin' over down there," Kirby reported.

"What is this man Gaines doing, Curtis?" Marcin asked.

"He may have steered clear of any formal blame hisself for the wrongdoings at Camp Verde, but he's always been up to no good. Fancies himself a man of the law. Since the war, he's been making a livin' as a bounty hunter, tracking horse thieves and other common criminals."

"Josiah Gaines is the furthest thing from a man of the law, Sergeant Kirby," Stanard said.

Movement erupted among the trees. They could see Ahmad being dragged from the wagon to a fallen tree trunk, where he sat with his hands still tied behind his back. One of the men, not Gaines, struck Ahmad across the side of his head with a pistol, knocking him on his side. The man struck a second blow under Ahmad's chin, sending him backward onto the ground. Two more men grabbed the unconscious wrangler and dragged him toward a large tree at the edge of the grove, his head slumped against his chest. Gaines jogged out from behind the wagon with a long rope over his shoulder, tying one of its ends in a tell-tale loop.

"He's got himself a coil, Sergeant," Stanard said, running toward his horse. "Gentlemen, we must make haste before it's too late."

"Zachek, you stay with the wagon. Do not even think to come down there, you understand?" Marcin ordered, swinging his leg over his saddle. Sergeant Kirby, Khalil, Stanard, and his men were already kicking up dust ahead.

"Tato," Zacharias said, grabbing Marcin's arm.

"Zachek, I will be back. Don't worry."

Marcin watched what was happening in horror as he rode toward the grove. Gaines and his men placed the loop around Ahmad's neck, threw the rope over a large branch, and lifted his limp body into the air, his feet a few inches above the ground. Stanard, Kirby, and the others began whooping and hollering to distract the posse from its purpose. As they closed in, Kirby raised his pistol and fired a shot into the air. Gaines signaled for crew to take cover as he tied the other end of the rope around the tree. Stanard and two of his men peeled off to the left toward the ambulance wagon, and Sergeant Kirby and Stanard's two other hands headed around to the right.

Marcin and Khalil raced straight ahead toward Ahmad. Shots rang out from behind the ambulance, and Marcin could hear screaming, one more shot, then silence. On the right, Marcin watched three men gallop south with Kirby and his team in close pursuit, firing from their mounts.

Khalil was soon standing beneath his brother's twitching body. He grabbed Ahmad around the waist and raised him to create slack in the rope, and Marcin loosened the noose. They laid the wrangler in the grass and untied his hands. John Stanard and his men stood watch with their pistols drawn. Stanard said something to one of his ranch hands and pointed at the hill. The man galloped toward Zacharias, calling out, "Bring the wagon, kid! Bring the wagon!"

Marcin kneeled next to Ahmad, choking back his tears. The wrangler had been beaten severely about the head, and his hands and feet were bent and bruised from kicking and scraping at the wagon's walls. A dark purple ligature ringed his throat. His eyelids were swollen shut, and his thick tongue protruded from his mouth.

Ahmad grabbed for Marcin's hand. "Shabah," he croaked, struggling to speak. "Brewer here. Shabah," he repeated.

Marcin laid Ahmad's hand on his chest. "Stay calm," he said.

The wrangler continued to struggle. "Chief? Where Chief?"

Marcin heard the wagon approaching. "He's coming, Ahmad. Chief is coming."

Zacharias blasted into the clearing and wrenched the wagon to a stop. Marcin and Khalil quickly lifted Ahmad into the wagon bed. "Chief," the wrangler moaned.

"I'm right here," Zacharias said, climbing over the seat.

"Shabah," Ahmad rasped. "Fight him, Chief. The angel will help," he said, stroking the boy's cheek with his broken fingers.

"Angel? What angel?" Zacharias pleaded.

Khalil intervened. "We must go. No time."

Marcin helped Zacharias onto the ground as Khalil started toward the road.

"I will fight Ahmad," Zacharias promised, running alongside the wagon.

"Good boy, Chief," Ahmad replied before losing consciousness.

*   *   *

Marcin could see from the look on the doctor's face that the news was bad. It was the same look Doc Adolph had had the night Lena passed. Khalil lifted his head from his hands and understood without a word being said that his brother was gone.

Khalil stumbled into the examination room. "Ya akhi!" he wailed and fell across Ahmad's broken body.

"Come, let's step outside," Doc Adolph said, leading Marcin, Zacharias, and John Stanard onto the street. "There was nothing to be done," he continued. "Your man was gone before he got here, I'm afraid."

Marcin's head was spinning. "Thank you, doctor," he finally managed. "I know you did your best."

"Yes, thank you, Hans. We're most grateful for all you've done." Stanard added and signaled for Marcin and Zacharias to follow him. "Give Khalil a minute."

Tears streamed down Zacharias' cheeks, and Marcin held him close. "We must be brave, Zachek."

Stanard patted the back of the boy's head. "I'm real sorry you had to see this ugliness, son."

Footsteps approached. Sergeant Kirby crossed the street with a man in a broad-brimmed hat, a silver star pinned to his coat. Zacharias ran to Kirby, nearly knocking him over with an embrace. "Sergeant, you're here! Did you find Gaines and his men?"

Kirby could not look the boy in the eye. "We chased those bastards as fast as we could, Chief, but they split up and headed across the river. We lost 'em. I'm so sorry."

"And the others by the trees?" Marcin asked.

"We circled back after that. The other two behind the ambulance were already stone cold. We decided to leave them for the buzzards and get ourselves back here to tell the sheriff what all happened."

"Welcome back, Sergeant. Evenin', Sheriff Holcomb," Stanard greeted.

"Evenin', John," the sheriff replied and turned to Marcin. "Mr.

Anderwald, I was comin' over to see how your man is, but I can tell
by the look of things—"

"He is dead," Marcin said.

"Damn it!" Sergeant Kirby groaned and bent forward. He
braced his hands on his knees, and Marcin could see his chest heaving. The other men stood back and gave the sergeant time to collect himself. After a few minutes, he returned to the group. "How's
Khalil holdin' up?" he managed to ask.

"Not good, Curtis. Come, we must help bring Ahmad to the
wagon. Zachek, wait here with Mr. Stanard and Sheriff Holcomb."

"Wait, Tato." Zacharias wiped his face with his shirtsleeve and
turned to the sheriff, fists clenched at his sides. "How are you going
to catch and punish those men?"

Marcin did not intervene. He wanted the same answers.

"We're puttin' the word out. I don't expect to see Major Gaines
around here any time soon. He's well aware he'll be accountable for
taking the law into his own hands." The sheriff rocked in his boots.
"There's not much more we can do for now, though."

"So, you're doing nothing," Zacharias said defiantly.

"Hold on now, son," the sheriff began but stood down when
Stanard stepped forward.

"You just do your best, Sheriff," he said.

"On my word, John. On my word."

*   *   *

The sun receded below the horizon, and the shadows of the
gnarled oaks on the hilltop stretched out in longing. Marcin floated
back and forth on the porch swing and watched Khalil kneel, his
back to the setting sun, and place his forehead and nose against the
soft earth that covered his brother's fresh grave. Khalil's mournful
prayer, mixed with the desperate cry of the peacock atop the farmhouse roof, erupted. A woeful cacophony of sadness and fear re-
bounded from house to hill and back again. "Allah! Hee-yelp! Allah!
Hee-yelp! Allah! Hee-yelp!"

PART TWO

The Lord is a God who avenges.
O God who avenges, shine forth.
Rise up, Judge of the earth;
pay back to the proud what they deserve.
How long, Lord, will the wicked,
how long will the wicked be jubilant?

—Psalm 94:1-3

CHAPTER 10

Three Taps

The showdown with Josiah Gaines and his men was neither the start of vigilance nor the end of violence in Bandera County. A bounty was issued for the suspected murderers of Ahmad, but no one, including the residents of Peacock Bend, harbored any illusions that justice with any due speed was in the offing, especially for an Arab camel wrangler. By the summer and fall of 1873, Comanche raiders and cattle rustlers of all stripes were running amok in Bandera Pass and along the Medina, and they were the top priority for the county's Minute Company, the more respectable successor to the virulent Vigilance Committees that had plagued the Texas Hill Country after the South's humiliating defeat.

In the five years following Ahmad's murder, Zacharias Anderwald, son and eldest child of Marcin and Agnieszka, beloved brother of Beata, Victoria, and Lena, and descendant of all who preceded him in the distant lands of Upper Silesia, struggled. The occasional levity that had returned after mourning his mother and baby sister's deaths faded once again after the loss of his friend. Although the constant work alongside his father, Sergeant Kirby, and Khalil at Peacock Bend and at the Stanard Ranch provided regular distraction, and his growing infatuation with Liza Stanard filled some of the emptiness in his heart, Zacharias sought revenge. Pure and simple.

In the precious few moments of solitude that Zacharias could find, he faced this unbecoming truth. Father Adamietz had taken great care to relate God's position on the matter during Zacharias' increasingly rare visits to the confessional at St. Stanislaus. "'It is to Him belongeth vengeance and recompense,' Master Anderwald," the priest cautioned. Nevertheless, Zacharias prayed that God might strike down the venomous Josiah T. Gaines slowly and painfully. To Zacharias' thinking, it was fitting that Gaines would know the same terror that Ahmad faced that day along the Bandera Road. Trouble was that Father Adamietz was not the only one listening to those prayers.

Common to all recollections of the time shared among the church pews and along the streets of Bandera was that Zacharias Anderwald was a boy, then a man, who did his damnedest to judge not and condemn not and give and forgive as best he could. But what most come to know through the trials and tribulations in their own lives—whether they admit it or not—is that all mortals, at one time or another, come up short before the Lord and fall prey to darker forces. Zacharias Anderwald was no exception.

*   *   *

"Kochanie, don't go!" Marcin implored from down the hall.

Zacharias did not go to his father. It didn't seem like a nightmare this time, and besides, he was too tired and his bed too warm. A gust of wind howled around the eaves beyond his bedroom window, and tree branches laden with winter ice scratched against the glass panes. Zacharias tucked the blankets around his neck, exposing his gangly legs and bare feet to the chilly room. The thick hair on his feet and shins stood on end. He settled back onto his pillow, and his mind began to wander as it was wont to do when he could not sleep. He always returned to the same scene.

"Get out, boy," Gaines' directive would pierce the silence, followed by Ahmad's stricken plea, "Chief, get Kirby!"

Zacharias pulled the pillow around his ears and shut his eyes tight. "'He will come with vengeance. He will come with vengeance,'" he repeated, rocking back and forth in the bed.

A draft whistled through the cracks in the window frame, ushering in the faint, putrid stench of decay. Zacharias' whole body was on alert. That smell—always the same when the shadow was hovering—was followed by a light tap on the top of his foot.

"Go away," he said through clenched teeth, but he did not dare look.

Another tap, more insistent this time. Scenes from Zacharias' childhood flashed behind his eyelids: him calling desperately for his father, and Marcin bursting into the room like a spooked animal.

Zacharias could hear himself as a small boy. "Tato, come quick!"

"No one is here, Zachek," Marcin always tried to reassure him, but Zacharias could sense his father's fear.

Soon, a woman would cry out, "Leave him," and everything would end as suddenly as it had started.

A third tap.

Zacharias opened his eyes. He would have to face whoever or whatever had come to call. The moon hung heavy in the frigid night sky, casting a bluish glow across the room. A man in a tattered soldier's cap emerged from the shadows. The figure listed to the side and had no face, only a black emptiness where his features should have been.

"Leave me alone, you sonofabitch!" Zacharias fumed.

The soldier raised his arm and pointed. "Mine," he hissed with a hollow laugh.

"Mamusiu, help me," Zacharias cried. He yearned to recall his mother's face and the sound of her voice—anything that would drive this creature from what he desperately hoped was only his imagination.

Distant humming floated across the hills in the darkness outside.

Zacharias blinked, and the figure vanished.

* * *

Zacharias no longer spoke of these encounters, resigned to silent solidarity with his father and consumed by new and far more enchanting diversions during his waking hours. One morning, he put his back into a last thrust of the shovel. The final post hole was dug for the new holding pen at Stanard Ranch. Marcin and Sergeant Kirby were already raising and leveling the fence posts on the far end of the line.

"All done there, Chief?" Kirby shouted.

Kirby and Khalil continued to call Zacharias by the nickname Ahmad had given him. It was a way to pay tribute to their friend and brother. It always brought back painful memories.

"Yes sir!" Zacharias said with a wave.

"Zachek," another called to him.

Zacharias smiled. It was Liza Stanard making her afternoon rounds. He turned to watch her approach from the main house. Liza had certainly changed since those early days of playing tag at Peacock Bend while his mother fitted hers with one outfit after another. Her bright blond hair flew in all directions, and a lock wet with saliva was tucked into the corner of her full lips. She was dressed in a printed frock cinched at the waist with a canvas apron, its pockets filled with pencils and colored chalk. She walked briskly with a sketchpad tucked under her arm. Liza never went anywhere without that pad. She was always drawing something.

As Liza approached, Zacharias noticed that one of her cheeks was smudged with graphite, but the other was bright red. He tucked his shirt back in and smoothed his hair. "Hey there," he said.

Before Liza could respond, John Stanard popped his head out of the barn. "Thought that was you, Liza Lou. What brings you out this way? Hopefully, you've got something cool and wet from the kitchen. I've been helping Khalil shoe the trail horses, and it sure is thirsty work."

Liza scoffed whenever her father said he was helping the men. "More like standing around, watching, and yammering on about something he's told you at least thirty times," she would say under her breath to Zacharias and laugh. Liza was clearly not in a laughing mood this afternoon, though. Zacharias could see she had been crying. Her eyelids were swollen, and clumps of wet eyelashes glistened in the sun.

"No, Daddy," she replied dismissively, turning her inflamed cheek away from her father. "I've come for Zachek. I need his help with something. Can you spare him?"

"Sure, but we'll need him to help to set the rest of the posts," her father said. "Don't keep him too long."

"Come," Liza grumbled, motioning Zacharias to follow her.

When they rounded a bend in the creek path, Liza led Zacharias down to the water's edge. She climbed onto a large boulder under a tree before she said another word.

"You've been cryin'," Zacharias said.

Liza scowled. "I certainly have not."

"I can see plain as day that you have. Wanna talk about it?"

"Not really."

"What happened there?" Zacharias pointed at Liza's cheek.

Liza touched her inflamed skin and winced. "She slapped me is what happened."

"Your mother?"

Liza's bottom lip began to quiver. "Who else, Zachek?"

"I'm sorry," Zacharias said softly and reached out.

Liza slapped his hand away. "I hate that woman!" she screamed, throwing her sketch pad into the brush. "How dare she say those things!"

"Calm down," Zacharias began, but Liza cut him off, her nostrils flaring like an angry bull.

"Do not even think about defending her, Zachek."

"Why don't you tell me what your mother said," Zacharias suggested.

"Believe me, you do not want to know."

"Go on. Tell me."

"Fine, then. For starters, in case you weren't aware, you're a Catholic. Did you know that?"

Zacharias smiled. Liza had an incomparable gift for sarcasm. He retrieved her sketchbook and gently brushed the dust off its cover before setting it on the rock.

"That's the lowest rung my mother can imagine, you understand? Barely a step above Injun, I suspect. Doesn't want her precious daughter sparkin' with the likes of you."

"Ah, my likes. I see."

Liza's breath slowed. "Mother says you're not one of us. None of you from Peacock Bend are 'our kind.'"

It was harder for Zacharias to hear what Eugenia Stanard thought about him out loud than to assume what it might be. The woman barely spoke to him when they passed on the streets of Bandera. Occasionally, she would nod with a perfunctory "Master Anderwald" and saunter past, her thin frame bent in a way that looked like her spine was too weak to hold her head. Her hair had gone entirely white after Liza's brother Robert died of diphtheria shortly after the Stanard family's last visit to Peacock Bend. He wondered if she blamed his family for that somehow.

"I see," Zacharias said. "So, why did she slap you?"

"I told her I'd rather be an orphaned guttersnipe like you than a snobby old coot like her," Liza snorted. "That was good, huh?"

"Yeah, I guess." Zacharias understood why Liza couldn't resist fighting with her mother, but it certainly wouldn't help. It was already hard enough to see a future together. Something he'd been thinking about more and more lately.

Liza removed her shoes and stockings. She dangled her feet in the cool water, opened her sketchbook, and thrust a pencil across a blank page. Zacharias watched images come to life with each violent stroke. It was an unflattering drawing of her mother with sagging skin and sharp fangs.

Zacharias kicked off his boots and waded into the middle of the narrow creek. He collected a few smooth, flat stones from the riverbed and skipped them across the surface, waiting for Liza to finish her drawing. He knew better than to interrupt. After several more throws, he turned back to the bank. Liza kicked her feet back and forth in the water, sending choppy ripples across the slow-moving current. Zacharias stared at her tender thighs exposed to the afternoon sun. He knew that she knew he was watching her. When she caught his eye, he blushed. Liza laughed and lowered her skirts so only her ankles showed.

"Liza, it's not funny," Zacharias said. "Your mother already hates me. Just think, if your father caught you like that here with me. He'd hate me, too."

"Never! Don't you know he adores you?"

"Still, it's not right. Not proper."

"Oh, for goodness' sake, I've talked enough about what's proper and what's not today. Don't you start."

Liza jumped off the boulder and joined Zacharias in the shallow water. She bent over to collect a few skipping rocks of her own, and the neckline of her dress fell open. Liza met Zacharias' gaze for a second time.

"Best two out of three skips win," she said, racing back to the riverbank. "After that, you can go back and help Daddy with the fence."

Zacharias overtook Liza with four giant strides and extended a hand to help her onto the bank. She lost her balance and fell against him, bracing her fall with a hand on his chest. Zacharias hesitated before pulling Liza closer and brushing his lips against hers. When she did not back away, he pressed his lips against hers again and held them there.

Zacharias and Liza sat hand in hand and watched the sun start to drift toward the horizon. A massive male bullfrog emerged from its watery hole at the creek's edge and began to roar, beckoning its future mate and fending off potential rivals. Further along, a female bullfrog leaped into a small puddle, her olive-green skin and white throat luminous in the dappled sunlight peeking through the trees. Her aspiring mate joined her, jumping onto her back, his yellow throat pulsing as he bellowed to signal his conquest. The two frogs remained locked together, rocking in the muddy water. Liza turned to Zacharias.

"Don't cry," he said, wiping a tear from her cheek.

Liza placed Zacharias' hand on her chest.

He pulled back. "We can't," he said. "I want to, you know it, but it wouldn't be right."

Liza covered her face and began to sob. "It's not fair, Zachek. It's cruel what she is doing to us. You must talk to my father."

"I will. Soon. I promise," Zacharias assured her.

A branch snapped in the clearing above. "Chief? Where the hell are you?" It was Kirby.

Zacharias jumped and almost sent Liza tumbling into the

water. "Right here," he replied, pulling his boots on and scrambling up the bank through the tangled underbrush.

"Whatcha up to, son? Playing hide-and-seek down there?" Kirby teased.

"No, just getting some water," Zacharias said, glancing back toward the creek, his fingertips caressing his lips.

* * *

Zacharias urged the wagon team along the Bandera Road as dusk fell. Marcin and Khalil were way ahead, and Kirby trotted along behind. The turnoff to Peacock Bend approached over a rise, and so did the familiar grove of trees. Zacharias pulled to a stop.

"Aw, damn it!" Kirby grumbled. "Chief, we should keep moving. Sittin' here rememberin' won't bring him back and won't do you no good either."

Zacharias stared out into the distance.

Kirby tried to lighten the mood. "I know what you were doin' down by the creek today," he said. "Is there anything we need to talk about?"

Zacharias couldn't look the sergeant in the eye. "None of your—"

A flock of birds burst from the treetops below. Zacharias spun his head around.

"Chief, don't. It ain't good for ya," Kirby started, but Zacharias raised a hand to stop him.

"Did you hear something?"

"Nope."

"I heard some kind of animal growling." Zacharias leaned forward and listened intently. "You sure you didn't hear that?"

"I don't see or hear nothin' but a bunch of birds, and an ant could spook them. You always do this. Stop lookin' for somethin' that's not there. He's gone, Chief. And there's nothin' any of us can do about it." Kirby kicked his horse and continued toward home. "Zacharias Anderwald," he called back. "You've got more important things to think about now. Like that girl."

Zacharias slapped the reins and steered the wagon back onto the road. That girl, yes, she was something, he smiled to himself. His mind wandered, thinking about Liza and what a life with her would be like. As he made the final turn for Peacock Bend, Zacharias' thoughts were interrupted by the glint of sunlight across the waters of the Medina and movement in the tree line along the riverbank. A thread of a shadow darted back and forth only to disappear into thin air as another figure emerged from the underbrush and onto the edge of the lower pasture. It was a woman in a long white dress, her arms extended in a manner suggesting an embrace.

The scent of clean, scrubbed skin and a familiar whisper floated on the breeze. "Jestem tutaj," the woman said.

It was her. She would help him. For the first time in many years, Zacharias could remember every detail of his mother's face.

CHAPTER 11

Blessings

Zacharias watched the patrons gather at the Bandera Saloon. The new bar in town catered to a more refined set with its stylish interior, trademark lager, and two-drink minimum. No women, reputable or otherwise, were welcome, of course, "nor any Negroes, Mexicans, Indians or known criminals or cheats," as the sign on the door read. Unlike its competition further along the road, a rundown rum hole next to the blacksmith's, this was a respectable establishment, its proprietors—two investors from Fredericksburg—would assure their silent partner. This partner was the very man Zacharias had come to meet.

The front doors swung open, their custom stained-glass panes rattling. A tall and imposing figure entered. Several customers looked up, some scowling, to see who had come to call. "It's the mayor," several muttered and turned to watch John Stanard wind through the crowd.

"Good afternoon, all," Stanard greeted each table of constituents, still relishing his recent post to the helm of Bandera's local government. "Hope you're enjoying yourselves this fine day."

Stanard approached the bar and signaled to the bartender. "Raymond, fetch me a glass of lager, would ya?" Zacharias stood a few stools down and offered a nervous smile when Stanard looked his way. "Howdy, Zacharias," he said, hand extended.

"Hello, sir. Thank you for meeting me." Zacharias gripped Stanard's hand harder than he intended.

The barkeep slid a tall glass of beer and a towel across the bar top. "Anything else, Mayor?"

Stanard eyed Zacharias. "Won't you join me for a drink?"

"No, thank you."

Standard raised his chin and sucked air through his teeth. "I guess that'll be all for now, Raymond. After you, Zacharias."

Zacharias led the way to an empty tabletop in the back of the saloon.

"So, what is so darned important?" Stanard lowered his glass with a thud and tossed his topcoat over the empty chair beside him. He settled into his seat and sipped his beer, wiping the foam from his mustache as he continued to speak. "I'm all ears," he said.

Zacharias took a deep breath and began. "Mister, erm, Mayor Stanard, thank you for coming to meet me. I've been meaning to talk to you about something."

Zacharias had practiced what he would say at least a hundred times but still felt ill-prepared. He hadn't sought his father's advice but now wondered if he should have. He quickly regrouped. It was time to stand on his own two feet. Besides, he and Marcin never spoke much about personal matters in any case.

What Zacharias worried most about in that moment was losing Liza. "Zachek, I cannot wait forever," she said one day at the creek after things had once again gone a little too far. "You must talk to my father. Alone," she insisted. "My mother will never agree, but I don't care a spit about her. My father will say yes, though. He likes you. Respects you and your father. Always has."

It was true. Since the first day he met the Stanards, the day the eponymous birds arrived at Peacock Bend, Zacharias always felt warmth and kindness from and toward Mr. Stanard. After Agnieszka's passing, he became a faithful customer, hiring Marcin for all the carpentry projects on his ranch. Zacharias also knew Mr. Stanard lent his father the money to buy the Hawleys' farm.

"I insist, Marcin," Zacharias overheard Mr. Stanard say to his father on the porch one night. "You are good for it, and this will be something for Zacharias and the girls. Let me help you. Let me help them. My Bobby is gone, and I already have plenty for my girls."

After a long silence, Marcin replied. "You are kind, Mr. Stan—"

"Call me John," Stanard interrupted. "We are business partners now, Marcin."

"John. Yes. Thank you, John."

There was no bringing Eugenia Stanard around, however. In the wake of their fight, Eugenia forbade Liza to see Zacharias anymore and never spoke to him again. The Baroness of Bandera, as folks referred to her with both envy and ire, would glide past the Anderwalds on the street with nary a glance. Beata recounted that Mary Rose, the Stanards' eldest and most beautiful, but not their brightest, had confessed that Mrs. Stanard would not allow her children to be seen with the riffraff of Peacock Bend in public anymore. "Mother says we don't mix socially with the help. Or Papists," Mary Rose said.

It was all Zacharias could do to remain silent when he saw the woman, but he knew that saying anything would only make things worse. He couldn't risk it. Liza was the most important person in his life.

"Spit it out, Zacharias. No need for such formalities," Stanard insisted.

Zacharias began to lose his nerve but managed to maintain his composure. "I need to talk to you about Liza, uh, Elizabeth."

Stanard belched into a closed fist and furrowed his brow. "Liza? Why do you need to talk to me about her?"

Zacharias could see wheels begin to turn behind the man's eyes and quickly forged ahead. "I would like to ask your permission to call on her."

"Well, Zacharias," Stanard said, eyebrows raised, "I had not realized your childhood friendship with Liza had progressed in this direction." He stood and headed back to the bar.

"Sir?" Zacharias called after him.

"Zacharias, we will both need a drink to finish this conversation. I'll be right back." Stanard walked behind the bar, poured two large whiskeys, and returned to the table. "Now, why don't you start over and tell me what the hell's going on."

Zacharias wiped his sweaty palms along the tops of his thighs.

"You know, sir, that Liza and I have been friends since we were small children. Of late, it is clear that our feelings have changed." He paused for a response.

"And you are certain Liza feels the same way about you?"

"Yes, Mr. Stanard. Quite certain." Zacharias realized he may have conjured up a worry the man had not yet considered. "Given that she will be eighteen in the spring, and I am soon nineteen, we are of courting and marrying age. And furthermore, sir, I am settled with a good income, and with the last project out at your ranch, our family is free of any significant debts." Zacharias was speaking so fast he was out of breath.

"You finished?" Stanard was frowning again.

"Yes sir, I'm finished." Zacharias willed himself to look Liza's father straight in the eye.

"Have you talked to Marcin about this?"

"Yes, er, no. I have not spoken to him about my specific intentions, but I suspect he has some idea," Zacharias replied.

"That would be an important next step from where I sit. You need to tell your father."

Zacharias nodded.

"As for me, there are many reasons why I might support this idea, Zacharias, but a million more why my wife will object, and I'm not sure what we're gonna do about that." Stanard pinched the bridge of his nose with his fingers. "If I allow this, I will never hear the end of it from Eugenia," he said, speaking to himself.

Zacharias' knee bounced nervously beneath the table.

"It helps that Mary Rose is settled with that idiot Parnell boy and his insufferable family over in Castroville. Did you know they have another baby on the way?"

"No, sir. I did not."

"Never mind. A story for another day. Anyway, that's one impediment cleared." Stanard threw back his whiskey in one swallow and held the glass to his lips before placing it on the table. "Zacharias, I think highly of you, son. I hope you know that. And I think you would make Liza a happy woman." After a long pause, he continued. "I'm inclined to give you my blessing, but you need to keep things quiet for a bit so that I can work on her mother. This won't be easy, but you have my solemn promise to try my best."

"Yes, Mr. Stanard. Thank you." Zacharias bowed his head.

"You and Liza steer clear of each other and don't attract any attention, you hear? And you need to tell your father. I don't want any secrets between us."

"I understand," Zacharias said and sniffed his whiskey.

Stanard snapped his fingers. "Raymond, another please." The bartender ran out to their table with a bottle from the top shelf and poured him another shot. Stanard raised his glass and signaled Zacharias to do the same. "Drink up, Zachek, this is gonna be a wild ride."

* * *

"Chief!" Kirby beckoned from the wagon. "Khalil and I been done for over an hour, and I gotta get back before the Mrs. feeds my supper to the pigs. And Zee will be expecting Khalil. Don't want her to worry."

Both Sergeant Kirby and Khalil had finally found their own mates. The sergeant had taken up with a Mrs. Cora Cryer from up in Boerne, whose husband drowned in the lake when he was fishing drunk. How exactly the two were introduced was a mystery. The former Mrs. Cryer, now Mrs. Kirby, arrived in Bandera one day on horseback along with the post. As for Khalil, he won his mate from some cowboys in a card game. The story went that she was the product of a forbidden affair between a Navajo medicine woman and a runaway slave. And while neither the woman nor Khalil understood a word each other spoke at the start; loneliness was common language enough. Everyone knew Khalil's wife—or they assumed they were married—by the name Zee, short for zawja, which Zacharias later discovered simply meant "wife" in Arabic. He never did know her real name. Zee herself was a healer and a renowned midwife across Bandera County.

"Sorry, Sergeant. I had to take care of something important," Zacharias replied, trying to hide a smile.

"What're you on about, kid?" When Zacharias did not answer, Kirby leaned in. "Wait a sec. You didn't. No, wait. You did?" The sergeant hoisted Zacharias onto the seat next to him. "I'll be blam-jammed! What'd Stanard say?" Before Zacharias could answer, a brawl erupted at the end of the road. "Aw, shit. Khalil's at it again." Kirby jumped to the ground and tied the team to the rail. "You can't leave him with that much time on his hands and a poker game that close by. He may forego the drink in the name of his God, but somehow them rules get murky when it comes to cards." The sergeant jogged toward the skirmish with Zacharias close behind. "We gotta hurry now, Chief. Zee will never forgive me if he gets thrown in jail again."

"Thief!" Khalil shouted as he staggered out of the dark lean-to beside the smith shop. He quickly regrouped and started back toward the bar's entrance. "You cheat me!" he bellowed.

Kirby jumped in front of his friend and pushed him back.

"Git the hell outta here and don't even think about coming back," the greasy bartender ordered, charging into the road, his shotgun raised. Two vaqueros exited next.

"Whoa! Whoa, fellas!" Kirby pleaded, his hands in the air. "Take it easy."

"This one here's a sore loser, Sergeant," the bartender pointed at Khalil. "You best get him off home, and I don't wanna see him round here again. He always starts a fight."

"Henry, I got it. You go on back inside with those two." Kirby waved the other men back toward the entry. "Adios, muchachos," he said, and when they hesitated, he took another step forward. "Go," he insisted. The sergeant turned to Khalil and pointed toward the wagon. "We're finished here."

Khalil shook his fist above his head. "Eat shit!" he roared, Kirby pushing him along from behind.

*　*　*

"Tato?" Zacharias called.

"Out here," a voice emerged from the darkness, startling a swarm of fireflies floating in the still night air. Marcin was sitting alone on the front porch.

"What are you doing?"

Marcin shrugged. Zacharias understood that his father still missed his mother terribly, even after all these years. Despite the unambiguous interest among the widows of Bandera County, Zacharias also suspected Marcin had yet to bring himself to be with another woman.

"I need to talk to you. It's important," Zacharias said.

"Come." Marcin struck a match and lit a small lantern on the side table. "What is wrong?"

Zacharias sat down next to his father. "Nothing's wrong. But I need to tell you something. I've already spoken with Mr. Stanard—"

"About Liza."

"How did you know?"

"Sergeant Kirby saw you down by the creek. Khalil saw you sneaking away from work. Who doesn't know, Zachek?" Marcin put a hand on his son's knee. "Is it love?"

"Yes."

"Great love?"

"I think so."

Marcin sat back and scratched his cheek. A shooting star ignited among the blanket of stars that shrouded Peacock Bend and trailed into the rolling hills beyond the Medina. "You look at Liza like I looked at Mama," he finally said.

"We want to get married."

"What does John say?"

"I am not worried about Mr. Stanard. It's Mrs. Stanard who will be the problem."

"She is not a nice woman, Zachek, but she is Liza's mother. You must get her blessing, or it will be bad luck for your marriage."

"Since when do you believe in luck?"

"Only bad luck, Zachek. I'm not sure good luck exists."

"What should I do?"

"Go to the church to pray, Zacharias. Pray that Mrs. Stanard changes her mind."

CHAPTER 12

Over Her Dead Body

Zacharias did pray. Hard. But his pleas to God veered toward the vindictive and at times, dangerously close to the vengeful. It was difficult to forgive Eugenia Stanard for how she treated his family and impossible to forgive her cruelty to Liza. Between heaving sobs, Liza had recounted to Zacharias the story of a recent gathering of the few women of means in town for their monthly afternoon tea at Stanard Ranch. Comparing her daughters, Eugenia had joked, "My Mary Rose has been a swan from birth, but my Elizabeth was our ugly duckling, who I fear may remain an ugly duck." When Liza confronted her mother, Eugenia replied dismissively, "Don't be so sensitive, dear."

In the end, the Lord saw fit to answer Zacharias' prayers. The evening after the next tea party, Eugenia Stanard desperately scratched at the welts from numerous mosquito bites. Her head was splitting, and her brow burned. Within another twenty-four hours, the black vomit began as Doc Adolph predicted. It was yellow fever. Liza faithfully nursed her mother, tending to the dreary duties of emptying the chamber pot and washing the soiled sheets, and doing her best to ignore Eugenia's vicious hemorrhagic ramblings.

"What did I tell you, John?" she had seethed when she learned of Zacharias' request for Liza's hand. "This was my worst fear. The answer is no. Absolutely not."

"Eugenia, darling, please. Give our Liza this one thing. You have nothing more to lose on this earth. We both know it." Stanard had done his best to mount a defense of the match in the last hours of his wife's life, but it was for naught.

"John Stanard, I tell you this now. Our daughter will marry that filthy Polack over my cold, lifeless corpse. Even then, I will still protest from the Heavens above. Am I making myself clear?"

And so, it was literally over Eugenia Stanard's dead body that Zacharias and Liza finally received John Stanard's blessing. Though Zacharias never said so out loud, he did wonder on more than one occasion if the woman simply had it coming. Of course, as those thoughts crossed his mind, he shuddered, knowing that they would likely not put him in a favorable light with the Lord.

Eugenia was laid to rest in the family plot behind the First Baptist Church. Her grave was placed beside her beloved son, Bobby, in accordance with her stated wishes. Many of the Stanards' fellow parishioners and Bandera dignitaries attended the funeral, and the Reverend Potter offered a perfunctory eulogy. After the final prayers, John Stanard invited the group to stay for refreshments in the fellowship hall. Liza remained in the churchyard and watched her father, Zacharias, and Marcin refill the grave.

"'For dust thou art, and unto dust shalt thou return,'" Marcin recited as he and Zacharias emptied the last shovels of soil and tapped the loose earth.

"Thank you. I'm grateful for your help," Stanard sighed and shook each of their dirty hands.

Zacharias noticed the gray pallor of shock and sleep deprivation on Stanard's face. "You're welcome, Mr. Stanard. We are sorry for your loss."

"Zacharias, you're a good man to offer a kind word for a woman who treated you so poorly. I am sorry for that."

Zacharias nodded.

John Stanard looked at his daughter Liza and released another heavy sigh. "Your mother was a good woman deep down, but she had a hard time showing it," he said, sprinkling a handful of dirt over the fresh grave before turning back to Zacharias. "Now that this is done, I've got something to say, and it's good Marcin is here, too.

Besides Eugenia's refusal to consider the idea, I've tried hard to find a reason why I should not give you my blessing. Truth is, I don't have a good one, so I am prepared to give it."

"Oh, Daddy!" Liza cried.

"Wait a minute, Liza," Stanard said, holding up a hand. "Zacharias, I trust you have spoken with your father?"

"Yes sir."

"And Marcin, you've no objections?"

"No, John. I want Zacharias and Liza to be happy. They are not happy apart."

"There it is. I do have one request, though." Stanard pointed at Zacharias. "I'd like you to wait until next spring for the wedding. A proper and public engagement will give things time to settle, and Eugenia might rest a little easier."

"Thank you, Daddy." Liza rushed forward and threw her arms around her father. "I love you."

"Love you, too, Liza Lou. All right, then. It's time to get on inside." Stanard brushed the dirt from his overcoat and led the way.

✳ ✳ ✳

The couple wed the following spring on the eve of Liza's nineteenth birthday. The ceremony was a small but happy affair, the first conducted in St. Stanislaus' new home, a beautiful limestone building with a soaring bell tower. The construction had stalled a year earlier due to a lack of funding, but an anonymous benefactor fortuitously came forward to complete the project. Zacharias suspected Mr. Stanard had something to do with this turn of events after seeing him huddled with Father Adamietz one afternoon, but he never pried about the details. What did they matter after all?

Mary Rose agreed to plan the service, and Beata and Victoria accepted Liza's invitation to make her bouquet and arrange the flowers. Out of courtesy, Zacharias invited Randall Parnell, Mary Rose's husband, to offer a reading during Mass, hoping that Randall could keep his finger out of his nose during the service. He was never able to do so at other family gatherings. Khalil declined Zacharias' invitation to join the wedding party, and Zacharias and Liza both agreed it was probably for the best. It might have been too much for the St. Stanislaus community to take in, and neither could ever imagine Khalil wearing proper trousers.

The reception took place on the great lawn in front of the Stanards' sprawling ranch house. Mrs. Kirby and Zee saw to the refreshments, and lunch awaited the guests upon their arrival. Most of the congregation was in attendance, especially the young folk. Weddings were the venue of choice for meeting and taking stock of future husbands and wives under the elders' watchful eyes. Zacharias was sure this was where the match between Anatol Dugos and Beata was plotted. Their nuptials would follow six months later.

After the plates were cleared, the cake was cut, and the champagne was poured, John Stanard clinked the side of his glass with a spoon and signaled to Marcin to join him on the veranda.

"Family and friends," he began. "I welcome you all here this afternoon to celebrate the union of Zacharias and Liza. Please join me in wishing them a life of happiness and prosperity together. And, most of all, many, many grandchildren!"

"Here, here," the attendees cheered.

"Marcin, I'd also like to invite you to say a few words."

Marcin stepped toward the railing, pausing to withdraw a folded sheet of paper from his breast pocket. "I will first say a few words to my son, Zacharias. Forgive me, John. I will speak in Polish. It is easier for me. I will ask my beautiful daughter Vicky, who will soon become a teacher, to help with the English." Marcin cleared his throat. "Zachek, mój synu," he began with uncharacteristic emotion.

When he was finished, Victoria translated. "My father says, Zachek, my son. I wish you happiness." The youngest Anderwald steeled herself before continuing. "I wish you happiness, and I know your mother, our mother, is here, watching over us all."

"I can feel her, too, Tatuś," Zacharias smiled and gently squeezed his father's hand.

Marcin turned to Liza and continued in English. "And Liza, you have brought happiness to my son, to me, to my family. I can never repay this debt. My Aga would have loved you like a daughter because I love you like mine." His hands trembled as he refolded the paper.

Liza threw her arms around Marcin. She kissed each of his cheeks. "Tato," she said. "Thank you. For everything."

* * *

Once the last of the guests had departed, Liza and Zacharias retreated to what was now their bedroom to prepare for a brief honeymoon in Galveston, an unexpected wedding gift from Mary Rose and Randall. But their excitement at the prospect of traveling to the sea was overshadowed by an even more exciting first event, their wedding night.

Zacharias worried that the unsolicited advice and counsel he'd overheard Mary Rose offering earlier in the afternoon may have given Liza pause. The sisters had been tucked away in the parlor, Zacharias within earshot on the front porch.

"It will hurt something terrible," Mary Rose blurted out. "And you cannot say no because it is your wifely duty."

"What are you talking about, Rosie?" Liza laughed.

Mary Rose ignored Liza's question. "Make sure it is dark so he cannot see you naked. And believe me, you do not want to see him either. It's disgusting."

"What's disgusting?" Liza urged.

"His *member*, of course," she said, her nose wrinkling. "It either hangs there loose among more hair than you can imagine, or it is full and hard and sticking out in front, which means you must lie back and take off your underclothes quick before Zacharias becomes frustrated. Frustrated men are not happy, and neither are their wives."

Zacharias had listened in bemused silence, recalling the many stolen touches with Liza in their secret place on the creekbank.

"Oh, and keep a small bottle of perfume by your bed just in case. You want to be sure you don't stink when your husband wants to lie with you," Mary Rose continued, pausing before offering a final tip to ensure a happy married life. "I wish Randall would mind his hygiene a bit more. Hopefully, Zacharias will. If not, when he is sleeping, you can put some perfume under his arms if the odor is too fierce, but you can never say anything about that. It is not a woman's place."

Zacharias clutched a hand over his mouth to muffle his laughter and stumbled back to the guests on the lawn.

The door creaked, and Liza closed it gently behind her. She wore a light shift that flowed over the curves of her body, her full breasts loose beneath. Her hair cascaded over her shoulders, but a strand was tucked into the corner of her mouth, betraying her nerves.

Zacharias rose from a chair in the corner of the room where he'd been waiting for her. He reached for the lamp at the bedside.

"No, leave it," Liza said.

Zacharias felt a twinge of self-consciousness. Marcin's only advice, offered haltingly, was to allow Liza to invite him into the bed for the first time. Kirby's instructions had been to scrub himself extra clean and shave close. Zacharias stepped forward and took Liza's face in his hands. Saying nothing, she reached out to untie his undershirt and lifted it over his head. She placed her cheek against the center of his bare chest, dragging her fingernails along his spine. Zacharias lifted Liza's chin and bent to kiss her, his tongue darting between her lips and pecking lightly at the tip of hers inside her mouth. The taste and feel of Liza were familiar and unknown all at once.

Liza took Zacharias' hand and guided him onto the bed. They lay side by side, giggling before Zacharias turned and pressed the entire length of his body against hers. He could sense Liza's hesitation mixed with her urgency when she turned to face him. Zacharias laid Liza back and lifted his body on top of hers. She parted her legs, allowing him to press even closer. As they moved together, Zacharias gently raised her nightgown around her waist, his fingers grazing her naked hips and his breath quickening with excitement.

"You're beautiful, Liza," he whispered in her ear. "You have always been my swan."

*   *   *

Upon their return to Peacock Bend from Galveston, Zacharias and Liza set to work on a new home. Marcin's wedding gift to the couple was a small plot of land further down the path from the original farmhouse and closer to the river. Liza deployed her sharp, artistic eye to draw the plans, and within a few months, the house started to take shape. The design included an expansive front parlor with a massive stone fireplace and three bedrooms. The house would also have running water and a flush toilet—gifts from John Stanard.

"No outhouses or wooden barrel dips for my Liza Lou," he said with a boom of a laugh over a whiskey too many one night.

Most important to Zacharias, however, was the spectacular wrap-around porch that offered the perfect perch from which to listen to the river below.

With the help of his father, Sergeant Kirby, and Khalil, Zacharias spent months dragging river rock up from the Medina for the new foundation. Zacharias could not believe the progress they had made. The undulating patterns of the smooth river rock—a mix of deep browns, blues, and blacks, joined with a dark gray mortar—evoked the movement of the waters from which the rocks had been collected. Framing was also well underway, and the house was larger than he had envisioned with all the rooms laid out.

Zacharias found himself on his own one morning, laying floorboards in one of the bedrooms.

"Oh, Mr. Anderwald," Liza beckoned. "Get yourself on up to the main house. Lunch is ready."

"Thank the Lord," Zacharias said to himself. His stomach had already been rumbling for over an hour. "On my way, Mrs. Anderwald," he replied.

"Where is everyone?" Zacharias asked, stomping the dust off his boots at the door.

"Bea and Vicky are helping at the church, and your father has gone over to visit with the Kirbys this afternoon. Oh, and Khalil's tending to one of the camel cows that's about ready to burst. He says the calf should arrive before dark."

"Poor thing," Zacharias said. "Birthin' one of those hump-backed beasts must hurt somethin' awful. Can't even think about it."

"Thing is, Zachek, we might have to start thinking about it whether we like it or not." Liza ran her hands across her abdomen and up onto her hips.

A jolt of shock rippled through Zacharias' body. "What? A baby?" he stammered.

Liza beamed. "Doc Adolph says I'm about three months on. We should have a little one right after Christmas."

"I can't believe it!" Zacharias said, tears pooling in his eyes. He scooped Liza into his arms and carried her triumphantly to their bedroom. "You wait here," he ordered, laying her on the bed and jogging back to the kitchen.

Zacharias returned with a tray filled with food and drink. He plumped the pillows behind Liza and made sure she was comfortable. He stretched out beside her and watched her eat.

After lunch, Liza dozed off. Zacharias' mind raced as he watched her sleep. His father was right. Aga would have loved Liza. It also occurred to Zacharias that the shadow had made itself quite scarce of late. It had not stirred since the confrontation with the woman in white that day he'd resolved to ask for Liza's hand. In the face of true love and happiness, had the demon returned from whence it came defeated? Zacharias hoped so but feared not. He shuddered. With a child coming, the stakes were so much higher. His father had been powerless to save little Lena and Agnieszka. Should the shadow come to call again, would he be strong enough to repel the malevolent force?

Liza stirred, and Zacharias reached out and stroked her belly, humming the tune his mother used to sing to him as a child. "Lulaj, lulaj. Go to sleep, go to sleep, my little one," he recalled the words. "I love you, Liza Anderwald," he said. "You rescued me from the darkness."

"We rescued each other," Liza replied, a soft smile on her lips.

CHAPTER 13

And They Brought unto Him Also Infants

Frantic shouting from the street in front of The Menger Hotel shattered the pre-dawn quiet. "Zacharias Anderwald!" a familiar voice bounced off the cobblestones lining San Antonio's Military Plaza. "Chief!"

Zacharias sat bolt upright in his bed and immediately knew this trip had been a terrible mistake. Liza was too far along for him to be traveling. Registering the new cattle brand for Peacock Bend could have waited, should have waited, until after the baby arrived. Hearing the urgency in Khalil's summons, he now feared the worst.

"Tato, wake up," Zacharias shook his father in the adjacent bed. "It's Khalil. Down on the street. Something is wrong." Zacharias grabbed his boots and threw his coat on over his nightclothes. "Hurry!"

"You go, Zachek. I will follow," Marcin replied, scrambling to dress.

Zacharias rushed to the hotel lobby. The night manager was standing guard at the front door, holding it closed. Khalil pounded on the other side. "Let him in!" Zacharias demanded. "Can't you see he's on urgent business?" He grabbed the manager, who continued to resist. "The man's frozen through. Let him in!"

"Sir, I'm not lettin' no Injun in here. It's against company policy," the man said. "The Menger is a respectable—"

"I don't give a goddamned spit about your company policy," Zacharias barked. "You open the door immediately, or there'll be hell to pay, you hear me?" Zacharias was close enough to see the remnants of the manager's midnight snack between his crooked teeth and smell tobacco on his breath.

Marcin arrived and stepped between the two men. "Sir, you see something is wrong. My son's wife is pregnant. We must know if something has happened. The lobby is empty. No one will see you break these foolish rules."

The manager reluctantly loosened his grip, and Marcin signaled to Zacharias to open the door. Khalil tumbled through. "Chief, Liza's not good. You must come," he sputtered.

"Is it the baby?" Zacharias asked, but he already knew the answer.

"Come, Chief. Come," Khalil insisted.

The men were back on the road within the hour.

*   *   *

By late afternoon, when Zacharias arrived home, driving sleet pounded the earth from a blackened sky. He found Liza prone on the bed, breathing in through her nose and out through pursed lips. Zee had stopped the bleeding and given Liza something for the pain, but she was weak and drifting in and out of consciousness. Zacharias sat at the bedside and watched the wetness of the rain run down the outside of the bedroom window. Lightning exploded from above. "One, two, three, four," he counted aloud before a distant clap of thunder boomed. The storm was on the move. He'd only gotten to the count of two last time.

Zacharias regretted leaving Liza in such a state. The baby had been quiet off and on in her belly for hours earlier in the week, and she had been fretting. But Liza was constantly fretting. Zee had come to the house to check on her. Said nothing was amiss and that Liza should get some rest.

"Stop fussing, Liza," Zacharias had implored. "You're gonna

find yourself in the lunatic asylum before long if you keep worrying like this."

"But why can't your father go with Sergeant Kirby? Why do you have to be there?" she had complained.

"My father and I are co-owners of the ranch. I need to be there, too, to sign the documents. I already explained all this." Zacharias was rarely short-tempered, but he was close.

"I know, I know, Zachek. I just hate being alone with the baby coming. The Kirbys have taken Bea and Vicky to Mary Rose to help with her new arrival. Of course, I'm happy to have them practice on somebody else's child," Liza tried to make light but failed.

"Liza, please," Zacharias soothed.

"And I can't communicate with Zee for the life of me," she said. "She never says a darned word I can understand. So that leaves me with poor Khalil. Is he the company I'm to keep while you're away?"

"Liza, I'd trust Khalil with your life."

"Of course, Zachek, and so would I. I was speaking about companionship. That's all," Liza sighed.

"Yes, unless you wanna chat about camels or cards, Khalil might not be the best conversationalist. But you'll be safe. Don't worry. Enjoy some time to yourself. You won't have much of that once the baby comes. Maybe finish some of those sketches you've been workin' on?"

Zacharias could tell Liza had forced a smile when he kissed her forehead before heading out the door.

The rain slowed to a drizzle. Zacharias relieved Zee and sent her to the apartment over the barn she shared with Khalil to get some rest. A hush fell over the house, which did not yet feel like home. Zacharias had rushed to finish construction before the baby arrived, but much was still to be completed. He started to nod off in his chair when Liza began to toss and turn. Zacharias reached out to stroke her head. She was burning with fever.

"The smell!" Liza groaned.

Zacharias sniffed and sensed a foul odor building in the room—a stench that was all too familiar. The hairs on the back of his neck stood on end. The shadow was back.

"I'm going to be sick," Liza gagged and lurched over the side of the bed, grasping for the basin she'd kept on the floor during the morning sickness she suffered in the first months of pregnancy. As she did so, something unseen grabbed one of her forearms from under the bed and began to pull her over the side. Zacharias gripped Liza's shoulders and tried to pull her back. "Hold me, Zachek," she pleaded, clutching Zacharias' ankle to keep herself from being dragged onto the floor.

"God, help us!" Zacharias screamed.

The grip suddenly released, and Zacharias and Liza tumbled back onto the mattress, facing the ceiling. The smell had worsened, and Liza began to retch, liquid surging into her throat. Zacharias rushed to sit Liza up, fearing the vomit might trickle back into her lungs, but this time, someone or something held her fast. Zacharias panicked. If he could not get Liza upright, she might choke. She gasped for air and inhaled the lumpy fluid. Zacharias plunged two fingers into the back of Liza's mouth to try and clear her airway, but she continued to gag, and her skin turned blue.

The room began to spin, and a dark cloud appeared above the bed. "Kara," a disembodied wheeze rattled from above.

The force holding Liza down released, and blood began to soak through the entire bottom half of her nightgown. Zacharias forced her to stand, holding her tight around the hips as more liquid poured out from between her legs. Liza doubled over, and he could feel her abdomen seize and twist. Zacharias wrapped Liza in a blanket and dragged her outside. The only hope was to go to Zee.

Zacharias lifted Liza over his shoulder and stumbled into the storm. Blasts of freezing air tore at his skin, and his bare feet slipped and slid in the mud as pelting rain soaked them both through. Zacharias managed to reach the barn, where he collapsed with Liza at the entrance. "Help me!" he pleaded with what little strength he had left.

The lock scraped, and the door opened. "Come, Chief," Zee beckoned.

The following hours were a fog. Zacharias sat in the corner; his head cradled in his palms. He watched the scene before him as though in a trance, with only bits and pieces registering.

Liza was lying on a small cot before a cast-iron stove. "No!" she protested.

"Drink, Miss Liza," Zee instructed, tipping a cup of water against Liza's lips.

After Liza took a few sips, Zee moved to the end of the cot and knelt on the floor. Her ebony skin shimmered in the firelight as she worked quickly, her head and hands between Liza's legs. The room smelled of burnt oil and herbs.

"My baby," Liza moaned.

After what felt like an eternity, Zee rose to her feet, her forearms cradling a tiny bundle wrapped in a white cotton sheet. She laid it gingerly on the floor beside the stove.

"Dear God, no," Liza whimpered.

Zacharias bowed his head and began to weep. He was consumed by an overpowering sense of loss and longing unlike any he had ever experienced, even in the wake of his mother and Lena's deaths. Total and complete emptiness collided with absolute truth and knowing. Their child was lost.

"Zachek, Jestem tutaj, I am here," a woman's voice called out.

"Mamusiu," Zacharias sobbed.

*   *   *

Peacock Bend stood silent in the morning light, damp and cold from the night's storm lingering over the hills. Doc Adolf and Khalil had arrived at dawn. Liza lay on her side, clutching the wrap of sheets. She stared unseeing at the wall, her lips moving, but there was no sound. A painful memory of his mother collapsed on the floor, talking nonsense after Lena's death, ripped through Zacharias' mind.

Zacharias lowered himself onto the floor next to the cot. "Liza," he said softly, seeking to draw her out. "It's me. Zachek." Liza did not move or react.

"Let me see to her," Doc Adolph said.

Zacharias moved to the small table at the opposite end of the loft where Zee had laid out some food and drink. The doctor closed the thin curtain that separated the sleeping quarters from the small kitchenette to shield Liza from view.

"Eat, Chief," Zee insisted, patting his arm.

Zacharias pushed the plate away and sat in numb silence. Doc Adolph soon opened the curtain again, and Zee took her cue to step away.

The doctor spoke slowly and calmly. "Zacharias, thankfully, it will only be the baby. I'm not sure what that woman Zee did, but I am duly impressed. She was able to extract most of the fetus, so I think we're past the threat of hemorrhage or infection. The worst is over, but Liza has experienced a significant shock. That will take more time to resolve."

"How far along was she, Doc?" Zacharias steeled himself for the answer to his question.

"Seven months, I'd say."

Zacharias bent forward, his forehead resting on the tabletop. "Was it a girl or a boy?" he asked.

"A little girl." Doc Adolf paused. "Zacharias, there was nothing Liza or Zee could have done to save that baby. The cord strangled her. Sometimes, in the end, hard as it might be to understand, it's nature's way."

"Nature's way or God's will?" Zacharias said.

"A little of both, I suspect. A little of both." The doctor patted Zacharias' shoulder.

Zacharias sat back in his chair, his jaw clenched and shoulders tight. "More like God's vengeance," he muttered.

Doc Adolph gave him a puzzled look. "Liza will need you to be strong. This is always hardest on the woman," he said.

Zacharias exhaled slowly and folded his hands in his lap. "Thank you, Doc. I'm much obliged, although I wish we didn't see as much of you as we do."

The doctor made to leave. "I'll be back around in a week or so to check in, but send for me if you need anything," he said, buttoning his coat.

Zacharias waited until Doc Adolph's footsteps faded and the barn door slammed before returning to the bedside.

"Zachek?" Liza croaked.

"I'm right here," he said, gently stroking Liza's arm.

After a few minutes, he tried to wrest the baby's body from her embrace, but Liza only tightened her grip. Zacharias looked to Zee for help.

The midwife bent down, her lips beside Liza's ear. "Let me hold her now. You get some sleep," she said, lifting the bundle into her arms.

Zacharias tucked the blankets tighter around Liza, who was still shaking. "Our baby," she wept. "I couldn't stop it."

"Don't talk like that. I should never have left you alone. It's my fault," Zacharias said.

"No," Liza turned to him. "It was…" Her voice faded.

"It was what, Liza?" Zacharias could not hide his alarm.

Liza hesitated again, her eyes searching the corners of the room. "A shadow."

Zacharias hoped and prayed he'd misheard, that Liza was delirious.

"A shadow man took our baby," she rasped.

Terror surged through Zacharias' entire body at the mention of the dark figure. He would never forgive himself if Liza had fallen into the sights of this vile spirit. "Liza, tell me what you saw," he pleaded but realized she had fallen asleep.

Zacharias stood and descended into the barn. He needed air. The horses and camels huddled close together for warmth, grunting and shifting nervously in their stalls. As he checked the latches on the gates, he heard what sounded like laughter and spun around. He was sure someone was standing behind him, but he was alone. A familiar odor pricked his nostrils, like when the soldier would come to him as a child. He then remembered what the woman in white would cry.

"Leave us!" Zacharias repeated the charge into the darkness. "Leave us, you sonofabitch!"

The animals kicked and snorted, and the peacocks began to shriek from the rooftop.

*　　*　　*

Zacharias and Liza gave their baby a proper burial and mourned her as though she had lived. However, no name would be carved on the wooden cross on the hilltop grave.

It simply read "Baby Girl Anderwald, d. 1876."

Father Adamietz rode out to Peacock Bend to offer the funeral rites. Zacharias held Liza close at the graveside. The wind whipped across the icy ground and sliced through his coat like a thousand blades. Marcin, John Stanard, the Kirbys, Khalil, and Zee stood nearby, stomping their feet to keep warm.

"Dear Lord, we are gathered here today to mourn a terrible loss," the priest began. "Oh, merciful Father, give this child your peace and let your eternal light shine upon her." Father Adamietz paused.

Zacharias fought to hold Liza steady. "Please hurry, Father," he urged. "I must get Liza inside."

"Yes, of course," the priest said, raising his hands toward the sky. "May God give us peace in our sorrow, consolation in our grief, and strength to accept his will. Amen."

"Amen," the group replied in a grim chorus, all except Zacharias.

Liza's father took her arm and led her back to the house. The others followed, leaving Zacharias and Marcin alone. The two stood without speaking for a long time.

"Zachek, I know this pain," Marcin finally said.

Zacharias stood silent.

"Zachek, you must listen to me."

Zacharias pointed a trembling finger at each of the graves. "How can that stupid man say that I must accept any of this as the will of a merciful God?" he said.

Marcin reached out, but Zacharias turned away.

"Lena? Mama? Ahmad? What kind of mercy did any of them receive?" Zacharias spat. "And now this poor little child is strangled in the womb. She didn't even have a chance."

"It is not fair," Marcin said.

Zacharias stooped to grab a handful of rocks and hurled them at the trinity of massive oaks. He quickly exhausted himself and, with one final throw, stumbled forward onto his hands and knees. "Tatusiu, I am to blame. This is my punishment."

"Who is punishing you?"

"God," Zacharias said, wiping his nose on his sleeve.

"What do you mean, God?"

Zacharias sat back on his heels, facing the gray skies above. "When Lena died, I hated Mama for not watching out for her by the river, and I hated you for not saving her. And I hated any God who would let a child suffer like that. So, when Mama died, I knew I was being punished for my sins."

"Zachek, don't do this," Marcin begged.

"And after Ahmad, I prayed for vengeance. Father Adamietz told me that it was not my place, but the Lord's alone, in His time, but I still pray for it if I'm bein' truthful. I still pray a little every day that Josiah T. Gaines and his men suffer for what they did."

"It's enough, Zachek—"

"No! Listen to me! I also prayed about Mrs. Stanard like you said I should. But I didn't ask God to make her change her mind about Liza and me. I asked him to punish her for her wickedness. Tato, it's me. I did this." Zacharias slipped down onto the ground, his fists sinking into the mud. "And here we are, on our hilltop once again. This time, we are burying my baby girl, an innocent who has suffered for my sins."

Marcin kneeled and took Zacharias into his arms. "No, you did not do this," he said. "Nor did God. It was me, Zachek. I brought this evil here."

Zacharias shook his head. "No, Tato."

"Yes, I did. But we will fight this demon together—you, me, and Mama."

"Mama?"

"She is here, Zachek," Marcin replied. "Aga is here. We will all fight together."

CHAPTER 14

Dziecko

The ritual remained the same for the four stillborn babies to follow, all girls, each of whom Zacharias and Liza laid to rest on the hilltop. Over nearly two decades, there would also be the countless unknowns Liza's body would surrender to miscarriage. With each loss, the couple's desperate hopes for a child faded. The silence between them grew more impenetrable, and the emotional scar tissue thicker. Zacharias would escape to the river to fish, to his room in the old farmhouse, or sometimes to sleep alone in the loft of the cowshed for days on end until Marcin would retrieve him.

"Zachek, it is time to come home," he would say, and Zacharias would follow in silence.

Liza withdrew to one of the bedrooms in the main house she had converted into a studio to sketch or paint during the day and to sleep at night. Like Zacharias, she would remain sequestered, alone in her grief.

One spring morning, upon returning from the river, his creel overflowing with large river bass, Zacharias found Liza on the front porch. She was seated behind an easel, painting. He slowed his pace to observe her. Liza's hair, revealing more than hints of gray, was pinned on the top of her head, and the cool morning air flushed her cheeks. A desiccated memory of their first meetings by the creek flared.

The gate scraped on its hinges, and Liza looked up. "Oh, it's you."

Zacharias continued into the house without a response but glanced back at the textured sheet of paper clipped to the easel frame. Hazy watercolors seeped into its absorbent surface, their muted, soothing tones dissonant with the bleak significance of the scene Liza chose to paint over and over. It was the bend in the Medina River where little Lena succumbed to the serpents. Zacharias let the screen door slam behind him.

"Good to chat with you, too," Liza mumbled.

What was there to say? Zacharias couldn't think of anything to heal their wounds or bridge the aching distance between them. For Liza, the search for peace had somehow come to mean indifference to the losses they had endured. Zacharias, however, would no longer accept that the most profound grief was a condition solely afflicting the one who physically bore the children. He had not carried their babies in a womb, but he kept them in his heart. Zacharias knew he should turn around and take Liza in his arms, but he couldn't bring himself to do so. His resentment of her was fierce and blinding. He could not explain why, not to himself or anyone else.

"Don't forget your father and Daddy are coming for supper," Liza said. "Daddy says he's got an announcement. Not sure what that means, but I hope he's not thinking about politics again. The last run nearly killed him."

Zacharias set to gutting the fish in the kitchen sink.

* * *

"Liz Lou, dinner was delicious." Stanard laid his napkin beside his still half-full dinner plate.

"Daddy, you barely touched your food. Are you sure I can't get you something else?" Liza's tone was full of concern. Her father had lost even more weight since he'd visited three weeks prior.

"No, thank you. I'm fine. Maybe some coffee, but don't make a pot solely on my account. Marcin and Zacharias, will you join me?" he gestured to both men.

"Sure," Marcin said.

Zacharias stared at the tablecloth. He could feel Liza watching him as she began to gather the plates. "Fine. Coffee for two, I suppose it is," she said. "I'll go put the pot on, and then I want to hear this big announcement."

The three men sat in silence. Liza dropped the dishes in the sink, slammed the cabinets open and shut, and banged the kettle onto the stovetop. When she returned with the coffee, she set the tray in the middle of the table and did not offer to pour. Liza took her seat and glared at Zacharias before turning to her father. "So, what's your news?" she asked.

Stanard offered up a devilish grin, his signature response whenever there was tension in the air. "I've made the decision to quit ranching. Last week, I was in San Antonio to draft the papers with my lawyer."

"Daddy, what's wrong?"

"Nothing, Liza. You keep telling me that I look terrible, so I'm gonna put my feet up and rest a bit."

"Well, but you have been out of sorts," she admitted. "And what does this mean?"

"I'm dividing the ranch between you and your sister. The house and the few acres between it and the main road are in Mary Rose's name. She gets all that after I pass, seeing that I need a place to live until I go to my maker. She and Randall can move there or sell it, whatever they like. As for the rest, the fields, barns, equipment, and livestock are in your name, Liza Lou. I hope you and Zacharias will run my cattle business from here. Of course, Zacharias should have some say about that."

Liza caught Zacharias' eye. "Daddy, this is so generous. Are you sure?" she said.

"Yes, Liza. I am sure, and there's no arguing about it. It's already done."

Liza turned back to Zacharias. "Zachek?"

"Mr. Stanard, thank you," Zacharias said. "I'm honored. Of course, I accept." He knew he'd misstepped when he saw the vein in Liza's temple start to pulse. "I mean, we accept."

"I've talked to all my men, and they're prepared to stay on. They trust you, Zacharias, and they get on with Kirby and Khalil if those Saturday poker games are any indication." John Stanard started to laugh but was quickly overcome by a coughing fit.

Marcin stepped into the parlor and returned with four glasses and a bottle of Irish whiskey, a gift from Stanard to Zacharias the previous Christmas. "We must make a toast," he said. He opened the bottle and poured four healthy portions.

"Absolutely," Stanard said, raising his glass.

After dinner, Marcin headed to his house, and Liza's father retreated to the guest room. He was soon snoring. Liza returned to the sink, and the crashing and banging of pots and pans resumed. Zacharias brought the last of the glassware from the dining table and set it on the counter. As Liza reached for one of the wine glasses, it slipped from her soapy hand, shattering on the countertop and sending shards of glass into the sink.

"Goddammit!" she grumbled and wiped a wet palm across her forehead.

Zacharias didn't move.

"Are you going to stand there, or are you going to help me?" Liza asked through gritted teeth.

Zacharias grabbed a dish towel and began to sweep up the broken glass.

Liza untied her apron and hung it on the back of a chair. "I'd appreciate your finishing up here, if you don't mind. I need to go to bed," she said and retreated to her studio, the door slamming in her wake.

*   *   *

Zacharias sat alone at the kitchen table, replaying the events of the previous night. His train of thought was disrupted by the shuffle of Liza's feet along the hallway.

"Morning," she mumbled as she drew herself a glass of water from the tap and sat down. She took a sip, staring over the rim, as though in expectation of something. Zacharias wasn't sure what.

"Fine, then. I'll start," she said. "I suppose I owe you an

apology after my behavior last night."

Zacharias set his coffee cup down. "I'm listening," he said.

"I'm not sure what came over me."

"It's not about last night, Liza."

"I don't think you can really understand," she started.

Zacharias slammed his fist on the table, and Liza jumped. "Enough!" he snapped. "Liza Anderwald, I am not your punching bag."

Liza looked stunned. "Why are you so angry, Zacharias? So cold?"

"I might ask you the same. You are not alone in your suffering but act like you are. I cannot take much more of this, and you must understand that." Zacharias paused, realizing the threat, while empty, was harsher than intended. "I fear if we each keep trying to face the pain by ourselves, it will consume us," he said.

Liza sniffed and dabbed her nose with a handkerchief. "I can't bear this. It's too hard."

Zacharias stood and headed for the door.

"I love you, Zachek," Liza called after him. "More than anyone or anything else."

Zacharias turned back before closing the door behind him. "Then I think it's about time we try to rescue each other again."

*   *   *

Dim light glowed beneath the door to Liza's studio. Zacharias inched closer, listening to see if she was awake. He could hear the scratch of a pencil, which stopped when a floorboard squeaked under his feet. He took a deep breath and turned the knob. It had been yet another four weeks of silence. It had to end.

A cloud of graphite dust floated in the air, and the room smelled of linseed oil. Liza was sitting in bed, her legs propping up a sketchpad. She watched Zacharias warily. He knew she would be too stubborn to speak first.

"May I see?" he asked.

Liza moved to the center of the bed and patted the edge of the mattress with her blackened hands. Zacharias eased in beside her, and she began to flip through the sheets of paper. They were all sketches of him working in the shop, sitting on the porch, fishing at the river, sleeping. All were from a distance but revealed that she had never been far away.

"Losing our babies broke me to pieces, same as you," Zacharias said.

Liza placed her fingers on his lips, smudging his chin.

Zacharias rubbed his hands back and forth along his thighs. "Thing is," he confessed, "I'll never be able to put myself back together without you."

With her other hand, Liza untied her nightdress. He could see her naked breasts beneath, listing gently to each side. When he leaned forward to kiss her, Liza's breath quickened. She took his hand and guided it toward her bare skin.

* * *

A renewed lightness soon permeated the pastures of Peacock Bend. The chatter of life returned, and Liza stopped sleeping in her studio. During a New Year's snowstorm, she launched her most ambitious project to date—a large mural that would soon grace the parlor wall opposite the stone fireplace. The preliminary outline, which Liza had spent over a week drawing, revealed a massive peacock, its full plumage on bold display. Zacharias watched her as she knelt and put the finishing touches on the bird's massive claws.

"I think it fitting, don't you, Zachek?" she said when she noticed him. "And this cock won't make any noise," she laughed.

It had been a long time since he'd heard that laugh. "Need any help?"

"Sure," Liza said, stepping back, surveying the final sketch. "I think I'll start at the top, so I'm gonna need the ladder. Can you run to fetch it from the shed?"

Zacharias looked at Liza but did not answer.

She waved her hand in front of his face. "Hello?"

He grinned.

"Yes? What's on your mind, Mr. Anderwald?"

Zacharias swept her hair out of her face and pinched her pink cheeks. "Back in a jiffy, Mrs. Anderwald."

The ladder secured, Liza began painting the intricate crown that crested the bird's head. She brought her face within inches of the wall and leaned back to take in her progress for each series of brush strokes, gripping the top step to keep her balance. Zacharias stood nearby, handing Liza pots of paint upon request. On one exchange, he noticed Liza had started to sway and braced herself against the wall.

"You alright up there?" he asked, offering a hand to help her down.

"A little dizzy," she said. "Probably time for a break." Liza eased onto the window bench. "And my stomach is sure in a lurch. Must have eaten something that turned."

"You stay put," Zacharias ordered, gathering the dirty paintbrushes and heading to the kitchen. "I'll get these washed and get you some tea."

Zacharias stared out the window as the water splashed over the brushes. Looking up toward the hilltop, he noticed something moving among the tombstones. He bent forward, his nose pressed against the windowpane.

"Mamusiu?" he whispered. His warm breath clouded the glass.

Zacharias dropped the paintbrushes and rushed out into the brittle winter day, the tap still running. A light wind stirred through the bare branches of the trees, and he could hear humming as he approached the graveyard. It was the beautiful melody of a familiar lullaby. Zacharias squinted at the figure. It was a woman floating above the ground and running her hand along the tops of the wooden crosses. Her face was blurred, its features indistinguishable, and she wore a diaphanous cream-colored gown.

The humming faded, and the figure extended her arms toward Zacharias. "Dziecko," she said. Zacharias was more curious than afraid and continued to stare. "Dziecko," she repeated. Zacharias understood her meaning. How many times had the old grannies of St. Stanislaus patted Liza's abdomen during her pregnancies and asked, "When is dziecko coming?"

Zacharias edged closer, but the woman's form began to fade. "Don't leave me," he said, but the figure dissolved into the frigid air.

*   *   *

Zacharias was ripped from his first full night of sleep in weeks by a deafening and desperate chorus of honks and shrieks blaring from the rooftop. The peacocks were at it again. Almost immediately in response, the peahens commenced a flurry of scratching along the side of the house.

Liza rolled onto her back next to him, her full belly pulling the blankets and exposing the entire left side of his body to the brisk morning air. She licked her lips and released a quiet grunt. Zacharias got out of bed, doing his best not to wake her.

"What is it, ladies? Whatcha got there?" he greeted the birds in the yard. The frantic scratching continued, followed by a menacing rattle. The birds had stumbled upon a rattlesnake in the brush. "Whoa, I see what's going on."

Zacharias dashed to the garden shed to grab a metal hoe and an ax and hurried back to the side of the house. The peahens continued to caw and peck in the dirt.

"Move aside, girls, so I can get in there," he said and inserted the hoe into the center of a large blackbrush, its treacherous thorns drawing blood along his forearm. "Lord Almighty!" he cried out in pain.

The rattling intensified, and Zacharias returned to the task at hand, slowly teasing the serpent from its lair and out into the open. The snake coiled around the blade and prepared to strike. Zacharias did not hesitate. He raised the ax in his other hand and brought it down behind the snake's head with one forceful blow. The head and body ceased movement immediately, but it would be another few seconds before the tail stopped shaking.

Shadows flickered beneath the bush's twisted branches,

followed by a flurry of black and white baby rattlers slithering from the nest within. Out of nowhere, two large peacocks lumbered through the air to join at least four peahens and several little chicks in a noisy swarm on the ground. Zacharias gave way, and the bevy began to gulp down the newborn serpents head-first. He watched the feeding frenzy for some time, overcome by a sense of relief and sadness at the death of the rattler. The serpent, off to feed in the first light of day as nature would have it, had likely just given birth to her young since they were still with her. She fought a good fight, but those poor babies never stood a chance.

"Zachek?"

Zacharias jumped. "Liza, what's the matter?"

"Nothing," she said. "Tired is all. The birds woke me." She stepped back as she took in the carnage.

"That was one of the biggest rattlers I've seen in years, for sure, and those birds are the best snakers I know," Zacharias said.

Liza noticed the streaks of blood on his arm. She gently touched his broken skin. "You hurt?"

"No, I'm fine. A few scratches is all."

Liza's mind seemed elsewhere.

"You sure nothing's wrong? You're kinda quiet," Zacharias said.

"I said I'm tired," Liza shot back.

"Hey, Doc Adolf says it's going perfectly this time. The baby is growing. You can see it. And you can feel it. I can feel it." Zacharias reached out and touched Liza's stomach.

"Stop. I don't want to talk about it," Liza said, pulling away.

Zacharias set the tools down and hopped over the birds, still enjoying their victory feast. "Come on inside. I'll get you some breakfast. Food usually gets the little one going for the day."

Zacharias knew he had to keep Liza distracted in these moments of panic. Other than the inspections of her urine for blood, waiting for the baby to move was the most excruciating time of the morning. The doctor assured her the baby was sleeping, but this did little to calm Liza's mind, or Zacharias', for that matter.

Liza gripped the kitchen door frame as she entered. "Whoa," she groaned.

"Somebody awake now?" Zacharias asked.

"That was the swiftest kick yet, sweet one. You must be hungry, too," Liza cooed, cradling her stomach.

Zacharias sent Marcin to fetch Zee when Liza's waters broke at midday. Khalil set off to alert John Stanard, who returned with the wrangler to Peacock Bend to await the baby's arrival. Zee took charge at Liza's bedside, making clear that the men should make themselves scarce.

Zacharias paced back and forth across the front yard for the entire afternoon and evening, his father and father-in-law sitting close by on the porch, trying to offer distractions from the groans and cries coming from the house. Khalil checked in every few hours, bringing food Mrs. Kirby prepared and wood for the kitchen stove, where Zee's iron pots popped and bubbled with boiling water and bitter potions. He would promptly return to the Kirbys' house by the river to report back to the sergeant, who was laid up again with a twisted back.

At daybreak, the daily volley of calls from the roosters on top of the barn and the peacocks on the roof of the house began, and soon after that, the first rays of morning sun reflected off the waters of the Medina River. Zacharias stood and stretched. His father and John Stanard both dozed in their chairs. Zacharias leaned against the porch railing and yawned. It was then he noticed the silence, and his breath seized in his chest. A loud smack and a startled cry rang out a moment later.

"Tato! Mr. Stanard! The baby," he said.

The two men startled awake and gathered with Zacharias to watch the latch on the front door for any movement. After a few minutes, Zee beckoned from inside, "Chief, come!"

Zacharias ran his fingers through his hair before opening the door. He tentatively entered the house and stopped in the middle of the still-darkened parlor. The door to the bedroom opened, and Zee poked her head out.

"Chief, come," she said, waving with her free hand. Zacharias hesitated when he saw the wad of bloody towels tucked under her arm. "No worry, Chief. Baby here. Liza good," Zee said, opening the bedroom door wider. "Come," she urged again.

He stopped at the end of the bed. Liza, her hair drenched in sweat, was maneuvering a delicate skull covered in dark wisps of hair toward her bare breast. "Hey there," he said.

"Come see, Zachek," Liza said weakly.

Zacharias approached the bedside and reached out to touch the baby's head.

"He's perfect, Zachek. And he looks like you."

"A boy?" Zacharias blinked the tears from his eyes.

"I know we talked about calling him John after my father, but I'd like to call him John Marcin if you agree," Liza said.

"Of course. Whatever you wish. It will sure make those two out on the porch happy," Zacharias chuckled and sat on the edge of the bed. He reached out to caress the back of the creased hand kneading the flesh of Liza's breast. "Welcome, my beautiful boy. Welcome, John Marcin Anderwald," he choked. "And bless you, my beautiful wife."

CHAPTER 15

Son of My Brother

And so, it was. He was. The child Zacharias and Liza had longed for all those many years arrived with a mighty trumpet of a cry on a sweltering August morning of 1896. Six weeks later, the extended Anderwald family and a small delegation of Stanards gathered at St. Stanislaus to celebrate and, of course, to do everything in their collective power to secure the boy's salvation. Zacharias agreed with Liza that they should err on the side of caution and wait to baptize John Marcin until they were sure he was strong enough to make the trip into town. Zacharias would never confess to Liza or anyone other than God that he had tucked a shovel and timber for a coffin under the front porch the day before his son was born and did not retrieve them until well past the child's first birthday.

Among the celebrants stood Marcin, who was still tall and handsome even with his silver curls and hunched back, Beata and Anatol and their twin boys, Victoria, and Mary Rose and her eldest son. Mary Rose's husband, Randall, had remained behind at home with their girls. His gout had flared again after the many indulgences on summer holiday in Rockport. Sergeant and Mrs. Kirby were also in attendance, although the sergeant could no longer stand for long periods, and Mrs. Kirby tended to wander, so they sat together in the front pew next to Liza's father. And despite a mild protest from

Father Adamietz, Khalil and Zee joined for the private service after all.

Father Adamietz donned his threadbare vestments stained with years of sacramental wine and hobbled to the nave's west side where the small stone baptismal font stood. "Please join me," the priest invited the group forward. John Stanard rose and stood beside Marcin, and Khalil and Zee made their way from the rear. The circle around the font parted to allow the Kirbys to watch from their seats.

"Zacharias, you and Liza, stand here next to me," Father Adamietz pointed with his crooked forefinger. "Ahem," he continued, calling everyone to attention with unnecessary exaggeration, and opened his prayer book. "What name have you given this child?"

"John Marcin Anderwald," Zacharias announced.

Marcin bowed his head and John Stanard beamed.

"And what do you ask of God's Church for John Marcin?" the priest asked.

"The grace of Christ, Father," Liza replied.

Father Adamietz dipped his finger into a small pot of oil and leaned over the infant squirming in Liza's arms. "And so, I claim you for Christ, our Savior, by the sign of his cross," he said and traced a cross on the baby's forehead. The child began to howl.

"Shh, John Marcin. Shh, my sweet boy. Mama is here," Liza soothed.

Zacharias moved closer and stroked his son's cheek. The baby immediately quieted upon his father's touch.

The priest moved to his closing. "Baptism is God's most beautiful and magnificent gift of grace. It is a gift because it is conferred on those with nothing to give in return. And it is grace because even those guilty of sin may receive it. Peace be with you all. Amen."

Zacharias took John Marcin in his arms and started toward the exit where Khalil stood, holding the door open. As Zacharias crossed the threshold, the old wrangler gripped his arm. "Ahmad would be proud, Chief," he said.

Zacharias swallowed hard. The memories were still painful. "Ya akhi," he whispered.

Khalil caressed the infant's head with a cracked and callused hand. The child gazed intently at the wrangler. "Son of Chief,"

Khalil said, his voice like a song. "You are son of Ahmad's brother, son of my brother. You are one of us." A soft smile crossed the wrangler's thick lips. "Allah ma'k, God be with you."

CHAPTER 16

Farewell, Dear Sergeant

The menagerie of lost souls who came together at Peacock Bend formed what no one could dispute was a kinship in its truest essence, and for several years following the birth of John Marcin Anderwald, they were blessed with a modicum of calm in their lives. Respite would be elusive, however. The vagaries of life on the frontier, and specifically the impetuous weather in the Texas Hill Country, conspired to disrupt whatever measure of grace and peace the Anderwalds had fought so desperately to secure.

In early August 1900, angry storm clouds appeared on the horizon. Torrential downpours pummeled the arid lands to the west and swelled the waters of the Medina River. The rains arrived in Bandera at midday, and the river's tempestuous current quickly overflowed its banks, with waves rumbling nearly three feet in height. Soon after, the streets were engulfed and formed temporary tributaries with bits and pieces of lives bobbing on their surface. Most of the farms along the lowlands were ravaged, and even the old mill was swept away. The Bandera Courthouse and St. Stanislaus occupied the highest ground and were spared, but many of the newer buildings along Main Street succumbed to flooding, including the home of the town's fledgling newspaper, the *Bandera Bugle*, which would have to be rebuilt entirely. As for the flood's human toll, it was certainly of consequence for Bandera as a whole, but for the inhabitants of Peacock Bend, a profound and most personal loss was incurred.

Khalil burst into the barn, drenched. "Chief, come! Kirby," he gasped. "Trapped."

Zacharias had sent Khalil to fetch the sergeant to help rescue several cows stranded in the lower pasture. He was assembling rope to help pull them out of the mud. "Trapped? What do you mean?"

"Water too fast and too high. I cannot get to the cabin. And too deep for the horses," Khalil panted.

Zacharias had only seen this look on his friend's taciturn face once before, and that was the day Ahmad was taken. A flutter of panic tightened Zacharias' throat. "Take this," he ordered, tossing a large coil of rope to Khalil. "Let's see if we can get over there on foot."

The men rushed toward the river. They tied the rope around each of their waists to ensure that if one was swept away, the other had a chance to reel them back in. The water rushed over their boots and within twenty yards was up to their thighs, and they were still a good hundred yards from the Kirbys' cabin. The storm clouds had erased the sun from the sky, and the driving rain limited their range of vision. They could barely see their hands in front of their faces. It took them over an hour to reach the turnoff to the cabin, and by then, the water was nearly at their hips. They were forced to swim from tree to tree, grabbing at limbs and pulling each other along by the rope.

"Khalil, stop," Zacharias ordered. "We gotta rest, or the river will take us," he cried.

The two men gripped an old scrub oak for dear life. A rip of lightning tore through the clouds and illuminated what lay ahead. In the pasture below, the Medina had consumed nearly the entirety of the Kirbys' cabin. Only the dark peak of its roof could be seen above the water. "Curtis, no!" Zacharias wailed into the whipping wind and started across the raging current.

The burn of rope seared the skin of Zacharias' torso. He looked back to see Khalil struggling to maintain his grip on the tether binding them. "No, Chief," Khalil insisted. "They are gone."

Sergeant Kirby would have known that the water would come

fast, and the window for escape would be narrow. He would also have done everything in his much-diminished physical power to save the second but no less dear Mrs. Kirby. It would never be precisely clear what transpired that tragic afternoon, but the Kirbys and their home were overcome.

Two days later, when the storm finally passed, and the waters receded, Zacharias and Khalil set off in search of their friends. They soon came upon the sergeant and his wife at a sharp bend in the river. The couple was tangled among several large tree roots below its surface, arm in arm as if in an embrace. The two men wept silently on the riverbank.

The loss of Sergeant and Mrs. Kirby weighed heavily on Zacharias, poking at old wounds and tearing open new ones. Cold silence greeted the priest's prayers among those gathered in the Anderwald family cemetery, their heads bowed low. There simply were no words. Zacharias held fast to his father, whose shoulders shook as he quietly sobbed. His young son John Marcin stood stalwart between Liza and Zee, each holding one of his hands. John Stanard leaned on a cane, a gift from the sergeant several years before, its handle carved into the shape of a longhorn's head. Khalil remained at some distance, his thick fingers tightly gripping the spade he'd used to dig the graves.

Another unwelcome guest was also present that morning, Zacharias was sure. At first, the menacing figure slipped in and out of the surrounding brush, inspecting the scene from afar, but as the Amens faded, Zacharias also sensed someone or something approaching from behind. He turned quickly to try and catch a glimpse of the visitor, but they remained elusive. Zacharias shuddered and pulled his father closer. He watched the first shovel of dirt cascade into the open grave and was quickly overwhelmed by a powerful whiff of putrid air billowing from the dark hole in the ground. It was then he heard a distant growl echoing up from the river.

"I am here, and you are still cursed above all," it hissed.

The shadow was lurking once again.

CHAPTER 17

The Summons

Zacharias stood with John Marcin on the lawn of the Bande-ra Courthouse and looked up at the balustrade above the entrance. A canvas banner tied to the top rail fluttered in the breeze, and its blue-painted lettering read "10th Anniversary, 1891-1901." The impressive building stood on the corner of Main and Pecan Streets, and its dome could be seen for miles, soaring even taller than the steeple of St. Stanislaus Catholic Church. The town council decided to host a celebration of the famed courthouse to boost the community's spirits after the devastating flood the previous year, and no one was in greater need of boosted spirits than the residents of Peacock Bend. The empty silence left in the wake of Curtis Kirby's death was deafening. Zacharias kept expecting to see the sergeant at every turn on the ranch and along the streets of Bandera, but his dear friend never appeared.

Peals of raucous laughter rang out at the building's entrance, where a group of young boys was playing tag on the marble stairs.

"There's Frankie and Tater," John Marcin said. "Can I go play?"

"Yes, but you boys stay out of trouble," Zacharias instructed.

"Frankie! Tater!" John Marcin waved and set off at a run.

"Look at them fancy britches," the boy Frankie cackled, pointing at John Marcin's new striped trousers.

"And a neckerchief, too," his brother Tater said, joining the fun. "Aren't you the dandy!"

Zacharias chuckled as John Marcin admonished the boys, "Oh, shut up, you big lumps."

The Kalkas were like the brothers John Marcin never had. Franz Kalka, who everyone called Frankie, was a year older than Tater and John Marcin. He was tall for his age and athletic, with thick blond hair and rosy cheeks. Tomas Kalka, who most called Tater, was shorter and chubbier than his brother, with a weak chin and mousy brown hair, but smarts beyond compare. That boy was rarely seen without his nose in a book. His unfortunate nickname had stuck from the first day of elementary school. John Marcin had nearly wet his pants when he relayed the story to Zacharias over supper.

"Papa, listen to this," John Marcin giggled. "Delia Stevens, one of Sheriff Stevens' girls, told Tomas he looked like a potato. Everyone's been callin' him Tater since!"

"You shut up, John Marcin," Zacharias heard Tater shouting from the courthouse steps.

Frankie stepped into the fray, putting his younger brother in a headlock while John Marcin tickled him under the armpits.

Zacharias noticed a group of older women scowling at the boys. "A bunch of delinquents," one said to no one in particular.

Frankie stuck his tongue out in reply.

"I never," another biddy snarled. "Where are their parents?" she said, craning her neck to see over the crowd.

"John Marcin Anderwald, I said no nonsense," Zacharias scolded. "Get on back over here."

"Shucks, gotta go. I'll catch up with ya later," John Marcin said, kicking up a cloud of dust.

Zacharias led the boy toward the refreshment tables, which were filled with an assortment of baked goods and bowls of fruit punch. They joined Liza, Marcin, and John Stanard, who were chatting with other locals dressed in their Sunday best.

John Stanard raised his glass. "This sure is a good thing us all comin' together," he said.

Marcin nodded from where he was seated. "It is time to put this unfortunate year behind us."

"Agreed," Zacharias said, stuffing a piece of lemon cake into his mouth. When he turned to grab seconds, he spotted Judge Malcolm Duffy, one of South Texas' most esteemed jurists and a frequent drinking companion of his father-in-law's, winding his way through the crowd at a purposeful pace with another unknown man at his side.

"Gentlemen, might we have a word," the judge said, gesturing toward a quiet spot under a nearby tree.

"Sure thing, Duff," Stanard agreed and led the way.

Zacharias helped his father stand and followed.

"Thank you for breaking away from the celebration," Judge Duffy began. "Kindly allow me to introduce my colleague, Jeremiah Ramsey, Esquire. Mr. Ramsey is the prosecuting attorney riding the circuit with me. He'd like to have a word."

The stranger was a slim man with long white fingers and a perfectly coiffed mustache curled at its ends. He wore a gray pinstripe suit with a thick gold chain clipped to his vest. The other end of the chain was tucked into a side pocket, and the shape of a large round watch bulged through the fabric.

"It is a pleasure to make your acquaintance, gentlemen." The man spoke with no discernible accent that might reveal his origins.

"I'll leave you to it, Jeremiah," Judge Duffy said. "I don't want to risk any prejudice on my part regarding the matter at hand."

The prosecutor waited for the judge to step away. "I'm not sure if word has arrived up this way yet, but there's to be a murder trial in Helena next Thursday. The Rangers brought in a band of thugs believed to be the outlaws who've been terrorizing folks along the southern forks of the Chisholm Trail for some years."

"What's all this got to do with us, Mr. Ramsey?" Zacharias asked.

"If I may, Mr. Anderwald, the gang's alleged leader, is someone I think you all might have a keen interest in. Does the name Josiah Thomas Gaines ring any bells?"

Zacharias felt faint at the mention of the name. His father and John Stanard also appeared stunned, the color draining from their faces.

"Where did you find this Gaines?" Marcin finally said.

"Some weeks back, the sheriff in Helena received complaints of drunken crowds gathering at the edge of town. Things were getting rough, so he commandeered the Rangers to ride with him to investigate. Sure enough, they stumbled upon a group of some twenty or so spectators at what they call a Helena Duel."

"What in the heck is that Ramsey?" Stanard interrupted.

"A form of frontier justice in those parts, Mr. Stanard, common among the underbelly of society. Disputing parties are stripped to their waists and wrists bound together. The men then set to wrestling and stabbing each other until someone bleeds to death."

"Never heard of such nonsense," Stanard huffed.

After taking a long sip of punch, the prosecutor continued. "Usually, a fair bit of gambling is involved, and the Mr. Gaines in question was caught with three other accomplices collecting the bets. This Gaines asserts he was in the wrong place at the wrong time. Holding the bag of money for another man, he said, but several folks have sworn on a stack of Bibles that those boys are the infamous Gaines Gang."

Marcin looked unsteady on his feet. "Tato, do you need to sit?" Zacharias asked.

"No. Stop fussing," Marcin said, batting him away.

"And so, gentlemen," the prosecutor added, "we are presented with the rare opportunity to bring these men to account, in essence, for the totality of their crimes."

"Why waste time on all of that nonsense?" Stanard asked. "There may be somethin' to this frontier justice idea. Let the sonofabitches stab each other to death."

"Hold on there, John," Zacharias raised his hand. "Mr. Ramsey, how can you be sure it's him?"

"This is the matter I've come to discuss, sir," the prosecutor replied. "The wife of the man in custody and several character witnesses have come forward. They say we have a case of mistaken identity, and the man we're holding at the jail is Jacob Gaines, a simple farmer from Goliad, not the leader of a thieving and murderous gang of outlaws. They have hired a defense lawyer to come from San Antonio for the trial."

"Seems like you might not be certain you have the right man," Zacharias said.

"There is no disputing that the other men are who we think they are. Credible witnesses have come forward to testify. However, in Mr. Gaines' case, though he may have overseen his gang's activities over the years, he was not often present during the commission of crimes. We believe this is why finding him has taken so long. For now, we only have the word of his fellow defendants, and their motives are suspect, of course. We have an equal number of witnesses who swear we have the wrong man. I must confess, given that this will be a matter of life and death, I am somewhat uneasy."

Zacharias looked at Stanard, eyebrows raised.

"What in God's name are you saying, Ramsey?" Stanard bellowed. "If there's enough of a chance it is the right Gaines, the man should hang!"

"In all candor, Mr. Stanard, I'd feel much better about bringing my case if I were sure we have the right man. The three of you are the only individuals known to have witnessed Mr. Gaines committing an actual crime who have survived their encounter," Ramsey replied.

"But it's been over twenty-five years since we've seen this man. He must be seventy by now," Stanard said.

"John," Marcin spoke up. "I will never forget that day or that face. And I know you have not forgotten. Mr. Ramsey, we will come and help you."

"No, Tato, it's too far," Zacharias intervened. "I can go with John."

"Zachek, you were only a boy. How can you remember? And if this is the man who killed our friend, I want to see justice with my own eyes."

Zacharias' voice trembled. "Tato, I, too, will never forget that bastard's face. We'll all go together. And we must take Khalil. He also saw what Gaines did to Ahmad."

"Ah, yes, the brother." The prosecutor pursed his lips and twisted the end of his mustache. "I do hope you understand that although my invitation includes lodging at a small boarding house in Helena for you and your family, the Negro would have to make other arrangements."

"Khalil is family, and he's not a Negro," Marcin protested.

"I'm not sure that matters, you see." Ramsey's calm composure faltered, and he fidgeted with his pocket watch.

"We take your point," Stanard interjected. "We'll figure all that out, but Khalil has a right to confront this man. I assume you agree, sir."

"I suppose so," Ramsey replied.

Zacharias closely observed the prosecutor but remained quiet. To him belongeth vengeance. But when? He was tired of waiting. No one hoped more than Zacharias that Josiah Gaines might finally answer for Ahmad. Perhaps his father-in-law was right, and the specifics of which crime Gaines would hang for were irrelevant. This pure evil, manifest in the loathsome Gaines, must be destroyed. There was no other choice.

CHAPTER 18

Crime and Punishment

The road veered south out of San Antonio across flat, dry terrain. Zacharias urged the team of horses along, John Stanard at his side and Marcin and John Marcin wedged onto the back bench. Khalil brought up the rear on his own horse. A massive red-tailed hawk swooped low overhead, its wingspan almost the width of the carriage. As the bird descended in pursuit of its next meal a few hundred feet ahead, its sharp claws protracted with timed precision. The hawk dove into the brush, and all was still for a single beat before the bird began to flap its wings violently. A threatening screech rang out, followed by an angry rattle.

The mighty tussle was still underway when the traveling party approached, and no one spoke as they watched the life-and-death struggle ensue. The hawk had plunged its talons into a giant rattlesnake, the serpent refusing to submit without a fight. It thrashed wildly and struck desperately, but the bird's grip was too firm. The hawk continued to try and take off without success, only managing to bounce with the snake into the open dirt road, dust clouds exploding with each impact. After a few more failed attempts to take flight, the bird resolved to peck the remaining life force out of the rattler without further fuss and dragged its kill back to the roadside.

"I hate snakes," Marcin muttered.

"Show's over," Stanard announced. "We should keep moving, Zacharias."

Khalil kicked his horse hard and darted out ahead. He had yet to say a word the entire trip, but as he passed the dead snake, he raised his fist and cried out, "Allahu Akbar!"

Zacharias noticed Marcin had slumped forward in his seat. He reached back and touched his father's arm. "Tato, what's the matter?"

Marcin looked away from the macabre scene. "This is a sign," he said.

"What sign, Grandpa Marcin?" John Marcin asked.

The boy. Zacharias wondered if it had been a mistake to bring him along. How many nights of terror had been visited upon him after witnessing the horrors of Ahmad's murder? And his prayers of vengeance had been an open invitation to the shadow man. Zacharias feared Liza had been right.

"Zacharias Anderwald, that boy's got no business going to a hanging at his age. It might scare him to his own death," she had pleaded that morning before they left for Helena.

Zacharias felt the same impulses of anger and resentment from those early years of his marriage lick at the edges of his memory. He would stand his ground. "Liza, John Marcin has to learn about right and wrong and consequences."

"Ah, I see. You've already made up your mind. Don't insult me by pretending you have some principled reason for exposing our child to such a gruesome display. You know damned well it's revenge you're after." Liza stomped off to her studio.

Revenge. Zacharias could hear Liza in his head. "Leave your grandfather be, John Marcin," he snapped. Zacharias loosened the reins, and the horses set off once again.

The group arrived in Helena at dusk. The main street ended at a square, where the courthouse, a modest two-story white brick building, stood at the center. A broad wooden staircase led to a second-floor main entrance centered along a balcony that stretched across the entire front elevation. A smaller door underneath the stairs was padlocked and flanked by two barred windows. Two men sat in wooden chairs on either side of the locked door, smoking, their rifles propped against the building's exterior. Upon closer inspection, Zacharias noted that all the windows around the first floor were barred. Mr. Ramsey was perched on the courthouse steps, awaiting their arrival.

Ramsey stood and dusted off the seat of his trousers. "Good evening, gentlemen. I appreciate your making the long trip."

"I see preparations are almost complete for tomorrow," Stanard said, looking toward the activity on the square.

Across the street stood a raised wooden platform, one set of steep steps rising on the side closest to the courthouse. There were no steps on the opposite end. Two thick wooden posts roughly fifteen feet tall towered over each end, and a long crossbeam ran the distance between them. One man was on a ladder securing nooses to the beam. The other two tested a lever that opened a wide trap door at the center of the platform. The click and slide of the door mechanism skipped off the courthouse's masoned walls and down the road.

"Yes, tomorrow's events should draw quite the crowd," Ramsey said. "We've got folks camped all the way to Goliad. With the potential for multiple hangings in one week, word gets around. And it's already been a busy stop with three yesterday alone. A couple of horse thieves and a cattle poacher."

"So, there's no question about the verdicts," Zacharias said, his comment more a statement than a question.

Ramsey adjusted his watch chain before responding. "Mr. Anderwald, there is no debate about the identity of three of the men, so there is an expectation, you see." Ramsey changed the subject. "What do you say we head to the boarding house for something to eat? You all must be hungry. Our hostess, Mrs. Grange, has prepared some dinner."

The group started across the street, but the prosecutor stopped when he noticed Khalil. "Yes, your ranch hand. I almost forgot." He signaled to one of the men sitting under the courthouse balcony. "Cody, show that man to the shed out back. He can sleep in the extra cell."

"You got it," the guard said, motioning for Khalil to follow.

"No need to lock the door, of course," Ramsey quipped but reverted to a more professional tone when he realized his joke had landed flat. "And see to it he gets something to eat."

"Will do," the deputy replied.

Zacharias watched until Khalil disappeared behind the court-house before rejoining the rest outside a small clapboard house on the far corner of the square. Mrs. Lucinda Grange, proprietress of the Grange Boarding House of Helena, greeted them at the front door. "Come on in. Your supper is gettin' cold," she said.

After their meal was inhaled and the dishes were cleared, Mrs. Grange poured drinks, and the men discussed the plan for the following morning. "How's all this gonna work?" Stanard began.

"Again, I am grateful for your help," the prosecutor replied. "The sheriff has impaneled a jury who will hear these men's cases tomorrow morning at ten o'clock. It is my hope that once you have had a chance to see the prisoner in question, you will be able to offer confirmation of his identity. I'm of the mind to focus on direct testimony from each of you. Judge Duffy does not tolerate any nonsense in his courtroom, and he and I are due at our next venue by Monday, so he'll want us to keep things moving. Of course, the defense lawyer will have a chance to call his witnesses and say his piece," Ramsey added.

"What happens after that, Mr. Ramsey?" John Marcin asked from the far corner of the room.

"Young man, if this Mr. Gaines and his accomplices are found guilty, they will be hung until they are dead. That's the law of this here land," the prosecutor explained.

"So, whether or not this Gaines lives or dies depends on what my father and grandfathers say tomorrow?"

"They are an important part of the evidence we will give the jury. But this will be a fair trial, I assure you, or as fair as I can make it."

Stanard grabbed the drink before him and tossed it back, slamming the empty glass on the table without a word.

Marcin took a short sip of his drink before speaking. "If this is the man who killed Ahmad, he must be punished." His hand began to shake, liquid sloshing over the side of his glass.

Zacharias jumped up from the table. "Come, Tato," he ordered, lifting Marcin from his chair. "Mr. Ramsey, we'll see you in the morning."

* * *

The party from Bandera arrived at the courthouse to find the gallery packed with spectators. At the front of the courtroom, a massive wooden desk with a ladder-back chair faced the room. To the left, a second chair stood, and two benches, one behind the other, were lined up under the window for the jury. On the desk's right, another heavy bench was bolted to the floor, with a line of iron rings fixed to the floorboards in front. Mr. Ramsey and another man in a dark suit were seated at either end of a narrow table facing the judge's desk, their backs to the crowd. Each was sifting through a thick stack of documents.

Zacharias led John Marcin by the hand and followed Stanard and Marcin into the second to last row of seats for observers. Mr. Ramsey turned to survey the room and looked relieved to see his witnesses. He hurried toward them. "Good morning," he greeted, pulling his pocket watch from his vest. "We should be getting started shortly. Make yourselves comfortable."

"Where's Khalil, Mr. Ramsey?" Zacharias looked around the room.

"He's given his statement already," the prosecutor said. "The boys brought him through the jailhouse last night, and when he reached Mr. Gaines' cell, there was a scuffle. Judging by your wrangler's violent reaction, there is no doubt he believes the prisoner is the man who killed his brother. I thought it best not to create any more commotion," Ramsey confided.

The door latch scraped at the side entrance, and a hush fell over the crowd. Judge Duffy entered the courtroom. He had a Bible bound in leather and a folder stuffed with papers tucked under his arm. After straightening the folds of his robes, the judge sat behind the desk and pounded his gavel against a small wood block on the desktop. "Ladies and gentlemen, I'll ask you to take your seats," he announced. "I will also ask our distinguished jurors to take theirs at this time. Court is in session." The judge signaled to the guards. "Deputies, bring the defendants."

Chatter hummed around the room, and bodies pressed against

each other in great anticipation. Zacharias could only see the backs of most people's heads, but two individuals attracted his attention during the brief lull before the proceedings began. He first noticed a woman in a large brown bonnet that covered her entire face. She was seated in the front row, a small boy at her side. Zacharias could not see the details of the child's face through the crowd but could not miss the unruly tangle of luminescent red hair atop his head.

The clank of metal arose outside, and the spectators turned toward the main door. Two deputies entered, flanking a tall man in a tattered shirt and torn trousers, and escorted him down the center aisle. The prisoner's filthy hands and bare feet were bound by heavy iron shackles. He was unshaven, and his stubble was the same shade of snow-white as his copious eyebrows and thick, tangled mane. The man walked slowly and looked straight ahead. As he passed their row, Marcin grabbed Zacharias' arm. Zacharias leaned forward in his seat, straining to get a look at the man's face. When the accused reached the bench in front, the guards helped him sit and attached the chains from his leg irons and handcuffs to the rings on the floor with heavy padlocks.

The deputies retraced their steps and exited back out onto the balcony. They returned with three more men shackled together from hip to hip. They, too, were unkempt and unwashed. They were seated next to the other man, and the deputies chained them to the floor as well. None of the defendants looked at each other.

Judge Duffy straightened his wire reading glasses, pushing them further along the bridge of his nose, and reviewed the papers in his folder before addressing the lawyers. "Gentlemen, shall we begin?"

The cases of the accomplices, whose identities were never in doubt, as Mr. Ramsey would state in his opening remarks, were heard first. In their own defense and in the desperate hope of avoiding the noose, each claimed that Josiah Gaines had committed the crimes in question and that they had simply been bystanders, but the jury visibly scoffed and shook their heads. When the defendants' fates appeared determined, their subsequent offers to confirm that the infamous gang leader Josiah Gaines was, in verifiable fact, the man sitting with them in the courtroom and to bear witness to his

other notorious crimes committed over the years earned them neither favor nor mercy from the judge.

What consumed most of the remaining two-hour trial was
whether the right Gaines had been apprehended and, if so, to determine the man's guilt or innocence. As the court turned to his case,
Gaines remained silent and unmoving, save the faint rise and fall of
his chest.

"Mr. Gaines, do you understand you have been accused of several crimes, including horse and cattle thieving, assault, torture, and
murder?" Mr. Ramsey began his questioning of the fourth defendant. When Gaines did not reply, the prosecutor continued. "Given
the seriousness of these crimes, both individually and together, I
am compelled to remind you that if you are found guilty, the punishment for any of these crimes is death by hanging. Again, do you
understand the severity of your situation?" Gaines still did not react.
"Sir, I repeat. Do you comprehend the gravity of these charges?"
Ramsey demanded.

"Judge, if I may?" the defense attorney raised a hand from the
table, and for the first time, the prisoner's countenance shifted ever
so slightly.

"Yes, Mr. Connors," Judge Duffy replied, peering over his
glasses.

"I have advised my client that he is within his rights to remain
silent on these matters."

"So noted," Judge Duffy said, scribbling something in the file.
"Thank you, Your Honor. Further, I must object. My respected colleague is making some dangerous assumptions about facts. We have
not yet confirmed the identity of the man sitting here today. I fear
we may be getting ahead of ourselves," the defense attorney stated.

Mr. Ramsey was visibly shaken. "Judge Duffy, the defense has
not provided any proof that the veracity or accuracy of the prosecution's witnesses should be questioned."

"Mr. Connors, what have you to say to this?" the judge asked.
Connors rose from his chair. "May I approach, Your Honor?"
"You may."

The defense attorney walked toward the judge's bench with
several sheets of paper in his hand. "Your Honor, I have here three

sworn statements. One from Mrs. Susanna Gaines, the wife of Mr. Jacob Theodor Gaines, a second from Mr. Joseph Phelps, a neighbor of Mr. Jacob Gaines, and a third from Pastor Falk from the First Baptist Church of Goliad, where Mr. Gaines is in regular attendance. Each confirms that the man you have in custody is Jacob Theodor Gaines, not Josiah Thomas Gaines."

Judge Duffy took several minutes to review the statements before giving them to Ramsey. "Mr. Connors, are any of these witnesses present?"

"Yes, Your Honor. I have Mrs. Gaines here with me today." The defense attorney pointed to the woman in the large brown bonnet who was bent forward over her lap. "She is, however, too distraught to testify in public, having endured the shock of her husband's arrest and seeing the poor treatment he has received since. She is a fragile woman in the best of circumstances."

"And the others?"

"Mr. Phelps fell ill several weeks ago and, unfortunately, passed."

"And the preacher?" The judge's delivery became ever more clipped with each question.

"Your Honor, Pastor Falk is elderly and in fragile health. He was unable to make the trip from Goliad. But each witness has signed their statement," Connors said, pointing at the bottom of the papers.

The judge flipped through the written statements before responding. "Mr. Connors, as you surely know, I cannot accept statements that cannot be verified from witnesses who cannot be cross-examined. I understand how difficult this must be for Mrs. Gaines, but she must summon some semblance of strength to testify."

"Yes, Your Honor."

"Mrs. Gaines, please come forward," the judge ordered.

The woman in the bonnet, uneasy on her feet, approached the witness chair.

"Mr. Connors, I'll ask you to give Mrs. Gaines her statement." Judge Duffy lifted one of the sheets of paper in the air.

Connors passed the paper to the woman.

"Mrs. Gaines, please look at the statement your counsel has

provided. Is that your signature on the bottom?"

The woman bobbed her head.

"Ma'am, I need you to speak up," the judge insisted.

A weak and barely audible "Yes, Your Honor" came from beneath the bonnet.

"And did you write or dictate this statement to Mr. Connors?"

"She dictated it, Your Honor," Connors replied.

"I am asking the witness, counselor," Duffy scolded. "I'll ask again. Mrs. Gaines, did you write this statement yourself?"

The woman shook her head but did not speak.

"I'm sorry, Mrs. Gaines?"

"No, sir," she mumbled.

"Mrs. Gaines, I believe you understand what I am getting at. Did you dictate this to Mr. Connors? Are these your own words?" The judge was growing impatient.

The woman pitched forward, her head between her legs, and began to moan. "Judge, I think you have what you need," Connors said as he helped Mrs. Gaines back to her chair and returned to the counsels' table.

The red-haired boy remained still. The only time he moved was to place his hand back onto the woman's lap and lace his fingers through hers. Judge Duffy signaled to Ramsey that he should carry on.

"Your Honor, gentlemen of the jury, I am prepared to refute the statements provided by Mr. Connors, including that of Mrs. Gaines, which claim, dubiously, I might underscore, that this defendant is not the man we say he is. It has taken some time, but I have found what I believe to be the only remaining eyewitnesses to one of Mr. Gaines' heinous crimes."

Mr. Connors raised his head and looked at his client, who offered the briefest flinch in response. The prosecutor proceeded.

"Mind you, this has not been an easy task given what I understand is the defendant's unfailing, or should I say, Mr. Josiah Thomas Gaines' unfailing success over the years in silencing potential witnesses. I have invited these men here today to offer their testimony and to confirm once and for all and beyond a reasonable doubt that this man seated here before you is the Mr. Gaines in question." Ramsey looked at the prisoner. "Your Honor, I call Mr. John Stanard of Bandera County to the witness stand."

Stanard walked briskly to the front of the courtroom. After swearing an oath, to tell the truth and only the truth, he faced the prosecutor.

"Mr. Stanard, is this man known to you in any way?" Ramsey crossed the room and pointed at Gaines' chest.

Stanard paused before responding. "While it has been some time since I had the extreme displeasure of meeting this Mr. Gaines, I can say with relative certainty he is the man who abducted Mr. Marcin Anderwald's tenant and ranch hand, Ahmad, beat him and strung him up in a tree with the intent to murder him."

"Your Honor, might I ask this witness to clarify his answer?" Connors interjected.

Judge Duffy gestured in the affirmative.

"Mr. Stanard, did you say, 'relative certainty'?" Connors asked.

"Yes. Gaines would have been much younger then, but this man here certainly resembles the individual I gave chase to on horseback those many years ago."

"So, you encountered him during a skirmish, riding a horse at speed," Connors looked at the jury skeptically.

"Yes, that is true," Stanard replied.

"No further questions," Connors said, looking across the courtroom at Gaines and back at the judge.

The prosecutor appeared unfazed by the defense counsel's questions. "Thank you, Mr. Stanard. That will be all."

Before returning to his seat, Stanard approached the prisoner. The deputies rose to hold him back. "It's you, Gaines, you bastard. You tortured and killed that poor man in cold blood. Left him danglin' and suffocatin'. Same's comin' round for you in a couple hours. Same's comin'," he threatened.

The room erupted, but Gaines displayed no reaction.

"Mr. Stanard. I'll ask you to take your seat," Judge Duffy intervened. He then spoke to the audience. "Quiet, ladies and gentlemen, or I will clear this courtroom."

"My apologies, Your Honor," Stanard replied.

Ramsey proceeded, "The prosecution calls Mr. Marcin Anderwald, also a resident of Bandera County."

Marcin took his place in the witness chair and was sworn in.

"Mr. Anderwald," Ramsey again pointed at the defendant, "can you tell me if this man is known to you and if so, how?"

"Yes," Marcin said, looking directly at Gaines. "His name is Josiah Gaines."

"And how did the identity of this man become known to you, Mr. Anderwald?"

"From the war. I first met this man at Camp Verde when I was in the employ of the Confederate Army."

"Is this the man you also encountered on that terrible day along the Bandera Road?"

"He most certainly is," Marcin replied, pounding his fist on the judge's desk. "He murdered my good friend Ahmad."

The defense counsel raised his hand. "Your Honor, might I also ask this witness a few questions?"

"Fine, Mr. Connors."

Connors stood and approached the witness chair. "Mr. Anderwald, did you arrive at the scene together with Mr. Stanard?"

"No. John went first with Sergeant Kirby. I came second with Khalil, Ahmad's brother, to cut Ahmad down from the tree." Marcin began to weep. "Ahmad was still alive, and we tried to save him."

"But, Mr. Anderwald, help me understand something." The defense attorney faced the jury in advance of his next question. "Mr. Stanard has said that he had already given chase, and Mr. Gaines had fled on his horse. How can you be sure this is the same man?"

"I, I," Marcin stumbled.

"Ah, I see. So again, Mr. Anderwald, you never engaged with the defendant directly at the scene," Connors smirked. "No further questions for this witness."

The crowd began to stir. Zacharias went to his father. "Tato, come," he said and helped him back to his seat.

"Judge, I'd also like to ask the younger Mr. Anderwald a few questions," the prosecutor announced.

"Proceed, Mr. Ramsey," the judge instructed, and Zacharias returned to the witness chair.

Ramsey stood behind Gaines. "Mr. Anderwald, tell the court how you know this man seated before you today."

"Mr. Ramsey, I remember every terrible moment of the day Ahmad was murdered. I met the man on that bench on the road with four other men. They stopped our wagon on the way to school. Mr. Gaines was in charge and said he was representing the Bandera Vigilance Committee. He had bright red hair at the time, not white like it is today, and fewer creases and wrinkles, of course, but the eyes...." Zacharias paused to compose himself but continued staring at the man across the room. "Those blank, pale-blue eyes, betraying no emotion, are exactly the same as those of the man I met that horrible morning and watched torture and kill Ahmad."

"Thank you, Mr. Anderwald. That will be all," the prosecutor finished his questioning.

"Wait!" Zacharias insisted. He could not leave what weighed on his mind unsaid. Gaines was not worthy of mercy, but this could not be about vengeance alone. No. It had to be about justice. Zacharias had to make them all understand.

"Go on, sir," Ramsey said.

Zacharias turned to the jury, his hands gripping the arms of the witness chair. "Judge, members of the jury, I want to say something else. That man made a choice." Zacharias was now pointing at Gaines. "He could have changed his mind when he saw Mr. Stanard and his men approaching. Coulda dropped that noose and had an even greater head start on his escape, but he didn't. Gaines rushed to finish the job, ensuring the knot around the tree was tight before mounting his horse. I remember clear as day."

"Your Honor, I object," Connors said. "The witness was a boy at the time. He could not possibly recall such details."

"Overruled, Mr. Connors. Given the younger Mr. Anderwald is a confirmed eyewitness, I am inclined to offer some latitude here."

"Thank you, Judge," Ramsey said with a slight bow. "Mr. Anderwald, is there anything else you can tell us?"

"Yes, there is." Zacharias sat forward in the chair. "The man who murdered Ahmad in cold blood for no reason at all had a peculiar pattern to his speech—a kind of soft swooshing, if you will. I have often heard this sound in the nightmares that have plagued me since. I would like to ask you to have the prisoner say his name out loud, Josiah T. Gaines."

Connors jumped out of his seat. "Your Honor, I must object once again. This is a farce. There is no way this man can remember a voice from his childhood. And it means nothing anyway."

The judge scowled at the defense attorney. "Mr. Connors, you are overruled. The defendant will do as the witness asks."

When Gaines did not respond, the deputies approached from behind and forced the prisoner to his feet. Gaines resisted, his face flushing with anger. "You're a fucking liar," he said under his breath.

"Excuse me, is there something you'd like to say, Mr. Gaines?" the judge prompted.

The defense attorney approached his client. "No, Your Honor. My client has nothing—" he started, but Gaines interrupted.

"Shut your mouth, Connors, you pathetic piece of shit," Gaines seethed, the words "Connors" and "piece" sounding more like "Connersh" and "peesh."

Zacharias began to tremble. "Judge Duffy, now that I have heard this man speak out loud, I have no doubt. He is Josiah T. Gaines. May his soul rot in hell."

Suddenly, the prisoner exploded. "MY NAME IS NOT JOSI-AH. I AM JACOB. JACOB THEODORE GAINES!" he roared.

Connors took his seat. He extracted a small handkerchief from his breast pocket and wiped his upper lip.

"Your Honor, I rest my case," Ramsey said, returning to his seat.

A buzz surged through the crowd, and Judge Duffy pounded his gavel. "Quiet in the courtroom! Quiet, I say!" He turned to the jurors. "I'll ask you, gentlemen, to take some time to discuss and render your verdict. Mr. Anderwald, your testimony is concluded."

Zacharias returned to his seat. He watched the jurors deliberate among themselves for less than five minutes before a man on the front row proclaimed, "We don't need any more time, Judge. We're in agreement."

"All defendants, please rise." Judge Duffy said, and the deputies stepped forward to pull the prisoners to their feet. "Mr. Foreman, what are your verdicts?"

"We find all four men guilty on all counts, Your Honor."

The room burst into whoops and hollers. Judge Duffy pounded

his gavel. "Order or I will clear this courtroom!" he warned, turning to the foreman. "Thank you, sir," he said, scribbling a note before addressing the defendants. "Gentlemen, you have all been found guilty of multiple crimes. The penalty for each is to hang by the noose until you are dead, and so each of you must prepare to die this afternoon."

Gaines did not move. Two of the other men began to cry, and the third lowered his head in defeat.

"You need not hope legal trickery will further delay your sentences, as there will be no further trial. A jury of your peers has based their determination on the evidence presented here today. You have answered to the law and the citizens of Helena and the great state of Texas, and now you must answer to God." The judge banged his gavel for the last time. "This court is adjourned," he announced.

The deputies released the accomplices from the iron rings on the floor and took them away first. The sheriff took hold of Gaines next and led him toward the exit at the rear, the prisoner exerting more resistance with each step. Gaines paused when he reached the row where Zacharias and his family were seated. A sudden recognition Gaines could not hide flickered across his face, and his lip curled ever so slightly.

* * *

Outside on the square, the crowd pushed and jostled, seeking the best vantage point to view the gallows. Zacharias stood in front at the center of the platform, John Marcin beside him. Marcin and John Stanard stood to his right next to Mr. Ramsey. A sharp wind gusted, and the four empty nooses dangling from the crossbar whipped back and forth.

John Marcin pulled on Zacharias' sleeve. "Papa, lift me up. I want to find Khalil."

Zacharias hoisted John Marcin onto his shoulder. As he turned the boy around, he, too, surveyed the scene. Like the cold, gray skies above, it felt like all the color in the world had been drained away.

Some two hundred people were packed into the square, donning dark wool cloaks with hoods or brimmed hats to shield themselves from the intermittent precipitation. Small children and even adults sat atop the roofs of surrounding buildings. They also perched among the limbs of the tall pecan trees on either side of the gallows, displacing several ravens that darted into the upper branches. Many more observers stood on flatbed wagons parked at the rear, and among them, Zacharias spotted Khalil on his horse.

"There he is, Papa," John Marcin said, pointing at the wrangler.

The low hum of conversation emanating from the gathering was interrupted by a scream from the direction of the courthouse. Zacharias released John Marcin and turned toward the noise to find the woman in the brown bonnet clutching the red-haired boy to her side.

"Jacob! Jacob!" she wailed.

The boy stood tall, staring at the barred entrance to the jail cells. He was not wearing a hat, and his glowing locks stood out in even starker contrast to the gloomy surroundings.

The door opened, and the crowd fell silent. One of the guards emerged, climbed into an empty wagon, and drove it around behind the platform. Next, the condemned men filed out behind a preacher. A second guard and the sheriff brought up the rear. The men were escorted across the road to the gallows. Another shriek rang out when Gaines stepped onto the stairs leading up to the platform. The woman in the bonnet had collapsed into the arms of a man standing next to her. The boy with her remained at attention, watching Gaines. Distracted, the prisoner stumbled. The guard helped him to his feet and pushed him and the others forward. The four prisoners now stood facing the crowd, their hands bound behind their backs. As the preacher offered last rites, their faces showed no outward signs of fear, only resignation.

Zacharias stood transfixed. One by one, the guard placed the nooses around the condemned men's necks and slid the knots under their jaws. When the rope touched Gaines' skin, he looked at the red-haired boy, who raised his small hand above his hip and waved. The guard adjusted Gaines' knot one final time, and he winced. Zacharias swallowed hard. He ran his fingers over his throat and felt his Adam's apple bob beneath his skin. The sheriff followed, placing black hoods over all the prisoners' heads before positioning himself by the trap door lever, awaiting the preacher's signal.

Zacharias felt John Marcin's body tense. "Son, you don't have to look," he said. "I'll tell you when it's over."

Zacharias held his breath. He'd been praying for this since he was a boy, but somehow, he feared it would not solve anything. He also wondered if things might get worse. But it was too late now. The trap door squealed, and the condemned men dropped. There was a gash of silence before a burst of cheers exploded around the square. The ropes groaned ominously, and Zacharias watched the four bodies swing back and forth. One at the far end of the platform continued to twist violently, and he could hear choking beneath the hood.

"That fella's rope was too short. The poor soul is stranglin'," a woman standing behind Marcin said.

Zacharias bent down and touched John Marcin's shoulder. "It's all done," he said, but when he looked back at the platform, only three bodies were hanging from the crossbar. The fourth was missing. The noose that had been around Gaines' neck was empty and bouncing back and forth beneath the crossbeam, and his head-less body was wedged through the trap door of the platform.

"That is most unfortunate," Ramsey said. "He was too heavy, and the rope too long. Alas, this happens occasionally."

Suddenly, there was a thud in the dirt and a bone-rattling shriek of terror from somewhere nearby. It was Marcin, who had collapsed, convulsing and frothing at the mouth. Zacharias started toward him, stumbling over what had so terrified his father: a sev-ered head covered in a black hood rolling along the ground. Blood splattered over the tops of Zacharias' boots and oozed into the dirt.

"Don't look, John Marcin!" Zacharias shouted.

Zacharias, too, turned away. When he did, he spotted the shad-ow figure slithering behind a tree near the courthouse steps, its head peeking out from behind the trunk. Zacharias rubbed his eyes. He might be able to convince himself that he was seeing things but could not deny what he smelled. A blast of wind shepherded the fa-miliar stench of death and despair across the square. When Zacharias looked again, he froze. The shadow stood at the red-haired boy's side, pointing at John Marcin. The young Gaines' thin lips quivered ever so slightly as if holding back a smile.

"He's mine," the shadow's whisper floated on the icy breeze.

John Marcin clutched Zacharias' arm. "Did you hear that, Papa?"

CHAPTER 19

She Is Here

Shadows grew long across the pastures of Peacock Bend, and the color of the Medina River eased from blue to black in the approaching twilight. Crickets chirped along the path from the main house, past the original homestead, and up to the barn. A peacock shrieked, "Eee-you, eee-you," from somewhere in the distance.

Watching the sunset with his father had become a silent ritual for Zacharias in the months since their trip to Helena. Marcin had not uttered a word since the incident at the gallows. The doctor diagnosed his condition as apoplexy and did not offer much hope he would ever speak again. The episode also weakened Marcin's legs, and he had difficulty standing and walking. Zee moved into the old farmhouse to help care for him. Without a word, she fed and bathed him, took him to the toilet, and sang him to sleep. With Liza often preoccupied with her own father, who remained adamant that he would stay put in his own home until the Good Lord came to call, Zacharias was eternally grateful to the healer.

One evening after Zee put Marcin to sleep, Zacharias lingered on the front porch, a rare nightcap in hand. He lowered himself onto a chair with a heavy sigh and set his glass on a rickety wooden side table. His father had insisted on keeping the old thing, vehemently rejecting Liza's suggestion that it might better serve as firewood. It was one of the first pieces of furniture Marcin had built for

Agnieszka when they moved to Bandera. Zacharias closed his eyes and tried to picture his mother's face. It was more difficult with each passing year.

Something brushed against Zacharias' shoulder from behind, disrupting his train of thought. It was John Marcin. "You spooked me, son," Zacharias said. "Come and sit."

The boy remained standing. "I just came to say goodnight, Papa. Zee says I gotta go to bed."

"Right, she is," Zacharias smiled and tousled John Marcin's curls. It was like looking in a mirror at his younger self. "Listen, you make sure to include Miss Zee in your prayers tonight and every night. She's a blessing."

"I will," John Marcin replied, appearing to have more on his mind. "Papa, can I ask you something?"

Zacharias took a sip of his drink. "Shoot, kiddo."

"Is Grandpa Marcin dying?"

The liquid caught in Zacharias' windpipe, and he began to cough violently.

The boy remained quiet.

When the fit passed, Zacharias squeezed John Marcin's hand. "Listen, son, all I know is that he's not getting any better. Why don't you say a prayer for Grandpa Marcin, too, while you're at it?"

"Yes, Papa," John Marcin said and retreated.

The evening gatherings grew less frequent as winter approached, and Marcin's health further faltered. "Tato, put this over you. It's cold tonight." Zacharias tucked a blanket around his father's body, and Marcin offered a much-labored smile. It was in these moments Zacharias knew his father was still in that broken body somewhere. A breeze picked up, and something caught Marcin's attention in the yard.

"What is it? What do you see?" Zacharias asked.

Marcin became agitated and tried to stand.

Zacharias jumped. "Tato, no, wait. I'll get Zee. Let us help you."

When Zacharias and Zee returned, John Marcin close behind, they froze at the front door. Marcin was standing at the porch railing, reaching out into the darkness.

Zacharias rushed to his father's side. "Tatusiu, what's the matter?"

Marcin shook his head.

"You must sit," Zacharias pleaded. Marcin ignored him and started down the porch steps. Zee reached out to grab him, but Zacharias stopped her. "No. Let him go."

Marcin walked out the front gate for the first time since his collapse in Helena. He continued toward the river, and Zacharias and John Marcin followed. When Marcin reached the riverbank, he raised his fists. "Leave them!" he croaked. "Take me!"

"Papa, what's going on?" John Marcin said.

Zacharias lifted a finger to his lips.

"Zachek," Marcin called to his son.

"I'm right here," Zacharias replied, joining his father at the water's edge.

Marcin pointed across the river. "Zachek, she is here."

"Yes, Tato. She has always been here."

"Kochanie," Marcin cried into the night. "I am coming."

*   *   *

Beata and Victoria made their long, somber sojourns home to bury their father, and on the morning of the funeral, as they had done for their mother many years ago, they picked small bouquets of sage grass and a few last marigolds hanging on around the perimeter of the house. They tied them with remnants of indigo blue ribbon they'd found in their mother's old sewing box and placed them in each of Marcin's hands before Zacharias nailed the wooden coffin shut. Father Adamietz made haste with his prayers at the graveside in the Anderwald family plot as freezing rain began to fall.

After the final Amen, Zacharias led John Marcin back toward the house, but something distracted the boy, and he stepped away to take a closer look. Several small pieces of fabric were snagged on the rough bark of one of the old oak trees. A worn piece of cream-colored muslin was tangled together with two lengths of faded yellow ribbon. John Marcin removed the remnants from the tree and showed them to his father. "Look, Papa, someone has torn their dress," he said.

Zacharias took the scraps of fabric and placed them against his lips. "Mamusiu," he choked.

Father Adamietz approached from behind to offer comfort. "Marcin has gone home to God, Zacharias. He is at peace now," the priest said tenderly.

"No, Father," Zacharias smiled. "He has gone home to her."

PART THREE

For nothing is secret, that will not be revealed,
Nor anything hid, that will not be known and
come to light.

—Luke 8:17

CHAPTER 20

The Bandera Ball

John Marcin Anderwald, the namesake of the two men whose prayers and machinations had had as much to do with his being as his parents, would offer solace to a mother and father who nearly collapsed from heartbreak in the years before his arrival. He also served as a beacon of light amidst the darkness for those who had already sought the safety of Peacock Bend and those yet to find their way. Over his lifetime, John Marcin would be summoned time and again to hold the wicked to account and guide the lost and wounded to a place of peace.

It would, however, take more than a great flood, a hangman's noose, or even two world wars to ease the weight of grief, grudges, and guilt, let alone the spirits agitated during those difficult years along the Medina. For John Marcin Anderwald, a true reconciliation—or as close as any man can hope to come to such a thing—would take a lifetime of questions and prayers, both answered and unanswered.

*   *   *

John Marcin burst out of the door. He'd heard the engine clicking long before his Granddaddy Stanard's Model T crested the hill. Liza hurried over from the garden in time to see her father's car fly into the air at the top of the lane and land with a loud crack. John Stanard had pledged to hang up his driving gloves on his eightieth birthday the previous summer, but he'd yet to make good on that promise, much to the collective dismay of his family, fellow citizens, and complete strangers alike. He was, without question, the most reckless driver in all of Bandera County.

"Good gracious, that man is going to kill himself one of these days," Liza said. "John Marcin, if I ever catch you driving that fast, I'll skin you alive."

"Never, ever, Mama," John Marcin mocked. "I promise to drive just like you."

"And how might that be, young man?"

"Slow, slow, slow like a slug on a leaf." John Marcin grinned and pecked his mother's cheek.

Liza feigned insult and rapped her knuckles on the top of her son's head. "Oh, my, you're drowning in hair tonic! But you sure do smell gorgeous," she teased, nuzzling John Marcin's ear. "I guess you've figured out that girls don't like boys who reek of camels."

"Quit it," John Marcin whined, smoothing his curls back into place.

Stanard slammed on his brakes and slid to a stop in front of the ranch house. "Lord Almighty, that girl can fly!" the old man laughed as he tumbled out of the car. "Did you see that, Liza Lou? I think all four wheels may have taken flight."

"That's enough showing off, Daddy. We don't want to give this boy any ideas. I'd like him to make it home from the dance tonight in one piece."

"Yes, the dance. You best be on your way, John Marcin. The gas tank is full, so you should be fine getting to town and back, but no joy ridin', you hear?"

"Yes, Granddaddy."

John Marcin could hardly contain his excitement. This was the first time his grandfather allowed him to take the car out by himself, even though he'd been practicing for over a year on their weekend drives along the back roads. Cruising down Main Street would be quite the spectacle. There were only twelve or thirteen cars in all of Bandera and the surrounding county, so he was certain to cause a stir.

"Howdy, John," Zacharias greeted from the porch. "You comin' in for a drink?"

"Don't want to be rude, do I?" Stanard said before turning to John Marcin. "You have yourself a good time, young man, and be home by dawn."

"Daddy," Liza bristled. "John Marcin, you are to be home by eleven and no later."

"Liza, let the boy be," Zacharias said. "He's sixteen for goodness' sake. Old enough to take care of himself. Do drive carefully, though, son."

"I will, Papa." John Marcin jumped into the car and pressed the starter.

The night's first stop was Frankie and Tater Kalka's nearby farm. John Marcin squeezed the bulb of the car horn in three successive blasts to announce his arrival. The boys tumbled out their front door and climbed in, Frankie in front, and Tater relegated to the back. John Marcin noticed Tater had misbuttoned his shirt, leaving a gap and exposing his cavernous belly button. "Tater, fix your shirt. You look like a goof," he laughed.

"Aw, nuts, I can't do anything right. Look here. I cut myself four times shaving this afternoon." Tater pointed to several spots of crusted blood on his cheek.

"Maybe you should get your nose outta the newspaper during your beauty regime, eh?" Frankie said. "But don't worry about it. The posh gals won't be interested, and the pug-uglies won't give a damn about how you look. They'll just be grateful for a dance partner."

Tater smacked his brother on the back of the head. "Why don't you shut yer yap, Frankie."

"Goddammit, Tater," Frankie snapped, throwing himself back over the seat to strike a blow and knocking John Marcin's arm off the steering wheel.

The car swerved off the road and back onto it. "Stop it, you two," John Marcin howled. "If I wreck my grandfather's car, I'll have hell to pay. Frankie, sit!"

"Sorry, John Marcin," Frankie said, straightening his collar.

"You should be sorry," Tater muttered.

All had been forgiven and forgotten by the time the boys reached the Bandera Courthouse. The dance had already started in the upstairs hall. Lights were strung along the front sidewalk, and the entire second floor was glowing from within. Music pulsed through the open windows.

Frankie jogged ahead. "Shake a leg, you two!"

"Dammit, Frankie, wait for us," Tater yelled at his brother.

John Marcin slammed the car door and straightened his tie. "Leave him be, Tater. You know he's always gotta make a grand entrance."

The Bandera Ball, as it was known, had become something of an occasion for the young folks across the Hill Country. Most of John Marcin's classmates and a good number of teenagers from the surrounding area were in attendance. A group of girls dressed in their Sunday finest huddled in the corner nearest the stage where the Schulte family band, the Pipe Creek Posse, was playing. Albert, the oldest brother, scraped away on the fiddle, and younger brothers Louis and Joe plucked hard on the rhythm guitar and kept the beat on the stand-up bass, respectively. The girls swayed and tapped their feet to the music, some ogling the band members and others pulling at their dresses, waiting for one of the boys to work up the nerve to ask them to dance.

The boys gathered on the opposite side of the room, drinking punch, laughing, and joking among themselves. Several older boys were sneaking sips from metal flasks hidden in their coat pockets. Frankie and Tater blended into the merriment, but John Marcin was content to stand back and observe. He did not have Frankie's grace and confidence, nor Tater's complete lack of self-awareness. Frankie always had the perfect thing to say and the prettiest girl on his arm. Tater, on the other hand, was always yammering on about the news of the day or some recent invention he'd read about, whether or not folks wanted to hear about it. John Marcin leaned against the back wall and observed the scene. He watched Frankie scan the throng for his first conquest, crossing the room and inviting a gorgeous blonde onto the dance floor. Five more couples followed suit, and the crowd gathered around the stage began to thin.

It was then that John Marcin noticed her. A girl he'd never seen before stood by herself, reading what looked to be sheet music. She was tall and slender, with long, wavy black hair falling to her waist with an unusual casualness as though she had just rolled out of bed. She had twisted two sections in front and tied them back with a red ribbon matching the dark red stain on her lips. She wore a pink cotton dress with a more open neckline than was considered proper, in Bandera anyway, and short flowing sleeves that gapped to expose a white lace slip beneath.

"Don't drool on the floor," Frankie said, taking a break from dancing to catch his breath.

John Marcin blushed. "You worn out already?"

"Yeah, well, I'm givin' old Sophie's feet a rest. And her back-side," Frankie winked. He pulled a pack of cigarettes from his shirt pocket and offered one to John Marcin.

"No, thanks."

"Suit yourself." Frankie slipped a cigarette between his lips and lit the end. "Never seen her before," he said, gesturing toward the girl next to the stage. "You?"

"Nope. Me neither."

"You sure have been lookin' tonight, though," Frankie chuckled and prodded John Marcin with an elbow. "And so have all these other fillies in here. They're gonna be in a right state. They hate any kind of competition for my affections."

John Marcin looked sharply at his friend.

"Ha!" Frankie laughed. "I'll give you first crack, but you better move quick, or I'm gonna go talk to that girl." Frankie dropped his cigarette butt to the floor, twisting it under the toe of his boot. "I best get back to Sophie. She's already poutin' over there." Frankie skipped away and swooped his statuesque dance partner back into his arms.

John Marcin had no idea how Frankie did it, but he sure hoped he might someday. He turned back to the stage and was startled to see the girl in the pink dress standing on it. Albert Schulte placed his fiddle on a chair and stepped forward. "Ladies and gents, may I have your attention?" He waited until the room settled. "We have a special treat for you all tonight. My baby sister Anna will be joining me for a few vocal numbers we've put together. Please give her a big Bandera welcome!"

The boys began to whoop and clap as Anna stepped toward the center of the stage. The girls in the audience were slightly less exuberant in their welcome, looking her up and down. Anna stared at the floor as she waited for the band to tune their instruments. Albert Schulte ushered his sister closer and pointed at the front of the stage. When she hesitated, he turned his back to the crowd and said something that made her jump and quicken her step.

Albert turned back to the audience with a wide grin. "This first number is a song that some of you might have heard of," he said. "It's called 'By the Light of the Silvery Moon.'" At his count the music began.

Albert sang the first verse, his baritone clear and bright, "Cast two, me, you, sound of kisses floating on the breeze," he crooned, leaning toward Anna, his cheek against her temple.

Anna only looked up when they reached the chorus. She raised her head and locked her almond-shaped eyes on John Marcin out in the crowd before opening her mouth and releasing the most agile and rich alto. "I want to spoon, to my honey I'll croon love's tune," she sang in perfect harmony with her brother. John Marcin could feel Anna's voice move through his whole body.

At the song's end, the room erupted in applause, none louder than John Marcin's. Anna looked as if she wanted off the stage. Albert whispered in her ear. She started to exit, but her brother grabbed her arm, pulling her back and goading the audience to clap louder.

"Wouldn't you like to hear one more, folks?"

The crowd roared in agreement. John Marcin recognized the tune. It was 'Put Your Arms Around Me, Honey.' He'd listened to the song with Granddaddy Stanard on his new Victor phonograph. His mother had disapproved. The lyrics were sassy, she said, but his grandfather had laughed and increased the volume. Albert and Anna began to dance together. "It's just about the time for making love," Albert sang. "Someone is a-waiting all along for me. No more hesitating, I must go and see." In the few beats before the chorus, Anna looked out again into the crowd. When she spotted John Marcin, she began to sing out strong and loud.

After the final chord, Anna rushed off the stage. The band kicked off another old-time fiddle tune, and couples swarmed back onto the floor. "Dumbass, go over there," Frankie mouthed over the music.

John Marcin knew he had to act quickly before he lost his nerve, or worse, before another boy beat him to Anna. He forced his way across the room, dodging pairs of dancers.

"Hey, watch it!" one boy yowled when John Marcin stepped on his foot.

"Get outta the way," another couple warned.

"John Marcin, where ya goin'?" Tater inquired from behind the refreshments table where he'd been stationed most of the evening.

"Leave him be, Tater," Frankie scolded.

Anna glanced up as John Marcin approached. "Hey," he began, forgetting what he'd planned to say next.

"Thank you," she said warmly.

"Uh, for what?"

"I was so nervous, but I did what my brother Joe taught me. He always says to find someone in the crowd with a kind face and focus on them when you sing. And there you were," Anna smiled.

John Marcin buried his hands in his pants pockets and swayed back and forth. "You're welcome," he replied.

"What's your name?"

"I'm John Marcin. John Marcin Anderwald."

"Oh, yeah," Anna said, acting as if she were reminded of him rather than meeting for the first time.

Anna Schulte was beguiling and elusive at the same time. John Marcin tried to conjure up what Frankie might say next. He shifted on his feet. "So, um, do you wanna get some punch?" was all he could think to ask.

Anna laughed. "I want a drink, but not punch. Come with me." She looped her arm through John Marcin's and guided him across the front of the stage toward the exit. He noticed Anna's brother Albert watching them. "Catch me if you can," she said and pushed John Marcin aside, racing down the stairs ahead of him.

"Wait for me!" he cried.

John Marcin was willing to play whatever game this enchanting girl had in mind. He followed her to the lobby. She was nowhere to be seen. He continued outside onto the courthouse's front lawn. Looking left, John Marcin saw no one, but to the right he spotted Anna as she rounded the building. He caught up to her behind the courthouse where a large wagon was parked. She was rooting around in a carpetbag in the back.

"Aha! Here we go. Even better than punch," she said, waving a flask. "Let's find a quiet place for a *real* drink."

"Wanna go for a ride?" John Marcin offered. If there was ever a time to show off Granddaddy Stanard's Model T, this was it. "I have my grandfather's automobile." When he saw Anna's look of shock, he laughed and said, "Time for a *real* ride."

John Marcin grabbed Anna's hand and led her to the car. "I've always wanted to ride in one of these," she said.

"Where would you like to go?"

"Wherever you see fit to take me, John Marcin Anderwald," she replied with a coquettish curtsy.

John Marcin opened the passenger door for Anna and climbed behind the wheel. They sped toward the river. Anna leaned out through the window, the air coursing through her hair.

"Stop here," she ordered when they reached the riverbank.

John Marcin parked in a grove of trees, and they sat in silence, looking out over the water glinting in the dappled moonlight.

"How about that drink?" Anna broke the awkward silence, kicking off her shoes and unscrewing the top of the flask. She took two large swallows and offered John Marcin a turn.

He took a quick sip and began to cough. "I'm not much of a drinker," he confessed.

"Great, more for me," Anna said and grabbed the flask back.

"You might wanna take it easy there," John Marcin suggested but quickly realized he'd overstepped. Anna glared at him. "I'm sorry. I only…" he fumbled.

"I'm sorry, I only," she mocked him like an insolent child. "Aren't you the goody-two-shoes! Your mama must be so proud."

John Marcin wasn't sure what to say. He gripped the steering wheel. Anna swung her stocking-covered feet onto the seat and pulled up onto her knees, her whole body facing him. Head cocked to the side, she stared at John Marcin. "What?" he asked.

Anna's only response was to take another slug of whatever they were drinking. John Marcin opened his mouth to speak again, but before he could say a word, Anna bent forward and kissed him full on the mouth. Her lips were soft and wet, and she tasted of alcohol. It was his first kiss, but clearly not hers. Anna leaned back. "Are we done fighting?"

"Who said we were fighting?" John Marcin was confused and could not contain his exasperation.

"Feels like we were," Anna said, and a cloud descended between them.

"We should be getting back," John Marcin started to say, but Anna burst into tears. "What's wrong?" he asked, reaching across the seat.

Anna pushed his hand away and shook her head. "I'm sorry. I've had too much to drink," her voice cracked. "Things like this always happen when I drink."

John Marcin withdrew a handkerchief from his pocket and offered it to Anna. "I didn't mean to upset you."

"Thank you," she sniffed, dabbing her face. "You're right. We should go."

John Marcin started the car. When they reached the courthouse, people were already streaming out of the front entrance. The dance was over, and the clock in the tower was striking ten. "I better find my friends," he said. "They'll be wondering where I've gotten to, and I'm their ride home."

Anna reached for the door handle.

"Wait, wait, I'll get that." John Marcin jumped out and ran around to the passenger side of the car.

Anna cast a quick glance at John Marcin as she got out, and the last vestiges of her earlier boldness dissolved into the cool night air. John Marcin lost any nerve he might have had to kiss her again amidst the uncomfortable silence between them.

"See ya," she finally said and ran off toward the courthouse.

"Hope so," he smiled, watching Anna dart across the lawn.

Frankie approached from the courthouse steps. "Hey, Ander-wald! Where in the hell have you been?"

"Yeah, we've been looking all over for you," Tater added, struggling to keep pace with his brother.

"I was getting some air. Hustle up. We gotta go," John Marcin hurried his friends toward the car.

"Air? What air?" Frankie groused. He flopped into the front seat and loosened his tie.

"Hang on a minute," Tater said, dancing on the side of the road. "I gotta take a piss. I'll be right back. And you better not leave me behind, or I'm tellin' that you skipped out on the dance, John Marcin." Tater ran across the street to a clump of bushes.

"Seriously, where'd you get to? We were starting to worry," Frankie said.

"I told you. I went for a walk."

"Hmmm." Frankie was clearly suspicious. He leaned forward and grabbed something off the dashboard. "What do we have here?" he said, holding a handkerchief out of John Marcin's reach. Would you look at that? Dark red lipstick. I've never seen your mama wear that shade."

"Give that to me!" John Marcin lunged across the seat and snatched the cloth from Frankie's hand. "And not a word to Tater," he urged as he stuffed it back into his pocket. "He'll tell the whole county."

"I won't say nothin', but you might wanna wipe your face before he gets back." Frankie pointed at John Marcin's cheek with a devilish grin.

Chapter 21

To the Border, Boys!

Anna disappeared after the Bandera Ball as suddenly as she had appeared. John Marcin concocted countless excuses to head into town in hopes of running into her, and he kept an eye out at church picnics and other events on the off chance her brothers' band might be playing. He mustered the courage to take a drive out to Pipe Creek to try and find the Schulte place, but upon asking for directions at the post office, learned the family had cut and run a month prior. They'd sold their ragged farm to settle some debts.

"Huh," the postmaster scoffed. "They owe you money, too?"

"No, sir," John Marcin said with a frown. "I take it they didn't leave a forwarding address?"

"Nope, and if you want my opinion, it's a good thing they've gone. Somethin' wasn't right about those folks, especially with the father and the older boy."

"Much obliged," John Marcin replied and left without further inquiry. He'd heard a few rumors about the Schultes, but his mother always cautioned against paying gossip too much mind.

Soon enough, Anna Schulte was a faint memory for John Marcin. There were more pressing concerns in his life. The world beyond Bandera County had come calling. The first call came from Heaven above in the summer of 1914. Granddaddy Stanard was gone. The end was quick and true to form. It happened one afternoon as John

Stanard raised a glass of his favorite whiskey with friends at the Bandera Saloon.

"I am confident your father suffered a massive coronary attack, Mrs. Anderwald," the doctor explained. "He was gone before he hit the ground."

Liza stood next to her father's body in the bar's storage room, Zacharias and John Marcin equally stunned and numb at her side. They had all rushed to the saloon the minute word reached them at Peacock Bend. The barkeep, Raymond, had driven out in the Model T to deliver the news.

"I'll give you some time alone," the doctor offered and exited, closing the door behind him.

Liza kissed her father's lifeless cheek. John Marcin could not look. He wanted to remember Granddaddy Stanard's sparkling smile, not his face fixed in death. The air was sucked from John Marcin's lungs, and he could feel yet another tear in the fabric of his world. Sergeant Kirby, Grandpa Marcin, and now Granddaddy Stanard. It was too much to bear. Who would be next? He rushed out onto the street, his mother's anguished wails of grief rising behind him.

John Stanard was buried in the graveyard behind the First Baptist Church on Pecan Street but was abundantly clear in his last will and testament that he was to be laid to rest next to his beloved son Robert and not his wife. John Marcin was versed in the many stories about Grandmother Eugenia from his mother. Still, none was more telling than when he asked her why his grandfather had insisted on such a specific placement of his grave. "I don't blame him one bit, John Marcin," Liza said. "And I'm telling you as clear as I can. When I go, don't you dare bury me in this wretched place. I know Daddy wanted to be near Bobby, but I will not spend eternity lying anywhere near that awful woman."

*   *   *

The second call came a year later when tensions flared along the U.S.-Mexico border, and armed raids from the Mexican side escalated. Tales of Pancho Villa and his ragtag bandit army elicited fearful cries and false bravado in equal measure among the good citizens of south Texas. Young men were recruited from near and far to help build forts from Brownsville to Big Bend to defend their great state from the villainous Villa. Several boys who'd been in school with John Marcin joined the Texas National Guard over at Camp Travis and were dispatched to the lower Rio Grande Valley. Adam Moravietz was the first to sport his new uniform at Mass the Sunday before leaving for the garrison in Harlingen.

"Would ya take a gander at all that finery," Tater exclaimed from the pew behind John Marcin.

Every head in St. Stanislaus turned. The young man was dressed in a brand new, crisply ironed uniform: a coat, collared shirt, and pants all in the same olive drab color. Adam acknowledged his fellow parishioners with a quick bow of his head as he joined his family in the front of the church.

Tater whistled through his teeth and received a sharp punch from his brother. "Would you be quiet," Frankie said.

"You be quiet," Tater began to protest, but both young men were silenced by a swift smack on their heads, their mother's thick palm still capable of commanding their attention.

After the service, the friends found each other in the small churchyard. Adam and Frankie were smoking near the cemetery gate. "Hey Adam, that's a right smart uniform you got there," Tater said.

"Yeah, I suppose," Adam replied with a quick smile, "but it itches somethin' awful. My mother insisted I wear the darn thing to church. I think she's more excited than I am about all of this."

"The fabric's khaki. It was invented by the British Army over in India," Tater continued.

"What in the hell are you dronin' on about?" Frankie laughed. "Always with your random facts. You sure are the dumbest smart person I know, brother."

"And you're the dumbest dumb person I know," Tater shot back.

"Will you two cut it out?" John Marcin intervened before turning to Adam. "So, when you headed out?"

"First thing tomorrow morning to San Antonio, and after that, the afternoon train south."

"You scared?" Tater asked.

"Are you joking?" Frankie shoved his brother backward.

"Aw, Frankie, don't be like that," Adam said. "Maybe a little, Tater. More curious than anything, though. Basic training over at Camp Travis was the furthest I've ever been away from home."

The group fell silent and watched Adam smoke his cigarette. A car horn blared from the street. "That's my cue. I gotta drive my parents back home," John Marcin said, extending his hand toward Adam. "You keep yourself safe and come back and tell us all about it."

Adam shook John Marcin's hand.

"And stay away from them brothels. You don't wanna come back with the French pox," Frankie chided.

"That's right, them painted ladies are nothin' but trouble, and there are no known cures for the pox yet," Tater added.

"Enough with the science lessons," Frankie said. "Besides, what experience have you got with any painted ladies? No whore would even touch your fat ass no matter what you paid her!"

"Quit it, Frankie. I'm warning you," Tater replied.

John Marcin smiled as he walked back toward the church, the Kalka boys' banter fading into the distance.

*   *   *

The third call came the following spring of 1915 off the coast of Ireland when a German U-boat sank the passenger liner *Lusitania*, killing over one thousand civilians, including many Americans. Zacharias knew of two men who'd been on the ship. The stories of their heroism topped the front pages of the nation's newspapers.

"Liza, listen here," Zacharias said. "You remember a Mr. Timmis who used to come around your father's ranch on his way to Galveston?"

Liza looked up from her book. "The cotton man from Gainesville? The one with the accent?"

"That's right, the one from England."

"How did Granddaddy know him?" John Marcin chimed in from the desk where he was filing invoices from Camp Travis' latest orders. As more and more men were mobilized at the border, the army's need for beef to feed them was insatiable. Peacock Bend was supplying almost half of the camp's monthly requisitions.

"Says here Timmis did business with your grandfather for years. He was on that boat the Germans sank with another Gainesville man named Moodie. Looks like they are quite the heroes. Gave their lifebelts to two women who survived."

"What happened to the men?" John Marcin asked.

"Apparently, Timmis jumped into the water and swam unaided for hours till a rescue boat found him. Moodie is still missing and feared drowned."

"Such a terrible way to die," Liza said.

"Yep. Not sure how we're gonna stay outta this God-forsaken war over in Europe now." Zacharias flipped the page.

Liza was discernibly agitated. "I don't even want to think about getting entangled in all that craziness. It's none of our affair after all."

"Mama, it might not be up to any of us. They say the Governor might be calling for more men to help at the border, and there's even talk that President Wilson might have to send some troops over to help fight the Huns."

"And what talk is that, John Marcin," Liza challenged.

"Mama, we've already sent a bunch of boys to the border."

"Oh, for goodness' sake," Liza interrupted. "You and your friends keep jabbering on about Pancho Villa and that saber-rattling Kaiser. You're too young to understand the dangers."

"Too young? Seriously, Mama."

"Enough. I mean it," Liza said.

"You know I'm old enough to join the Guard on my own if I wanted to," John Marcin began but decided against engaging his mother further on the subject of the impending war. At least for the moment. Liza had always believed something terrible would be less likely to happen if you didn't speak about it. And John Marcin was never inclined to argue with her unless necessary.

* * *

The fourth call came on January 10, 1916, from San Isabel, Mexico. The newspaper's headline read, "Eighteen Americans Massacred." All hell had broken loose on the southern border.

"I'll be damned," John Marcin said as he scanned the pages of the *Bandera Bulletin.*

Liza was sketching by the fire. "What is it?" she asked.

"Those sonofabitches!"

"John Marcin, language," Liza scolded.

Zacharias tossed a log he'd brought in from the yard onto the fire. "What happened?" he said, brushing small twigs off his sweater.

"Pancho Villa and his men abducted some American engineers from a train in Chihuahua." John Marcin traced his finger over the printed columns on the page. "Lord, have mercy! They shot 'em all, but one got away."

"Why on earth did they have to do that?" Liza asked.

"Hang on a minute. I'm still reading. It says here bandits stopped the train, pulled the Americans off, and shot them right there in the desert. Execution style. No reason at all. Unbelievable..." John Marcin trailed off. He worked up the nerve to broach what was on his mind. The ice hissed as the flames of the fire licked the fresh log. "Some of us have been talking about joining the Guard. Doing something more to help," he said.

"Have you now," Zacharias said, frowning.

Liza dropped her charcoal pencil, and her sketch pad fell from her lap onto the carpet.

"Yes sir," John Marcin replied. He could see his father and mother exchange glances.

"Foolishness," Liza grumbled as she retrieved her pencil and pad and settled back onto the sofa.

"I think we'll all have to do our part, sooner or later," Zacharias said, avoiding Liza's steely glare.

"John Marcin, there is plenty to do right here," his mother intervened. "Your father cannot manage this ranch by himself. He needs your help."

"Mama, Papa's got Khalil and the ranch hands. Besides, I cannot stay back when Frankie, Tater, and the others go. It's our duty."

"The answer is no," Liza said firmly.

Zacharias did not look at Liza when he spoke next. "I figured this was coming soon enough. It's the right thing to do, son."

"Zachek!" Liza cried, fear and frustration brimming in her eyes.

Zacharias displayed unexpected firmness. "John Marcin is a grown man, if you haven't noticed. He needs to make his own decisions."

Liza slammed her drawings on the coffee table and stormed out.

✳   ✳   ✳

The train whistle blew twice, and a signal bell clanged on the platform. Liza continued to fuss with John Marcin's uniform. She unfastened and refastened the dark bronze buttons on the front of his single-breasted coat and brushed the dust from his breeches, which were from the same heavy cotton twill. John Marcin's dark hair was cut short, parted to one side, and fixed with a thick pomade.

"I gotta go," he said softly.

"Don't you look handsome," his mother repeated for the third time.

"Mama," John Marcin took her hands in his. "I'll be fine. Don't worry so much."

Liza threw her arms around John Marcin and kissed each of his cheeks. "You write as often as you can, you hear?"

"Yes, ma'am. I will."

Another whistle blew, and a conductor scurried along the platform. "All aboard! Last call for the 9:15 to Mission, boys!" he bellowed.

Zacharias placed a hand around Liza's waist. "He's gonna miss his train if you don't let him go."

"You better hurry, then," Liza said.

"John Marcin, be careful and come home to us in one piece."
Zacharias embraced his son. John Marcin could feel his father's body
trembling.

"I plan to, Papa."

John Marcin stepped onto the train and searched for an open
seat. As he placed his bag on the rack running along the top of the
rail car, the train jolted and began to inch forward. He looked out
the window. Zacharias and Liza stood arm in arm, watching and
waving. John Marcin placed his hand against the glass and did his
best to smile. He noticed for the first time how his parents had aged.
The lines across his father's forehead and around his mouth had
deepened, and his tall frame had begun to bend across the back. His
mother's blond hair was now mostly white, and her midsection had
thickened. They looked like they could be his grandparents among
the others who'd come to see their sons off. A loud crash at the back
of the car distracted his attention. The Kalkas had made the train
after all and were slogging their way through the car with their bags,
sweaty and agitated. When John Marcin looked back toward the
station again, he could no longer see his parents.

"Would you move it, Tater!" Frankie growled, tripping over
his brother's drawstring barracks bag stuck in the aisle. "And pick up
your damned satchel. How many books you got in there anyway?"

John Marcin waved from the middle of the car, where he'd
found several empty seats together. "Hey, over here, you two."

"There you are," Tater huffed. "We've been through five wagons looking for your ugly mug." Frankie and Tater tumbled into
seats across from John Marcin after placing their gear on the rack
above.

"I was worried you were gonna miss the train," John Marcin
said.

"Yeah, so get this," Tater said. "Frankie here didn't get home
till dawn. Was out the whole night saying goodbye to Sophie." Tater
removed his jacket and laid it over his lap, exposing his uniform
shirt, which was soaked with sweat at the armpits.

"Tater's jealous, is all," Frankie rolled his eyes. "We got here in
plenty of time."

"I ain't jealous!" Tater protested. "I don't have time for all that
mush."

Frankie yawned and leaned his head against the window. He was soon asleep. Tater untied his boots and loosened his shirt collar. He extracted a thick book from his jacket pocket, something about a General Napoleon based on its title, and settled in to read. The train was filled with soldiers John Marcin recognized from basic training at Camp Travis over the past two months. All of them were now officially members of the Third Texas National Guard and headed to Harlingen to join several U.S. Army Infantry and Cavalry units that had been stationed along the border for over a year. John Marcin listened to bits of chatter here and there, but most of the men were taking the opportunity to get some shuteye.

John Marcin watched the world pass by outside the train car. It felt familiar, and he soon realized the tracks ran alongside much of the same road he'd traveled to Helena years ago. Not much had changed. It was the same dusty landscape. As the train picked up speed, the click and clack of the train's wheels lulled him into a deep slumber.

Out of nowhere, John Marcin was jostled awake. The train was racing toward a dark tunnel, a pinprick of light at its center. The cars penetrated a hillside, and the temperature dropped. He fumbled in the darkness, his fingers brushing against the window. He could feel frost forming across its surface and scraped the condensation off the glass with his fingernail. In a flash, the train shot out of the darkness and into a blinding white light. When his eyes began to adjust, John Marcin found himself standing in the middle of a vast field surrounded by tufts of dry grass and thick bushes with long, sharp thorns along their tangled branches. He had no idea how he had gotten there. In the distance, he could see a small grove of cedar trees. "Frankie! Tater!" he tried to cry out, but his throat locked. John Marcin ran toward the trees, thinking they might offer shelter and a higher vantage point to gauge where he was.

John Marcin did not hear the creature approach but sensed its presence a split second before two giant talons tore into his flesh and lifted him off the ground with such force that it felt like his arms were being wrenched from their sockets. The trees grew closer at high speed, and the beast's claws retracted upon approach. John Marcin crashed into the treetops, their branches scratching and ripping his skin. His body came to rest, and he looked around, seized with fear. He was hanging from one of the massive pecan trees on the square in Helena, his feet dangling above the lowest bough. Before him stood the empty gallows, and there was not a soul to be seen. John Marcin struggled to free himself, but the collar of his shirt was snagged on a broken branch. The pressure of the fabric tightened around his throat with each movement of his body.

Footsteps sounded, and a red-haired boy appeared beneath the empty nooses. Panic shot through John Marcin's entire body, and his ragged respiration quickened. The boy made his way to the edge of the platform. He peered at John Marcin in the tree and opened his mouth wide. The bottom half of his face began to dissolve into a dark space where his bottom jaw should have been, and a gust of air, smelling of rot, filth, and loathing rushed into John Marcin's nostrils. The taste of the foul scent coated his tongue, and his stomach soured. What followed was the most menacing of howls, spiraling into an angry roar interspersed with wicked laughter.

"Shabah! Diabeł!" John Marcin screamed in terror. Everything went black, and he could feel his body convulsing. Then he heard a woman calling out loudly and clearly from the direction of the courthouse.

"Leave him!" she cried.

"John Marcin, wake up," another voice implored.

John Marcin felt someone grab him and shake him hard. "Tater, I said leave him! He's having a bad dream." It was Frankie.

John Marcin blinked and tried to focus. Tater stood over him, a look of concern on his face. "Whoa, friend. You're white as a sheet. What the heck were you dreaming about? You look like you've seen a ghost," he said.

John Marcin looked around, still dazed and confused. The train had arrived at a small depot. The sign on the one-room station house read Beeville. He needed some air and pushed toward the exit. He threw open the compartment door, and a blast of wind chilled his lungs. A whistle blew, and the soldiers on the platform began to gather their bags and say farewell to loved ones. John Marcin noticed one young man, taller than most, standing alone near the ticket office. His uniform hat was too big for his head and sat low over his ears. He was watching John Marcin. A second whistle blew, and the crowd began to move toward the train. John Marcin was about to return to his seat when the young soldier lifted his hat in greeting, revealing a shock of red hair beneath. John Marcin's chest tightened.

"On or off?" the conductor frowned.

"Um, on," John Marcin stumbled.

A surge of bodies forced John Marcin back onto the train. He lost track of the red-haired man, but once the new passengers were settled and the train departed from the station, he set off to find the curious soldier. He searched each car twice on the short trip between Beeville and Harlingen without success. When the conductor announced the approach to their final stop, John Marcin returned to his seat and assembled his gear.

"Where'd you go?" Frankie asked. "We thought you'd jumped off the train."

"Restless, I guess. Had to stretch my legs," John Marcin replied.

Frankie offered him his canteen. "Drink some water. You look peaked."

"We're here! We're here!" Tater announced. "Would you look at all them boys with their rifles. Must be a hundred or more in front of the station."

*   *   *

The first few weeks at base camp floated by in a haze. Tater barely completed basic training at Camp Travis and fared no better during the additional training at the Harlingen garrison. He still couldn't run a full lap around the barracks, so off to the camp kitchens it was for him. John Marcin and Frankie, on the other hand, were deployed right away. John Marcin was assigned to a transport unit, given he was one of the few new recruits who could drive an automobile, and Frankie was placed in an infantry field unit after a near-perfect score at the rifle range.

The men were housed in temporary bivouacs that lined

Harlingen's streets and spread over several city blocks. John Marcin shared a canvas tent with five other men a few steps from the sprawling horse pens erected at the center of town. While the whinnies and scents of the animals were comforting and made him feel more at home, the general state of the crowded accommodations was primitive, the worst being the poorly planned latrines, which were few and far between and always at full capacity. When the new recruits complained, the drill sergeants reminded them that on the border it was even rougher, and daily constitutions out among the scrub brush presented the clear and present danger of a snake or scorpion bite with each squat, so they should be grateful. This reminder was often followed by a shower of profanity and a rotation cleaning the horse stalls or, worse, the latrines themselves.

Nevertheless, John Marcin soon settled into a routine. His mornings were filled with miles-long runs in the hills at dawn before the heat set in for the day, followed by calisthenics. Afternoons included rifle practice, field drills, and mechanics training in the truck depot near the train station. During his fourth week, he was assigned to the regular convoy delivering supplies to the units stationed along the border. Save a few tense days in March 1916 following Pancho Villa's attack on Columbus, New Mexico, and border crossings here and there along toward Big Bend over the early summer, John Marcin and the other men accepted that there would not be much excitement in the offing. The hardships and monotony of daily military life set in soon after.

By the fall, morale among the men had plummeted. The commanding officers decided it was time to boost the soldiers' spirits. They announced a jamboree on the main square one Saturday evening, with musical entertainment and special rations of steak, frijoles, and fluffy tortillas. The men were disappointed to learn that no liquor would be served, but that was to be expected. Soldiers had already been barred for months from frequenting local saloons and houses of ill-repute with the stated goal of maintaining discipline and curbing the rampant venereal disease plaguing the border garrisons.

John Marcin arrived late that Saturday from his supply run to Brownsville, covered from head to toe in dust from the road. He was starving, so he did not take the time to do more than brush his uniform and splash some water on his face. Tater stood behind a long table, scooping piles of meat and beans onto plates. "Look what the cat drug in, boys," he shouted over the music. A bluegrass band was playing on a makeshift stage in the square. "That was a long haul, eh?"

"Sure was. Give me a good piece, Tater. No gristle," John Marcin ordered.

"Got a nice juicy one right here for ya," Tater scooped up a thick, sizzling piece of steak from the grill and placed it onto a bed of steaming refried beans.

John Marcin scanned the crowd for any familiar faces and saw Frankie, who was sitting at a table next to the stage. He headed that way.

"How was the trip?" Frankie asked, a toothpick dangling in the corner of his mouth.

"Long and hot. Same as usual," John Marcin replied as he devoured his supper. He hadn't eaten since breakfast. As he drew his sleeve across his chin to wipe the drips of juice off his face, the officer in charge of the army band tapped the microphone to quiet the audience.

"Listen up, boys," the officer announced. "Our next band has traveled all the way from Wichita Falls for your listening pleasure. Please give a warm Harlingen welcome to the Pipe Creek Posse!"

Applause and cheers exploded from all directions. Frankie's head jerked around, and John Marcin sat motionless, staring at the stage.

"Hello, Harlingen!" Albert Schulte greeted the crowd with a swish of his fiddle bow. Louis Schulte followed with his guitar suspended across his stomach by a braided leather shoulder strap, and Joe Schulte after that with his stand-up bass fiddle under his arm. Anna arrived last and joined her brothers at center stage. She was taller and thinner than John Marcin remembered, and her dark hair was slicked back into a tight bun at the nape of her neck.

"This here is Miss Anna, and she's gonna sing a few for ya tonight," Albert announced.

Anna moved in front of the microphone, cradling it in her hands, and the crowd of soldiers exploded with catcalls.

"Is that…" Frankie pointed at the stage.

John Marcin nodded, mouth agape.

"Good evenin'," she said. "This one is called 'High on a Mountain Top.' I hope you enjoy it."

Albert counted down, and the band kicked off the first few bars.

Anna bounced to the beat. "As I look at the valleys down below, they are green just as far as I can see," she sang out into the night. "As my memories return, oh, how my heart did yearn for you and the days that used to be." As the song built to the chorus, "High on a mountain top," she sang louder. "Thinking about the days that used to be." When she reached the next line, she spotted John Marcin. "Well, well," she stuttered, losing her place in the song for a beat before catching herself. "Well, I wonder if you ever think of me."

When the set was over, John Marcin pushed his way backstage. Anna was helping her brother Joe lift his bass into the bed of a rusted-out truck. "Anna?" John Marcin said.

Anna looked at him with no visible sign of recognition at first.

Joe eyed John Marcin suspiciously and stepped between his sister and the presumed stranger. "How can we help you, soldier?"

"Relax, Joe," Anna said, a warm smile breaking across her face. "He's a friend from Bandera. Anderwald, right?"

"That's right," John Marcin replied, nervously passing his service cap back and forth between his hands.

Joe looked at John Marcin for another uncomfortable moment. "Hmm, big ranch along the Medina? Strange bird name?"

"Yes, that's right. Peacock Bend." John Marcin's gaze lingered on Anna.

"You got five minutes, Anna." Joe wiggled his fingers in front of her face. "Bertie will be back soon."

John Marcin waited until Joe was out of earshot. "I wasn't sure you'd remember me."

"Took me a minute, but sure. How are you?" Anna leaned back against the side of the truck. She was wearing heavy stage makeup, but John Marcin could see that she was still as beautiful as he remembered.

"Fine. Uh, other than I'm stuck here and there's no end in sight," John Marcin said. "And you?"

"No complaints, I guess. Been on the road for some time, so I know what it's like to be far from home." Anna nibbled at her thumbnail.

"Sure was a terrific show tonight, really great." John Marcin could not hide his exuberance. He waited for Anna to say something, but she only continued to bite her nails and watch him. "So, what happened? Why'd you leave Bandera?" he continued.

Anna raised an eyebrow and chuckled. "That's a long, long story I don't have time to tell right now, John Marcin."

His heart skipped a beat. Anna did remember him. "When might you have some time?" he asked.

Anna looked past John Marcin and fell silent. "Anna!" a man shouted from the rear of the stage. John Marcin turned to see Albert Schulte barreling toward them. "Anna, where the hell have you been?" he demanded, his speech slurred.

Anna jumped around to the back of the truck. John Marcin instinctively put more distance between them and donned his cap. He stood at attention with his hands clasped behind his back.

"I'm right here, Bertie," she replied, her head bowed.

"Who the hell is this?" Albert said.

"Nobody, Bertie. He's one of the soldiers assigned to assist the bands. That's all. He was helping Joe and me get the bass in the truck."

Albert stared at John Marcin as if trying to assess his intentions or maybe place his face. "Get the gear loaded already. I need a drink," he announced.

"Yeah, of course you do," Anna said with the slightest hint of sarcasm.

Albert started in her direction. "What'd you say to me?"

Anna extended her hands out in front of her body. "Nothin', Bertie. I didn't mean anything by it. You go on over to the hotel. Joe, Lou, and I will meet you at the bar." Albert glared at his sister before stomping off. "I'm sorry about that," Anna said, hurrying to load the truck. "He's a mean drunk."

John Marcin stepped closer. "Anything I can do?"

"I'm fine. Don't you worry about me."

John Marcin took a deep breath. "I'd like to hear that story of yours sometime. How long are you here for?" he said.

"Another day or so," Anna offered tentatively. "I'll be at church tomorrow morning if you want to join me. Maybe we could take a walk after that?"

"You go to church?" John Marcin regretted the question before he'd even finished asking it.

"The Lord intended a day of rest and prayers for forgiveness even for us lowly sinners, John Marcin, but if you're not interested…"

"No, no! I'm sorry. I'd love to. I didn't mean—" he stammered.

"If it won't shame you to be seen with me, be at First United at ten o'clock sharp," Anna said as she slammed the truck's gate closed and followed her brother into the night.

*   *   *

The final clang of the old bronze church bell summoning the parishioners of First United Methodist Church sounded from the belfry. The door, its massive cedar frame warped from years of exposure to the elements, opened with a violent yank. Anna was late. She entered the chapel, a whirl of untamed hair falling over her face. She was wearing the dress she'd worn on stage the night before. The lack of modesty in her Sunday attire caused several of the older folks to click their tongues. "Such impertinence," a woman seated near John Marcin remarked to her husband.

John Marcin was alone in the middle of the last pew on the right, save one withered farmer hunched over in the seat along the aisle. He watched Anna approach, the bright morning sun cascading in behind her. From the moment she crossed the threshold, John Marcin could not look away. He watched the swivel of her head, the way her long earrings shimmered in the light. Anna stepped into the row, failing to avoid the old farmer's toes. "Excuse me. So sorry. Oh, my goodness me," she giggled.

Anna took a seat. John Marcin could feel the heat of her body and smell the light perfume on her skin. He was mesmerized as she opened and closed her handbag, rooting for something she couldn't seem to find. She finally extracted a shawl from its depths. Anna tilted her head to the side, catching John Marcin's eye. In the brief seconds when he might have played off that his was a passing glance, he could not look away. Anna winked and blew John Marcin a flirtatious kiss. She reached for the hymnal and joined the congregation in song, singing louder than anyone else.

CHAPTER 22

Port Isabel

T he Pipe Creek Posse's next stop after Harlingen was the Elks Lodge on Market Square in Brownsville. The band's booking for a weekend of morale-boosting shows for the troops stationed at nearby Fort Brown had extended to five weeks and counting. After their first show, Anna's brother Albert had picked a fight with some soldiers from New York, accusing them of flirting with Anna. The Yankees broke one of his legs in two places, fractured his nose, and nearly broke his bowing arm before the police arrived. The Exalted Ruler of the Brownsville Elks, whom John Marcin suspected also had hopes in Anna's direction, offered to let the hobbled Posse serve as the lodge's house band in exchange for room and board during Albert's convalescence. Morale had never been higher.

For John Marcin, these months had been magical. His whole world was set right for the first time in a long time. After their first encounter in Bandera, he had often thought of Anna, or at least the idea of her, but assumed that night at the ball had been a fluke. Yet, there she had been, on the stage in Harlingen, her fiery green eyes seeking him out in the crowd. And now he was here in this miserable town on the Texas-Mexico border whenever he could get away on leave to be with her.

"I'm headed to Port Isabel on Thursday to deliver supplies. Why don't you ride along with me?" John Marcin suggested as they strolled around the square, close enough their elbows brushed against each other.

"Is that allowed?" she asked.

"Officially, no, but it'll be a fair exchange of mutual discretion. My lieutenant's got a standing craps game with a few of the officers stationed there. Goodness knows I've turned a blind eye his way a time or two."

"I'll see if I can get away. Bertie gets agitated if I'm gone too long."

John Marcin frowned. He didn't much care for Anna's oldest brother, always watching her and ordering her around. Anna made excuses for Albert's behavior, and John Marcin couldn't figure out why. He also had a feeling—nothing he could yet put his finger on—that she was afraid of her brother.

"Anna, Albert can certainly get around when he wants a drink. I've seen him do it more than once. I gather he could do the same for a bit of grub," John Marcin said. "And why the hell do you wait on him like you do?"

John Marcin could see Anna's defenses engage whenever they talked about her brother. She refused to explain why she gave in to his demands. "I said I would try, and I will," she replied.

"Fair enough. I'm sorry," John Marcin said and took her hand.

Anna pushed him away. The entrance to the Elks was only a few paces ahead. "I must go. It's late," she said, darting into the lobby and up the stairs.

The following Thursday morning, John Marcin stood at the base of those same stairs waiting for Anna. It had been nearly twenty minutes, and the supply truck's horn blasted for a second time from the street. John Marcin's passenger was clearly losing patience. John Marcin skipped halfway up the staircase, stopping when he heard Anna and her brother arguing.

"And what am I supposed to do all day?" Albert complained.

"You manage to get yourself to the bar every damned night," Anna replied. "You're not a cripple. Besides, I'll be back in time to fetch your supper, so quit fussing."

"Don't be like that, Anna. I need some company. Joe and Lou are off somewhere, too," her brother said in that sickening and deceptively sweet way of his. "Come sit a spell with me before you go."

"Seriously, Bertie?" she said. "It's not even ten o'clock in the morning, and you're already drunk. Get outta that damned bed, splash some water on your face, and go get some fresh air, will ya?"

Anna rushed out onto the landing and slammed the door. She looked startled when she saw John Marcin on the stairs. She hurried past him, repeatedly looking back at the door as if to make sure Albert wasn't following them.

"Everything all right?" John Marcin asked when he caught up to Anna outside where the truck was parked.

Anna jumped into the middle of the front seat. "I'm fine," she said, leaning forward to take one last look back in the direction she'd come.

John Marcin cleared his throat and gestured toward the other passenger. "Anna, this is Lieutenant Blakely. Lieutenant, this is my cousin Anna, the one I've been telling you about."

Distracted, Anna had not acknowledged the man seated beside her. She bobbed her head and offered a timid smile.

Blakely tipped his cap. "Hello, *Cousin* Anna. Anderwald, let's get a move on."

Anna remained silent during the drive but appeared to relax a little more with each passing mile. The skies were a bright blue, and the air was balmy as they bounced along the road running northeast out of Brownsville and ending at the docks of Port Isabel on the Gulf of Mexico. Thanks to John Marcin's adept navigation of the rough dirt track and his fearless penchant for top speeds, they arrived within the hour. The lieutenant disappeared into a small shack on the wharf with several other soldiers, and John Marcin unloaded the cargo while Anna waited for him on a bench near the water.

After his last load, John Marcin emerged from the central warehouse with an army-issue wool blanket tucked under his arm and a tin bucket swinging at his side. "Hey, Cuz! Shall we take a walk? I've got a picnic for us," he said.

Anna turned and smiled. The weight of whatever was going on with her brother seemed to lift ever so slightly. "I'd be delighted, Private Anderwald."

When they reached the beach, they kicked off their shoes. John Marcin tied his boots together with their laces and hung them over his shoulder. He watched Anna remove her shoes and stuff them into her bag. She wriggled her toes in the sand, their manicured nails painted bright red. They ambled barefoot, hand in hand, the cool water rushing up the beach and around their ankles. John Marcin guided Anna around a gentle bend in the shoreline toward a lighthouse looming over a rocky pier. They made their way around to the far side, hidden from the rest of the world, save the seagulls flying playfully above the foamy surf.

John Marcin laid out the blanket and began to unpack the contents of his bucket: enough sandwiches, fruit, and cookies to feed a regiment, along with several beers. "It helps to have a friend in the kitchens," he said and popped the caps off two bottles.

Anna drank too fast and let out a loud belch. "Oh, goodness," she blushed. "I'm so sorry."

John Marcin laughed. "Why are you always apologizing?" he said, stroking her cheek.

Anna shrugged.

John Marcin bent forward and kissed her on the mouth. "Outta my way. I'm starving!" he said playfully, reaching over her for a sandwich.

After they'd eaten the last bite of food and drained another two bottles of beer, John Marcin put his boots back on. He already felt light-headed from the alcohol. "Come," he said, helping Anna up from the blanket. "Last one to the top of the lighthouse is a rotten egg!"

A steep circular staircase constructed from heavy steel twisted into the dark interior of the tower. John Marcin could hear Anna's footsteps bouncing off the walls below as he arrived at the top. He stood at the window looking over the crystal-blue Gulf waters sweeping across the endless horizon. Anna approached him from behind and wrapped her arms around his waist, pressing her body against his. He could feel the blood pumping in her chest. She nuzzled him beneath his earlobe.

John Marcin turned to face her. "You're so beautiful," he said, holding her face and kissing her again, this time longer and harder.

Anna ran her hands over John Marcin's hips but quickly pulled away.

"What's wrong," he asked.

"I don't wanna ruin it," she said. "Like I always do."

John Marcin raised his hand to tuck a piece of Anna's hair behind her ear and glanced at his wristwatch. "Damn," he said.

"What is it?" Anna looked worried.

"Nothin'. We need to watch the time, though."

"I can't do this much longer," Anna confessed.

John Marcin frowned. "I'm sorry. This is the best I can muster for now."

"I know, but I don't like it," she said, turning toward the window.

"You know there's a chance I'll have to go and fight or at least stay on here to help guard the border, right?"

"Of course I do. I'm not arguing. I just said I don't like it."

"Point is, Anna, my situation will not change any time soon, and I can't start a real life with you until this war is over."

Anna appeared truly astonished. "You wanna have a life with me? Why?"

"What do you think this is, a fling?" John Marcin could not hide his growing frustration.

Anna turned away again and muttered something under her breath. All John Marcin could make out was a name. Bertie.

"What does that boozehound have to do with this?" he snapped.

"Please don't talk about my brother like that. You have no right," Anna whispered.

"Damn it, Anna!" John Marcin groaned and slammed his fist on the stone windowsill.

Anna raised her hands as if to shield her face from an impending blow. John Marcin stepped back and lowered his voice. "I didn't mean to frighten you," he said.

Anna raced down the steps.

John Marcin took a deep breath and followed. He found her kneeling on the sand, face toward the sky. He knelt beside her and touched the small of her back. "Please talk to me."

Anna swallowed hard before speaking. "I love you, John Marcin Anderwald. Or at least I think I do. I don't have much to go on when it comes to knowing what love is."

John Marcin rested his cheek on the top of Anna's head. Her hair smelled of gardenias. "I love you, too," he said softly. "And I'll take care of you. I promise."

Anna sniffed and wiped her nose with the back of her hand.

John Marcin gently lifted Anna's chin and kissed her for a third time. This time, things felt different. The instant their lips touched, Anna laid back on the blanket. John Marcin followed her lead, stretching out beside her, his arm resting across her stomach. She turned onto her side and grabbed his shirt, pulling him closer and kissing him back, her teeth sinking into his bottom lip.

"Do you want..." John Marcin didn't finish his sentence.

Anna smiled.

"Are you sure?" he asked, uncertain what to do or say next.

"Never been surer of anything," she said.

John Marcin traced the outline of Anna's waist before touching the buttons on the front of her blouse. Anna's chest heaved as he began to unbutton her shirt. She slipped her own hands under his waistband and stroked the tender skin of his stomach with her fingertips. They took their time, undressing each other slowly. Fully exposed, Anna took hold of John Marcin, pulling him on top of her. John Marcin had never felt such a fury of longing. He hoped Anna couldn't tell that he didn't have much experience and managed to control himself long enough—or at least tried his best—to ensure that she was satisfied before his quiet release. Afterward, they lay for some time listening to the waves crashing along the beach with increasing intensity toward the evening's high tide.

John Marcin reached for his uniform as the vermillion-tinged sun drifted toward the horizon. "We better get going," he said.

Anna shook the sand from her skirt and combed through her windblown hair with her fingers. They laughed nervously as they straightened their clothes and gathered the blanket and picnic bucket. When they reached the docks, Lieutenant Blakely was already standing near the truck, stuffing a wad of cash into his pocket.

"We won't have to worry about him, I see," John Marcin said with relief. "Looks like lady luck was with the lieutenant this afternoon. Heck, he might even buy me a drink tonight."

The drive back to Brownsville was as quiet as the drive out to Port Isabel, but the atmosphere was thick with satisfaction on all fronts. All of that dissolved, however, when they arrived back in town. Anna's whole body tensed. "Stop right here," she said, a few blocks from the square. "I can walk the rest of the way."

"Let me drop you in front of the lodge," he said.

"Right here," she insisted, pointing toward the side of the road.

John Marcin looked at Anna with confusion and concern. He pulled to a stop. "Whatever you want," he said. John Marcin helped Anna out of the truck and onto the sidewalk. He tried to kiss her.

She stiffened. "Not here. Someone will see," she said.

"Who cares?" he said and tried to kiss her again.

"I'm serious. Stop." Anna shoved John Marcin back. The look on her face was no longer playful. "I must go. I'm so late. Bertie will—"

"Forget about your damn brother, for God's sake! He doesn't own you." John Marcin could feel his anger rising.

Anna shrunk back against the side of the truck. "I'm sorry," she mumbled like a scolded child.

John Marcin sighed. "Listen, I'll be back in a month when I have my next leave."

Anna brushed her fingers across her lips.

John Marcin stepped closer and hugged her. "Four Sundays. That's it. Meet me at the church when I get back?"

"It's a date," Anna snuffled with a quick smile and slowly walked backwards along the sidewalk. "Last pew on the right, and don't you be late," she said with a shake of her finger.

Anna turned and hurried toward the entrance to the lodge, scanning both sides of the street like frightened prey. John Marcin watched her until she disappeared inside.

*　　*　　*

It would be nine weeks before John Marcin could return to Brownsville, including Christmas and New Year's. All hell had broken out overseas in Germany, and General Pershing's quest to capture Pancho Villa was abruptly halted. Troops and equipment were being diverted away from the Texas-Mexico border and in the Kaiser's direction. John Marcin and his unit had been caught in the shifting winds of war.

It was a cold Friday night in late January 1917 when John Marcin finally made his way back to Anna. He tumbled through the front doors of the Elks, scanning the crowd for her. Albert was on stage with another local act, fiddling away. The room was packed, tongues were loose, and the smoke was heavy. John Marcin spied Anna at the bar, surrounded by numerous gentlemen of varying ages, including the wizened Exalted Ruler himself, who were jockeying to buy her a drink and obviously waiting for the right opportunity to make their move. He approached her from behind and tapped her shoulder. Anna spun around in her seat, bleary-eyed and drunk.

"Look who we have here, boys," she seethed, eyeing John Marcin. A few men at the bar inched closer as if to form a barricade.

"Anna, what's going on?" John Marcin said, standing his ground among the other suitors.

"Go to hell!" she spat and slapped him hard across the cheek.

Anna prepared to strike him again, but John Marcin grabbed her wrist to prevent another blow. "What the hell!" he cried.

"Where have you been for over two months, huh?" Anna said, her words slurring. "You come in here after all this time without one goddamned word and think I'm gonna be all sweet and nice?"

All eyes were on John Marcin. "What are you talking about? Didn't you get my letters?"

Anna glowered at him. "Letters? What letters?"

"Can I have a word?" John Marcin took her by the elbow. "In private?"

"No, you cannot," Anna barked, yanking her arm away. "Anything you have to say to me, you can say right here in front of my friends." She pointed her finger around the room and teetered on the edge of her stool. The group of men, tempers on the edge from a night of drinking, began to press forward again.

John Marcin spoke softly but insistently. "Anna, I swear to you. I sent letters every week. Lieutenant Blakely brought them himself. Said he left them for you at the bar."

Anna took another sip of her drink.

"Listen to me. I know what you're thinking, but you must believe me. I got dispatched on a supply run to Fort Ringgold in Rio Grande City. From there, I got put on another troop transport to Fort Bliss way out in El Paso. Lieutenant Blakely will most certainly vouch for me. I couldn't get back here until this very minute."

Anna scowled at the barkeep. The man raised his arms in surrender. "Don't look at me, Miss Anna. I gave them letters straight to Albert the minute they arrived. Go on, you ask him."

"Anna, hurry," her brother Joe beckoned from the dance floor. "Break's over."

John Marcin reached for Anna, but she shoved him away and stumbled through the crowd. Stunned and confused, John Marcin followed her. Albert was standing on the side of the stage.

"What's he doing here?" Albert asked as he rosined his fiddle bow.

"Where are my letters?" Anna demanded.

"Burned 'em. No use in getting your hopes up. That soldier's only on the make like all the rest of them bums you raise your skirts for," her brother sneered.

"You sonofabitch!" Anna pounced, but Joe held her back.

Albert stood over Anna. "Listen good, Baby Sister. You want a smack right here and now in front of all these people? In front of him?" Albert spoke through his teeth without moving his lips. "Don't you mouth off to me if you know what's good for you."

John Marcin stepped between Anna and Albert. "Hey, don't talk to her like that," he said.

"You best keep your nose out of my family's business, soldier, and your hands out of my sister's knickers," Albert lashed back.

John Marcin started forward, but Joe put a hand on his chest. "Leave it. You'll just make things worse for her."

"Don't you threaten me, Bertie, you sick bastard!" Anna exploded. "You need more from me than I will ever have the stomach to give you. That's for sure. Let's get this damned show over with and get paid what we're owed 'cause I'm done!" Anna stomped onto the stage.

John Marcin retreated to the bar and watched Anna and Albert warily during their performance. Anna kept her distance from her brother, crossing to the opposite side of the stage every time he eased her way. As soon as the last chord of their set rang out, Anna ran out to the alley behind the lodge.

John Marcin ran after her. "Anna?" he called.

"Go away," she said, steadying herself against the corner of the building.

"I wanna make sure—"

"I said, go away. Leave me alone," Anna pleaded and bent forward, retching into the gutter.

"Let me help you." John Marcin took Anna by the waist. "Here, drink this," he said, offering his canteen.

Anna took a short sip and swished the water around in her mouth before spitting it onto the ground. "What do you want from me?" she moaned.

The night air was chilly, and Anna started to shiver. John Marcin took off his uniform jacket and covered her shoulders. They stood in silence for several minutes. "A little too much to drink?" John Marcin finally spoke, trying to be tender.

"Yes... Er, no. That's not it."

"What is it? Tell me." John Marcin gritted his teeth. His patience for Anna's evasiveness about anything she feared might not be well received was wearing thin. "Tell me what's wrong."

"It's nothing. Forget about it." Anna could not look John Marcin in the eye.

"I'll tell you what's wrong," he insisted. "I don't get how you could think for even a second that I'd up and leave you without a word. Have you not been listening to anything I've told you? I love you. I would never...." John Marcin went quiet again. Would I never? he began to wonder.

It was like Anna was reading his mind. She panicked and could barely catch her breath to speak. "J- J- John Marcin, I'm not drunk," she stumbled. "All right, maybe I am. A little."

"What is going on?" he pleaded.

"I figured you'd left me."

"That can't be all of it. You need to be honest, or I can't help you." Anna buried her face in John Marcin's chest. "God damn it, Anna! Tell me right now!" he said, pushing her away.

Anna shrunk back against the brick wall of the building and took a deep breath. "I'm pregnant."

The words struck John Marcin like a punch to the face. "You're what?" he finally managed.

Anna recoiled, her head bowed, and her arms folded tightly across her chest like armor. "I'm so, so sorry."

John Marcin's mouth ran dry, and his palms were sweating.

"Please say something," Anna whimpered. "I really am sorry."

"There's no need to apologize," John Marcin said, his mind racing. "It's as much my doing as it is yours. We'll fix this."

"What do you mean?"

"I'll speak with Albert and—"

"No!" Anna gripped John Marcin's arm. "Bertie can't find out about this. He'll kill me. I mean it."

The moon peeked out from behind a cloud, its sharp winter light revealing bruises along Anna's arm, on her cheek, and under her eye that she had tried to hide with thick makeup. John Marcin touched the black and blue patches with his fingertips. "Anna, did Bertie do this?"

Anna didn't have to answer. John Marcin bolted back into the bar.

"John Marcin, don't! Stop!" she begged.

A crowd gathered around the scuffle that erupted on the dance floor. Albert was lying on the ground and trying to fend off John Marcin, who straddled him, landing blow after blow about his head and face.

"That's enough," Louis Schulte finally said, stepping into the melee and pulling John Marcin off Albert. When John Marcin continued to throw punches, Louis grabbed him by the collar and threw him onto the dance floor. "I said enough," he grunted.

John Marcin struggled to his feet. It was then he saw Joe Schulte holding Anna by the shoulders near the stage. "Let go of me!" she demanded.

"Show's over, folks," Louis announced, pulling Albert off the floor and steering him toward the exit. He was barely conscious, and his face was covered in blood.

"Anna, stay back," Joe warned. "He'll never let this go. You know that."

"I should at least make sure he's not hurt too bad," she said.

"No, Anna. We must leave," John Marcin intervened.

"Don't tell me what to do! He's still my brother, and it looks like you hurt him bad. Bertie! Bertie!" Anna cried.

"He's right, Anna," Joe broke in. "John Marcin, you gotta get her away from here. She'll never be safe around Bertie again. Nor you, so go. Far away as you can get."

CHAPTER 23

Safe Harbor

John Marcin helped Anna gather what few belongings she had. Albert was still out cold in the adjoining room, but Louis stood guard at the door as a precaution. Anna yanked open the drawers of a large wooden dresser, their warped sides scraping against the frame and dislodging flakes of peeling paint into the air. Out of the top drawer, she scooped underwear and stockings into her arms and stuffed them pell-mell into a tattered red leather suitcase. She reached into the back of the drawer one last time and extracted a small tin box, immediately flinging it against the wall and scattering small keepsakes and a photograph bent and ragged at its corners across the floor. The photo landed at John Marcin's feet. It was a picture of a little girl leaning over a porch rail, an older boy standing behind her. Both were grinning from ear to ear. John Marcin recognized the faces. It was Anna and Albert.

"You bastard!" Anna screamed and gripped the sides of the bureau.

John Marcin took her in his arms. "Easy, I'm right here."

"Bertie," Anna sobbed. "Bertie, why?"

"You better get going," Louis said.

"Bertie," Anna repeated over and over as she and John Marcin descended the stairs and headed into the unknown.

John Marcin sped north and did not ease up on the gas until

the lights of Brownsville had dissolved in the rearview mirror. He drove straight through the night, with only a short stop at the garrison to secure a weekend pass. As they raced toward Bandera, John Marcin began to formulate a plan. Anna could not, of course, stay with him at the base. He would have to hope that his parents would take her in. He was not sure what he would do if they said no.

John Marcin and Anna crested the road leading to Peacock Bend at sunrise. The cattle lowed across the pasture as they approached, and a peacock raised an alarm from the roof of the barn. "Eee-you! Eee-you!" it shrieked, sending the camels and the goats into a restless whirl in their pens. Anna began to stir. "Are we there?" she asked, stifling a yawn.

Smoke was already rising from the chimney of the main house. "Yes, we're home."

Anna took John Marcin's hand in hers. "Will you tell them straight away?"

"No. I think we'll have some breakfast first," John Marcin answered with a nervous chuckle. When Anna didn't laugh, he squeezed her hand. "Don't worry."

The brakes squealed as they came to a stop. The front door opened, and Zacharias stepped onto the porch. "Liza, come quick! It's John Marcin," he hollered back into the house as he hobbled across the yard.

"Papa!" John Marcin threw his arms around his father.

Liza ran outside, still tying the belt around her bathrobe. "What a wonderful treat," she said, showering her son with kisses on each cheek.

"Mornin', Mama," John Marcin said with a soft smile.

Anna remained by the passenger door.

Liza squinted in her direction. "And who might we have here?"

John Marcin beckoned Anna forward. "This is Anna. Anna Schulte. Anna, these are my parents, Zacharias and Liza Anderwald."

"Pleased to meet you both," Anna said with an awkward curtsy.

Zacharias gestured toward the house. "Why don't you come on in out of the cold?"

John Marcin could feel his parents' eyes on their backs as he and Anna entered the house. He was not sure what to say next, but time was short. A forty-eight-hour pass was the best Lieutenant Blakely could do.

Liza excused herself to get dressed, and Zacharias put the kettle on. John Marcin sat beside Anna at the kitchen table.

"Where's your family from, Anna?" Zacharias asked.

"From around here. We lived over on Pipe Creek when I was a girl."

"Wait, you're Hans and Mary Schulte's daughter?" Zacharias said with a look of guarded recognition. "The singer?"

"Yes, sir. My family has, or I should say, had a band." Anna began to wring her hands in her lap. "The Pipe Creek Posse, but I don't expect you've heard of us."

Liza emerged from the bedroom. "I knew I recognized you, dear," she said as she retrieved an apron from a hook on the wall. "I think John Marcin's father and I may have seen you perform at one of our church socials. But that would have been some time ago."

"Yes, ma'am. It's been a few years since I've been back to Bandera."

Liza watched Zacharias prepare to pour the coffee. "Goodness me! You put out those old, chipped mugs for company?" she scolded. "John Marcin, run to the cupboard in the dining room and fetch the good china. Bring saucers and plates, too. And Zachek, you've forgotten the cream and sugar."

John Marcin hadn't seen his mother this nervous in a long time. Liza set to preparing a spread of bacon and eggs.

"So, how did the two of you become acquainted?" Zacharias asked, doing his best to make conversation.

"We met some years back when I was in school but lost track of each other when Anna moved away," John Marcin replied. "One night a few months ago, there she was again, singing away on the main square in Harlingen."

"Do you live in Harlingen now, Anna?" Liza chimed in.

"No, ma'am. My brothers and I were traveling and performing most of the past year until—" Anna glanced quickly at John Marcin.

"Anna and her brothers have been renting rooms in Brownsville since the fall. One of her brothers was injured, and they've been staying there while he recuperates," John Marcin explained. "I have regular occasions to stop through on my supply route, and it's been nice to have a familiar face from home," he added.

"Here we are," Liza said, setting the food on the table. "Dig in before it gets cold, dear."

"It looks delicious, Mrs. Anderwald. Thank you," Anna said, inhaling her first helping.

Liza and Zacharias watched Anna push a last piece of bacon onto her fork with her fingers. "Would you like some more?" Liza asked.

"Yes, please," Anna replied, her mouth full. "I can't remember the last time I had a hot breakfast."

John Marcin joined her for seconds, and the conversation around the table again stalled. The only sound was the clanging of silverware against his Grandmother Eugenia's china. Liza rose to clear the dishes after all the plates were emptied, and John Marcin noticed Anna trying to stifle a yawn. "Mama, it was a late night and a long drive. I think Anna might like to take a bath and rest a bit. Can I put her in the guest room?"

"Of course, of course. Let me help you get settled," Liza offered.

"Mama, stop fussing. I can show her the way."

"I'll go and fetch her things from the truck," Zacharias said as he pushed his chair out.

"No, no. I'll bring them later. You sit and relax, Papa."

John Marcin led Anna down the hallway. They didn't speak until they were behind closed doors.

"You should have what you need in the bathroom there," John Marcin said, pointing toward the hall.

Anna crossed the room and stared out the large window. "It sure is nice here," she said. "You can see all the way to the river."

John Marcin joined her. "You can see the Medina from almost every room in this house. My parents wanted it that way." John Marcin took a deep breath and exhaled slowly. "That river is why my family is here."

"Makes sense," Anna said. After a long moment of silence, she cleared her throat. "I think I'll go run a bath. Then I might lie down for a bit. I'm so tired."

John Marcin heard the water start in the tub and leaned back against the windowsill. He hadn't been in this room since the day Grandpa Marcin passed and was laid out on the same patchwork quilt that now covered the bed. His grandparents' photos stood in tarnished silver frames on a small desk brought from the old farmhouse. John Marcin knew the pictures well. The one of his Grandpa Marcin was taken on the Bandera Courthouse's front steps just before the trial in Helena. The one of his Grandma Aga, whom he'd never met, was much older. It had been taken at a St. Stanislaus summer picnic on the banks of the Medina at some point during the Civil War. The third always made him smile. Sergeant Kirby, Khalil, and another wrangler, Khalil's brother Ahmad, posed with a herd of camels on the parade ground at Camp Verde.

An ornately carved wooden box, its brass hinges blackened from age, stood next to the frames. John Marcin lifted the top and peered inside, where he found a pair of scissors and a small fabric ball stuck full of rusted pins and needles. There was also a notebook with a thick lock of blond hair bound by a strip of yellowing muslin tucked inside its cover. John Marcin slowly leafed through the pages filled with Polish phrases written in his grandfather's precise hand and their English translations beneath. Toward the end, one page included a list of names and birthdates, including his own on the last line.

The bed springs squeaked. John Marcin tucked the notebook back inside the wooden box. He hadn't heard Anna return from the bathroom. "What's all that?" she asked as she climbed under the covers.

"Some old things of my grandfather's. Brings back memories."

Anna coughed. John Marcin noticed the faint cloud of her breath on the air and realized how cold the room was. "You'll freeze in here with that wet hair. I'll run and fetch some wood for the stove," he said.

"John Marcin, wait," Anna said. "I want you to tell me the truth. Are you sure it's no trouble for me to be here?"

Anna started to sit up, but John Marcin urged her back onto the bed. He could feel how thin she had become. Her collarbones protruded from under her skin. He sat on the edge of the mattress.

"Of course, it is," he assured her.

"It's obvious your parents have heard the rumors about my family. I can see it on their faces. I expect they disapprove of me."

"You're imagining things."

"I'm not sure about that," Anna muttered.

"Stop worrying," John Marcin said, tucking the blanket tighter around her body and kissing her forehead. "You'll feel much better once you've had some rest."

Anna was soon asleep, and John Marcin headed off for a much-needed bath of his own. Afterwards, he checked in on her, adding wood to the stove and watching the slow and steady rise and fall of her chest for a few minutes before making his way out to the parlor. He heard the clink of a crystal decanter, followed by liquid trickling into glasses. His parents rarely drank, and the fact that they were imbibing before the sun had set told him all he needed to know. He'd avoided the conversation long enough. John Marcin entered and poured himself a finger of whiskey before joining Zacharias and Liza by the fire.

Liza started. "Are you gonna tell us what's going on?"

"They're sayin' if things keep getting worse over in Europe, some of us might be headed over." John Marcin knew he was not answering his mother's question.

"Your mother was talking about the girl, I believe," Zacharias said.

John Marcin took a short sip of his drink. "Right. The girl." He paused again and pretended to wipe something off the rim of his glass. "I've been calling on Anna for a few months, and things are getting serious."

"What do you know about her? About her family?" Liza asked.

"I've heard all the rumors, if that's what you're asking, and that's all they are," John Marcin insisted.

His parents exchanged looks of concern. "The Schulte family has had a long and troubled history in these parts," Zacharias said. "There were more than rumors regarding the treatment of Mrs. Schulte by Mr. Schulte."

"What does any of that have to do with Anna?" John Marcin interrupted.

"Son, if you would let me finish." Zacharias looked hard at John Marcin. "After Hans Schulte ran off, Sheriff Stevens was out to that farm on a regular basis. Those boys were always scrapping. Bills were never paid."

"Papa, I've heard those same stories."

"John Marcin, you also need to be aware that the sheriff was directed on several occasions by concerned parties to investigate complaints about the oldest boy. I can't recall the name."

"Albert," John Marcin said, not realizing he'd spoken the name aloud. His stomach turned. He'd never heard anything specific about Albert, only the vague stories about the violence between Anna's parents and the family's money problems.

"Yes, that's right. Albert Schulte. Sheriff Stevens was investigating alleged improprieties between Albert and his young sister. And my understanding was that they were serious improprieties."

Liza crossed herself before swallowing the rest of her drink, and John Marcin sat frozen in his chair, staring at the bottom of his glass.

"The family fled before an investigation was completed, but the questions, or rumors, as you say, were never put to rest," Zacharias continued. "Mind you, I am not blaming that girl, but—"

"Enough!" John Marcin said and jumped up. He stood before the fireplace, the flames warm against his skin.

"Why exactly have you brought her here?" Zacharias asked.

It pained John Marcin to see his parents worry. "Anna's not safe in Brownsville. She needs a place to stay. Especially now. I can't leave my post in Harlingen, and she can't stay with me there."

"What do you mean by 'especially now'?" Liza's tone betrayed a growing sense of dread.

John Marcin lowered himself back into his chair and cradled his head. He knew the news he had to share would shock and disappoint his beloved parents, perhaps offend them. He had to tell them, beg for their charity and grace, and someday hope for their forgiveness. "Anna is with child," he confessed.

"Oh, John Marcin. No," Liza grimaced.

"Mama, I am sorry, but I did not come here for your judgment, harsh and deserved as it may be. I came for your help," John Marcin replied.

Liza and Zacharias did not say a word. John Marcin dropped his head once again into his hands.

The heavy silence was shattered by screams coming from the bedroom. John Marcin ran toward the noise, his parents on his heels. "Anna! Anna!" he cried and burst through the door.

The room was freezing cold again, and wisps of what looked to be black smoke wafted toward the ceiling from the bed. Anna was sitting upright, wide-eyed like a trapped animal. "He's trying to take the baby," she whimpered.

"Who is?" John Marcin pulled Anna close. She burned with fever and shook with chills.

"The shadow," she croaked.

John Marcin looked at his father, who was standing in the doorway. "Get some more wood for the fire," he said. "Papa!" he shouted when Zacharias did not move.

Liza leaned over the bed and felt Anna's forehead with both hands. "You poor dear," she soothed.

"The shadow," Anna sobbed. "He's here."

Liza laid Anna back onto the pillow and took charge. "No, John Marcin, you go fetch the wood," she instructed. "Zachek, you run and get Zee."

Zee came straight away, her leather medical bag—willed to her by Doc Adolph upon his passing in honor of their unofficial, but longstanding professional partnership—in hand. Her first directive was for Liza to bring fresh water and clean towels. Her second was to send Zacharias and John Marcin out of the room. "Leave. I will take care of things," she said, pushing them toward the door.

Anna moaned. John Marcin turned to say something but was met by the door closing firmly in his face. "Come," his father beckoned and headed toward the kitchen. "Zee will take good care of her." Neither father nor son spoke of the shadow.

By the time Zee emerged from the bedroom two hours later, night had fallen. John Marcin and his parents were seated at the table, sipping tea. Zee unfolded and buttoned the cuffs of her dress and joined them.

"How is Anna?" John Marcin asked, nearly toppling his cup.

"She'll be fine," Zee said. "Needs food and rest, but her strength should come back soon."

"And—"

"Baby's fine. Lucky that girl is as far along as she is. Hard to tell at first. She's so skinny," Zee said. "Fever can take a fetus when it's starting, but this one was a few months on."

"A few months?" John Marcin knitted his brow.

The midwife peered at John Marcin. "Six, maybe seven. Baby will come before summer."

Zee had brought John Marcin into this world and helped raise him. She knew him better than most. John Marcin immediately understood that the healer had discovered what neither he nor his parents had considered but would undoubtedly have to face. This child could not possibly be his.

"That baby's gonna need more than its momma. Somebody to keep the Devil away, I suspect." Zee's attention remained fixed on John Marcin until Liza placed a plate of food on the table and distracted her. "If you don't mind, Miss Liza, I'll take my supper home," Zee said. "Already past my bedtime, and Khalil will be wonderin' where I've gotten to."

"Yes, of course. You go on. Thank you for your help," Liza said, wrapping Zee's plate in a dishtowel.

John Marcin did not say another word. He followed Zee out the door. She headed to the barn, and he started toward the river.

CHAPTER 24

I've Decided I Will Love Her

John Marcin cracked the door to Anna's room. He peered in from the darkened hallway, his wet clothes dripping on the floor. The glow of the few remaining embers in the stove offered the only light in the room. The twinkle of distant stars beyond the window caught John Marcin's attention. He tiptoed past the bed and placed the palms of his hands and his forehead against the cool panes. He saw something stir in the pasture. It wasn't the longhorns. They were still in their pens near the barn. John Marcin's heart began to pound in his chest as he looked closer. A woman was approaching from the river. She wore a long white dress with puffed sleeves and a full skirt. He blinked, and the figure jumped. She now stood at the front gate, her head pivoting from side to side as if scanning the house. How had the woman reached the gate so quickly? He blinked again, and the woman was outside the bedroom window. Her face was blurred, but he saw two large dark eyes staring back at him.

"He is gone now," the figure said, her voice muffled by the glass.

John Marcin blinked a third time, and the woman vanished. The blankets rustled on the bed behind him, and he turned around. Anna sat up and brushed her hair away from her face, still sticky with sweat. She licked her lips and reached for the glass of water on the nightstand. "Hey, there," he said.

216 J. E. Weiner

"Hello," she replied after a few sips.

John Marcin remained at the window. "I didn't mean to wake you."

"You didn't. What time is it anyway?"

"Nearly five-thirty."

"In the morning?"

John Marcin looked at his watch. "Yep. After Zee left, you slept the whole night through."

"Zee?" Anna seemed confused.

"You don't remember what happened last night?" John Marcin moved to the bedside.

"You're all wet. Where have you been?" Anna asked.

"Down by the river."

"Why?"

"Couldn't sleep. Got caught in the rain."

"You and your mother are gonna catch your deaths running around outside with no coats, getting soaked to the bone."

"My mother?" John Marcin knew the woman he'd seen was not Liza. A sharp burst of fear surged in his belly.

"She was out in the yard in her nightdress earlier. You didn't see her?"

John Marcin did not want to burden Anna or himself with talk of ghosts. There were more pressing issues to address. "My mother has been in bed for hours," he said.

"Never mind, I must have been dreaming," Anna sighed. "Won't you sit with me? I've been alone in here all night. I've missed you."

John Marcin remained standing. "You must be hungry," he said. He could feel the strain between them.

"What is it?" Anna asked, appearing to brace herself for the answer.

John Marcin kept his distance. "Nothing. I'm wet and cold, is all."

"You sure that's it?"

"Jesus, Anna. What do you want me to say? I was worried about you," John Marcin paused before continuing. "And your baby—" He did not finish his thought.

Your baby. The words landed like an anvil between them. John Marcin could see the shame and sadness on Anna's face.

"John Marcin, I—"

"Don't. We're gonna make this right, but I need the truth. Is it mine?" John Marcin watched the wheels spin in Anna's head. He knew that her first impulse would be to lie. It always was when it came to difficult topics. Her childhood, why her family fled Bandera, Bertie. John Marcin raised his hand before Anna could answer. "No, don't tell me. I don't want to know," he said.

"How is that even possible?" Anna whispered.

John Marcin reached out tentatively for Anna's hand. "So, I've been thinking about this all night. I don't much care about how we become a family, but I..." John Marcin bit his lip. "I am clear minded about one thing. I want to be with you. I love you."

"But why?" Anna whimpered. "I'll ruin this, and I'll surely ruin you."

"Stop it," John Marcin said. "None of this is your fault, no matter what that manipulative brother of yours told you."

Anna recoiled like she'd been slapped. "I'm sorry."

"How many times do I have to tell you to stop apologizing to me? There's nothing to be sorry about," John Marcin barked but immediately softened. "Marry me before I go back to Harlingen. No one will be the wiser."

"How? Where?" Anna looked stunned.

"It won't be in a church, but I suspect that might be for the best given the circumstances. And you'll stay here at Peacock Bend. My parents and Zee will care for you until I return."

"But—"

"Trust me. It's settled," John Marcin said.

Anna nodded.

✳ ✳ ✳

John Marcin struggled with his tie. He addressed the haggard reflection staring back at him in the mirror. "It's the only choice you've got. Buck up," he said out loud.

"John Marcin," Liza spoke through the bedroom door. "It's Mama. May I come in?"

John Marcin dropped the ends of his necktie in frustration. "Um, yes, ma'am," he said.

Liza opened the door. "Don't you look handsome," she said warmly. "I wanted to check and see if you needed anything."

John Marcin fought back his tears. For pity's sake, he was a grown man. He would not cry in front of his mother.

Liza began to tie a knot in his necktie. "Tell me. How can I help?"

John Marcin shrugged. "I'm not sure. All I know is that she needs me. She needs us."

Liza smoothed John Marcin's curls. "Oh, I almost forgot," she said, reaching into her dress pocket. She withdrew a long hairpin capped with a small peacock, its tail feathers spread and dotted with tiny blue sapphires. It was a final birthday gift from Granddaddy Stanard. "Give this to Anna," she instructed.

"Mama, you don't have to do this," John Marcin said.

"Something borrowed and something blue all in one." Liza pushed the pin into John Marcin's hand. "Those confounded birds!" she laughed nervously, wiping a tear from her cheek.

"That's not what I meant."

"I know. Listen, I was hoping the two of us would have an opportunity to talk a little bit, and now seems as good a time as any."

John Marcin steeled himself for the worst.

"I lost and mourned many a child before I was blessed with you, my beloved and only son, whom I love more than anything on this earth," Liza sniffed, taking John Marcin's hands in hers. "And because of that love I feel for you, I've decided a few things over the past couple of days." Liza took a deep breath. "First, I will honor and respect your choices in life, even if they would not have been mine. And so, I offer you and Anna my blessing on this marriage without condition."

"Thank you, Mama," John Marcin said, his head bowed.

"Second, I have also decided that I will accept the child like my blood with no further explanations required."

John Marcin looked away, overwhelmed by his mother's kindness.

"And I have decided that I will love Anna. Of course, it would have been easier for us all if things had happened in a natural order, but that cannot be helped now. Besides, I suspect that girl has suffered a deficit of affection in her life to date. It is time to start anew," Liza said softly. "She is welcome here in my home and in my family."

John Marcin collapsed onto the mattress and covered his face with his hands.

"Hey, hey, don't go messing up your father's suit or, more importantly, that perfect hairdo," Liza smiled and patted his leg. "Come. Everyone's waiting."

John Marcin retrieved Anna from her room. She was wedged into the one stage dress that still fit, and the hairpin from Liza sparkled atop her head. She looked beautiful. John Marcin tried to explain how everything was happening so fast but even he was not entirely sure. A man named Steiner, a clerk of some kind and Zacharias' longtime business acquaintance, arrived at midday. He'd agreed to expedite a marriage license and officiate. John Marcin overheard the man remarking to Zacharias that fast-tracked nuptials were becoming more common because of the impending war. But John Marcin assumed his father had asked for a favor.

Zacharias, Liza, Khalil, and Zee were already gathered in the parlor. The clerk got right to the formalities as soon as John Marcin and Anna joined them. Signatures were affixed to the various documents, champagne was poured, and toasts were offered to Mr. and Mrs. John Marcin Anderwald. The remainder of the impromptu event went by in an immemorable flash.

After his parents retired, John Marcin joined Anna in the spare room. He would be leaving in a few hours for Harlingen. Both were a bundle of nerves. Anna was pacing and fidgeting with her nightgown, and John Marcin was uncertain whether he could muster any desire to touch her knowing what he knew. The idea of Anna with another man was difficult enough, but the thought that it might have been Albert made him sick. John Marcin silently scolded himself. He understood that Anna's misfortunes were not wholly of her own making, but still. He made the first overture, climbing between the sheets and holding them back so that Anna could join him.

"You will come back for us, won't you?" she asked tentatively as she slipped into the bed, her eyes searching John Marcin's.

"We are a family now, and that's that," he said and kissed her softly on the cheek.

Anna wriggled her gown over her head and tossed it to the ground. She turned to face John Marcin. He could feel the lump in her abdomen pressed between their naked bodies, connecting them and keeping them apart at one and the same time.

"Oh, my," Anna said, touching her belly. "The baby. It moved."

John Marcin rolled onto his back and stared at the ceiling. The delicate soul dancing within Anna's body was an innocent in all this mess. There was no turning back.

CHAPTER 25

Thy Lovely Face

John Marcin heard the garage door open and close with a loud bang, followed by the thud of army boots at a fast clip across the cement floor. "Anderwald, you under there?"

John Marcin seized the truck's rear axle and pushed the mechanic's trolley from under the vehicle. One of the young clerks from the garrison's main office stood over him. "What do you want?" John Marcin asked.

The clerk waved a tell-tale yellow envelope back and forth in the air. "This came a few minutes ago. Lieutenant said I should run it over to you straight away."

John Marcin sat up and wiped the grease from his hands with a rag. "Thank you," he said. The clerk remained in place, watching expectantly as John Marcin ripped the envelope open. "I believe I can read this without any assistance from you, so, that'll be all."

"Suit yourself," the boy snapped and retreated, the metal door slamming behind him.

John Marcin unfolded the telegram and took a deep breath. His eyes skipped over the page.

1917 MAY 21=SPC JOHN MARCIN ANDERWALD=NATIONAL GUARD GARRISON HARLINGEN TEXAS=IT'S A BOY BORN YESTERDAY [STOP] MOTHER AND BABY WELL

J. E. Weiner

[STOP] WORD FROM YOU MOST WELCOME=PAPA.

He reread the message before stuffing it in his pocket and rolling back under the truck. There was no point in asking for a leave. With enlisted troops already being gathered up right and left for transport to France and news of the impending draft blasted across newspaper headlines, the commanding officers had been clear that all soldiers were to remain on duty until further notice. No exceptions. A few of the boys sent home earlier in the spring had already been reactivated. Tater had a tantrum when he got word of his recall as he stepped off the train in San Antonio on his way home. Frankie volunteered to stay behind and was soon deployed to a new field artillery regiment in the U.S. Army's 36th Division. John Marcin followed orders and submitted a copy of his marriage certificate that his father had sent by post. He would take the telegram to the registration office to ensure it was also included in his file. This likely meant that he'd avoid being sent over to the trenches.

John Marcin stared at his tin plate in the mess tent at dinner. Charred steak and beans again. The garrison's menu had grown tiresome. Without warning, three shot glasses slammed onto the table from above his head. John Marcin found Frankie and Tater standing before him. "We hear congratulations are in order," Tater announced and sat down. "When were you gonna tell us?"

"Only got word earlier this morning," John Marcin said.

"This calls for a celebration, yes?" Frankie dug a small flask out of his jacket and filled the glasses.

The three men hunched forward and downed the shots in one quick swallow. "Ah, that hits the spot," Tater said.

Frankie held up three cigars, and Tater produced a box of kitchen matches. John Marcin snipped the ends of the cigars with a pocketknife and the friends puffed away at the sweet tobacco.

"What're you gonna call the boy?" Frankie asked.

"I think Tomas is the perfect name, don't you?" Tater giggled. "Regal and elegant, I'd say."

"Shut up, Tater," Frankie chided. "John Marcin doesn't want to jinx the kid. Of course, if you want a name that will bring your boy luck, best choose Franz."

John Marcin did not refuse when Frankie offered him a second shot. He would write to Anna tonight. It would be his first letter home since a brief note sent two months before to say he'd arrived safely back at camp. Now that the baby was here, his silence could neither be excused nor forgiven.

Later that evening, John Marcin stared at a blank page, pen in hand. Several sheets of paper lay crumpled into balls on the corner of the small metal desk. *Dear Anna,* he began again and went back to change *Dear* to *Dearest,* squeezing the additional letters into the small space between the words. He paused before scribing the note in one final draft.

> *Dearest Anna,*
> *Please forgive the long silence. I've no excuse worth offering.*
> *I received my father's telegram and am relieved that you and the baby are safe. I'll leave the choice of name to you, as you have shouldered the more considerable burden in bringing this child into the world.*
> *War appears inevitable, and we all await news of what's next. I am not afraid, but I am also not easy. I don't relish leaving you alone for so long, but nothing to be done about it.*
> *Give my best to all at Peacock Bend.*
> *Yours,*
> *JM*

John Marcin tucked the note into a small envelope without rereading what he'd written. He extinguished the gas lantern and flopped into bed, his bunkmates snoring and worse in the cots beside him. He stared at the tent's ceiling, the glow of streetlamps outside distorting the folds of the canvas. John Marcin had done his fair share of worrying for one day—Anna, the baby, his parents, the war, all of it. Fatigue tugged at his eyelids, and he ceased resistance to sleep or to dreams.

The next thing he knew, he was standing in the hallway of the ranch house at Peacock Bend. His father and Khalil were whispering in the kitchen.

"You heard same as me, Chief," Khalil said.

"It was a bad dream. Nothing more." Zacharias sounded exhausted.

"Shabah is back. We must protect the boy," Khalil said more insistently. "He is not strong enough to fight such things. You know when evil comes here, Chief, it is strong."

"Leave it, Khalil," Zacharias said.

The room began to tilt, and John Marcin felt like his head was splitting, and the deepest and blackest of darkness descended. "Papa?" he called.

It was Khalil who replied. "Come."

John Marcin found himself in the camel pen outside the barn.

"We go to Zee. She has something for you," the wrangler said, signaling for John Marcin to follow.

Zee was waiting at the door to the apartment behind the hay loft. "John Marcin, my love," she cooed. A calm immediately descended. Zee had always treated John Marcin like her own, the child she had never borne herself. All the babies she brought into the world were hers in some way she always said. Zee led him to a small table near the stove and sat down across from him. "Hands!" she demanded and smacked the tabletop. John Marcin reached toward the medicine woman, and she grabbed his hands, hers cracked and leathered from a life of struggle but warm beneath the skin. She ran her index fingers across the lines on his palms, and when she was finished, she placed her own palms over his and began to chant in a language John Marcin did not recognize.

Zee stood and retrieved a glass jar from the fireplace mantel. She rejoined John Marcin at the table and unscrewed the top of the container. She dipped her forefingers inside and withdrew an oil-like substance that smelled of sage. "Close your eyes and mouth," she ordered.

John Marcin felt Zee's two fingers touch his forehead and descend over his eyelids to the tops of his cheeks. She did the same over each nostril and across his lips, then pushed the tips of her fingers into each ear canal.

"Stick out your tongue," Zee said and placed a drop of oil on its tip.

John Marcin felt rough hands on his face and opened his eyes. Khalil stood before him. "Zee protects you from the demon. You are safe now," he said.

"Anderwald, time to head out," another man squawked. John Marcin squinted into the sliver of sun darting through the flap of the army tent. It was Lieutenant Blakely. "I said get your ass moving, soldier!"

It had only been a dream.

A reply to John Marcin's letter did not come for nearly two weeks. This time, the telegram had been tossed onto his desk a few days after its arrival, soiled with greasy fingerprints and a dark ring from a coffee cup.

1917 JUNE 12=SPC JOHN MARCIN ANDERWALD=NATIONAL GUARD GARRISON HARLINGEN TEXAS=LETTER RECEIVED [STOP] JOHN MARCIN ANDERWALD JR BAPTIZED SUNDAY LAST [STOP] REGRET TO REPORT KHALIL DIED A WEEK AGO TUESDAY [STOP] PASSED QUIETLY IN SLEEP [STOP] WRITE MORE, WILL HELP [STOP] STAY SAFE=PAPA

As he read the words printed on the yellow slip, John Marcin felt the bottom fall out of his stomach and his throat clench. He had dreamed of the wrangler on the night he had passed. "Khalil," he said out loud. "Ya akhi, my brother, no." John Marcin lowered himself onto his cot and wept. He wept for Khalil, his parents, Anna, and the child he'd not yet met. For the first time in months, he longed for home.

* * *

By the summer's end, John Marcin, Frankie, and Tater found themselves back on a train, this time heading north out of Harlingen. The Kalka boys had been assigned to the Guard's Lone Star Division and were due at Camp Bowie in Fort Worth for training within the week. They would shortly be on a ship to Europe. John Marcin had received orders to report to Camp Travis outside of San Antonio. His Lieutenant had put in a word so that John Marcin

might be stationed closer to home, given his new baby and the hardships his elderly parents faced with the loss of their ranch foreman.
John Marcin was not scheduled to report until the end of August,
and he had a week's leave ahead of him. None of the men had much
time to pack, let alone alert their families before they departed the
garrison. John Marcin doubted he'd have sent word in any case.
Anna never replied to his letter. He planned to hitch a ride to Bandera from San Antonio and make his way to St. Stanislaus for Sunday morning services.

"Next stop, San Antonio," the conductor announced.

The train began to slow upon its approach, the grinding of
steel on steel along the rails followed by a long whistle announcing
its arrival. John Marcin sat alone, and Frankie and Tater slept in the
row behind. They would continue to Fort Worth.

"This is my stop," John Marcin said. The Kalka brothers stirred
and yawned as he removed his bag from the rack. "Don't get up. I
just wanted to say goodbye."

Frankie moved into the aisle and grasped John Marcin's hand,
pulling him into an embrace. "You take care of that beautiful girl
and that baby, you hear?" he said, slapping John Marcin on the back.
"You've been blessed."

"I know," John Marcin replied.

"So, if you know that, stop acting like a condemned man."

John Marcin smiled weakly. "Stay safe over there, you hear?"

"Don't you worry," Tater declared with a snort. "We're gonna
kick that Kaiser's ass all the way back to Berlin!"

"Oh, Jesus, Tater," Frankie scoffed. "The only assaults you'll
be making will be on our boys' bellies with the crap food you'll be
cookin'. Probably send us all back to the trenches with the runs."

"You shut yer yap, Frankie!"

"No, you shut up!"

"Both of you shut up," John Marcin interceded. "Save it for
the Krauts. Keep your heads down and get yourselves back home as
fast as you can."

John Marcin exited onto the empty platform. As he raised his
arm to offer a final wave, he observed another soldier taking the
seat in front of the Kalkas where he had been a moment ago. John

Marcin's hand stopped in mid-air. He could see the passenger's profile—bushy eyebrows, a sharply angled nose and chin, and thick red hair. The train began to pull away. John Marcin walked along the side of the car, trying to get a better look. The man turned and looked out the window, slowly blinking his pale-blue eyes. Shivers cascaded along John Marcin's spine and left him paralyzed.

"It can't be," he whispered.

* * *

John Marcin tipped his cap to the old sharecropper in the driver's seat. "Thank you kindly," he said and watched the pickup pull away. He removed his uniform jacket and brushed off the hay he'd been sleeping on in the back of the truck, threw his duffel bag over his shoulder, and jogged across the street.

The morning sun reflected off the bronze bell suspended high in the belfry above the entrance to St. Stanislaus. The windows were open, and the door at the entrance was ajar. John Marcin could hear a familiar soloist rounding the last verse of 'Come Thou Fount of Every Blessing.' He eased inside and immediately spotted his parents standing in a pew a few rows from the front. A head peeked out from the crook of his mother's arm. Liza swayed back and forth, trying to keep the infant quiet. Anna was standing before the altar with the choir. John Marcin took a seat in the last row. He saw Anna notice him. She looked him straight in the eye and began to sing the final lines of the hymn. The words and their haunting melody burrowed deep into John Marcin's brain, along each nerve in his body and back to center, filling his aching heart.

Oh, that day when freed from sinning
I shall see Thy lovely face.

Yes, John Marcin smiled to himself, thy lovely face, indeed.

CHAPTER 26

Homecoming

As the final clouds of the war to end all wars gathered over the Argonne Forest and receded east over the Meuse River in the fall of 1918, a new bank of storm clouds rolled across the hills of Bandera County and settled over the Medina. While John Marcin dutifully traveled back and forth from his wartime post at Camp Travis whenever he could to see Anna and the baby, he was also forced to confront what most folks politely referred to as the difficult circumstances of his home life.

The baby, Junior as he was known, was not right from the start, and most could tell with one look. The child's pinpoint pupils stared out from a head disproportionately compact atop a stocky body. Worse, the poor thing mewled, night and day, depleting his parents of their last reserves of patience and much of their affection for him and each other.

Then there was Anna. Gossip continued to swirl about the drink and the dalliances but talk of her mental instability started up after word of Albert Schulte's suicide by a shotgun blast to the face reached Bandera on Halloween. He'd been buried by Anna's brothers somewhere out in West Texas. Anna locked herself in her bedroom for nearly a week and dissolved into a booze-fueled depression. John Marcin confessed he could not understand Anna's grief over the loss of the brother who had visited so much trauma upon her, nor could he remedy the self-loathing that lingered long after. He desperately hoped that his love for Anna, all-consuming and blinding as many considered it to be, would be enough to rescue his young family. Alas, it was not. Anna would often fall silent, withdrawing to the dark corners of the ranch, or bolt for parts unknown, returning hours or sometimes days later with the faint whiff of whiskey on her breath and occasionally another man's coat draped across her shoulders.

John Marcin awoke one night to the sound of running water in the kitchen. He brought the rocking chair to a complete stop and stood, careful not to jostle Junior, who had settled at last. John Marcin gingerly placed the child in the bassinet under the window and tiptoed down the hall.

Anna was bent over the sink, drinking from the spigot. Her hair was tangled, and the hem of her dress was loose.

"It's almost midnight." John Marcin's tone was flat and even.

Anna jumped, banging her forehead on the faucet. "Dammit, don't scare me like that."

John Marcin flipped on the kitchen light. "Where've you been?"

Anna shielded her eyes from the glare of the bulb. "Out. But I'm back, as you can see." When John Marcin did not respond, she added, "Why can't you trust me for once?"

"I think you owe me an explanation. That's all."

"Oh, I see what's going on. All those folks yammerin' in your ear, 'that Anna Schulte's no good.' You're starting to believe them." Anna began to cry. "Why am I always to blame?"

"Nobody's blaming you," John Marcin said. He was tired of the waterworks.

"The hell they aren't," Anna lashed back. "You, too. You think I can't see the disgust on your face? Don't notice how you don't touch me when you come home?"

"Enough," John Marcin said. "All I'm asking is that you have the decency to tell me the goddamned truth," he insisted through clenched teeth. "So, I'll ask you again. Where were you?"

"I believe I already said." Anna became more combative.

"Tell me again, 'cause 'out' is not a satisfactory answer as far as I'm concerned."

"As far as you're concerned," Anna mocked. "Fine. If it will ease your insecurities to have an accounting of my evening, I went over to Boerne to pick up some sheet music for the choir from St. Peter's. The stupid motor car wouldn't start 'cause I couldn't get the crank to turn. And who's fault is that, huh? You were supposed to fix it."

"Right," John Marcin said. "Thing is, Anna, your story doesn't make much sense, seein' that you're three sheets to the wind. Did you also pick up some of the church's altar wine?"

"Oh, for God's sake!" Anna cried. "The only place open was a bar on the main street, and no, I don't recall the name. Some bar. So, I went to see if anyone could give me a hand. A nice gentleman offered to help. The least I could do was buy the man a drink to say thank you. There. Satisfied?"

John Marcin did not reply.

"Is this interrogation over? Can I go to bed?" Anna asked.

Again, John Marcin said nothing. Anna groaned in frustration and pushed past him. He listened to the click of her high heels receding and the slam of the bedroom door. John Marcin tensed, worried she might have woken the baby. After a few minutes of quiet, he turned to the dirty plates in the sink. The fireworks were over for the night.

*　　*　　*

Soldiers soon began to trickle home from Europe's battlefields over the winter of 1919, some broken in body and some in mind, and with them came a sickness even more deadly than the Great War itself: influenza. The residents of Peacock Bend were hit harder than most. Zee was the first to succumb. She had traveled from ranch to ranch to nurse the youngest victims of the outbreak in those early days but fell ill on Good Friday and was gone by Easter morning. John Marcin helped Zacharias carve a wooden cross topped by a crescent moon and star to match Khalil's, and father and son headed to the hilltop, shovels in hand. Liza joined at midday to say her goodbyes. Anna refused to leave the house for fear of sickness and stayed back with the baby.

"I guess we should have sent for Father Adamietz," Zacharias said as he pushed the grave marker into the soil.

"I don't think he would have come to say prayers over a healer," Liza said.

Zacharias sighed. "But I don't have the words myself to do her justice. She was a remarkable woman. And Khalil," Zacharias turned to the wrangler's grave, now overgrown with sage grass, "my dear friend, you loved Zee more than anything in this world, so I suspect your being together in whatever afterlife awaits is what you would have wanted. I wish you both peace, ya akhi."

Liza smiled and took Zacharias' hand in hers, their gnarled fingers gently twining together. "I think those are the perfect words, Zachek."

John Marcin longed for the love his parents had for each other. He wished for the connection beyond language, religion, and homeland that Khalil and Zee had forged during their life together, for the devotion Sergeant Kirby showed his wife to the bitter end. Tears pricked at John Marcin's eyes. He knew he would never have any of that with Anna, but still, he hoped that things might change. John Marcin placed a bouquet of daffodils he'd picked on the mound of freshly turned clay. The instant the flowers' delicate yellow trumpets caressed the loamy soil, hollow, vengeful laughter floated up the hill from the river. Closer, among the trees on the hilltop, shadows flitted about their branches. John Marcin's pulse raced. He bowed his head and thrust both fists into the soft dirt. When he looked again, he saw the woman in white standing close, watching him.

Five weeks later, Anna Anderwald dispatched a ranch hand to Camp Travis to bring John Marcin home. Zacharias and Liza were failing fast. John Marcin arrived at dusk and rushed to his parents' bedside, donning a white cotton mask he'd taken from the army base's infirmary to try and forestall exposure to infection. Liza was already delirious with fever by the time he arrived, and an ominous cough rattled every bone in Zacharias' body. John Marcin immediately understood Anna's decision not to send for the doctor. There was nothing to be done.

John Marcin pushed the bedroom door open. "Mama, Papa, it's me," he said.

The creak of the door startled Liza. "My son," she rasped, her breath labored. John Marcin lifted his mother's hand to his cheek. The putrid smell of sickness seeped from the pores of her skin.

John Marcin moved to the other side of the bed and stroked his father's hair. "I'm here, Papa. It's all gonna be fine."

Zacharias began to hack, struggling for each intake of breath. He twisted and turned in the bed. "No," he managed before his chest seized again, propelling sputum from the depths of his lungs into the claggy cloud of death hovering about the room.

John Marcin remained with Zacharias and Liza for the entire night and did his best to make them comfortable. He washed their faces and hands and changed their pillowcases, but as the black of night descended, any expectation that they would survive to see another day evaporated. Although he arrived home in enough time to say his goodbyes, neither his efforts nor prayers could save the two people he cherished above all others. John Marcin threw himself across the end of the bed, his parent's feet against his chest. He needed to feel them in both mind and body.

At some point before dawn, John Marcin awoke to the sound of a woman humming in the darkness.

"Mamusiu!" Zacharias croaked.

John Marcin rushed to light the oil lamp on the bureau. No one else was in the room except his parents, who were lying slack-jawed and motionless in the bed and most certainly gone from this world.

*   *   *

The authorities' continued pleas to avoid public spaces fell on deaf ears, and the genuine prospect of contamination did little to deter the good people of Bandera on the morning of Zacharias and Liza Anderwald's funeral. Carriage after carriage, interspersed with the occasional automobile, made their way to Peacock Bend from the highway. The entire county had come to pay its respects.

Two faces in the crowd offered significant comfort to John Marcin. Frankie and Tater Kalka, who'd returned from Europe on a recent troop transport out of France, were among the early arrivals. It was the first time John Marcin had seen the brothers in nearly two years, and he barely recognized them in their civilian clothes. At first glance, Frankie looked the same, although thinner, but he could not hide the tremors in his hands.

"Lieutenant Kalka, good to see ya." John Marcin pumped Frankie's hand.

Frankie offered a vacant look, conveying uncertainty. John Marcin was not sure about what.

"Talk later, after all of this?" John Marcin gestured toward the gathering assemblage of mourners.

Frankie stepped back without a word.

"Oh, don't mind him," Tater broke in with a slap at the center of John Marcin's back. Tater was trimmer at the waist and had lost most of the pudge around his cheeks. "Our Frankie's a man of few words these days, and I am mighty grateful for that," he joked. Tater's belly still bounced when he laughed.

Anna approached with Junior on her hip, his nose stuffed from crying. "Well, well. Who have we got here?"

"Oh, right. Frankie and Tater, you remember Anna? And that's our boy, Junior."

Frankie seemed confused by the child, but something softened when he looked at Anna.

"Thank you for comin'," Anna said, her attention drawn to the elder Kalka. She bounced the child roughly on her hip.

"Course I remember you," Tater interjected. "And would ya look at this little guy," he said, tickling Junior under the chin.

Junior burst into another round of howls.

"Aw, June. Not again," Anna stomped her foot and quickly retreated.

The boyhood friends glanced at each other in awkward silence.

"Right, we'll leave you to it," Tater finally said, and he and Frankie moved to the rear of the group standing at the graveside.

The ancient Father Adamietz, who'd insisted on making the trip out to Peacock Bend to preside over the burials, began the service. "In this solemn grief over the loss of our dearest friends and community members, we find solace in the knowledge that they have gone to be with our Lord Savior, Jesus Christ."

A swarm of hands crossing chests passed through the gathering. John Marcin stood alone at the edge of the wide opening in the earth where Zacharias and Liza's coffins lay side by side. He had insisted that they share the same grave. It would have been their wish. He could not see Anna nearby but could hear Junior's interminable bawling.

"You will recall the story of Zacharias and Elizabeth in The Gospel According to Luke," the priest continued, "both of whom were 'righteous before God, walking in all the commandments and ordinances of our Lord blameless.' So, too, were Zacharias and Liza Anderwald. Take comfort in knowing that our blessed friends are walking among the angels in Heaven. Amen."

Another dissonant voice, quiet and angry, caught John Marcin's attention as a chorus of Amens rang out. "I am here," it hissed.

John Marcin was overcome by an oppressive sense of loss, loneliness, and despair that was greater than most would wish upon their worst enemies. Was this the demon Khalil had spoken of? The shadow that had so terrified his father and grandfather. He was not sure he had the strength to find out. John Marcin's head began to spin.

"Whoa, there. We got ya," Tater said as he and Frankie pulled John Marcin to his feet.

CHAPTER 27

Brothers Anderwald

Like the armies of Europe who'd returned to their native soils to lick their wounds, John Marcin and Anna Anderwald managed to maintain a cold détente between them despite the shroud of grief and regret hanging heavy over Peacock Bend. However, the years continued to unravel, as did John Marcin and Anna's relationship. Frustration was often expressed in silence, but tempers flared when Anna drank. The ominous shadow also never strayed far, waiting patiently for any chance to do harm, and the woman in white hovered ever close, desperate to repel the menacing force.

The spectacular break in the somber mood that appeared some eight years later when John Marcin and Anna welcomed a second son was a great surprise to one and all. Lucas Zachary Anderwald—great-grandson of Marcin, grandson of Zacharias, and though second in line in the fourth generation of Anderwalds, the first biological son of John Marcin as best anyone could vouch—burst into the world a vibrant child. His grip was firm, his latch upon his mother's breast tight, and his slumber deep. In the initial years after Luke's birth, the congregants at St. Stanislaus remarked that the color returned to Anna's cheeks, and for the first time anyone could recall, the young Mrs. Anderwald appeared to be happy. So did John Marcin, who stood a little taller and walked with renewed lightness in his step.

Alas, this respite from the storm at Peacock Bend would be fitful. And so, the fate of the Anderwalds of Bandera County continued to hang in the delicate balance between good and evil.

*   *   *

April 1936. At long last, the relentless spring rains had moved on from Peacock Bend. The pecan trees lining the path from the barn were in full bloom, and the bright green pods that would encase the year's crop were sprouting along their branches. John Marcin watched his son Luke deftly hop between the muddy puddles dotting the ground, the splash of his boots alternating with the creak of the rusty tackle box swinging at his side. Together with Junior, who had darted ahead, they were headed to the river for an afternoon of fishing.

Luke paused to fix his suspender strap, which had slipped off his shoulder. "Geez, Junior. Wait up, would ya," he said and set off again.

Junior trudged on without a glance back. This was part of a game he insisted Luke play. "Master and Servant," Junior called it. "I'm older and much smarter, so I'm the master, and you're a stupid little pipsqueak, so you're the servant," he would say.

Pipsqueak—or Squeak as Junior referred to Luke—and stupid would be the last two words most would use to describe John Marcin's younger son. He was a robust and handsome boy with smarts and savvy beyond his nine years of age. Strawberry blond curls framed his face, and deep-set blue eyes sparkled above broad cheekbones. While fairer, Luke bore an uncanny physical likeness to his Anderwald ancestors, but his infallible instincts for rhythm and harmony were all Anna.

A few years back, Anna had given Luke an old guitar she'd tucked away in the barn and showed him a few basic chords. From there, he taught himself to play by ear. Luke would listen to old Jimmie Rodgers' records over and over on the ancient phonograph in the front parlor, strumming and yodeling along. He'd even written a song for his mother's birthday the spring before. "Anna, my banana, so sweet you are to me," was the first line. Anna laughed so hard that she got a case of the hiccups that lasted for two days.

The blessings of health, vigor, and smarts bestowed in abundance upon Luke remained in relative deficit when it came to Junior. When the Great Depression hit, and the school closed because Bandera County couldn't pay its teachers, John Marcin decided not to send Junior back after classes resumed. The boy never did take to the strictures of the classroom, and John Marcin figured he'd be better suited to pitching in around the ranch in any case. Tater Kalka had also hired Junior to unload deliveries each week at his new dance hall in town, aptly and somewhat ironically named The Fox Hole. The extra money was a big help during those lean years.

"You're a good friend, Tater, taking him on like that," John Marcin said.

"Never you mind. I need a stock boy, and Junior's my man," Tater smiled reassuringly.

John Marcin lingered at the lower pasture. A small herd of longhorns ambled across the open field. The last of the camels at Peacock Bend, the ranch's third generation of the odd beasts, instigated arguments here and there but quickly stood down. Their geriatric teeth were long gone, so they did not present any real challenge or threat, and the longhorns knew it. A new herd of Angora goats grazed further along toward the river. Those goats saved Peacock Bend. The army couldn't get enough of their wool after the First World War, and when things got rough after the stock market crashed, fresh goat milk and cheese brought in more than a few much-needed dollars. John Marcin watched a nanny goat steering her two kids away from the herd and toward the far end of the pasture, her nervous bleating piercing the still air. Several of the cows began to bellow and snort in reply. The remains of the long-collapsed Mormon homestead peeked over the tall grass, hawks circling above the rotting wood searching for a midday snack.

"Everyone doin' fine up there?" John Marcin spoke into the clouds. He missed his family, found and otherwise. All of them. On days like this, he realized how blessed he had been as a child and how alone he was as a man.

A peacock cawed from the direction of the barn. "Oh-wow, oh-wow!" it crowed. John Marcin looked back toward the house, and a figure caught his eye. Anna must be out on one of her walks again, he thought and continued toward the river.

Junior lay on an outcrop of limestone on the bank, his head extended over the water. He was inspecting a dark pool churning beneath the rocks.

"Hey, June," John Marcin greeted his eldest.

"Where the hell you been, Pop?" Junior said, waving him over. "I've been waiting for hours! Squeak, hurry and get them poles ready. We gots us a bunch of large-mouth bass under there."

Luke scowled as he threaded the fishing lines through their guides and pushed sharp fishhooks through the midpoints of two fat, juicy worms. Junior jumped to the ground, grabbed the first rod, and scurried back onto the rocks. Luke went to join him, but Junior waved him away. "There's not enough room here, Squeak. Besides, this is my hole. Go find your own fish," he ordered.

"I hate when you call me that," Luke grumbled and headed further down the riverbank. John Marcin joined him under a colossal bald cypress, its roots twisting out from the mud and into the water below, creating a perfect spot from which to cast out into the slow-moving current.

"You know Junior. He gets a little crazy about his fishing," John Marcin said, trying to reassure Luke.

"I understand, Pop. He's simple, is all."

John Marcin flinched. "Who told you that?"

Luke hesitated before answering. "Uh, Ma did."

"Your mother should know better," John Marcin said.

"Yes sir," Luke mumbled but was distracted when his line began to whir.

The still unseen catch snagged beneath the surface darted toward the opposite bank. John Marcin leaned forward to help Luke reel in his prize, but the challenger resisted with gusto and nearly dragged them into the water. The fish's tail thrashed above the water line, sending wide ripples across the river's surface, followed by its entire body bursting into the air and plummeting back into the depths of the Medina. John Marcin and Luke continued to pull and wind together until a massive bass flopped onto the muddy bank, its gills pulsing and its mouth opening and closing rhythmically at first, then in random sequence, and finally coming to a stop. Luke lifted the dead fish and proudly placed it into his tattered wicker creel.

"Pop, I'm sorry about what I said." The boy had obviously been stewing over their earlier exchange.

John Marcin patted his son's head.

The afternoon drifted away, and the fish stopped biting, likely scared off by Junior's outbursts each time his hook got tangled in the tree roots. As dusk fell, the trio returned to the house, their catch of the day tethered to a string.

"Come look, Ma," Junior said with a slam of the kitchen door. "We gots fish. I caught the biggest one."

"That's nice, June," Anna replied dismissively from the other room. "Go on and get them cleaned for supper."

"Aw, it's Luke's turn to gut the fish," Junior whined.

"No, Junior, it's yours," John Marcin said. "Don't push your chores off on your brother."

"But Pop!" Junior protested, hurling the fish into the sink basin.

"Pop, I'll—" Luke interrupted.

John Marcin cut him off. "No, you wash up and join your mother. She's been waiting on you to help finish the choir arrangement."

"I gotta do everything around here," Junior groused, slamming a frying pan onto the kitchen counter.

John Marcin followed Luke into the parlor. Anna was sitting at Grandaddy Stanard's old piano, tapping out a melody with one hand, holding her old blue hymnal open with the other. The last of the day's light shone through the picture window onto the songbook's yellowing pages. The scent of Listerine mixed with gardenia from Anna's favorite perfume hung in the air. On the wall behind her rose the peacock mural John Marcin's mother had painted long before he was born. After forty years, the original paint maintained its brilliant color and sheen, and the brush strokes were equally sharp.

The floorboard creaked under John Marcin's boots, and Anna turned around. Her eyes were bloodshot, and the creases at their corners were deep and pronounced. "Howdy, darlins," she said.

"How's my little posse?"

"All right," Luke replied.

"Catch anything?"

"Yeah, we already said." Luke kicked the corner of the braided rug with the toe of his boot. "I caught the biggest one, but Junior keeps sayin' it was him."

"Don't pay your brother's braggin' no mind. Your Pop always sniffs out what's what in the end. Can't fool him." Anna winked at John Marcin and patted the space on the piano bench beside her. "Get on over here, Luke. I need your help."

The boy slid onto the bench, his hips brushing against his mother's. Anna bent over to kiss the top of his head.

"I gotta get this one straight," she said, launching into the first verse of a familiar hymn. "Will you sing the harmony line? You're always so good at that."

John Marcin watched as Anna and Luke dissolved into their own world among the stanzas of the old standards. A recurring flicker of hope sparked in his heart that today, this week, this month might be the moment when the savage grip of Anna's past would be released, and things righted, allowing her to return to him and their family.

*   *   *

A conspiracy was afoot at Peacock Bend—the good kind, as far as John Marcin was concerned. Though Junior could barely read or write, he was a whiz with all things mechanical, mastering everything John Marcin had taught him about fixing cars and trucks. He had a bustling auto repair business running out of the barn, stunning everyone with his new-found business acumen. John Marcin decided it was time for genuine celebration and planned to gift Junior Great Granddaddy Stanard's old Model T for his nineteenth birthday. John Marcin enlisted Luke's help to get the old jalopy cleaned up, with assurances the boy would keep his lips zipped about his brother's present.

After Junior's birthday feast of his favorite fried chicken, John

Marcin jingled the keys in the air. "If you can get it going, it's yours," he announced.

Junior was flabbergasted. "Really, Pop?"

"I'll believe that when I see it," Anna snickered between cigarette puffs.

"How about giving the boy some encouragement?" John Marcin resisted the urge to scold Anna, doing his best to turn her sour mood around. "If anyone can get that old thing running, it's Junior."

"Sure," Anna replied.

"Listen to this, boys," John Marcin said with a rare gleam in his eye, "I took your Ma out on our first date in that car. It sure was something, right Anna?"

"Yeah, it was somethin', I guess." Anna tossed back another swig of beer. She leaned across the table and ran a finger along the top of the birthday cake, licking a dollop of icing perched on its end and looking straight at John Marcin, daring him to reprimand her.

John Marcin refused to take the bait and surrendered first. He always did. "Shall we go take a look under that hood, June?" John Marcin patted the birthday boy on the back and stood up from the table.

"Sure thing," Junior said, swinging his bent legs over the bench. "I'll go grab my boots."

Anna sat silently, picking at the beer bottle's label with her long Firehouse Red fingernails. After draining the last of its contents, she headed into the parlor, leaving the cake and dishes strewn across the table. John Marcin could hear a cigarette package ripping, followed by the scrape of a match. "Luke?" Anna called. "Be a good boy and bring me another beer."

Junior rushed back through the kitchen and out the back door. "Ready, Pop!"

"Only one more," John Marcin mouthed to Luke before heading to the barn.

After a couple hours of tinkering with the Model T, John Marcin returned to find the house in complete darkness. He turned on the kitchen light and reached for the refrigerator latch. Both hands were required to break the seal around the heavy steel door. The bottom shelf, usually lined with amber-colored bottles of Anna's favorite Pearl Lager, was empty. He moved into the front room, where he found Anna snoring in her armchair, the end of a cigarette smoldering in her hand. He stood over her and watched her sleep. In these quiet moments, the heaviness that hung about her would lift. She was still a beautiful woman who turned heads in every room she entered.

John Marcin lifted the cigarette from between Anna's fingers and stubbed it out in the already overflowing ashtray on the side table. He tried to lift Anna and nearly tripped over Luke, who was fast asleep under an afghan at his mother's feet. John Marcin grabbed the table to steady himself, and the lamp and empty beer bottles covering its surface came crashing to the floor.

Anna moaned and curled further into her chair.

"Luke," John Marcin said as he folded the blanket back, "wake up now."

Luke coughed and the stench of alcohol wafted into the air. John Marcin clenched his jaw, blinded with fury. He grabbed the boy by the collar, dragged him to his room, and threw him across the bed. "Don't you dare come outta here until you've slept this off. You hear me?" he shouted, slamming the door and storming back into the parlor.

"What is it? What's wrong?" Anna asked.

The last vestiges of respect for his wife had finally disintegrated for John Marcin. "You're wasted again. That's what's wrong."

Anna muttered something under her breath.

John Marcin yanked Anna to her feet. "Our child is passed out drunk. Shame on you!"

"John Marcin, I didn't—" Anna began.

"No, nothing you can say will excuse this. I'm tired of your excuses, Anna, and your useless promises. They don't mean anything anymore."

"Please," Anna whimpered.

"Go on," John Marcin spat, shoving her toward the bedroom. "Get out of my sight!"

*   *   *

John Marcin awoke on the couch with a splitting headache. He made his way to the kitchen but stopped in the doorway. Anna was at the stove, flipping pancakes, a cigarette in one hand and a spatula in the other. Her hair flowed over a red silk robe cinched around her narrow waist. The radio crackled on the counter; its antennae crisscrossed to pick up the signal from Austin. It was her favorite Saturday morning show, featuring old-time folk music. She sang along to one of her favorite songs, 'Little Darling Pal of Mine,' by The Carter Family, and danced as she cooked as though the night before had never happened. Luke slunk in behind John Marcin and crawled into a chair at the table. He did not look at his father.

Anna spun around to grab a bowl filled with batter from the counter and spotted Luke. "Good morning," she said, spreading her arms and sauntering toward him. "Come dance with your Ma." Luke stumbled into his mother's embrace. She placed one of his hands on her hip and extended the other out, leading him in a two-step around the kitchen table. "My little darling, oh, how I love you. How I love you, none can tell," she sang. On the second turn, she lifted Luke's arm and twirled beneath. He was tall enough that she did not have to bend anymore. Anna rubbed the tip of her nose against her son's as she sang the last line, "Oh, how I love you, none can tell."

The back door slammed, and Junior burst into the kitchen. He'd been tinkering under the hood of the Model T since daybreak.

"Would ya look here. Another pal o' mine," Anna announced.

"Mornin', Ma," Junior replied cheerily. "Whatcha cookin'? I'm starved."

An up-tempo fiddle and banjo instrumental kicked off on the radio, and Anna extended her hand toward Junior. "You're gonna have to give your mama a spin first. Sing for your supper, as they say."

Junior stepped forward with a broad grin. He plodded around the room, doing his best to keep to the beat of the music.

J. E. Weiner

"Watch it," Anna said. "Damn it, Junior! Keep those enormous feet off my new slippers."

"I'm tryin'," Junior whined.

"Ouch!" Anna stopped and pushed Junior away. "What did I say about my feet," she complained. "Look what you've done. I think my toe's broke."

Junior's face fell. "Can't we dance some more?" he pleaded.

Anna softened when she realized John Marcin was watching her. "Maybe after breakfast."

"Hey there," her greeting and apology were joined.

John Marcin remained silent.

"Go on and sit, boys. The flapjacks are ready," Anna said.

Anna poured a fresh cup of coffee and set it before John Marcin, who had taken a seat at the table. She looked at him with expectation. Of what John Marcin could not be sure. She extended her index finger to offer a brief but tender stroke over his earlobe. John Marcin ignored her and took a sip of the steaming black liquid. Anna stood for another long beat before sitting down. They all ate in silence, save the music on the radio.

CHAPTER 28

Flipping the Switch

Anna held herself together for a good long patch after what John Marcin would come to call the "flapjack jamboree." The beer did not return to the icebox, hiding places under the tree roots for hard liquor remained empty, and a hot breakfast was on the table most mornings.

John Marcin also gave Anna credit for her efforts to stay busy outside the house. She volunteered to direct the St. Stanislaus choir and led rehearsals on Thursday afternoons. When Junior worked at The Fox Hole, John Marcin ran them both into town, and after school, Luke joined his father and brother at the bar until Anna finished at the church. Choir rehearsals often ran over time, but John Marcin didn't mind. It gave him time to chat with Tater. Frankie, too, when he was in the mood to socialize.

John Marcin never had to twist Luke's arm to hang out at The Fox Hole. It was impossible for the boy to resist endless pretzels, peanuts, and root beers for supper and the opportunity to peruse Tater's library in the back office. Its shelves were filled with rows of history books and piles of the back issues of *Life Magazine*. Even more enticing, Luke would also get to help set the stage for the dance hall's most popular event, a weekly talent show. Anna was late enough some nights that John Marcin and the boys could watch some of the acts. Aspiring musicians, singers, a few magicians, and even a juggler or two flocked to Bandera from across three counties to compete for the five-dollar prize at night's end.

Frankie Kalka ran the back of the house at The Fox Hole. He had a more disheveled look of late, his square jaw dusted with blond whiskers and his long locks often unkempt, but still drove the ladies wild. When Frankie moved furniture or boxes, he would strip down to his undershirt, revealing several large tattoos dancing along his still-muscled arms. A rattlesnake was coiled tight and ready to strike on his left bicep, and on his right forearm, a red heart hung from a small cross, dripping with blood. Women would sit at the bar and bat their eyelashes whenever he would come close, but he never paid them any attention. Frankie only spoke when it was necessary and usually only when preparing for a show. Luke was one of the few people Frankie would engage. "Run 'em," he would grunt and point, which meant Luke was to set the microphones, clip them into place and tape their wires across the wooden floor to the side of the stage. "Check 'em," Frankie would order, and Luke would snap his fingers in front of the microphones and call out, "Testing one, two, three," repeatedly. Frankie would tinker with the amplifiers until the feedback settled and then disappear without another word for the rest of the evening.

"Leave him be, son. He's not so good with people anymore," John Marcin consoled Luke one night after Frankie slammed the office door in his face.

"Yeah, it's for the best that my brother keeps behind the scenes. Takes the pressure off talkin' to folks, you know?" Tater agreed.

"Uncle Tater, what happened to Frankie in the war? Why's he like he is?" Luke asked.

John Marcin wondered the same things about his childhood friend, who seemed increasingly lost, unable to shake the memories of battle.

"Can't say for sure, Luke. Never was right after we got back. Always nervous," was all Tater would or could say.

* * *

The week of Thanksgiving 1941, John Marcin arrived at the dance hall with his sons to find a new face, or what was left of a face, unloading crates behind the bar. Junior jumped back when he saw the man and rushed from the room. Luke stared open-mouthed but didn't move.

"Afternoon," the man said. He stood over six-and-a-half feet tall, and his face looked like it had melted. His left eye and nostril were blocked by thick white scar tissue descending from the crown of his bald head and over half of his face like a mudslide. A piece of his top lip was also missing, exposing several broken teeth inside his mouth.

John Marcin heard footsteps approaching. "Behind the bar, Uncle Tater," Junior said, pointing at the stranger.

"Ah, yes," Tater nodded with a click of his tongue. "I should have warned ya. This is our new barkeep. Tiny's his name. He's a fright, I know, but no need to be alarmed."

The newcomer offered a brief bow and continued unpacking crates.

John Marcin inspected the stranger from behind. The back of his head was covered in the same white scars winding through patches of brutally inflamed skin. At the base of his skull, a ragged patch of wiry red hair caught on his collar when he moved his arms.

"It's not polite to stare," the man said, facing the shelves. He was talking to Luke, who had snuck around the bar to observe the stranger more closely.

Luke reached into a crate and pulled out a bottle of whiskey, gripping the neck of the bottle so hard it shook. He handed it to the man.

"I'll get the rest of this. You go on," the stranger said, wrenching the bottle from Luke's fingers.

Luke still didn't move.

The man stepped closer, his frightening face right in front of the boy's. "I said git!" he yelled.

Luke backed away and retreated to the end of the bar, Tiny's sinister laugh following in his wake.

"He's only curious," John Marcin said. "We don't see too many strangers around here."

"You might wanna teach your kid some manners, respect for his elders, and the like," the bartender snarled.

John Marcin ignored the new arrival and made his way to the back office to find Tater. "Where on earth did you dig that fella up, Kalka?" he said with a thumb jerk toward the bar.

"Old friend of Frankie's from the war," Tater replied with a roll of his eyes and a puff of his cigarette. "Arrived out of nowhere last week."

John Marcin raised his eyebrows. "Friend? I've never heard Frankie mention anybody named Tiny."

Tater rested his forearms on the top of his desk. "They both ended up in the same trench on the western front at some point. Tiny got the wrong end of a shell. They say his wife wouldn't take him back looking like that, so he's been wanderin' ever since. Somehow, he found his way here. Frankie offered him work and a place to stay," Tater explained. "I'm letting him sleep on a cot in the storeroom."

"Tiny, huh. Nickname's a little too ironic, don't you think?" John Marcin said.

"Apparently, his head peeked over the trenches even when he was kneeling. That's how the Huns spotted him," Tater chuckled.

John Marcin heard Anna out front and headed in her direction. "Now, who've we got here," she vamped as John Marcin approached, but she was looking past him. John Marcin turned to find Frankie standing in the shadows behind the stage. "Excuse me for a minute," Anna said, smoothing her skirt over her hips. "I'm gonna go say hello to Frankie. Wait one more minute for me, would ya?"

"Sure," John Marcin said, his eyes narrowing as they followed Anna. When he noticed Luke watching him, he leaned over the bar and grabbed a bottle from the ice bin. "How about one more root beer before we hit the road?"

"That'll cost you a nickel," Tiny said.

John Marcin flipped the top off the bottle and handed it to Luke without a glance at the bartender. He was watching Anna and Frankie. "Put it on my tab."

*   *   *

Anna was singing along to the radio as she and Luke trussed chickens for Sunday supper. The signal crackled, and a series of bells rang. "We interrupt our program for this important news bulletin," the announcer began. "President Roosevelt says that the Japanese have attacked Pearl Harbor in Hawaii from the air."

"John Marcin, get in here!" Anna beckoned.

John Marcin had already heard the report from the other room and was tuning into the news broadcast on the big radio in the parlor. Anna and Luke joined him, and Junior was only two steps behind from the front porch.

"Pop, what does this mean?" Luke asked.

John Marcin frowned. "War. And it won't only be war with Japan. I fear we're also heading back to Europe."

"So, you're gonna have to go and fight," Luke said nervously.

"Squeak, you're so stupid!" Junior broke in. "He's too old, but I'll get to go fight, right Pop?"

"We'll have to see about that, June." John Marcin didn't want to dash the boy's hopes.

"Why wouldn't I, Pop?" Junior insisted. "I'm ready to fight like Uncle Frankie did."

"And look what happened to him," Anna said. "It's not your father's decision in any event. It's up to the army. But they're only gonna want the strongest and the smartest—" Anna stopped.

"You sayin' I'm not strong? That I'm not smart? I'm stronger and smarter than all of you put together!" Junior cried.

"I only meant—"

"No, Ma. You think I'm feeble-minded. You always have, but, but—" Junior stammered, spittle flying from his mouth. "But yer dead wrong!"

"Stop it, Junior," John Marcin said.

"You never take my side!" Junior stormed outside, slamming the front door so hard one of its panes cracked.

After a long and stunned silence, John Marcin turned to Anna. "Was that necessary?"

"For Heaven's sake! It takes so little to set him off. You can't say a word about anything to him," she said, waving her hands dismissively and retreating to the kitchen. After a few minutes, the back door opened and closed.

Luke stood to follow his mother, but John Marcin took his arm. "No, I'll go after your Ma this time."

John Marcin always worried when Anna wandered off. It never ended well, especially after a tiff. She had a switch, and though John Marcin could not always predict what would trigger it, he could always tell when it had been flipped. Sometimes, she would go quiet, staring out the window or sitting alone in the dark. Other times, she would pace frantically back and forth on the front porch or set off to walk the ranch for hours at a time.

Fumbling with the buttons on his winter coat, John Marcin followed Anna to the hilltop cemetery, where she had stopped at the low wrought-iron fence encircling the headstones. He had built the enclosure after Zacharias and Liza passed to keep the wild boars from rooting around the graves. Anna struggled with the gate, allowing John Marcin the chance to catch up. He reached out and placed his hands over hers, which were already ice-cold, and slid the latch aside. The gate swung open, and Anna walked past him and sat on a small wooden bench under one of the oak trees. She stared into the distance, her back straight and hands tucked into her jacket pockets.

John Marcin had not been inside the fence since it was built. This place reminded him of people he found difficult to remember and things he'd prefer to forget. Ambling between the two rows of graves nearest the trees, John Marcin tried to make out a few names and dates on the older wooden crosses battered by the elements for almost a century. The only stone marker was the one for his parents. A weeping angel, carved into granite, cradled a plaque bearing their names, dates of birth and death, and a short epitaph: *Rest together in peace.*

A cigarette butt teetered on the headstone's base, and a small black circle of ash stained its top. He would have to talk to Junior. He'd told that boy a million times he couldn't smoke in the graveyard. Too much dry brush. John Marcin reached out to sweep off the debris and felt a sharp tap on his shoulder. He turned, expecting to see Anna behind him, but she hadn't moved from the bench. John Marcin looked to see if a branch might have fallen from the tree above, but there was nothing. He felt another tap on his other shoulder. He spun around, but again, no one was there.

"Damn this place," he said, pulling his collar tight around his throat. "Anna," he said. When she did not respond, he became more insistent. "Anna!"

Anna's gaze was fixed on the river below. She blinked but did not speak.

"Somebody touched me. Was it you?"

Anna raised her wind-chafed hand and scratched her cheek.

"Was it?" John Marcin asked again.

Anna turned to look at him, but it was as if she was looking through him.

John Marcin flailed his arms above his head. "Anna, did you hear me?"

Anna bobbed her head, but her expression did not change.

"Which is it? You heard me, or you touched me?" he asked.

Anna shrugged.

"Aw, forget it!" John Marcin said with disgust. "I don't know where you've stashed the booze, but if you've come here to get swacked, be my guest. I'm goin' back to the house before I'm frozen through."

John Marcin wrenched the gate back open, the screech of its rusted hinges echoing across the pastures below. He heard a woman speak. "Don't be afraid," she said.

John Marcin turned back to Anna, "What did you say?"

Anna didn't answer.

The woman spoke again. "Jestem tutaj, I am here."

John Marcin understood that it was not Anna. He bolted toward the house and did not look back.

✳ ✳ ✳

The telephone rang in the parlor, the vibrations rumbling across the surface of the heavy oak desk on which it sat. "I'll get it," John Marcin said. Few folks outside of Bandera proper had a telephone, and calls were still a significant happening. John Marcin lifted the receiver to his ear. "Anderwald residence," he announced.

The operator came over the line. "Go ahead, Mr. Kalka."

"Hey, John Marcin. Tater here. How's everyone doin' this evenin'?"

"No complaints."

"I hope I'm not disturbin' your supper."

"Nah, finished a while ago."

Tater hesitated. "Listen, I was callin' for Anna. She around?"

"Sure, I'll get her." John Marcin set the receiver on the desk with a loud bang. "Anna, Tater's on the line for you."

Anna emerged from the kitchen, a dish towel in hand. "I got it," she said, shooing John Marcin away. "Why don't you go on and finish drying those dishes?" Anna waited until John Marcin was out of the room before speaking. "Hello?" she began. "Oh, hi, Tater. What can I do for ya?"

A minute or so of silence was broken by the occasional "uh-huh" from Anna. John Marcin strained to listen in.

"That's awfully kind of you to say, Tater, and I'm flattered," she said, "but I'm not sure about this. It's been a long time." She paused as Tater made whatever case he was making. "Let me talk to John Marcin. Can I call you back a little later this evening?" Another pause. "I understand. I'll call you back tonight."

Anna returned to the kitchen.

"What did Tater want?" John Marcin asked.

"Apparently, the act he had booked for the Friday after next has to leave for basic training. He's invited me to fill in for the night. A short set and probably only this once until he can find a new band." Anna looked uneasy as she waited for a reaction.

"Might do you some good," John Marcin said with unexpected tenderness. "Pick your spirits up a bit. You're always happier when you're singing."

"Yeah, I suppose," Anna said tentatively.

"Mama, you'll be great," Luke said excitedly. He'd been eaves-dropping from the hallway.

"You think I should?"

"Yes," John Marcin and Luke responded in unison and laughed.

"I guess I'm gonna need a band, then," Anna said. "How about

I start with you, Luke?" She looked at John Marcin. "If your Pop don't object, of course."

"Can I, Pop? Can I?" Luke begged.

John Marcin thought for a moment before answering. "Sure. I think that'd be fine, as long as you don't miss any school and save me a seat on the front row," he finally said with a smile.

Luke and Anna got to work that same evening and rehearsed past midnight for a week straight. It was the first time in months that John Marcin had seen a sparkle in Anna's eye, and she came more and more alive with each song. She and Luke selected a set of seven numbers—a couple of upbeat gospel tunes from the St. Stanislaus choir repertoire and a few folk and country standards. Anna would sing lead with Luke on the guitar, providing the occasional harmony line. They planned to close with a duet, Jimmie Davis' latest hit, 'You Are My Sunshine.' It was John Marcin's favorite.

John Marcin waited backstage with Anna and Luke the night of their first show. Anna looked stunning, her cheeks flushed with excitement and a new shade of burgundy lipstick brightening her full lips. Her still-raven hair was pinned back on each side, and small peacock feather earrings danced beneath her earlobes. John Marcin could hear the hum of chatter and the clink of glasses in the bar.

"My hands are shakin' somethin' terrible," Anna exclaimed. "Deep breath and hold for two," she said to herself, inhaling and exhaling dramatically. John Marcin could smell alcohol on her breath, and she seemed to read the worry on his face. "A little nip to take the edge off my nerves. Nothing to worry about," she said and squeezed his hand.

In contrast to his mother's jitters, Luke waited patiently, fine-tuning the strings on his guitar. John Marcin warmed with pride as he looked at his son, who was fast becoming a young man.

"Not scared, are you, kid?" Tiny growled from the shadows.

John Marcin noticed Luke flinch as the maimed bartender approached. "Leave him be, Tiny," he warned.

"Only makin' conversation," the barkeep huffed and set off toward the storeroom, slowing to look Anna over as he passed.

Anna moved toward the side of the stage where Frankie was standing. "Are there a lot of folks out there?" she asked.

Frankie dipped his head and blinked.

Anna grabbed his hand and pressed it to her chest. "I'm so nervous! Feel how fast my heart is beating, Frankie," she said.

Frankie kept his palm against Anna's body for a split second before yanking it away and looking nervously at John Marcin.

"Oh, you. Such a funny bird," Anna laughed and turned to Luke. "Listen now, Tater's gonna introduce us in a minute. You go on out first. I'll follow right behind."

John Marcin moved out to the front of the house to watch the show. As soon as the spotlights hit Anna and Luke's faces, the energy on the small stage exploded. Their set was over before John Marcin knew it, and the audience was on their feet, cheering and demanding an encore.

"Aren't you the nicest," Anna said with a grin. "That's all we've got for tonight, folks, but if Tater will have us back, we promise to put together some more tunes. What do you say to that?"

The crowd roared, and Tater gave a thumbs-up from behind the bar. John Marcin had never seen Anna so relaxed, so confident. Yet another switch to be flipped.

*　　*　　*

Anna and Luke Anderwald headlined The Fox Hole's Friday night lineup for nearly a year and a half. Anna invited a drummer named Jack Parsons out of Uvalde and a bass player named Dicky Reeves from Medina to join them. Both Jack and Dicky were too old to be drafted and played backup for several local acts. They were happy to jump ship for the chance to perform with Anna, though.

John Marcin bought Anna a second-hand truck to get herself and Luke to and from the bar. The ranch was busier than ever and getting away on time for their show was tricky. The Second World War had brought renewed prosperity to Peacock Bend. The U.S. Army came calling in constant search of beef, and John Marcin had trouble filling the orders, especially after most of his ranch hands were drafted. Junior was also too busy to drive. After three attempts to register for the draft without success, he soon forgot all about the army business. Automobile production for civilian use was halted, so folks had to make do with what they had. Junior's expert mechanical skills kept the whole county on the roads.

John Marcin missed the first set with greater regularity than he liked. He would often arrive to find Anna on a break at the bar, her laughter increasing in volume and insincerity, drink by drink. One Friday, he arrived to find Luke chatting with Tater, Anna nowhere to be seen.

"Where's your Ma?" John Marcin asked.

Luke quickly scanned the crowd. "Dunno, Pop."

It registered with John Marcin that Tater was tending bar. "Where's the help at, Tater?"

"Stepped out for a smoke, I suspect. Or maybe a crap," Tater laughed.

John Marcin rapped his knuckles on the sticky bar top. "I'll go see if I can find Anna," he said, heading toward the back of the bar.

John Marcin popped into the storeroom first before continuing past the stage entrance. As he approached the turn in the hallway, he heard a muffled cry coming from the direction of Tater's office. It was a woman. "Please," she said. But there was something else, a noise like an animal panting. Then, another voice, a male this time, but John Marcin could not determine what was said. He tiptoed further around the corner. A thin crack of light framed the closed office door. "But why not," the woman cried out from inside. "Anna, don't," the other voice sounded again. It was Frankie.

Head pounding and fists clenched, John Marcin continued forward against his better judgment. Another ten feet and he would be able to turn the doorknob, but something or someone moved ahead in the darkness. An imposing figure crouched on the hallway floor. John Marcin recognized the twisted outline of Tiny's head, bent forward, his right eye level with the keyhole. One of his hands gripped the door jam, supporting his massive frame. The other was in front of his body, hidden from view, but John Marcin could see the shadow of the bartender's upper arm moving swiftly between his legs. He also heard a soft grunt. Startled, John Marcin bumped back against the wall, and Tiny's head immediately spun around. Easing around the corner, John Marcin hurried back to the bar.

"You find her?" Tater shouted over the crowd.

John Marcin's stomach lurched. "Uh," was all he could manage.

"You okay, Pop?" Luke asked.

"Yeah, you look like you could use a good stiff drink, Anderwald." It was Tiny, a lascivious grin blooming across his mutilat-
ed face as he buttoned the top of his pants. "Listen, Tater. I think
somebody might have been back in your office," the barkeep said.
"Anderwald, you see anybody back there?" The quiver of flesh where
Tiny's eyebrows would have been served to underscore his question.

"No, nothin'," John Marcin said, biting the inside of his cheek
hard enough to draw blood.

Tiny peered at John Marcin. "Huh. And you didn't hear
nothin'?" he toyed and waited for a beat before continuing the interrogation. "Nothin' at all?" Tiny said and slipped behind the bar.
"Coulda swore I saw you back in that direction."

John Marcin met Tiny's sneer with an equivocal stare. "Nope.
Was taking a leak."

"Then maybe it was your wife back there," Tiny said with a
vicious, lipless grin.

"Not her either. She was in the ladies fixin' her face." John
Marcin hardened his stare.

Tater untied his apron and tossed his bar towel in the sink. "If
folks can't mind their business, I'll have to get a lock on that door, I
guess." He stubbed out his cigarette in a tarnished brass ashtray near
the cash register. "Break's over, Tiny. Get on back to work. I've got
other things to do," he ordered, waving the sullen bartender out of
his way.

Tiny glared at John Marcin as he turned and left the bar without another word.

CHAPTER 29

Wars of Attrition

The sun peeked over the ridge east of Peacock Bend, and mockingbirds dueled in the treetops, boasting increasingly complex sequences of chirps and tweets with each volley. John Marcin rolled onto his side after a night of tossing and turning on the sofa. The throbbing in his lower back intensified. He hadn't slept a wink after the fight with Anna. He'd demanded she quit performing at The Fox Hole, and she'd refused.

"A bar is no place for a teenager to spend so much time, Anna," John Marcin insisted. "Or a married woman," he added under his breath.

"Wait a goddamned minute," she said. Anna had sworn on every family grave she could tally that she had not been anywhere near Tater's office and certainly not with Frankie. "Don't you make insinuations you aren't prepared to defend. And don't bring Luke into this either!"

Anna stormed off on one of her walks in the middle of the night and didn't return until dawn. She was still in bed.

The peacock standing sentry in the yard issued an angry honk, and the other birds scattered into the sky like giggling schoolgirls. Footsteps approached from the kitchen. "Pop, time to get up," Junior announced. "And hurry. We've gotta leave for church by nine-thirty. Ma's got a solo."

John Marcin limped to the bathroom, slamming the door shut behind him. He let the water run in the sink until the initial flakes of rust surrendered to the drain. When the stream was clear, he cupped his hands beneath the spigot, splashed his face, and ran his wet hands through his hair. John Marcin caught his reflection in the mirror over the sink. He looked worse than he feared, but the delicious smell of bacon and coffee distracted him, and he made his way out to the kitchen.

"Hey, Pop," Junior said, lifting a large iron skillet from the stove and scraping a mound of scrambled eggs onto several plates.

Luke tumbled in next. "Mornin' all," he yawned.

"I thought we was gonna have to send in the undertaker to bring out a body," Junior said. "You were dead to the world."

Luke grinned and poured himself some milk from a jug on the table. "Where's Ma?" he asked, licking the remainder off his lip with his tongue.

John Marcin felt the cloud descend. "Probably still getting dressed," he said.

"Pop slept on the couch last night," Junior blurted, his mouth full of food.

"That's enough, Junior," John Marcin snapped, but when he noticed Luke's look of worry, he added, "Ma was having none of my snoring, so I came on out to the parlor. Not fair to bother her all night." John Marcin looked at his watch. "Finish up and get dressed, boys. Time for church."

A half-hour later, John Marcin tapped his thumbs against the sides of the steering wheel. Anna hadn't responded to his earlier honks of the horn, and he was tired of waiting for her. "Luke, run back in the house and get your mother," he ordered.

The front door flew open as Luke started up the porch steps. Anna hurried out, stumbling over the threshold. "Somethin' wrong?" Luke asked.

"That man is always ordering me around," Anna said, brushing past.

The drive to church was quiet. John Marcin stared straight ahead and drove faster than usual. Anna sat next to him, filing her fingernails, which were uncharacteristically free of color. She had complained the night before that she'd left her polish somewhere at the bar.

"Maybe it's somewhere in the office," John Marcin had suggested, setting off the fight that would land him on the couch.

John Marcin glanced in the rearview mirror. Junior brought the funny papers along and acted out the scenes of his favorite comic strip to himself in the back seat. Luke was next to him, pressing his face against the window, watching the Bandera Highway fly by.

When the Anderwalds arrived at St. Stanislaus, Anna headed straight to the choir loft, and John Marcin, Junior, and Luke found seats in a pew near the front. John Marcin turned back to ensure Anna was where she said she would be and as far away as possible from Frankie Kalka. He spotted Tater and Frankie walking their mother down the aisle. Tater bobbed his head, but Frankie avoided eye contact.

The service was quick and covered all the liturgical bases. Father Kurz—whom some old-timers still referred to as the "new priest" despite his having arrived after Father Adamietz collapsed during a sermon two decades before—had breathed new life into Mass of late. This included expanding the choir and increasing the number of hymns sung each Sunday. Anna's solo was always the highlight of the morning. When she moved toward the choir loft railing, John Marcin usually loved to watch people's faces. Expectation dissolved into rapture for most when she began to sing. This morning, one congregant attracted John Marcin's particular attention. Frankie stood transfixed at the end of a pew a few rows behind, watching Anna.

After the final blessing, John Marcin wound through the congregants gathered outside on the church lawn. Luke and Junior were standing in the shade near the car. "Isn't Ma with you?" Junior asked.

John Marcin stopped in his tracks. "She's not out here?" he said, his head swiveling in search of Anna. "Don't wander off. I'll go fetch her."

John Marcin rushed back inside the church. No one was left on the main floor, but he heard movement above. "Anna?" he called. Footsteps pounded down the stairs, and Anna appeared at the bottom. Her hair was loosened from her bun on one side, and the top button of her dress was undone.

"Where the hell have you been?" John Marcin said, looking past her and up into the loft.

"I had to put the hymnals away. It was a real mess," Anna explained as she grabbed John Marcin's hand.

John Marcin could have sworn he heard the scrape of a shoe across the floorboards upstairs, but Anna did not look back. "Come along, it's hot as blazes in here. I'm ready to get home and have some cool lemonade," she said, pulling John Marcin toward the exit. Anna crossed the lawn to where Luke and Junior were standing. "Sorry to take so long, boys. You must be starving. Let's head on home," she said, climbing into the car.

John Marcin blasted onto Cypress Street, his eyes remaining fixed in the rearview mirror. He could see Frankie Kalka step out of the side door of the church with some hesitation, cast a glance to the right and left, and jog toward his truck.

*   *   *

By the end of that hot summer of 1943, as the Allies' momentum was building in Europe, an intensely personal war of attrition befell the combatants of Peacock Bend. John Marcin did his best to extricate himself from the emotional chaos of loving and tending to Anna. He chose not to confront her about that day at church. No good would come from a confession or a denial. He felt like a fool either way.

Instead, John Marcin threw himself into managing Peacock Bend's expanding cattle operation and a new volunteer role for the Texas State Guard. He'd often be gone for a week at a time when he led training courses for army mechanics over at Fort Sam Houston. John Marcin would leave Junior "in charge" so as not to cause unintended slights or provoke any unnecessary outbursts, and members of the St. Stanislaus congregation would help when needed. John Marcin understood that most of the men felt obliged to help a fellow parishioner, and a few felt sorry for him. But all, without exception, had to overcome the severe protests of their wives who did not want their husbands anywhere near Anna Anderwald. At least that's what John Marcin overheard Joe Mazurek say one afternoon as he helped stack hay bales.

John Marcin observed Anna doing her best to ignore the rampant gossip following her every move. Her ability to maintain a brave face, however, was in direct proportion to a steady combination of alcohol and "happy pills" to calm her nerves. Her doctor prescribed the latter when Anna found herself in a deep funk following Frankie's sudden departure for points unknown a few weeks after the incident in the choir loft. She'd arrived for her show at The Fox Hole to find Tiny at the soundboard on the side of the stage. Even Tater had no idea where Frankie had gone. Anna could only make it through half of the set that evening. She excused herself with apologies and retreated backstage with a bottle of whiskey. John Marcin left Anna passed out in the bar's office and headed home with Luke, assuring Tater he'd be back in the morning to retrieve his wife.

The Friday night shows eventually grew unbearable, and John Marcin begged Anna to quit. It was hard enough to watch her collapse into despair, but there was also Tiny. John Marcin came to loathe even the thought of him for reasons far beyond the man's deformities and foul humor. The bartender was always lurking around the corner, taunting him or leering at Anna.

One night after a show, John Marcin waited for Anna to pack her things. Tiny was drying glassware. "She sure does sing like an angel," he said.

John Marcin offered no reply.

"I am impressed by a man who'll let his beautiful wife loose in a place like this." Tiny left the insinuation hanging in the air as he lifted a new keg into the cooler.

John Marcin reopened the sore inside his cheek with a sharp bite.

"I heard she used to be with another band before she met you. With her brothers."

"So?" John Marcin glared at the barkeep.

Tiny leaned in closer, his hideous face inches away and his hot and sour breath billowing into John Marcin's nostrils. "I also heard there was somethin' strange about that Schulte family. Dark secrets, they say."

John Marcin stiffened. "Don't you have work to do? I'm sure Tater isn't paying you to talk my ear off."

"No need to be snippy. I'm just making conversation." Tiny changed the subject when Tater emerged from the office. "How's Luke doin', by the way? Strikes me as a bit outta sorts these days."

"What's it to you?" John Marcin had nearly had enough of Tiny's bullshit.

"I'd think he'd be havin' a bit more fun, dashing as he is, with a wit, to boot. Especially when he's had a few."

John Marcin's head began to spin. Luke drinking? He'd tan that kid's hide if it was true.

"Will you leave it be, Tiny? Stop messin' with him," Tater warned.

"I didn't mean nothin' by it," the bartender said, raising his hands in surrender and retreating to the storeroom.

"Don't listen to him, John Marcin. He's got nothin' nice to say about anyone or anything. I'd send him on his way, but I need him more than ever now that Frankie's gone." Tater winced. Frankie was a sore and uncomfortable subject between the two friends. No one ever said an overt word about Frankie and Anna. They respected John Marcin too much. But no one, including John Marcin, had any doubts that there had long been something going on. John Marcin assumed Tater blamed himself somehow, figuring he could have stopped things, maybe. John Marcin knew Tater couldn't have done a darned thing about any of it.

*   *   *

The passage of time did nothing to help John Marcin and Anna Anderwald. In the year after Frankie's disappearance, John Marcin's bitterness and anger nearly consumed him, and Anna's fragile existence continued to crumble. One morning, when Anna had been gone from the house all night, John Marcin set out to scour the ranch and bring her back. He found her huddled on the riverbank, wearing a thin nightgown stained with blood and excrement and a pair of Luke's work boots. Her spine protruded from beneath her blueish-white skin—each individual vertebra visible as they descended beneath the fabric of her gown. She clasped her knees to her chest and rocked back and forth on the muddy bank. Anna's face was covered in deep red scratches, and the fingernails on her visible hand were broken and caked with dried blood and grime. Though alone, she spoke to someone unseen. "I beg of you," she pleaded. "Leave me alone!"

John Marcin edged forward but stopped when he heard a mocking cackle in the distance. He scanned the tree line and the low brush surrounding them, holding his breath to listen for the source, but all he heard was the rush of the water. He took another few steps and stopped again. "Whore," a growl rumbled across the river.

"No, please," Anna said, forcing her fingers into her ears, "I'm not to blame! I couldn't stop him!"

John Marcin went to Anna. He reached out, but she began to kick and punch him.

"Get the hell off me!" she howled.

"Anna, stop," John Marcin implored, trying to grab her wrists. "It's me."

"Please, no," she sobbed. "Don't hurt me, Bertie!"

John Marcin managed to subdue Anna by wrapping his arms around her entire frame. She stopped resisting and went limp, her whole body sinking into the mud.

"Make him stop, Mama," she said. "Make him stop." John Marcin held Anna tightly until her respiration slowed. "I'm so sorry," she whimpered.

John Marcin began to hum his favorite song, "You Are My Sunshine," the one Anna had performed that first night at The Fox Hole. It felt like a lifetime ago. They sat for a long while, watching the sunbeams dance across the current. The quiet was broken at last by the mournful cry of a peacock. "Hee-yelp. Hee-yelp," it beckoned.

"I think it's time we head to the house and get you cleaned up," John Marcin said, but Anna didn't move. He stood up and gently lifted her to her feet. "Here we go. I got ya," he urged.

Anna pulled away and looked at the river, her eyes widening in fear. At midstream, the head of a large cottonmouth broke through the surface, its long form weaving back and forth toward them on the riverbank. Anna stood frozen and silent until the snake turned downstream. "He'll never let me go," she said calmly.

"Who?"

"The one who lurks in the shadows."

Anna was scaring John Marcin now.

"And she cannot save me. Hard as she tries."

"Who are you talking about?" John Marcin was not sure he wanted to hear the answer.

"The lady in white. She comes for me, but it's too late."

John Marcin slowly coaxed Anna toward the house, leading her by the hand. "You're gonna be fine. Don't you worry."

Anna stopped. She reached out and touched John Marcin's cheek, the tip of her ring finger grazing his earlobe and the metal of her wedding band hard against his jaw. "Can you ever forgive me?" she whispered.

CHAPTER 30

In Anna's Wake

Anna vanished once and for all on August 10, 1945, the day after "Fat Boy" fell on Nagasaki. Her pre-dawn departure was like its own nuclear explosion over Peacock Bend—a massive blast and searing pain followed by an eerie, empty calm. Over the first few months, accounts of Anna in some town or another, from Fort Worth in the north to Galveston in the south, trickled in at a steady clip. Each time, John Marcin would tuck her photo into his breast pocket, pack a few sandwiches and a thermos full of coffee, and set off to try and find her. One sweltering Sunday the following spring, Dicky Reeves stopped in with the most promising but also the most disturbing report.

"Howdy, Dicky," John Marcin called from the front gate as Reeves stepped out of his truck, dust still settling around its wheels. "What brings you by?"

"Afternoon to ya," Dicky said, dodging a curious peacock pecking at his boots. "Hope you don't mind my comin' by unannounced, but I have some news."

John Marcin invited Dicky onto the porch. "Beer?"

"No thanks, I'm good." Dicky took a seat and brushed his sweaty bangs off his forehead. "How you holdin' up?" he asked.

John Marcin leaned a hip against the porch railing. "One foot in front of the other, I suppose."

"Saw Junior at the feed store last week. He seems good."

"June's a malleable sort. Nothin' much bothers him," John Marcin smiled.

Dicky cleared his throat. "And Luke? Sherriff said he got another ticket for joy riding around the Mormon Camp."

John Marcin stared across the river into the distance. "Word sure does travel fast here in Bandera."

"Right, understood. I don't want to take too much of your time, but I needed to tell you somethin'," Dicky said.

"I'm assuming it's about Anna, yes?"

Dicky fidgeted in his seat.

"Spit it out, Reeves. It's not like I'm unaccustomed to shock and disappointment when it comes to my wife." John Marcin crossed his arms over his chest.

"Jack and I were in Austin last night playing a gig. Coulda swore we saw Anna standing on a street corner near Sixth and Congress. Figured you'd wanna know."

"Did you talk to her?" John Marcin was more than intrigued. It was a first sighting by someone he knew and trusted.

"We tried, but she spotted us and blended into the crowd along the sidewalk before we could get to her. It was a busy Saturday night."

"What was she doing? Was she with anyone?" John Marcin could not contain his curiosity.

Dicky became visibly uncomfortable, hesitating to say anything further.

John Marcin redoubled his cross-examination. "Dicky, was Anna with someone?"

"Not him, if that's what you're askin'." Dicky could not look John Marcin in the eye.

"So, not Frankie. Who, then?"

"I can't be sure."

"I've made my peace, Dicky. Say what you came to say."

Dicky took a deep breath. "There's somethin' else, John Marcin."

John Marcin's body tensed. "I'm all ears."

"I can't be a hunnerd percent certain, but Jack and I coulda sworn Anna was with child."

John Marcin grabbed the porch railing with both hands, his knuckles whitening. "You don't say."

Dicky backpedaled. "Like I mentioned, we weren't sure. We coulda been wrong, you know."

John Marcin took a deep breath. "Could I ask a favor?"

"Anything," Dicky said.

"Maybe you and Jack could keep that little detail to yourselves? Would you do that for my family's sake?" John Marcin released his grip on the rail and rubbed the back of his neck with his hand.

"Of course. Not to worry about us," Dicky assured him.

Tater was the only person John Marcin could bring himself to share this story with, and he did so on a ride to Austin the morning after Dicky's visit. The pair spent two days walking every inch of Congress Avenue and Sixth Street, stopping into every bar, shop, and seedy hotel along the way with Anna's picture to ask if anyone had seen her. Tater also brought a snapshot of Frankie in his army uniform, taken somewhere in France. A few folks said Anna's face was vaguely familiar, but none could recall when they'd seen her or who she might have been with. No one recognized Frankie. Both John Marcin and Tater returned to Peacock Bend empty-handed and defeated.

"Luke, run and fetch me another whiskey." Tater raised his empty glass, the remaining ice cubes clinking against its side.

"You need a refill, too, Pop?" Luke asked. John Marcin was rolling his glass back and forth between his palms. "Pop?"

"Nope, I'm good."

"Grab me another ice cube from the kitchen while you're at it," Tater added.

Luke let the screen door slam behind him.

"Listen, I knew finding Frankie was a long shot, but I sure was hopin' you might get some word about Anna," Tater consoled John Marcin.

"Yeah, well," John Marcin muttered.

"It's not right what she did. What either of them did. And if she's with child..." Tater went quiet and, only after a long silence, continued. "I'm sorry I didn't say something when I first had my suspicions. I hope you believe that."

"Stop it," John Marcin said.

"But—"

"Tater, you did nothin' wrong. This is on them, and they'll have to live with it."

Drinks in hand, Luke returned, pushing the door open with his foot. He handed Tater his whiskey and eased onto the porch swing, the rusted chains straining against his now substantial form. He also sipped a short pour. "Uncle Tater, you think my mother is ever coming home?"

Tater's shoulders appeared to stiffen, and he paused to collect himself, taking a long slug of his drink before answering. "No, Luke. I don't think she is," he said.

"Pop, what about you?"

John Marcin downed the rest of his own drink and peered at the glass in Luke's hand. "Aren't you a little young for the hard stuff?"

"Seriously? I'm asking about Ma, and you've gotta harp on what I'm drinking?"

"Dicky was by the other day. Said he heard from the sheriff that you've been joy ridin' again," John Marcin replied.

"I don't mean no disrespect, Pop, but the folks around here need to tend to their own fucking affairs for a change." Luke slammed his glass on the table and headed back inside.

John Marcin knew that he should follow his son. Say something, call him back to reprimand him, but he could not find the strength. He heard the back door close and the truck engine rev around the side of the house. Luke sped off, fishtailing along the loose gravel road.

"I don't get it," John Marcin said.

"What specifically are we talkin' about here?" Tater asked. "There's a lot not to get."

"After everything with his Ma, he's drinking and carrying on as bad as she ever did. I can't take much more," John Marcin confessed. "I already lost Anna. I can't lose him, too."

"Stop, John Marcin," Tater said. "He'll come around. As for what happened to Anna, that's not your doin' any more than what Frankie did is mine. Something broke inside your Anna long ago, and no matter how hard you tried, you couldn't mend it. God only knows what damage that brother of hers did. Same for Frankie. His mind was shattered into bits over there in the trenches. And none of us could fix him. The doctors call it 'Shell Shock,' but the more accounts I read, I'm not certain they have any idea what befell those poor boys." Tater crunched the remains of an ice cube. "Maybe the two of them found a way to put their pieces together and make some kind of whole. I cannot explain or understand what they've done to you and, even worse, to Luke and Junior. What I do know is that those boys need you more than ever."

John Marcin wiped his mouth on the back of his hand. A silent and invisible weight settled once again dead center in the middle of his chest.

✳   ✳   ✳

After the trip to Austin, John Marcin stopped chasing Anna and did his best to return to some semblance of a routine after a year of constant tumult and crushed hopes. He insisted the family return to regular attendance at St. Stanislaus to keep the congregation from too much chatter, and he and Tater had more than the occasional meet-up at what was now The Silver Dollar Saloon, so he had company. After Frankie left, Tater took on another business partner who suggested a new name for the bar would be an excellent excuse to throw a grand reopening. Tater welcomed a fresh start. John Marcin also got back to work. Peacock Bend's cattle business expanded its menu of services thanks to three new bulls—one massive Longhorn and two black Angus—that, for a handsome price, had occasion to fraternize with heifers of age across Bandera, Medina, and Kerr counties.

For the most part, Junior lived independently, coming by for Sunday supper or a ballgame on the radio. His auto repair business was steady enough to cover his few expenses, and he even had a budding love interest, a gal named Doris Pittel, whom he'd met at a church social. Before their first date, Junior made a special trip into town to get a shave and haircut and buy his first bottle of Old Spice. He soon began to douse himself in the stuff, and John Marcin and Luke could smell him coming from a mile away. Both agreed, though, that Doris was good for Junior and good for them. She was no beauty queen and was simple as a rake, but she kept Junior company, laughed at his jokes, and stopped in regularly to cook a meal and give Junior's socks and underwear a wash. John Marcin considered everyone a winner except, perhaps, poor Miss Pittel.

Luke was equal parts favorite son and wild child of Bandera and uncontrollable either way. By his eighteenth birthday, he had crested six feet and bulked to nearly two hundred pounds of muscle. As the star point guard for the undefeated Bandera High School Bulldogs, Luke received calls from colleges across the state to recruit him to play for their basketball teams. He was smart, too, and rumored to be on the shortlist for valedictorian. "The full package," the coaches said. And where the young ladies were concerned, he was the catch of the county. His bright smile and wicked sense of humor won over most, and he garnered more than a few smooches under the bleachers.

John Marcin held his breath whenever Luke took off in Anna's truck to meet his friends, though. Every weekend looked the same for the young people of Bandera in those days: cruising down Main Street and boozing around bonfires along the Medina. Occasionally, one of the kids would host a barn party, and word spread like wildfire through the school cafeteria. At the start of Luke's senior year at Bandera High, Felix Knapp's old cowshed burned down after someone tripped over a kerosene lamp during an exceptionally rambunctious gathering. Bandera County Sheriff Garrison Hicks and his deputies shifted into high alert. Sheriff Hicks personally took the time to visit the alleged ring leaders and their parents at home.

"The next kid I catch doing something stupid like that is gonna spend a night or maybe even two in the old jailhouse. We'll see how you like sharing a cell with all the ghosts and the rats," Hicks threatened, standing over Luke in the parlor at Peacock Bend.

Luke was sprawled on the sofa, his feet propped up on the coffee table. "You gotta be kidding me. Get a load of this tough guy," he snickered.

John Marcin gave him a sharp shove with his boot. "Son, you best show the sheriff some respect."

Luke couldn't contain a loud snort.

John Marcin was losing patience. "You think this is some kind of a joke?"

"Luke Anderwald, I assure you that I'm quite serious." The sheriff took a step forward.

Luke sat up straight. "My apologies, sir. Forgive the interruption," he said with a salute.

"That's enough out of you, Mr. Anderwald," Sheriff Hicks glared at Luke. "Why don't you save some of that sass for the game against Eldorado this weekend, eh?"

"Yes, Sheriff," Luke said with a hint of deference and sat back in his seat, clearly aware of when not to push it.

Hicks pulled up a side chair and sat down. "John Marcin, if you don't mind," he said, gesturing to the seat next to Luke. "Why don't we try this again, Luke."

Luke offered a quick nod of compliance.

"How's your brother? Doin' good?" the sheriff asked.

"Seems like it."

"He still sweet on that Pittel girl?"

"I guess. Try not to stick my nose into other people's business," Luke replied.

Sheriff Hicks ignored the provocation. "And how about you?"

"I'm dandy. Why?" Luke peered out the window, pretending to investigate the peacock parading in the yard, its feathers on display, and avoided eye contact. John Marcin knew Luke hated these questions. He hated them. People were always asking, and frankly, it was none of their goddamned business.

"If you say so," Hicks replied. "But people are talking, Luke."

"Oh, yeah?"

"People are sayin' you might be drinkin' a little too much. Maybe also driving a little too fast on the back roads?"

Luke rolled his eyes. "Mm-hmm."

John Marcin could sense his son's simmering impatience.

"We're all worried about you. Me, Tater, your Pop. You know, with your mama bein'—"

Luke jumped to his feet, his shins banging on the side of the coffee table, and grabbed a duffel bag lying on the floor. "If all we're gonna do is chit-chat, Sheriff, I think we're done here. I need to get to practice," he said, throwing the front door open and slamming it closed behind him.

"Luke," John Marcin half-heartedly called after his son.

"Let him go," the sheriff said.

*　*　*

The blaze of light was blinding, and Earth felt like it was spinning out of control on its axis, gravity giving way. John Marcin's entire body floated through the air in slow motion. His head, neck, and limbs were fixed and unmovable, but he could feel a frantic pounding inside his chest. Voices followed. Unintelligible at first, building to a symphony of harrowing screams and angry growls interspersed with words and phrases, some of which he understood and others he did not.

The first words John Marcin could make out were "Murderers! Whore!" and "He is mine" soon followed. Angry growls surged from somewhere beneath his body, and zaps of electricity seared his insides as they flowed from his head to his toes. Then he heard a woman cry, "Go!" at the top of her lungs.

A bell trilled in short bursts. John Marcin opened his eyes. He had fallen asleep in his armchair. It slowly registered that the telephone was ringing. He lifted the receiver. "Mr. Anderwald?" a man said.

"Yes, this is he," John Marcin answered through the fog of sleep.

"Your son's been in an accident."

*　*　*

John Marcin tapped the elevator call button for a third time, hoping it would speed the car's arrival. He could hear the internal gears whir and spin behind the carved metal doors anchoring Nix Memorial Hospital's lavish main lobby. The policeman on the phone said Luke had been passed out in the back of his truck after a night out in San Antonio. His only slightly less inebriated friend was behind the wheel. "The driver lost control, and your son was thrown headfirst fifty feet into a cow pasture, Mr. Anderwald," the deputy reported.

The elevator creaked open and closed, and the ascent to the fourth floor seemed to take an eternity. When the doors finally parted again, John Marcin hurried to the nursing station, where a young nurse was seated. "I'm looking for a patient," he said breathlessly. "The name is Anderwald. Luke Anderwald."

"Are you family, sir?" the nurse inquired.

"Yes, I'm his father. The doctor sent me from the Emergency Room."

"Room three forty-five. On the left," the nurse said, pointing down the hallway. "He got to us in the nick of time last night. He's sleeping now."

The room was dark, save a strip of light seeping in between the drawn window shades and falling across the hospital bed. Luke lay motionless under a thin white sheet. His left leg, covered in a plaster cast, was exposed and suspended from a metal rigging bolted to the ceiling. He had yet to regain consciousness for any extended period, and the doctors were concerned.

John Marcin approached the bedside. "Oh, God," he gasped.

Luke's entire face was bruised and battered, and a wide swath of his curly blond hair had been shaved, revealing a deep purple gash that wound along the entire left side of his head like a serpent. The laceration oozed between a long line of black sutures.

John Marcin eased into a chair beside the bed and gently took Luke's hand. "Son, can you hear me?" he asked. "Luke, I'm right here. The doctor says they're gonna get you fixed up, so don't you worry." John Marcin pressed his lips against the back of Luke's fingers and began to pray for the first time since he could remember. The next thing he could recall, he was folded over the bed, still holding Luke's hand.

"Mr. Anderwald?" the nurse said with a tap on his shoulder. "I am sorry to wake you, but I need to check your son's vitals." She moved toward the head of the bed and flipped through pages attached to a clipboard.

"I'm sorry," John Marcin replied with a yawn. "It's been a long night."

"Why don't you get yourself something to eat in the cafeteria?"

"No, thank you," John Marcin replied. "I'm fine."

The nurse insisted. "Sir, I can't force you, but it won't do your son much good if you collapse from thirst or hunger, and they have to admit you to the hospital, too, will it?"

John Marcin smiled weakly. "Fair point," he said with a slight bow. "I think I will stretch my legs and get some coffee. I'd appreciate your keepin' watch for a minute."

"Of course. Take your time."

A lounge with a row of vending machines offering coffee, candy bars, and cigarettes was around the corner and down another linoleum-lined hallway from Luke's room. The rooms along the corridor stood empty, and the strong scent of disinfectant wafted through the air. A door swung open ahead, and as John Marcin passed, he sensed movement in his peripheral vision. When he turned to investigate, a puff of what looked like white smoke floated behind the door and disappeared. John Marcin shook his head. "I really do need some coffee," he said to himself.

The click of the coins, the thump of the Styrofoam cup into the dispenser, and the splash of liquid bounced off the white cinder block walls of the lounge. John Marcin grasped the sides of the vending machine and leaned his forehead against the glass case holding a picture of a steaming cup of coffee and some kind of pastry. His mouth started to water. He dug out a few more coins from his pocket and dropped them into the next machine, proffering an array of chocolate bars.

John Marcin retraced his steps with a coffee and a Mars Bar in hand. As he approached the room where he'd seen the white smoke a moment before, he heard a woman singing softly inside. He poked his head into the room. It was still empty. He was puzzled, not afraid, and somehow, a renewed calm flowed through his body.

"Do they know why he won't wake up?" John Marcin asked as he stepped back into Luke's room.

The nurse was entering notes into a chart and spoke as she continued to scribble. "He had a terrible blow to the head. Sometimes, the brain needs a little time to reset."

"I see," John Marcin nodded and set his coffee and candy bar on the windowsill. He'd lost his appetite.

"You'll need to be patient. When your son wakes up, the doctors will know more. For now, though, we need to let him rest," the nurse said reassuringly as she inserted the ear tips of her stethoscope and warmed the chest piece with her breath.

"And his leg?"

The nurse continued to lift and press the metal disc across Luke's chest and on each side of his torso before responding. "Sorry," she said, removing the ear tips. "I can't hear you when I'm wearing these."

"His leg. Will he be able to walk again?"

The young nurse made some more notes in the chart. "Most likely yes," she said and turned to leave. "I'll be getting on with my rounds. Excuse me."

Suddenly, Luke cried out. John Marcin rushed to his side. "Son, I'm right here," he said. Luke began to writhe in the bed.

The nurse hurried back, pressing her palm against Luke's forehead. "Are you in pain?" she asked.

Luke began to shake his head back and forth, desperately trying to communicate something. "Ah-na two yes," he whispered.

John Marcin stepped back from the bedside, eyes wide. "What's going on?"

"Your son is agitated for some reason," the nurse frowned. "I'm concerned he might be in pain."

Luke began to speak again. "Yes, I see you," he said.

John Marcin placed his mouth next to Luke's ear. "Who, son?"

"Ah-na two yes. Ah-na two yes," Luke repeated.

John Marcin became unsteady on his feet. "Mr. Anderwald, are you all right?" The nurse asked and gripped his arm. "Mr. Anderwald?" she repeated, trying to elicit a response.

Luke croaked, "I see you," and repeated, "Ah-na two yes."

"He's feverish again and not making much sense," the nurse said, retrieving a thermometer from the cabinet. "It could be delirium either from extreme pain or infection. Maybe both."

John Marcin braced himself against the bed with both hands. "It's not gibberish."

"What's he saying?" the young woman insisted.

"Ona tu jest. It's Polish. It means 'she is here.'"

"Oh, I didn't realize your son spoke Polish," the nurse said, glancing through Luke's chart. "It's not noted here in his record."

"He doesn't," John Marcin replied.

CHAPTER 31

Undone

The crickets chirped in the yard as the sun slipped behind the trees. John Marcin gripped a bottle of pain pills tightly in his fist and watched his son through the screen door. It had been two years since Anna vanished and nine months since Luke's accident. While the world had begun to right itself after total war in Europe and the Pacific, the battle continued at Peacock Bend. The demon that had tormented Anna quickly turned to Luke, who, like his mother, struggled fiercely against the impulses to excess that, in turn, fueled cycles of unfettered cruelty toward those most dear to him.

Luke sat alone on the porch with his leg propped on the railing, shifting his position for about the tenth time in as many minutes. He looked to be searching for the perfect angle to offer relief from the constant pain in his hip. No luck. "Shit!" he howled, gingerly placing his foot back onto the floor.

John Marcin stared at the label on the pill bottle. *Two tablets every six hours as needed for pain*, it read. He twisted the top off the bottle and shook two pills into the palm of his hand. He'd given Luke his last dose three hours ago, and this would be his fourth of the day. He returned one of the tablets to the bottle and replaced the cap.

John Marcin sat down next to Luke. "Pain bad again?" he asked, handing him a tablet.

"Yup," Luke said, placing the pill on the tip of his tongue and swallowing it with a sip of beer.

"Doctor said not to mix."

"I already got one doctor, Pop. Don't need two," Luke snapped but immediately softened. "Sorry, it's been a long day."

John Marcin stroked the stubble on his chin. "Dicky Reeves phoned again this afternoon."

"Yeah?" Luke's head started to bob and weave. The medicine never took more than a minute or two to kick in.

"Don't you want to hear what he wants?"

"I know what he wants." Luke was becoming agitated. "He and Jack want me to play some gigs with them in San Antonio."

"Maybe a change of scenery would be good for you?" John Marcin suggested.

"Pop, please." Luke turned away.

"Luke, you've been home for months, and except for one afternoon of fishing with Junior, you haven't left this porch. You need to get yourself up and around."

"You do understand I almost died that night, right? Takes a little time to set a person's mind straight after something like that," Luke shot back.

"I know what happened, but it was almost a year ago."

"I also gotta face the fact that my leg is shot. So that means no more basketball and no more college. If you didn't notice, all those coaches stopped calling the day after the crash was reported in the paper. *Bandera Teens Careen off Highway 16.* That headline's sure a grabber, but wait, *Team Captain in Coma?* Ooo, that was an even hotter story."

"Nothing is stopping you from going to college. You're sure smart enough, and we can afford it if that's what you want to do. All you have to do is finish—"

Luke cut his father off. "I already told you there is no way I'm going back to Bandera High School, head hung low and gimpin' around. I won't give those gossipin' vultures any red meat. I got the regular stink eye when I returned after the accident—from the kids, the teachers, and even the parents. They all blamed me, but I wasn't driving. I won't give them the satisfaction of taking me down a peg.

Tsk, tsks in the hallways? Screw that!" Luke finished off his beer.

"So, don't go back to school," John Marcin said, "but don't give up on your music. Give Dicky a call. I hear you playing at all hours back in your room, and those new songs seem like they might really be something good. You should try and get back out there." When Luke did not react, John Marcin took another tack. "What about we go and see Junior? Haven't had a proper visit with him since he and Doris moved into Grandpa Marcin's house."

Luke visibly tensed at the mention of Junior. John Marcin worried he might regret making this suggestion. His sons' last row hadn't been pretty. In fact, it had been vicious.

"Squeak, you gotta stop drinkin' and poppin' them pills," Junior had scolded. "I don't want you to be like Ma anymore."

"It is always so simple to the simple man, June," Luke had jeered.

"Whad'ya mean by that? You better not be calling me simple," Junior threatened and reeled his fist back.

Luke grabbed Junior's arm and wrenched it behind his back.

"You leave your brother be," Doris cried and pounced on Luke, scratching at his face.

Luke threw Junior and Doris to the ground before John Marcin could intervene. "Fuckin' half-wits, the two of you," he spat and limped out into the night.

Not long after the fight, Luke took another pass at getting sober. John Marcin was stunned when Junior stepped in to help with the worst of the withdrawal, but the moment Luke was in the clear, he disappeared again. It had been weeks since Junior had come around—the longest and coldest shoulder he'd ever turned his brother's way.

John Marcin treaded back in lightly. "Listen to me, Luke. I learned the hard way with your Ma that people don't take too kindly to stubborn silences."

"Maybe," Luke sighed.

"The truth is, son, that you cannot go on like this."

"Leave it, Pop," Luke said, shutting down again.

It was clear Luke did not want to have the conversation. Not then. Not ever. But John Marcin understood he would regret it if he did not force the issue. He'd given Anna her space, and he lost her for good. He would never forgive himself if he made the same mistakes with Luke. It was time to set things right.

John Marcin jumped up and grabbed Luke's chair, swinging it around violently. He hovered over him, the heat of his anger rising through his cheeks. "Nope. We're talking about this whether you like it or not."

"What are you doing?" Luke protested.

"Lucas Anderwald, if you won't talk to me, you're sure as hell gonna listen to me."

"I said no!" Luke tried to stand but immediately grabbed his leg and tumbled backward into the chair. He reached out for the pill bottle on the table.

John Marcin grabbed the bottle, his veins now throbbing in his neck. "I am warning you. I am at my wits' end."

Luke lurched toward his father. "Give me my goddamned pills!"

John Marcin didn't move.

"Whatever. I've got more where those came from," Luke said and slammed his head against the back of the chair.

"Not anymore. I flushed the ones in your medicine cabinet this afternoon. I also found the stash in your boot, so those are gone, too. You're done with these." John Marcin rattled the pills in the bottle before stuffing them into his back pocket.

Luke smiled—a hollow, haunting smile—and a distorted sound gurgled up from his chest: "Suit yourself, Anderwald. If that makes you feel like the tough guy you most certainly are not, nor ever will be, so be it."

John Marcin retreated into the house, Luke's laughter following in his wake.

*   *   *

A stony silence fell over Peacock Bend. John Marcin would rise before the sun and head out to the far reaches of the ranch, returning long after dark and immediately retreating to his bedroom without a glance in Luke's direction. Luke himself laid low and undertook a renewed regime of self-enforced sobriety. He didn't have a choice about the pills. John Marcin had taken care of those. So, his first act of demonstrable contrition was to haul all the beer and hard alcohol out of the house to where Anna used to keep her reserves in the graveyard. He poured out the contents of each bottle into the tall grass.

The initial week or so was pure hell. The purge of the painkillers almost immediately opened the floodgates of withdrawal, and once the headaches and nausea started, Luke spiraled. Junior rallied like he always did. "Aw, Squeak," John Marcin heard Junior call out to his brother. "You puked again! Time for another shower." At some point later—John Marcin was unsure when—Luke was tossing in the bed. Junior arrived with some warm broth. "Easy, Squeak. You're burning with fever and still gots the shakes. Pop says it'll pass. Here, have some soup." John Marcin watched Junior spoon the salty liquid through his brother's cracked lips. Luke immediately perked up and reached for the spoon. Junior gently pushed his hand away. "Hold on. I got it. I don't want you spilling all over the clean blankets," he said.

After weeks of torment, the worst was over. John Marcin peeked into Luke's room one morning as he slept, the creak of the door announcing his presence. Luke opened his eyes and stretched in the bed. "Hey, Pop," he said.

"Feelin' better?"

"Yes sir, I—"

"Get dressed. Looks like you could use some coffee," John Marcin said and headed to the kitchen without waiting for a response. He set the coffee pot on the stove to boil and watched the flames dance beneath the kettle. Here we go again, he thought.

"There's a saying about a watched pot, right?"

John Marcin startled. Luke was standing behind him. He was a disturbing sight, his skin brittle and wan and his cheeks sunken into his skull. The whoosh of coffee boiling over on the stove quickly refocused John Marcin's attention on the task at hand. He filled three large mugs and handed one to Luke. He grabbed the others and headed out the back door. "Let's take one of these to Junior," he suggested.

Luke followed his father out the door, and they headed to the old farmhouse.

"June?" John Marcin called through the screen door. A plump woman with stringy brown hair and large glasses approached from inside but did not move to invite John Marcin or Luke inside. "Oh, hi, Doris. I didn't know you were here," John Marcin said.

"I live here." Doris pursed her lips twice in rapid succession, a curious tic when she spoke. "Where else would I be?" she asked, her lips pulsing so close to the screen they almost touched it. "You feelin' better?" Doris looked past John Marcin at Luke. "Junior said you was sick again."

"Yes, much better, thanks," Luke said. "Where might we find my brother?"

"In the shop," Doris replied and turned away.

John Marcin and Luke headed to the barn. Junior's boots were sticking out from under a sedan, its axles straddling four large wooden blocks. "Mornin', June," John Marcin announced.

Junior's feet jerked, and his whole body began to wriggle out from under the car. He peered at Luke from the ground. "He's awake?" he asked John Marcin.

"Looks that way." John Marcin smiled and held out one of the steaming cups. "We brought you some coffee."

Junior sat up and wiped his hands on his overalls. "With sugar?"

"No, black," John Marcin said.

"Pop, you know I like it with two sugars but give it here. I'll drink it anyway." Junior took one of the mugs, spilling some of its contents.

"Why don't we sit for a spell?" John Marcin gestured toward an old wooden bench near the corral gate. It was draped with Khalil's moth-eaten saddle blanket from all those years ago. John Marcin felt a pinch in his chest. The last of the camels had died off the summer before, and like with the wranglers, memories of those times popped to mind only infrequently.

"Sure," Junior said suspiciously.

The two brothers sat in awkward silence, drinking their coffee. Junior made a loud slurping noise as he finished the last sip.

"Listen, June," Luke broke the silence. "I wanna thank you for all you've done. Taking care of me and all."

Junior released an exaggerated exhalation of breath. "That's my job, Squeak."

Luke gave his brother a puzzled look.

"I'm the big brother. I'm supposed to take care of you."

"Well, thank you, big brother. I appreciate it."

"It's not me you gotta worry about, Squeak. You gotta make things right with Pop," Junior said, pointing at John Marcin. "He was real mad you done what you did. Real sad, too. You gotta 'pologize to him."

"I understand, June. I will. I promise."

"Don't promise. Do it," Junior said. "Right now."

Luke looked at his father, a familiar sadness descending. "I'm sorry, Pop," he said.

John Marcin nodded. "That's a start."

"I need to get back to work," Junior interrupted. "Thanks for the coffee. And don't forget. Two sugars next time," he grinned and slithered back under the car.

Luke lit a cigarette and took several long drags before straining to pull himself up from the bench. "I'm gonna head back to the house," he groaned.

Junior popped his head out from under the chassis. "Yeah, yeah," he said. "I'll be down for lunch in a bit. You can make the soup this time, Squeak."

"You got it," Luke laughed.

CHAPTER 32

Unexpected Encounters

The Bandera Highway shot straight as an arrow westward into the swelter of the late summer day. The black asphalt sizzled in the heat, and the roadside was an explosion of yellow and orange sunflowers atop thick stalks protruding from scattered clumps of spotted bee balm and switchgrass. Luke finally contacted Dicky Reeves and Jack Parsons after another few months of cajoling by John Marcin, and within a week, The Medina Ramblers were launched with Luke as the frontman. Jack printed a stack of posters advertising their debut show at The Liberty Saloon in downtown San Antonio the following month. Luke volunteered to post them around Boerne, Pipe Creek, and other nearby towns. He'd invited John Marcin and Junior along for the ride. After a morning of nailing flyers to telephone poles, the trio was headed back to Bandera and their favorite swimming hole along the Medina.

Luke jammed the accelerator to the floor, and the pickup's engine roared. He stuck his head out of the driver's side and howled, "Woohoo!" into the rush of air. "Your turn, June," Luke said, pointing toward the passenger window. "Ye-ahhh! Give it a go," he said and laid on the horn.

John Marcin sat between Luke and Junior in the truck cab, enjoying their banter. He couldn't remember the last time his sons had enjoyed each other's company.

"All right, all right," Junior agreed, pushing his face through the window. When he opened his mouth, the hot wind rushed into his nose and mouth in one gush. "Wuh," was all Junior could muster before his throat seized, and he began to cough. He flopped back against the seat, and John Marcin and Luke burst out laughing. "What?" Junior frowned.

Luke turned his attention back to the road. "Find some music, would ya, June?" he said, pointing at the dashboard. Junior twisted the tuning knob back and forth, searching for a station. Static gave way to a blast of music. Tennessee Ernie Ford's 'The Shotgun Boogie' pulsed through the speakers. "Turn it up. I love that song," Luke said. "The big fat rabbits are jumpin' in the grass," he sang along as Junior bopped back and forth in the passenger seat. "Wait 'til they hear my old shotgun blast!"

A few miles before the turnoff to the ranch, Luke eased onto a narrow farm road that led to the river. Even in the hottest summer months, the Medina's waters ran cool and deep. The swimming hole was located where the road crossed the river via a narrow, one-lane bridge lined with short cement bollards meant to prevent cars from going over into the water. It was common knowledge that you didn't even try to cross if you couldn't see the bollards above the waterline. The bridge also provided the perfect jumping-off point into the current below.

"Here we are," Luke announced as he parked in the shade. "I'll grab the grub, and June, you bring the blanket."

John Marcin slipped out of the cab and stretched before following Luke and Junior down a dirt path that cut through the undergrowth and opened onto a flat patch of crushed limestone near the riverbank. The boys dropped their picnic gear and stripped to their swim trunks before jumping into the water, the gleaming white skin of their torsos and legs in stark contrast to their tanned faces, necks, and forearms.

"Last one to climb the bridge is a rotten egg," Luke challenged Junior, scurrying up the opposite bank toward the overpass.

John Marcin kicked his shoes off and folded his pants legs around his knees. Junior had joined Luke on the bridge and was prancing back and forth across the tops of the bollards.

"Jump, jump, jump!" Luke egged his brother on.

"Bombs away!" Junior announced, plunging into the river feet first.

"That's a six," Luke said after Junior's head popped to the surface.

"Are you crazy?" Junior protested. "That was at least a nine."

"Too much splash," John Marcin chimed in. "Try it again, June."

Junior swam back to the bank and crawled out of the water. He shook his fist in the air. "You are blind as a bat, Squeak," he said, storming onto the bridge. "You, too, Pop. Look closer this time."

After two more jumps, the judging panel agreed that the snacks promised had been earned. John Marcin grabbed the picnic basket and waded over to a large boulder at the water's edge, where Luke and Junior were perched. Junior flipped open the top and revealed stacks of sandwiches Doris had wrapped in thin wax paper, a half-eaten bag of potato chips on top.

"Pop, Luke already got into the lunch," Junior protested.

"Shut up, big baby," Luke teased.

Junior shot back, "You're the baby. Not me!"

Luke rolled his eyes. "Geez, I was kidding. Take it easy, June."

John Marcin watched Luke rummage through the picnic basket. "Egg salad, eh? My favorite," he said, unwrapping a sandwich and stuffing half of it into his mouth. He patted Junior's cheek and skipped back toward the water, flipping down the back of his trunks and exposing his bare backside. "Back to the competition, jackass. That bridge is calling my name," Luke laughed. "Pop, you're the final judge."

*　　*　　*

Four weeks later, The Liberty Saloon was hopping. The Medina Ramblers' first big show in the big city was opening for some good ol' boys from Nacogdoches. The main act had kicked off their second set. John Marcin tapped his boot to the beat of the music and watched Junior spin Doris around the dance floor in a jumbled two-step. The bartender drifted by and pointed at his beer glass. It was tempting, but he needed to stay sharp enough for the drive home. Places like this brought out the worst in Luke, and John Marcin suspected it was only a fifty-fifty proposition that he was still sober after his show. Luke had disappeared into the back of the bar some time ago. John Marcin looked at his watch and decided to give his son another ten minutes before going to look for him.

John Marcin turned his attention back toward the stage. He spotted an older woman approaching from the dance floor, her hips gyrating seductively. He looked away, trying to ignore her. A soft and ample breast crammed into a tight sweater brushed against his arm. "Hey, there," the woman's boozy breath floated past his ear. "You tryin' to play games, pretending not to notice me over here?"

John Marcin grimaced. She reminded him of Anna at her worst. He tried to push the woman gently along.

She gestured toward the bathrooms and tried again, coquettishly twisting a long lock of hennaed hair around her index finger. "Wouldn't you like a little company tonight?"

John Marcin shoved her away. Harder this time. "I said no."

"Sweetie, take it easy. I was only makin' conversation," she grinned and rubbed her hand along his inner thigh before moving further along the bar.

John Marcin took the opportunity to go look for Luke. He gradually wound his way through the throng of patrons, around the backstage area, and before long, found himself standing in front of the men's room door. He heard people inside. He pushed the door open and spotted Luke's boots pointing in one direction in the stall and a pair of stilettos pointing in the other. Luke was leaning against the wall, and the redhead from the bar was squatting before him. John Marcin hoped he was only imagining the scene, but he wasn't.

"Change your mind?" the woman said, winking at John Marcin. She stood and extended her hand toward Luke. "Like we agreed, that'll be five dollars." Luke pulled his jeans up and retrieved several bills from his pocket. The redhead grabbed the whole stack and skipped out of the stall. "Thanks for the tip, handsome. Hope to see you again sometime." The bathroom door slammed, and John

Marcin heard the woman cry out, "Oops, sorry about that, honey. Wrong address!"

"Get out of there," John Marcin ordered.

Luke fumbled with the buttons on his jeans. "What's the problem, Pop? Didn't wanna wait your turn?" Luke laughed.

John Marcin curled his lip in disgust.

"Jesus, can't a man have a little fun?" Luke appeared to change tactics. "You can't seriously be angry, Pop. There's no crime in fraternizing with a fan after the show. It's part of the job."

John Marcin stood his ground. "Do you expect me to believe that load of horse shit?"

"Pop, are you honestly upset about this?" Luke flung his arms into the air in frustration. "Because if you are, that's ri-di-cu-lous. Do you hear me? Ridiculous. The stupidest thing I ever heard come out of your mouth. I'm a grown man with needs. Who cares how I get them met?"

"You're drunk," John Marcin said.

"Enough!" Luke cried and pounded his fist against the wall beside John Marcin's head, clearly catching himself off-guard as much as John Marcin.

John Marcin shrank back. "Luke Anderwald, you're scaring me, son."

The hateful shadow stirred. "Go to hell," Luke sneered and started toward the bar.

John Marcin grabbed his arm. "Wait," he pleaded.

"What the fuck is wrong with you?" Luke lashed back. "You made things so hard for Ma and drove her away. Now it seems like you're trying to get rid of me, too."

Luke's face was flushed and his eyes betrayed profound anguish. John Marcin again was reminded of Anna's darkest days and instinctively tightened his grip.

"Will you just leave me alone!" Luke shouted, wrenching his arm away and bolting for the exit.

* * *

John Marcin stumbled after Luke into the night, completely undone. He wandered along St. Mary's Street toward the River Walk for hours, searching every bar and hovel. The night soon subsided, and the first hint of dawn kissed the base of the Navarro Bridge on the east side of the San Antonio River. A flickering red sign over a doorway beckoned just ahead. It was the last bar on the strip.

As he entered, the smell of stale beer and urine rushed full force into John Marcin's nostrils. A portly man in a rumpled plaid shirt emerged from the back room. "Evening," he said with a yawn. "Come to think about it, I guess I should say mornin' to ya. What'll it be?"

"I'm looking for a man. Young twenties, tall, blond hair."

"Nope. Nobody like that's been in here. It's been a slow night. A few regulars earlier, but that's it."

John Marcin was out of ideas and places to look. He collapsed onto a barstool in defeat. "I'll take a shot of Jack," he grunted, "and a beer chaser."

The bartender drew a beer from the tap and set an empty shot glass in front of John Marcin. He retrieved a bottle of Jack Daniels from the shelf behind the bar and poured a generous portion. "Long night?" he asked.

John Marcin tossed back the shot.

Someone else coughed nearby. John Marcin turned and could just make out the outline of a figure seated in the back corner of the bar.

"You still here?" the bartender said. "I thought you'd be long gone by now. Give me a sec, and I'll turn the table lights back on."

The bartender flipped a light switch on the wall behind the cash register. An older man with a full head of hair slicked into a limp pompadour was sitting in the last booth, facing the front door. A nearly empty bottle of bourbon stood before him on the table. The man coughed again and reached for his glass. When his arm extended into the circle of light from the pendant hanging above the table, John Marcin could see the bottom half of a large tattoo on the man's bicep peeking out from beneath his shirtsleeve. It had faded with age, but it was clearly the image of a rattlesnake coiled and ready to strike. John Marcin's hand began to shake, and he sloshed beer over the rim of his glass.

"You okay there, sir?" The bartender extracted a towel from under the bar.

John Marcin gave a quick nod and finished his beer.

"Who's that over there?" he said, gesturing to the man in the booth.

"Him? That's Frank. He works the early shift."

"Where's he from?"

"Hell, if I could say," the bartender said. "Doesn't talk too much. Not to me, anyway." He offered John Marcin another pour.

John Marcin finished the second shot, trying to summon the courage to see if his hunch was correct. The man in the corner tipped his head back against the wall and squinted at the ceiling. John Marcin seized the opportunity to move closer and get a better look. He saw the man's other arm resting atop the table, grasping the bottle. A second tattoo—a red heart hanging from a cross—covered the length of his forearm. It was him. The man turned his head as if sensing John Marcin's presence, and recognition followed by panic flashed across his face. He glanced at the front door, seemingly searching for an escape route.

John Marcin approached the booth. "Frankie," he said and slid onto the bench seat on the opposite side of the table.

"How'd you find me?"

"I wasn't exactly lookin'," John Marcin replied. "At least not anymore."

Frankie circled his index finger in the air. "Coupla beers here," he rasped.

The bartender approached with two drafts balanced on a serving tray. "Whose tab?" he asked before setting the glasses on the table.

"Mine. These and the ones before," Frankie said.

"You better be prepared to settle up this time, Frank. No more advances."

"I told you already, Bill. I'm good for it. Now leave us be," Frankie barked.

The bartender clicked his tongue and shuffled off.

"So, what brings you in tonight?" Frankie spoke like he was on duty behind the bar, chatting with some stranger.

John Marcin could only muster a hostile glare in response.

Frankie took a sip of his beer. "Listen, I—" he began but stopped. "Shit, I don't have any idea what to say to you."

John Marcin continued to stare across the table. Frankie had not changed much at all other than looking a little older and more haggard; his hair had only hints of gray around the ears and a few fine lines across his brow.

"Looking for Luke," John Marcin mumbled.

"What's that?"

"I'm looking for Luke. He was playing over at The Liberty. He had too much to drink, we had a fight, and he stormed off. It's a familiar drill."

"Luke's playing music again? You don't say." Frankie paused, crumpling a napkin. "So, how are you?"

"What do you care?" John Marcin shot back.

Frankie reached for the near-empty bottle of bourbon. "It might be hard for you to believe, but I do care," he said, downing the final sip.

John Marcin leaned across the table. "Bullshit!" he said through gritted teeth, his face in Frankie's. "Why'd you leave?"

"I guess I didn't think I had much of a choice."

"A choice?" John Marcin slammed the tabletop with the palm of his hand and took a deep breath, trying to control his anger. "You sure as hell did have a choice. For starters, you had a choice not to sleep with my wife," he seethed.

Frankie flinched at the mention of Anna.

"Or what about Tater? After all he's done for you. All those times he kept you from blowin' your brains out after you got back from the war. No choice? Frankie, you're a selfish bastard!"

Frankie didn't respond.

"Whose idea was it to run away? Yours or Anna's?" John Marcin goaded.

Frankie opened his mouth to speak but remained silent.

John Marcin leaned back in his seat, his hands gripping the edge of the table. "Where is she?"

Frankie scratched his cheek. "John Marcin, I swear. I would tell you if I could. I haven't seen Anna in years. We were only together for those few short months after—"

Frankie's eyes suddenly locked onto something near the bar's entrance. John Marcin swung his head around to find Luke standing a few paces away.

"Luke," John Marcin sprang out of the booth. "Where have you been? What are you doing here?" John Marcin was confused. The drinks had gone to his head.

Luke glared at Frankie. "I've been lookin' for you, Pop, and this is the last place open. Junior's in a real state of panic."

"Luke, I, I—" Frankie stammered as he stood up.

Luke stepped around his father, reeled back, and punched Frankie square in the jaw, sending him flying back into the booth. Frankie, out cold, rolled off the bench and onto the floor. The bartender started toward them but reconsidered when he saw the look on Luke's face. John Marcin reached into his pocket, counted out several bills, and threw them onto the table. "Let's go," he ordered, grabbing Luke by the collar and dragging him out of the bar.

CHAPTER 33

Final Inventory

"Eee-you! Eee-you!" came a frightened cry from the rooftop above, followed by a frantic "Hee-yelp! Hee-yelp!" from somewhere in the hills.

"Damned birds," John Marcin grumbled and propelled a ball of sweat-drenched linens onto the floor with a violent kick. He reached for the alarm clock. It was 4:25 a.m. The last time he'd checked, it had been 2:50 a.m. John Marcin turned on the reading lamp beside the bed, knocking over a bottle of pills the doctor had prescribed for Luke. They were a new treatment for alcohol addiction called Disulfiram.

"Oh-Wow!" another peacock replied.

Maybe Luke was finally home, and that's what all the ruckus was about? Luke had resolved once again to try and lay off the booze after that night at The Liberty. He was willing, he said, to try anything. In addition to taking the medication, Luke had even agreed to join the new Alcoholics Anonymous group that met at St. Stanislaus. He'd been at a meeting the night before but hadn't come home yet. John Marcin recognized this was Luke's problem to fix now, but he was still worried sick.

John Marcin blinked, trying to adjust to the light of the lamp. The inside of his eyelids felt like they were lined with sandpaper. He pried each lid open, one at a time, and stumbled out to the kitchen.

He prepared a lethally strong pot of coffee in the percolator and sat at the table in the waning hours of darkness. Yesterday's newspaper was splayed across the tablecloth. He began to sift through its pages in search of the crossword puzzle and discovered Luke's copy of *The Big Book*, A.A.'s manual for sobriety, lying underneath. A sheet of paper that looked like it had been crumpled and flattened again was sticking out from the book's cover. *Moral Inventory of My Defects and Sins* was scribbled at the top of the page, and a list followed. John Marcin recognized Luke's handwriting.

The squeak of brakes startled John Marcin before he could read what was written. He shoved the sheet of paper back into the book and replaced it under the pile of newsprint. The kitchen door flew open, and Luke burst inside. He stumbled to the stove and proceeded to pour a cup of coffee.

"Where've you been?" John Marcin asked.

Luke jumped, spilling the hot liquid down the front of his shirt. "Shit, Pop!"

John Marcin remained fixed in his chair. "You've been drinking. I can smell it from here."

"No lectures until I've had some caffeine and a shower. Can you do me that one courtesy?" Luke said. He leaned back against the counter and shook a cigarette out of a crumpled pack of Camels. He struck the match and touched it to the frayed tobacco.

John Marcin observed Luke's profile cast in shadow in the kitchen window, save the glow from the end of his cigarette. A beacon? Maybe, but John Marcin didn't know whether the light signaled safe or perilous shores.

After several drags, Luke exhaled a cloud of smoke toward the ceiling and dropped the butt into his cup. It fizzled among the dregs of wet grounds at the bottom. "I'm going to bed," he announced. "Tell June he's a dead man if he even thinks about waking me."

John Marcin watched in silence as Luke weaved toward his room.

✳ ✳ ✳

Junior had agreed to bring supper over later that evening. Before he arrived, John Marcin intended to confront Luke. He'd waited long enough to say his piece.

Luke was lying down in the parlor, rubbing his temples and trying to soothe his aching head. John Marcin smacked his stocking feet off the arm of the couch. "Sit up," he ordered.

"Quit it, Pop," Luke said, kicking his feet in the air and landing a blow on John Marcin's hip.

John Marcin grabbed Luke's big toes and wrenched them hard in their joints.

"Fucking hell!" Luke cried, recoiling in pain.

"I said, sit up. We've gotta talk about last night."

Luke massaged his toes. "You're insane," he snarled.

"You will not disrespect me, you hear?" John Marcin could feel his pulse throbbing in his neck. "And as for the booze, we're done. I won't stand idly by and watch you destroy yourself like your mother did."

Luke glowered at his father. John Marcin could see a dark cloud of uncontrolled hatred gather around his son, a malicious grin dancing across his lips.

John Marcin did not relent. "You got somethin' you wanna say to me?"

"Yeah, as a matter of fact, I do,"

"Go on, then."

"I need you to help me understand, Pop," Luke said. "When it came to Ma, isn't that exactly what you did do? Stand idly by and watch?"

John Marcin did not answer the question. He clenched his fists so tightly that his fingernails tore the flesh of his palms.

Luke leaned closer. "Maybe Ma was a shameless whore like they all said, and you just couldn't let her forget it. It's no wonder—"

The first slap across Luke's face, an autonomic impulse, rattled every bone in John Marcin's body.

"Goddammit!" Luke spat, holding his hand against his cheek.

The second slap followed in short order. This time, it was intentional, the culmination of the white-hot rage toward Anna and Luke that had been building in John Marcin for many years. The blow landed so viscerally that the couch tipped back off the ground. John Marcin returned Luke's stunned gaze and stepped away.

The back door creaked, and Junior started banging around in the kitchen. "Pop? Luke? Where you at?"

"Would you be quiet in there, June!" Luke bellowed.

Junior poked his head into the parlor. "You be quiet," he snapped back. "Don't take your feelin' poorly out on me."

"Not tonight, Junior," John Marcin said.

"Why are you always taking his side, Pop?"

"Steer clear is all I meant."

Junior stomped his foot. "This whole mess is Squeak's doin'. He's the one that's in the wrong, and you know it!"

John Marcin nudged Junior back into the kitchen. "Enough. It's been a long day."

"You always make excuses for him. He crashes his truck. You pay to fix it. He don't do a thing around this ranch, but you give him money whenever he asks. He don't even have a real job," Junior continued to fume.

"Easy, June," John Marcin said.

Luke had peeled himself off the couch and was standing in the doorway. Junior, his back to Luke, ignored his father's advice.

"And when he was in that hospital for months, no good to nobody, you had to sell two bulls to pay his medical bills. How'd he thank you? He came home a dang junkie! I had to clean up his puke and poop for weeks before he came to his senses. But did he give a rat's ass? Course not, 'cause he don't care nothin' about no one but himself."

"Junior," John Marcin tried to interrupt again.

"No, Pop, I'm gonna speak my mind."

"Your mind?" Luke laughed. "What mind are we talking about here?"

Junior jumped. "Luke, I didn't see you there."

"Spit it out, June. Say it to my face." Luke was like a mountain lion, stalking, preparing to pounce.

Junior fell silent and began to chew his thumbnail.

"Yeah, figures," Luke said. "So, you think I'm the burden, eh? Me? Maybe it's time you heard it straight, June. Pop's not ever gonna tell you the truth, that's for sure."

"Luke, don't," John Marcin cautioned.

Junior looked back and forth between his father and brother. "What are you talking about, Squeak?"

"You ever wondered why you don't look nothin' like Pop, big brother?"

"Luke, please—" John Marcin faltered. "I said stop it."

"Tell him, Pop. Tell him about Ma. How she whored around and got herself pregnant. How you came to her rescue even though you knew the baby wasn't yours."

John Marcin bit his lip. Anger drained from him like the warm air out of a balloon. All that was left was cold fear. "I'm begging you. Don't."

"And, of course, there's the more scandalous version of the story. Might explain why Junior here is not so smart."

"Do not say another word, or I swear—"

"What's he talking about, Pop?" Junior said, dancing from foot to foot.

"Your brother doesn't mean what he's saying. It's the booze." John Marcin stepped in front of Junior, eyeing Luke warily. "He's a drunk, and he needs help."

Luke hesitated, and for a moment, John Marcin felt as though he was inside Luke's skin. He could feel the shadow slithering along the arteries and veins in his body like an army of serpents. He could also sense his son's desperate but failed attempts to repel the dark force.

Luke struck with one last blast of venom. "Rumor was, Ma fucked her brother. And guess what happens when kin lie together? Their babies don't turn out quite right."

John Marcin exploded, flying at Luke and pinning him against the wall. Luke tried to resist, but John Marcin overpowered him. When Luke opened his mouth to protest, John Marcin forced his forearm against his son's throat with even greater force.

"Kara, punishment," a voice echoed in John Marcin's head.

"Pop, don't!" Junior pleaded.

The voice spoke more clearly this time. "He is mine."

John Marcin pushed harder.

298 J. E. Weiner

"Stop it!" Junior struggled to release Luke from their father's grip.

John Marcin finally backed off, and Luke collapsed to the floor, coughing and gagging. John Marcin stood over his son. He tried to step closer, but Junior held him back. "Luke Anderwald," he sputtered. "What you've done is unforgivable as far as I'm concerned. Only God in Heaven can save you now."

* * *

John Marcin sat alone in the parlor, the fire crackling and sending sparks dancing into the flue. Luke had disappeared into the night, and Junior had stormed back to his place, swearing he would never speak to his father or brother again. John Marcin knew where Luke was headed. Tater would keep an eye out. As for Junior, John Marcin counted on the ever-constant, if dull, Doris to offer aid and comfort.

The wind propelled freezing raindrops against the window-panes like the rhythmic crash of waves along the ocean shore. John Marcin laid back on the couch, his arm draped across his face. A memory of that afternoon with Anna at Port Isabel surfaced, and he tried to savor the image. It was not often that he had fond rec-ollections of their time together. Anna had been right in the end. He never could get past the gossip, and he had to admit that he did blame her, in part, for what happened with Albert. John Marcin had only known strong women in his life before Anna. His mother, Liza, had been his rock, his moral compass, and Zee, his faithful caretaker. Even Mrs. Kirby had triumphed over her misfortunes. John Marcin knew they would all fault his harsh judgment of his wife. At last, he understood that Anna had been the strongest of them all. He'd had it all wrong about her, but it was too late. He could only hope to make things right with his sons.

The last log split in the fireplace, and faint humming echoed inside the chimney. John Marcin closed his eyes and listened to the familiar tune. When the singing stopped abruptly, he sat up and blinked. Before him stood the woman in white. His breath caught in his chest, but not because he was afraid, only surprised. After all these years, John Marcin knew she never meant any harm to him or his family. She, like him, was desperately fighting to keep the evil stalking the hills of Peacock Bend at bay. The apparition's un-plaited hair billowed about her head and shoulders, and her long, ruffled dress floated as though on a breeze. Just in case, John Marcin pinched his cheeks to ensure he was fully awake. The woman remained before him, insistent, and extended her arms. She gripped a piece of paper in her hands.

Another image fired in John Marcin's brain: Luke's list. He rushed to the kitchen and dug into the pile of newspaper still strewn across the table. He fumbled with Luke's A.A. book and extracted the paper wedged between its pages. He spread the sheet on the table and began to read.

Number One: I am an alcoholic, the list began, and in parentheses Luke had scribbled, *fucking obvious*. John Marcin could hear Luke in his head. "They told me to write it all down, Pop. It makes it real."

The second entry on the list was etched on the paper with a slightly dulled pencil tip.

Number Two: I belittle my brother, who has never done anything but love and take care of me.

John Marcin swallowed hard. "Aw, June," he said to himself.

A small rip through the paper indicated that the pencil tip had snapped before the next addition to the list. The narrow line of a freshly sharpened pencil resumed and scripted, *Number Three: I continue to break my father's heart.*

"Eee-you!" one of the birds shrieked in the front yard.

John Marcin ignored the cock's cry. He felt sadness and anger, followed by more sadness and more anger as he recalled the last time he saw Anna—that day by the river when she clutched and grabbed at him in terror. He had been powerless to help her, and now he feared he was failing Luke. John Marcin thought about the weight of Anna and how her traumas and addictions had burdened their marriage from the start and their son for his entire life. Tears streamed down John Marcin's face as he read the next item on Luke's list. *Number Four: I can never forgive my mother for leaving me.*

"Hee-yelp! Hee-yelp! Hee-yelp!" the peacock warned.

John Marcin wiped the wet from his eyes and refocused on the last two entries at the bottom of the tattered page. *Number Five: Continuing to live this life is a selfish act,* and *Number Six: I hope God will forgive me for what I must do.*

"Luke, no!" John Marcin cried out into the darkness. He grabbed his overcoat and sped to The Silver Dollar.

* * *

Bruise-colored storm clouds inched over the horizon, and the temperature began to plummet. John Marcin clutched the steering wheel of his pickup and stared at the entrance to the dance hall. He desperately hoped he was not too late but was terrified that he might be. Not wanting to risk spooking Luke, John Marcin continued past his son's truck parked askew along Main Street and pulled around behind the bar. He jumped out of the truck cab and hurried through The Silver Dollar's back door. It was early yet, so there were only a few customers inside. Tater pointed toward the end of the bar where Luke was sitting on his favorite stool near the stage. John Marcin exhaled, and his pulse slowed.

Tiny peered at John Marcin as he approached. "Lookee who we have here, boy. Yer daddy's come to fetch ya again."

Luke ignored him and began to scratch his palms.

Tiny pointed at the shot glass in front of Luke. "Another, I assume?"

Luke nodded, and the bartender filled the glass with amber liquid. Luke threw it back in one swift gulp. Tiny poured another shot, and after that one was gone, offered yet another.

"Leave it, Tiny," Tater said. "No need to make any more trouble than is already on offer here."

Tiny's upper lip curled. "I'm sure I'll be back. Been bidin' my time with these Anderwalds anyway," he said and walked away.

John Marcin sat down next to Luke without a word. Luke did not acknowledge his father.

"Mind if I join the party?" someone else inquired over their shoulders.

John Marcin looked up to find Frankie Kalka's reflection in the cloudy mirror behind the bar. He bobbed his head, and Frankie hitched himself onto the stool on the other side of Luke.

Luke stared at Frankie in the mirror. "I don't recall extending any invitations."

"What'll it be, Frankie?" Tiny said.

"Beer," Frankie replied.

Tiny uncapped a longneck and slid it along the bar top. Frankie waited for him to step away before speaking further. "Luke, your Pop and I have come to terms," he finally said.

"So?" Luke scowled.

"Well, I—" Frankie paused and looked at John Marcin. "*We* wanted you to hear it from us."

Luke shrugged.

"Son," John Marcin said. "It's no secret that we've all had a tough time of late. If you can't talk to me about it, maybe you can talk to Frankie."

Luke shifted on his stool. "Yeah, right," he scoffed.

The three men sat in silence, and the bar began to fill around them. Frankie tried again to break the stalemate. He turned to face Luke. "I am sorry about your Ma. I want you to know that."

Luke lit a cigarette and blew a cloud of smoke toward Frankie.

"She never intended to hurt you, your Pop, or anybody," Frankie continued. "She was damaged. Like me, I guess." Luke didn't react, so Frankie took another approach. "You can't imagine the half of what she endured before she met your Pop. Couldn't shake it and loved him and you boys too much to drag you into her mess."

Luke glared at Frankie's reflection.

"All either of us could think to do was run away, which was wrong. I truly regret the pain we caused."

"Is she dead?" Luke finally blurted.

John Marcin moved to intervene, but Frankie stopped him. "I don't know, Luke. I haven't seen your mother for a long, long time."

Luke finished his cigarette and stubbed it out in an ashtray with

three forceful blows. He turned to his father, growing more bellig-
erent. "Let me ask you something, Pop," he said. "Do you seriously
think I could ever forgive this sonofabitch?"

"Maybe not," John Marcin shook his head, "but I think us all
coming to some kind of truce, and you knowing that your Ma was
suffering might ease a little of your pain."

"Luke, I've heard what's going on with you," Frankie said.

"What's going on, Frankie Kalka," Luke interrupted, lunging
off his barstool, "IS NONE OF YOUR FUCKING BUSINESS!"

Frankie shielded his face with his hands.

"That's enough," John Marcin said, pushing Frankie out of
range of Luke's fists.

Luke started to sway from side to side and grabbed his skull.
"Oh, God. My head."

"Come with me. You need some air." John Marcin helped Luke
outside behind the bar and propped him under the building's eaves
to keep him out of the sleet now pouring from the sky. Luke bent
forward and vomited into an icy puddle, the contents of his stomach
splashing over the tops of John Marcin's boots.

"It's that damned Disulfiram. Can't mix it with booze," Luke
moaned.

John Marcin helped Luke stand back upright. "Guess that's the
point, isn't it?"

"I'm sorry you're seein' me like this again, Pop. How'd you
know where to find me?"

"Frankie rang the house. Said you were in a bad way. I would
have figured it out sooner or later, though."

"Since when have you and Frankie been on speaking terms?"

"Since that night in San Antonio. I decided all that anger
wasn't worth it. Frankie's like family to me, and if you can't forgive
your family, that's a sad state of affairs."

Luke spit on the ground. "You're a better man than I am. I'll
never get past what he and Ma did."

John Marcin lifted the collar of his coat and pushed his hands
into his pockets. He rocked back and forth from heel to toe as he
fought to keep warm. "Luke, you are your mother's child in so many
ways. Plagued by the same impulses and desires. Don't let that darkness win. Don't let it destroy you like it destroyed her."

Luke covered his face with his hands. "I don't know if I can hold it back anymore. Feel like I might be too far gone."

"You're gonna have to find a way to defeat those demons, son. It won't be easy, and you'll have to accept what you've already lost, but you gotta cut away the bad and keep the good as best you can. And it's long past time for you to make that decision once and for all."

Luke sank into the mud and slush. "Help me, Pop," he pleaded.

John Marcin crouched next to Luke. "I cannot fight this fight for you, but I'm right here, and all the strength and love I have to offer is yours. I couldn't save your mother, but I'm not gonna lose you," he said.

"I'll be damned," Tiny jeered. He had followed John Marcin and Luke. "Would you look at the high and mighty Anderwalds? Rollin' in filth like pigs."

The bartender's massive form filled the open doorway, the light from the bar glowing from behind. John Marcin could hear his labored breath. "What do you want, Tiny?" he said.

Tiny ignored the question and moved closer. "Must be nice to have a father always savin' yer ass, eh, Luke?"

"Now's not the time," John Marcin shot back.

"No, I think right now is perfect," Tiny said, taking another few steps.

"Get the hell away from us!" Luke screamed, trying desperately to get off the ground.

Tiny's hateful countenance remained fixed upon John Marcin. "Maybe it's time you knew my name," he said. "It's Josiah. Josiah T. Gaines, Jr., to be precise." He looked to be waiting for some kind of reaction.

John Marcin was having trouble focusing but could feel his body instinctively stiffen and the muscles around his jaw contract. "What are you on about?" he asked nervously.

"I was named after my daddy," Tiny continued as he stepped into the open air, ice pellets bouncing off his massive bald head. "I assume that name must ring a bell or two?"

John Marcin looked hard at the disfigured barkeep. "It can't be," he said.

"Oh, yes, it can," Tiny smirked. "How's all this excruciating pain and unhappiness feel?"

John Marcin stumbled back against the side of the building.

"Pop, what's going on?" Luke asked meekly.

"What do the preachers call it? Ah, yes, divine retribution," Tiny hissed. "My family was destroyed that day at the gallows in Helena, thanks to your daddy and granddaddies."

"P— Pop?" Luke stuttered.

John Marcin didn't move.

"Do you remember that day?" Tiny continued, slowly moving closer to John Marcin. "When they hung my daddy, and his head was ripped from his body right in front of me? My poor mother drowned herself the next summer. I was left alone, a boy of six tender years."

"What do you want from me," John Marcin implored.

"Vengeance is what I'm after. I swore I wouldn't rest until I, with the Good Lord's blessing and the Devil's agile hand, punished you and yours, John Marcin Anderwald."

Tiny grabbed John Marcin around the throat, his thick fingers like a vice. John Marcin struggled, punching and kicking, but could not escape. His head began to spin, and his legs gave way beneath his body. As he slipped into the mud, he could feel his windpipe collapsing.

"Now you know," Tiny strained, squeezing harder. "Like a noose. Pulled tight."

"No! Stop!" Luke cried and, in one swift movement, sprang up and tackled Tiny.

Tiny was distracted by the unexpected assault and released John Marcin, leaving him prone and gasping for air. Luke pounded the murderous bartender's deformed face, but Tiny only began to laugh—a callous, vengeful, and familiar laugh. He threw Luke to the side like a ragdoll and straddled his body before starting to pummel him with his meaty fists. John Marcin could not move. He could only watch through his swelling eyelids.

"They're gonna blame you, Luke," Tiny grunted, each word landing together with a punch. "You're a violent drunk and a pill fiend. Maybe your father pushed you too far this time?"

After several more blows to the head, John Marcin could see Tiny's hands close around Luke's neck. Luke scratched at the bartender's arms and face but could not loosen his grip.

"Word of a war hero against the word of a drunk? I'll take my chances," Tiny wheezed through gritted teeth.

Blackness closed in around John Marcin with each weakening exhalation of breath, and all he could see was Tiny's twisted skull hovering in the air above Luke's, but someone or something else was looking out through the empty sockets. John Marcin watched in horror as Tiny's face began to dissolve, and thin wisps of black smoke floated out of his head and into Luke's eyes, nose, and mouth. Haunting wails and discordant shrieks suddenly tore through John Marcin's head. "Shabah! Diabeł!" one disembodied voice howled. "Cursed are you," another wailed.

Amid the terrifying din, John Marcin heard Tater scream, "Frankie, no!"

A crack of light flared, and a blast sounded an instant before Tiny's head exploded. Blood and brain matter splattered against the side of the building, and the bartender's body tumbled into the ice and muck.

"John Marcin," Tater said. "Can you hear me?"

John Marcin drew in a ragged breath and rolled onto his side. He was still not entirely sure where he was or what had happened. Tiny's body lay beside him, but it was unrecognizable. He had been shot from behind, and the exit wound was a mangled crater of burned flesh where a face had once been. Frankie stood a few steps away, a shotgun dangling at his side.

"Luke?" John Marcin rasped.

The back door to the bar opened, and light spilled out from inside, far enough to reveal Tiny's lifeless corpse.

"Holy shit!" a man shouted.

"Get back inside," Tater ordered, and the door to the bar slammed shut again. "John Marcin, look at me, friend. You hurt too bad?" Tater struggled to stand him up.

"I don't think so," John Marcin finally managed.

"Frankie, put that goddamned shotgun down and help Luke," Tater cried as a siren blared in the distance. "Damn, they already called the sheriff," he said, panic clearly overtaking him. "Change of plans. Go get Luke's truck and pull it around back. Quick!" Tater pointed to John Marcin's pickup, parked behind the bar. "Bring it over there."

The siren was moving closer. Frankie frantically fished in Luke's pockets for the keys.

"What happened?" John Marcin limped forward and stared at Tiny's headless body.

"No time to explain," Tater said, dragging John Marcin toward the trees and leaning him against the tailgate of his truck. "You don't need to get caught up in this mess. It's best you go on home and keep quiet. Lay low at Peacock Bend for a few days. Understand?" Tater ran back toward the rear of the bar.

"But Tater," John Marcin protested.

Tater returned with Luke in tow. "Listen to me. If anyone asks, you two came in for a drink around five o'clock and headed home together," Tater instructed, opening John Marcin's truck door and helping Luke into the front seat. "Let's get you on the road first, Luke. Everyone in there heard you yelling and carrying on. You take your Pop's truck."

Luke slammed the door closed and started the engine. As he backed into the road, John Marcin approached and waved for him to stop. Luke rolled down the window. "Pop, I gotta go."

John Marcin reached out and squeezed Luke's arm. "Be careful, son," he choked. "Get yourself home safe. I'll figure this out."

"I know you will. You always do," Luke said weakly and pressed the accelerator.

The siren was approaching fast along Main Street. John Marcin touched his neck with his fingertips. It was tender, the most painful spot where Tiny's thumbs had been thrust between his clavicles. He heard the screech of tires as Frankie sped around the side of the building, skidding to a stop and bounding out of the truck cab. The engine was still running.

"You fit to drive?" Frankie asked.

"He'll have to be," Tater said, pushing John Marcin forward.

John Marcin climbed behind the wheel. "What are you gonna tell the sheriff?"

"Not sure yet, John Marcin. Right now, you just need to go," Tater insisted. "Frankie and I will take care of the rest. Now get!" Tater grabbed Frankie, and the brothers hurried inside.

Unrelenting sleet and freezing temperatures made for treacherous travel along the trek back to Peacock Bend. Luke tore out of town along Eleventh Street, avoiding Main Street, where Sheriff Hicks' cruiser was now parked in front of The Silver Dollar, its lights flashing. John Marcin followed close behind, and neither driver turned their headlights on until they were headed west on Highway 16. John Marcin struggled to keep pace with Luke and to stay focused on the road. The smell of death hung heavy, and images of the night's events appeared before him in random sequence, more violent and disturbing with each burst.

"He's mine," someone murmured in his ear.

John Marcin shuddered and accelerated. Ahead, he could see Luke swerve into the oncoming lane and begin to slip and slide along the blacktop. John Marcin sped up. Luke's taillights pulsed as he pumped the brakes and managed to move back onto the right side of the road and regain control. Both pickups roared past a small sign indicating Ranch Road 470 was around the next bend. It was the turnoff for the swimming hole along the Medina, where he, Luke, and Junior had all laughed together for the last time.

Another sudden flare of brake lights blinded John Marcin for a split second as Luke veered off the highway and headed toward the river. John Marcin missed the turn. He jammed on his brakes and skidded to a stop. Quickly turning around, he raced to catch up. Over a rise a quarter of a mile ahead, Luke had stopped at the river crossing. John Marcin pulled his vehicle alongside. Their headlights illuminated the tops of the bridge's bollards, which were peeking out intermittently in the rush of the Medina's raging current, which had overflowed its banks and swallowed the narrow roadway before them.

John Marcin honked his horn and flailed his arms, desperately attempting to attract his son's attention. He rolled down the passenger window and screamed into the deafening wall of sleet, "Luke! What are you doing?" Luke bent forward and laid his forehead against the steering wheel. John Marcin threw his driver's door open and rushed into the road. He pounded on Luke's window. "Open the door," he shouted.

Luke slumped to the side, and his cheek smashed against the inside of the window. John Marcin could hear him through the glass. "She's here, Pop."

"Get out of the truck, Luke. Things will right themselves. I promise," John Marcin begged, pulling at the door handle. "Let me take you home. Everything's gonna be all right."

Luke slowly turned to face his father, but what peered out at John Marcin was not his child or completely human. It was the mangled form of a young soldier dressed in an old-fashioned military uniform. He had round, green eyes and jagged shards of bone and rotting flesh protruded from where the top of his skull had once been. The dark figure hissed, its long tongue flitting back and forth between bruised and bloodied lips.

"We are one," the soldier growled and dissolved into the darkness.

The truck's engine revved, and its tires squealed. "Dear God, no!" John Marcin screamed, slipping on the ice and falling to his knees. His fingertips grazed the rear bumper as the vehicle flew toward the bridge. The impact was swift, and the scrape of metal against stone deafening, but the instant Luke hit the water, the rain stopped, and all went quiet. The only sound was the rush of the river and the swirl of a familiar melody.

"Please help him," John Marcin wailed.

"Kochanie, jestem tutaj. My darling, I am here," a woman whispered. "I will protect him now."

EPILOGUE

The setting sun stretched through the windows of the Frontier Times Museum, and shadows lengthened among the bookshelves and curio cases. The elegant stranger's elbows rested on the counter, her chin in her hands.

"That's quite a tale," she said. "It sure does answer a lot of questions I've had. And not just about my ranch."

"How's that?" The curator was intrigued.

"Strictly between us?"

"You don't have to worry about me. As you've already heard at length, I've been keeping some big secrets for nearly half a century. Not lookin' to break my streak any time soon."

"Fair enough, then. You see, I've always been a magnet for ghosts for some reason and, of course, men who drink too much and do me wrong if you believe the papers. Have been my whole life." The visitor chuckled to herself, recrossing her legs and pulling at the cuff of her blue jeans. "So, it makes sense that all these spirits are riled up again at Peacock Bend. But how they got there in the first place is incredibly tragic."

"Yes, it is," the curator sighed. "The Anderwalds suffered more than their fair share of hardship, no doubt, but if their story has taught me anything, it's that all families harbor some secret or another."

"That's for sure," the woman muttered.

"You only gotta stroll over to St. Stanislaus and read the list of our founders' names etched into the granite memorial at its entrance and on the tombstones a little further along in the churchyard. My parents are in the first row of graves, and my older brother is buried in the new section along Cypress Street. At some point in their lives, all of 'em laid in sin polluted, as the old hymn goes, wretched and undone before our Lord."

The visitor's brow furrowed with lingering curiosity. "Can I ask what happened after Luke's suicide?"

"You mean his murder." The curator became unexpectedly agitated. "We all know well and good that was no suicide, ma'am, no matter what the coroner's inquiry ruled."

"I'm sorry, yes, the murder," she said, reaching across the counter and touching the man's arm.

The curator was distracted by the smooth skin across the back of the visitor's muscled hand. When his gaze met hers once again, he blushed. He could not shake the feeling that they had met somewhere before.

"Whatever became of John Marcin?" the woman prompted him again.

"Picked hisself up like all the Anderwalds did," the curator continued. "Felt his penance for Anna and Luke was to do right by Junior and make a life for him. The two of them and Junior's wife Doris kept the ranch goin' until John Marcin passed a few years back. Money from cattle and a little extra after his mama's paintings became so popular kept them comfortable. Were you aware that John Marcin's mother was a famous artist around here?"

"More than around here," the woman said. "Elizabeth Anderwald was a trailblazer on the early Texas art scene. She was my mother's favorite painter. That's how I got my first name, and that peacock mural of hers at the ranch is one of the reasons I bought the place."

The curator could not hide his confusion. "But I thought your name was—"

"You've been so kind to pretend you didn't recognize me this entire time, but you're thinking of my stage name. My given name is Elizabeth, but my mother always called me Liza."

"Ah, I see." The curator lost his train of thought for a moment, but quickly recovered. "I sure am glad to hear the mural remains. You said it was one of the reasons you bought the ranch. What were the others?"

"Mostly my mother. She passed away from liver cancer when I was sixteen. She would always say I was her 'never say never' child. I arrived late in her life, but that also meant she left mine far too early."

The curator bowed his head. "I'm very sorry to hear that. You were so young. It must have been difficult."

"It was. Still is after all these years," the woman said softly. "Anyway, after my mother died, I realized I knew almost nothing about her past. She raised me by herself in Dallas. I never had any siblings and never met my father. The only clues I had were that she had spent some time in this area as a child, and once, at the very end, she told me my father had been a soldier."

"Huh," the proprietor frowned. "A soldier, you say?"

The visitor quickly changed the subject. "And, of course, finding Luke's old guitars and sheet music were bonuses with my purchase. I'm thinking about recording some of those songs he wrote at the end of his life. They're wonderful."

"John Marcin woulda loved that idea," the curator said, his bright grin quickly dissolving. "I don't think he ever forgave himself for not saving that boy, but I'm not sure there was much to be done. Luke was hell-bent on self-destruction, like his mother."

"Speaking of Anna," the woman began.

The curator preempted her question. "Never came back. Still officially a missing person after all these years. Poor, poor girl."

The visitor looked away. "Mr. Kalka," she said, her voice catching with emotion. "I presume I've got that right?"

"Guilty as charged."

"Your friends and I have a lot in common—ghosts, demons, guilt, sin, doubts about God, faltering sanity. The whole lot of it. I'm glad to learn I'm in good company." The woman slapped her palms against her thighs. "It's getting late. I should let you close."

The curator held up a hand and eased off his stool. He un-hooked the photos of Agnieszka and the camel wranglers from the wall. "I want you to take them home where they belong, not gathering dust in this old place," he said. "Hang 'em next to that peacock. They'll all keep watch like they always did. Especially Agnieszka. She'll make sure you're safe."

"Thank you, Mr. Kalka. I believe she will," the woman said, gently tucking the frames into her handbag and heading for the exit.

"If you ever need anything, don't hesitate to come on by, you hear?"

The visitor stopped halfway to the door. "There is one more thing," she said. "I would love to meet Junior sometime."

"He and Doris live at the Medina River RV Park and run a diner further along Lakeshore Drive. Serve the best pies in the county. Tell 'em Uncle Tater sent ya."

"Will do," the woman smiled and receded into the fading afternoon light.

"Wait!" the curator called out to the visitor as the door slammed. He hobbled after her into the parking lot. "I forgot to ask. What's your family name?"

"Oh, it's Schulte. My name is Liza Schulte."

THE END

HISTORICAL NOTES AND SOURCES

The Wretched and Undone is a work of historical fiction that draws upon extensive primary and secondary historical sources, contemporary memoirs, and family oral histories to inform and shape the novel's characters—those drawn from real life as well as imagined on the page—and its narrative arc. A representative sample of the rich resources uncovered during background research for the book is included here:

General Sources

Regional and Local History

Baker, Lindsey T. *Ghost Towns of Texas* (Norman: University of Oklahoma Press, 1986).

Coleman, Marion Moore, "The Polish Origins of Bandera, Texas," *Polish American Studies*, Vol. 20, No. 1 (January - June, 1963): pp. 21-27.

Frontier Times Museum, *Bandera County*, (Bandera, Texas: Arcadia Publishing, 2012).

Hardin, Earl S., Jr., *On the Bandera Frontier: Contributions to the Bandera County Historian, 1992-2010*, (Bandera, Texas: Earl S. Hardin, Jr., 2019).

Hunter, J. Marvin, *One Hundred Years in Bandera, 1853–1953*, (Bandera, Texas: Hunter's Printing, 1953).

Texas Digital Newspaper Program, *The Portal to Texas History*, University of North Texas Libraries, https://texashistory.unt.edu/explore/collections/TDNP/

Texas State Historical Association, https://www.tshaonline.org/home

Memoir Accounts

Frontier Times Magazine, Memoir Features, 1923-1954, https://www.frontiertimesmagazine.com/

Maverick, Mary A., *Memoirs of Mary A. Maverick: A Journal of Early Texas*, (Maverick Publishing Co., 2005).

Withers, Anita Dwyer, "Diary of Anita Dwyer Withers, 1860-1865," *Documenting the American South*, https://docsouth.unc.

edu/imls/withers/withers.html

Bible References

Farstad, Arthur, ed., *Holy Bible: The New King James Version: Containing the Old and New Testaments*, (Nashville: Thomas Nelson, 1982).

Songs

Carter, A.P. "Little Darling Pal of Mine." 1928. *YouTube*, www.youtube.com/watch?v=DXqDFobYIeA.

Edwards, Gus Composer and Edward Madden Lyricist. "By the Light of the Silvery Moon." Jerome H. Remnick & Co., 1909. *YouTube*, www.youtube.com/watch?v=k6XSa0WFak8.

Ford, Tennessee Ernie. "The Shotgun Boogie." Capitol Records, 1949. *YouTube*, www.youtube.com/watch?v=AWPLCQP40jE.

Kelly, Thomas. "When We Lay in Sin Polluted." 1831. *Hymnary.org*, hymnary.org/text/when_we_lay_in_sin_polluted.

Reed, Ola Belle. "High on the Mountain." *My Epitaph*, Smithsonian Folkways Recordings, 1976, Track 1. *YouTube*, www.youtube.com/watch?v=0YSB94EH2_k.

Robinson, Robert. "Come Thou Fount of Every Blessing." 1758. *Hymnary.org*, hymnary.org/text/come_thou_fount_of_every_blessing.

Von Tilzer, Albert Composer, and Junie McCree Lyricist. "Put Your Arms Around Me, Honey." York Music Co., 1910. *YouTube*, www.youtube.com/watch?v=X0FS08D-ujY.

19th Century and Western Slang

"Common Words of the 1860s" and "Civil War Military Terms," *The Patriot Files*, http://www.patriotfiles.com/index.php?name=Sections&req=viewarticle&artid=6424

"Western Slang, Lingo, and Phrases – A Writer's Guide to the Old West," *Legends of America*, https://www.legendsofamerica.com/we-slang/3/

Part One Sources

Al-Saed, Mohammed, (translated by Asaf Zilberfarb), "The Story of 18 Saudis Who Participated in the American Civil War," *The Media Line*, https://themedialine.org/mideast-mindset/the-story-of-18-saudis-who-participated-in-the-american-civil-war/

Baker, T. Lindsay, *The First Polish Americans: Silesian Settlements in Texas*, (College Station: Texas A&M University Press, 1979).

Carroll, Charles C., "The Government's Importation of Camels: A Historical Sketch," *Report of the Chief of the Bureau of Animal Industry, United States Department of Agriculture*, Volume 20 (Washington, DC: U.S. Department of Agriculture, 1903).

Crutchfield, James A., *Comanche Captives* (U. of Oklahoma Press, 2005).

DeLay, Brian, *War of a Thousand Deserts: Indian Raids and the U.S. Mexican War*, (Yale University Press, 2008).

Gwynne, S.C., *Empire of the Summer Moon: Quanah Parker and the Rise and Fall of the Comanche, the Most Powerful Indian Tribe in American History*, (Scribner, 2010).

Hawkins, Vince, "The U.S. Army's 'Camel Corps' Experiment," *The Army Historical Foundation*, https://armyhistory.org/the-u-s-armys-camel-corps-experiment/

Hunter, J. Marvin, *Pioneer History of Bandera County*, (Bandera, Texas: Hunter's Printing, 1922).

————*The Lyman Wight Colony in Texas: Came to Bandera in 1854*, N.D., University of North Texas Libraries, The Portal to Texas History, https://texashistory.unt.edu/

Luther, Joseph, *Camp Verde: Texas Frontier Defense*, (Charleston, SC: The History Press, 2012).

"Panna Maria, Texas: A Polish Ghost Town," http://www.texasescapes.com

Perrine, Fred S., "Uncle Sam's Camel Corps," in Lansing B. Bloom and Paul A. F. Walters, eds., *The New Mexico Historical Review*, No. 4 (1926): pp. 434-444.

Sowa, Carol Baass, "Polish Immigrants Follow Priest's Call to Texas," *Today's Catholic*, September 14, 2018.

"Under the Rebel Flag: Life in Texas During the Civil War," *Texas State Archive and Libraries Commission*, https://www.tsl.texas.gov/exhibits/civilwar/dissent.html

Part Two Sources

Gard, Wayne, *Frontier Justice*, (Norman: University of Oklahoma Press, 1949).

Gilbreath, West C., *Death on the Gallows: The Encyclopedia of Legal Hangings in Texas*, (Fort Worth: Wild Horse Press, 2020).

Traub, Stuart H., "Rewards, Bounty Hunting, and Criminal Justice in the West: 1865-1900,"

Western Historical Quarterly, Vol. 19, No. 3 (August 1988): pp. 287-301.

Williams, R. H., *With the Border Ruffians: Memories of the Far West, 1852-1868*, (London: John Murray, 1907).

Part Three Sources

Alexander, Caroline, "The Shock of War," World War I: 100 Years Later: *A Smithsonian Magazine Special Report*, https://www.smith-sonianmag.com/history/the-shock-of-war-55376701/

Bandera Bulletin, 1945 to present, *The Portal to Texas History*, University of North Texas Libraries, https://texashistory.unt.edu/explore/collections/BAND/

Ball, Gregory W., *Texas and World War I*, (Austin: Texas State Historical Association, 2019).

Hartman, Gary, *The History of Texas Music*, (College Station: Texas A&M University Press, 2008).

Owens, William A., *Tell Me a Story, Sing Me A Song: A Texas Chronicle*, (Austin: University of Texas Press, 1983).

Texas Historical Commission, *Texas and the Great War Travel Guide*, (Austin: Texas Historical Commission, 2017).

————*Texas in World War II Travel Guide*, (Austin: Texas Historical Commission, 2005).

Treviño III, Geronimo, *Dance Halls and Last Calls: A History of Texas Country Music*, (Plano: Republic of Texas Press, 2002).

Whisenhunt, Donald W., *The Depression in Texas: The Hoover Years*, (New York: Garland Publishing, 1983).

ACKNOWLEDGMENTS

I am filled with boundless gratitude to so many for their support, encouragement, and, occasionally, tough truths in both writing and life. In the writing lane, thank you to Colin Mustful, Robin Henry, and the entire History Through Fiction team for your belief in me and this story. Your partnership has been invaluable. The same is true for members past and present of the Pacific Coast Writers Collective: Genio Borghi, Holly Brady, Scott Gordon, Marcia Kemp Sterling, Marc Morgenstern, JoAnneh Nagler, Ron Ott, Katrina Ryan, and Jacquie Walters. I am also indebted to the Stanford Continuing Studies Program, particularly two creative writing faculty. To Lynn Stegner, your generous advice, counsel, and mentorship have inspired me as a writer, and your expert editorial eye has made this novel better in so many ways. To Angela Pneuman, your "How to Start Your Novel and Keep It Going" course was where this all began (and continues). Special thanks as well to several trusted readers who kicked the tires on everything from storylines to medical and military terminology to Polish and Arabic translation: Nora Barakat, Jon Paul Buchmeyer, Gretchen Craford, Amir Eshel, Katherine Jolluck, Beata Skrzypacz, Andrzej Skrzypacz, and Itzhak Vardi.

In the life lane, it begins and ends with my beautiful family. To my sisters and fellow ghost magnets Martie Maguire and Emily Strayer, many of our stories are here, especially those from the many gatherings along that lonely stretch of Texas Highway 16. To my sister Tara Trask, thank you for the many moments of commiseration about our respective writing journeys. To my mother and sixth-grade English teacher, Barbara Trask, the fundamentals of creative writing and love of grammar and craft started in your class. But no one deserves my thanks more than my husband, Amir Weiner, and our daughters, Ya'el and Naomi. Many of our stories are here, too. Amir, you insisted I take that first writing course, and you have read and reread every word I've written since. You picked me up when tragedy struck and helped me find joy in writing and life again. And to my girls, we all would have remained wretched and undone but for your grace, strength, humor, and love.

About the Author

J. E. Weiner is a writer and novelist based in Northern California. Her debut novel, *The Wretched and Undone*, is a sweeping Southern Gothic tale set in the Texas Hill Country and inspired by real people and actual events. The book manuscript was named a Killer Nashville Top Pick for 2024 and a Claymore Award Finalist for Best Southern Gothic. Weiner's previous work has appeared in the literary journals *Madcap Review*, *Five Minutes*, and *HerStry*, as well as the recent grit lit anthology *Red-Headed Writing* (Cowboy Jamboree Press, 2024). Weiner is a founding member of the Pacific Coast Writers Collective, and while living and writing in blissful exile on the West Coast, her heart remains bound to her childhood home, the Great State of Texas.

https://www.jeweiner.com/

About HTF Publishing

Founded in 2023 as an imprint of History Through Fiction, HTF Publishing is hybrid publisher of compelling, high-quality historical novels. Following in the tradition of History Through Fiction, HTF Publishing seeks to provide readers with engaging historical narratives that are rooted in detailed and accurate historical research. As a hybrid press, we want to work with authors who are serious about their craft and aspire to share imaginative, important, and well-researched, historical narratives with the world.

If you enjoyed this novel, please consider leaving a review. It's the best way to support us and our authors. Plus, you'll be helping other readers discover this great story.

Thank you!

www.HistoryThroughFiction.com

Printed in the USA
CPSIA information can be obtained
at www.ICGtesting.com
CBHW021925071224
18535CB00004B/15